The Lig

the Waves

Stuart Farquhar

www.stuartfarquhar.co.uk
@WStuartFarquhar
www.facebook.com/StuartFarquhar.author

Stuart Farquhar is the author of The Ultimate Dreamer, Death Us Do Part and the Leo Self mysteries, as well as a semi-musical stage version of The Strange Affair of Dr Jekyll and Mr Hyde, and with Phil Scary, Faking History, Epsisode II: Attack of the Clowns and many Imaginary Frends sketches, some of which may or may not be published in due course.

He has been known to perform on the stage, write music and songs and design his own book covers, including the origami ones and the pastry dragon. He even tried his hand at stand-up comedy and people were polite enough to laugh.

He writes to get the voices out of his head.

THE LIGHT BENEATH THE WAVES

Published 2014 by The Imaginary Frends
email admin@stuartfarquhar.co.uk

Cover photograph by Phil Scary
Feejee mermaid created by Stuart Farquhar with thanks to
propnomicon
Edited by Phil Scary
Copy-editing and proofreading by Leigh Grieve
The Scary Clowns (Mr Coco & Mr Wobbly) created by Phil Scary

For Rosslyn, who saved me from drowning
For Andrew, her rock in the stormiest of waters
And for baby Murren, who never got to join the circus

In memory of Granda Thompson and the crew and families of the
Sapphire
Granda Farquhar on the Renown
The victims of the Stotfield disaster, Christmas Day 1806
And the Hopeman disaster

Thanks to Phil for permission to use the Scary Clowns
Rosslyn for making the beach look beautiful
Leigh for minding my p's and q's
Judith for writing faster than me

Special thanks to Sigurd Towrie's excellent Orkneyjar website,
www.orkneyjar.com, without which this would be a very different
book.
Also to the Nynorn Project for the language of the trows.

Mum and Dad for giving me somewhere to write it. Amy, Caleb
and Keir for distracting me from writing it. Debbie and Joshua for
distracting them from distracting me from writing it.

Karen Burke for housebreaking advice
Andrew, Maddy, Riley, Murren and Genghis
Lianne and Janice for keeping me informed
Julie and all at South Street
Jochen
Dene, Dave, Les, Miriam
Everyone who took part in the great title debate
propnomicon for showing me how to make a mermaid
Heartlanders, Missionaries and Antpeople
All the fans on Facebook, Twitter, the website and anywhere else

1

It was a dark and stormy night. No, really. The sun had slunk off to do whatever it does in its spare time, the overcast sky was filled with filthy black clouds that had sent the moon scuttling after its opposite number for safety, and the pummelling rain and jagged forks of lightning were a fair indication of the weather. It was a dark and stormy night.

The *Colleen* lurched wretchedly on the surging wave, lifted high into the murky darkness before crashing back down to the surface of the ocean with a bone-jarring crack. This time the Captain could have sworn that, just for a second, the trawler was actually raised clear of the water and hung briefly in mid-air. It might have sounded impressive as a story back on shore, but when you were there in the middle of it, it raised a grim, sickening feeling in the pit of your stomach. That crack wasn't just the sound of the splash. There had been wood in there too, and in this weather you wouldn't know if you were taking on water.

The Captain wiped the rain from his eyes and peered into the gloom, trying to catch a glimpse of one of the other boats. At first all he could see was more rain, the wind blowing it almost sideways. A gust blew some directly into his face and he cried out in pain. His eye still stinging, he looked again and this time saw a shadow. It was difficult to be certain but he reckoned the silhouette was the *Speedwell*. It was being tossed about like a cork. It shouldn't be sitting at that angle.

Something thudded against the hull and he looked over the side. A lifeboat was floating past. It was the wrong way up. He felt that knot in his stomach again. He looked back towards where the silhouette had been but it was gone now, swallowed by the dark and the solid curtain of rain. The only reason he knew it hadn't sunk was because it would take longer. He didn't really expect to see it again though.

There was a sudden cry from somewhere further back. '*Mermaid off to port!*'

The Captain ran to the other side of the deck, steadying himself against the wheelhouse wall as his feet slipped and skidded across the soaked wood. He gripped the side of the boat and looked along the length of the hull. The riding light bobbed furiously at the stern, illuminating the water close to the vessel. His eyes narrowed as he tried to separate the shadows and moving shapes. There it was! A flash of glistening forked tail. Could have been a porpoise but then a head broke the surface of the water. He couldn't make out features through the rainy gloom, but there was long hair and as the creature rose higher he could plainly see ample breasts. No porpoise, he thought as it flipped forward and dived again, its tail splashing behind it. Damn mermaids, bringing storms wherever they went. Just seeing one was bad luck but it was a bit late to worry about that now.

Lightning flashed again as the gale blew harder, becoming a terrible choir of the damned, all shrill wailing voices. He tried to stop his imagination from envisioning what the voices belonged to. Don't think of dead, eyeless souls riding the winds to bear you off to hell. Think of something good, something beautiful making the noise. A woman singing. And then the woman was a mermaid. Damn.

And then there really was singing. Over the noise of the wind came a sound he'd heard only a few times before but could never have forgotten. The mermaid song swooped on the air and snaked around his soul, wrenching it from his body and carrying it away into the heart of the storm. He didn't mind a bit.

There was a sudden splintering crack from behind. The Captain's head snapped around in time to see a section of the mast falling towards him. Then there was blackness.

He'd probably been unconscious for only a moment but there was no telling. No-one had come and moved him, which was ominous. His head was splitting as badly as the wood and his right eye stung with its newly scarlet vision. He wiped the blood as he staggered to his feet, but the view stayed red. Leaning on the side of the boat for support, he glanced down into the water again. More flotsam eddied past, this time broken pieces of wood and also items that would have been on board the boat. There were even some clothes. But as he stared they moved.

'Man overboard!' he yelled frantically, not knowing if there was anyone there to hear. 'Man over- ' But before he had time to take any action, he saw the sailor look up at him, reach out a forlorn arm and take in a lungful of water as the wave rose above his head and he sank forever. The feeling was in the Captain's mouth now.

For a few moments he just stood there, gazing helplessly into the waves. He'd had just enough time to recognise the man as the Captain of the *Sapphire*. Then his attention was caught by a new problem. There was another silhouette out there, and this time it was heading straight for the *Colleen*, and much faster than any fishing boat normally would. He recognised the shape and realised that there was no-one to steer the boat away.

'Brace for impact!' he shouted; but his voice was drowned by the hellish choir. He ran, or rather staggered, to the bell and rang it as loudly as he could, not caring that he might be the only person who could hear it.

The silhouette had detail now, and as it loomed out of the darkness he could make out the name painted on the side. *Sapphire*. It seemed much bigger than he knew it really was, somehow towering over a boat its own size. And then it ploughed through the side of the *Colleen*, sending splintered planks of wood flying through the air. The wheel-house windows were smashed and the rest of the mast gave way. One of the flying planks caught the Captain a glancing blow across the temple, and the rest of his vision turned dark crimson and began to blur. He grabbed the wheel and tried to pull himself to his feet. It spun a few times before he managed. As he struggled to stay upright and conscious, he was vaguely aware of the deck vanishing beneath him. He never felt himself hit the water.

As the *Colleen* broke up and began to sink, there wasn't an eerie silence or a gradual return to calm now that it was all over. There was still the howling gale, the projectile rain, surging waves and explosive sheets of light-ning. And there was still one more boat being sent to the bottom of the ocean.

It was a dark and stormy night.

I. The Mither o' the Sea

*T*he sea is alive. Oh, yes it is. It gives life to everything and it is teeming with life, so it is very much alive. It is powerful and dangerous and beautiful and peaceful. It has moods and it can be as vengeful as it can bountiful. And the source of all this life is the Mither o' the Sea.

The Sea Mither grants life to every living thing. She brings warmth to the ocean and she calms the storms. She is the onset of spring and the haze of summer. She is in the cooling breeze and in the leaping salmon and in the lapping waves.

But all that is good must have its opposite, and the Sea Mither's bitter enemy is Teran, the spirit of winter. Where the Sea Mither is gentle and calm, Teran is bitter and hostile. His screaming voice is in the winter gales and his rage is in the crashing waves.

Every spring, the Sea Mither returns to take up her summer residence in the sea. But first she must fight the Vore Tullye, the Spring Struggle, a fierce battle with Teran that lasts weeks and is seen in raging storms that tear across the land and churn the sea until it boils. And when she wins – for she always does – she leaves Teran bound at the bottom of the ocean where he can do no harm. She then spends the summer repairing the damage done by Teran's reign. She stills the storms and calms the sea. She warms the water so that life can return once more. And then all can enjoy the peaceful summer days, only disturbed by the occasional squall as Teran struggles to break free from his bonds.

But as autumn approaches, the Sea Mither, exhausted from her

15

summer labours, is forced to confront Teran once again as he breaks free and fights the Gore Vellye, the Autumn Tumult. The storms rage again and the seas boil once more, and this time Teran is victorious. The Sea Mither is banished and the spirit of winter holds the islands in his frozen grip, bringing cold and storms and ice and death.

Through the harsh winter days, the sea Mither hears the cries of every hungry child, every shivering woman and every drowning man, knowing that when spring returns, she too will return, refreshed, to do battle with Teran once more.

2

Wolfsburg was the commercial heart of the Empire. It wasn't the capital or even the biggest city; nor did it command the main port or principal foreign trade route, but it was more or less right in the centre of the vast alliance of provinces, and all roads – at least the ones that mattered – led there eventually.

Actually, it was a fallacy that Wolfsburg was in the centre of the Empire. It was relatively far north and a little to the west, but most people still *thought* of it as being in the middle. Its status had a lot to do with this, but so did the fact that most people overlooked the southern and furthest east provinces. Most of the south was occupied by the sprawling Province of Megara, which stretched as far as the eastern border. Its people and culture were of an entirely different stock to the majority of the Empire's citizens, so most considered it a different country and would have been surprised to learn it was part of the Empire at all. And a large chunk of the east was taken up by the Union of Moravia, a loose alliance of kingdoms that had never fully joined the Empire, and whose people had far more in common with the neighbouring Khazar Empire. If the Moravians couldn't make up their minds whether to be part of the Empire or not, then the real Imperial citizens couldn't be bothered working it out for them.

So if you ignored those two, as most people did, then Wolfsburg was pretty much the Empire's heart. Those who chose to extend the metaphor generally stated, more than a little unkindly, that Megara and Moravia were its bowels and its arse.

Wolfsburg was one of the city-states, powerful autocratic cities that were outwith the jurisdiction of any of the provinces, even if they were situated within the borders of one. Wolfsburg was entirely within the Duchy of Middenland but did not answer to the Duke. Instead it was ruled by the Graf Boris Fett-Kaufman who, like all the city-state grafs, had equal powers to the provincial rulers. And arguably more than some of them.

Every day, processions of merchants, traders, hawkers, tourists, farmers and beggars traipsed in and out of the giant wooden gates and along the cobbled streets that could cripple a mountain goat. There they mingled with the locals and relieved them of what little wealth they had, only to look in their purses at the end of the day and realise that anyone who lived in Wolfsburg would always come out best in a financial transaction. They had money in their veins. If you shook them they rattled. If you cut them you'd better have your hat ready to catch the jackpot.

Even the tourists came to Wolfsburg to make money. Of course, they did all the usual sightseeing and other touristy things, but you couldn't visit the City without a trip to one of its famous gambling houses, and if you went home with lighter pockets than when you came in, at least you could say you'd done it. And that the Watch had promised to do everything they could to find the pickpocket.

Wolfsburg's attractions were many and varied. At least they were as varied as the different coins in your pocket, because most of them were related to money somehow or other. Actually, a better metaphor would be to say they were as varied as the faces printed on the banknotes, because Wolfsburg was the first and only city to use paper money. The Bank of Wolfsburg, which virtually dictated the entire Empire's economy, had reasoned that paper was easier to produce than precious metals and also easier to carry, and would therefore be a more flexible and manageable currency. Many other people had pointed out, what with precious metals being precious, that's what made them valuable and worth using as money, as opposed to some glorified IOU. Not to mention the fact that paper was much more easily forged and liable to tear, burn or go soggy in the rain. Nonetheless, the Bank had forged ahead, and Wolfsburg effectively had a currency of its own. This wasn't a problem within the city, as virtually every currency was accepted here, even by the beggars. It was easy to take foreign money to any of the banks and exchange it for pretty much any other currency. The rest of the Empire had resisted the introduction of paper money, and technically it wasn't even legal currency outwith the City, but there were some places where just the mere fact that it came from Wolfsburg was enough for people to accept money they probably couldn't spend. However, the Bank predicted notes would be used across the Empire within five years.

The Bank itself was a huge building resembling a cathedral. Tours were organised for the public – for a nominal fee, naturally – and included a visit to the heavily-guarded vault where the Empire's gold reserves were kept, and to the ultra-modern printing press that produced the famous banknotes. You could buy them as souvenirs, although the gold reserves were unavailable even to those who could afford them.

Other attractions included the Weekend Market, which was on every day; the Travellers' Market, which pitched itself in a different location every week; and the Beggars' Market, which everyone said had forgotten its roots now that it played to the tourists. In the summer, the Festival Market set up for two weeks and in the winter the Ice Market pitched itself on a frozen lake. In between the two were an autumn Beer Festival and a spring Fruit Festival. But summer was when the city was at its most vibrant. All year round, street performers could be found on every corner and in every square that didn't already have a stall, but in summer the performers virtually took over the city for the Festival of Arts. Buskers busked, artists drew on the pavements, mimes annoyed everyone, and the theatres put on shows of every imaginable type. All testament to the art of making a profit.

More discerning tourists could avoid all of these events and look for the ones the locals frequented, the ones the city really revolved around. There were smaller, specialised markets to be found dotted all over Wolfsburg, and those searching for them could do worse than find streets with names like Fleshmarket Close or Tannery Square. If you wanted bread there was a bread market; if you needed household goods there was an iron market; there was even a fish market, with fish brought in daily along the River Wister. In some of the more residential areas, the markets would come to you, with various traders taking their carts around and stopping in the streets for people to come out and get their regular orders. It was said that if you couldn't make money in Wolfsburg you would be poor all your life; and there were worse places to be poor.

Perhaps the only establishment in Wolfsburg not dedicated to the pursuit of financial gain was the Imperial College of Magical Arts. This had been founded more than a century ago as a means of controlling the practice of magic in the Empire. Not that there were wizards on every corner, what with magic being hard to do and supposedly hereditary, but at the time people had felt it was important to ensure it was done properly. Safely. If people were going to go around turning people into other things, cursing each other and generally blowing things up in the hope of making gold, they should at least be taught how to do it by someone who had done it first and still had their own eyebrows. So it became law that a licence was needed to practise magic commercially within the Empire's borders. And such a licence was only granted on receipt of a degree from the College of Magic. (No licence was required to practise magic on a *non*-commercial basis, so anyone who didn't know what they were doing could do so with impunity, provided they weren't being paid money. This is called regulation.)

Ostensibly the College was a place of learning, like any other college or university. In reality there weren't that many students, what with hereditary and all that, and the staff stayed away as much as possible. Most of them were only lecturers because the law said so and besides it was regular money, so there was a strict Seventh Son of a Seventh Son policy to keep the numbers down. At least until people started harping on about equal opportunities. The pressure to allow non-hereditary students and even, say it under your breath, *females* led to the introduction of a rigorous entrance exam to put most of them off trying. Some did pass, but then they were offered the choice between an Academic Degree direct from the College or a Private Degree, which involved becoming an apprentice to one of its Fellows (and they were all Fellows and not Fellowesses) and living and working with them in their homes. This was promoted on the basis of fieldwork and individual tuition, although it usually meant donkeywork and more frequent rows, but most students fell for it because it was cheaper.

The College was intended to be a resource for the entire Empire and not just an elite club for its own lecturers and students. As such it also had a workshop that was open to the public. In theory anyone could come in and buy potions or magical artefacts (at least the smaller, less dangerous ones), learn some very basic herbalism or alchemy (the kind that didn't involve poisoning or really big explosions) and even engage the services of a qualified wizard. On Thursdays it was possible to book guided tours around the College to see research as it happened, and on Fridays it was possible to sue for any injuries incurred as a result. Thus the College entered into the spirit of Wolfsburg economics. During the Ice Market the wizards even staged public lectures for children, and hardly anyone failed to return to their natural shape at the end.

The College had the decency to look exactly as a College of Magic should look – all towers and turrets, wings and annexes, latticed windows, carved doors and lots and lots of gargoyles, all surrounded by a high stone wall with a black iron gate. Inside was all panelled wood and brass carvings, with doors that creaked just for the effect. Everywhere smelled of linseed oil and tobacco (well, apart from the bits that smelled of saltpetre and best-not-to-think-about-it-really) and the air tingled faintly. Not, as everyone assumed, from the magic but from the badly earthed lightning conductor on the roof and from the lump of uranium sitting forgotten in the cellar because no-one yet knew what uranium was.

Despite being one of its students, Adam had never actually been to the College of Magic. He had been apprenticed as long as he could remember and, being a Seventh Son, had not needed to sit the entrance exam. He had always lived with Malchus and learned magic. Except for those few weeks recently when he went off looking for information on the Skentys.

The Skentys was the ancient race believed to have created the world. Or perhaps they just created everything *in* the world. No-one was quite sure. They may have been gods, although no-one worshipped them, or they may have created the gods. No-one was entirely sure about that either, especially as no-one could work out what you called beings who created gods. Either way they had been very powerful until their Fall thousands, or possibly hundreds, of years ago, after some unspecified disaster. Or perhaps they just fancied a change and went on holiday. According to some, there were remnants of the Skentys civilisation far across the oceans in the so-called New World (which would presumably make it a very old world instead), and there were even fanciful descriptions of one-eyed lizard men in jungle temples. Although not descriptions from anyone you'd ever actually met or was even still alive to talk to about it.

Although the Skentys were not worshipped or even remembered much outside of academic circles, they were important to wizards because the one thing everyone was sure they *had* created was magic. Some surviving ancient magical artefacts were believed to have been made and used by the Skentys, although plenty of others had been made by Dr Wandernman, Reader in Design Technology, and many more by country folks who thought that a few twigs and a bit of string with a beetle in the middle was a powerful charm against the scrote. Some of these artefacts (the Skentys ones, not the scrote charms) turned up from time to time and were jealously guarded by the wizards who acquired them.

Adam had gone looking for a Skentys book, one that supposedly explained everything about creation and the Fall of the Skentys. His journey had involved being hunted by a witch-finder, nearly being sacrificed by killer monks, escaping from a burning library and half a city being destroyed by an extinct dragon, but had been otherwise uneventful. He didn't find the book and it got burned anyway, but he made some friends and met a were-rabbit, learned a dirty song and did at least discover some of the secret of creation, so not entirely unfruitful. The wizards at the College had watched most of this on a Skentys crystal ball and Malchus had even saved people from the dragon, but they still wanted a report.

The room they now sat in bore the legend BOARD OF STUDIES on a brass plaque on the door. The students liked to joke that the first word was misspelled. The large round table was covered with a heavy cloth that Adam had given up trying to determine the colour of, although he had narrowed it down to blue or black. Or green. No, not green. Blue.

Or black. Fifteen high-backed chairs were arranged around the table and the only sound came from the remorseless ticking of the grandfather clock in the corner.

Malchus had often spoken of the other wizards, but as this invariably amounted to him grumbling 'Blithering idiots,' Adam really had no idea what to expect. He was fairly sure Malchus was alone in his habit of dressing in pointed hat and midnight blue robes covered in yellow stars and moons. Or rather, he *hoped* he was, as Adam did not like the thought that one day he would be expected to do the same. So he was rather relieved when the door opened and in walked five men who were not wearing hats of any kind or images of any celestial bodies. Not that their attire was any more everyday than Malchus's. The most imposing wore fur-trimmed scarlet robes and had his hair so slicked back that an entire pig must have donated its fat to make this possible. The next wore a high collared green frock coat that made him look like a colour-blind undertaker, although his gaunt cheeks, sunken eyes and apparent unfamiliarity with the muscles that enabled one to smile gave him more the appearance of the dearly departed. Almost pushing to get in front of this apparition was a man so small Adam had to strain his neck downward to see him. He was dressed in a black tunic and tights, which, against all the laws of reason, managed to make him look slim when he was evidently the wrong side of thin. He had a waxed black moustache and Adam had to look twice to be sure he wasn't wearing a little mask over his beady eyes. He carried a small wooden chest. Behind him was a genuinely thin man wearing a grey tailcoat with a cravat that threatened to engulf the entire room. His white hair looked like it might uncoil itself into a cat any minute, and Adam realised there really were people in the world who wore pince-nez. Finally came a short man who looked completely out of place with the others. He was dishevelled and flustered and wore thick spectacles and a moth-eaten tweed jacket, giving him more the appearance of an office clerk than a wizard. He carried several roles of parchment, which he dropped twice just crossing the threshold.

The first man beamed as he saw Malchus and Adam. 'Malchus, m'boy!' he boomed. Good to see you! And this must be young Adam! Take a seat, both of you!' He frowned as he looked closer and realised they were already seated. 'Very good,' he said in possibly the only sentence in his entire life that had not been an exclamation. 'Well, gentlemen,' he continued as the others joined them at the table, 'shall we get on?' As he sat, he reached over and grabbed Adam by the hand, shaking it vigorously. Adam felt his fingers go numb as the blood supply was cut off. 'I am so very pleased to meet you, young Adam!' beamed the man, mercifully letting him go before the bones snapped. 'I am Garrick Tummelwit, Chancellor of the College, and these are my associates!' He indicated the near-deceased. 'Corban Torridon, Vice-Chancellor,' Torridon made no acknowledgement; 'Tapitlaw Credleigh, Principal,' the man wearing the cat smiled warmly; 'Melanin Psalter, the Bursar,' the moustachioed man nodded in a way that he apparently thought made him look superior; 'and our Warden, Marian Grimbly!'

The dishevelled man looked up from the papers he was frantically trying to arrange. 'Ah, yes,' he said, raising a hand and dropping everything on the floor. 'Oh ... ' He disappeared under the table.

'Good!' continued Tummelwit. 'Now – '

'Greetings,' intoned Corban Torridon in a voice so deep that the sun went dark for just a moment. He appeared to be responding to his introduction, and Adam wondered again if the man was at all well. The Chancellor looked at him over his spectacles before continuing.

'About this business at the monastery, eh?'

Malchus interrupted in his usual diplomatic manner. 'For crying out loud, Garrick! You know everything already, why do you need to interrogate the boy, eh?'

'Hardly an interrogation, Malchus!' said Tummelwit reproachfully. 'There are a few salient gaps in our knowledge of what happened at the monastery and, while we can work most of it out, it would be useful to have young Adam's account of matters! Besides,' he continued as Malchus opened his mouth again, 'that's only part of the reason we're here ... !' His voice had dropped a few hundred decibels to something approaching quiet, as if he were trying to inject an air of mystery into proceedings, although he still managed to make it sound as if there was an exclamation at the end of whatever he had left hanging, which was an impressive linguistic feat.

'What are you talking about?' asked Malchus suspiciously.

'Perhaps I should hand over to you at this point, Tapitlaw?' Tummelwit looked expectantly at the man with the cat on his head. The Principal inclined his neck and produced a white lace handkerchief with which he dabbed his nostrils delicately before speaking in a rich, plummy voice.

'We believe that events at the monastery were being manipulated by an unknown and dangerous power.'

'You mean the voice in the cellar?' asked Adam.

'Precisely,' smiled Principal Credleigh. 'The monastery at Kharesh was, as you know, a seat of ancient Skentys power known as the Causal Nexus. A power presided over by the monks, who were its guardians. That they had turned to murder and abuse of the power they guarded was unthinkable. We were unable to see what went on once you had descended into the tunnels beneath the building. Something was preventing us. You have told Malchus of a disembodied voice apparently controlling the Abbot.' He smiled at Adam, who realised he was expected to take up the story.

'Well, yes,' he said uncertainly. 'It was as if the Abbot worshipped it. And it controlled him. Directed his actions. Even killed him just to prove it could'

'Using the power contained within the monastery.' It wasn't so much a question as a statement for Adam to confirm.

'Yes. It said it was using it to experiment with evolution.'

'Did it say why?' asked Tummelwit, his voice only just showing concern.

'Not really,' replied Adam. 'At least, if there was any objective it never said. I think it was just because it could.'

'What happened to the voice when the monastery was destroyed?' asked Credleigh carefully. His eyes gazed unmoving at Adam.

'I don't know,' confessed Adam. 'We were too concerned with getting out alive and, well, I was unconscious for a lot of the time ... ' He faltered, realising he must sound like a very unreliable witness.

Credleigh smiled encouragingly. 'You were overcome by the smoke from the fire and were helped to safety by your friend.'

'Jana.'

'Jana. Just so. Please continue.'

25

Adam hesitated. He wasn't sure exactly *how* to continue. 'Well, that's all. No-one really knows what happened to the voice. We went back into the ruins but there was no sign of it. And since we don't know what it was we had no idea how to track it. If it had ever moved. I mean ... ' He tailed off, not knowing what he did mean.

'Just so,' repeated Credleigh softly.

He was still looking at Adam, who felt he was expected to say more. In the absence of anything better, Adam asked, 'Have you any idea what it was?'

Credleigh laughed gently. 'Alas no. We could speculate that it was perhaps some form of demon, or a wizard communicating magically from a great distance, but those would be wild guesses. This is nothing we are familiar with. But we do know it was capable of manipulating the Nexus. And that it knew of it in the first place.' He let these words hang for a moment before continuing. 'It seems unlikely it met its end in the destruction of the monastery – even in the destruction of the Nexus. But whether it did or didn't is immaterial. If there was one there will doubtless be others. Others with its knowledge and powers. And that is very dangerous for all of us.' He leaned in closer. 'I don't just mean all of us here in the College. I mean all of us in the Empire, and possibly beyond.' He leaned a little closer and looked deep into Adam's eyes. 'Possibly the whole world.' Whatever was in the monastery was most certainly not benign. If it has knowledge of the Skentys – knowledge perhaps in excess of our own – and has access to other powerful Skentys artefacts we are not even aware of ... ' He sat back, knowing he didn't need to complete the sentence.

There was a long pause before Malchus asked, 'What's that got to do with Adam?' His eyes were darting between Credleigh and Tummelwit, who was looking guilty. They were up to something.

Credleigh suddenly stood up and walked across the room. He stopped and stood looking out of one of the leaded windows, sunlight streaming in on him. Two sparrows were pecking up breadcrumbs on the windowsill. He smiled at them. His back still turned he replied, 'We believe Adam has shown great talent and resourcefulness, and has proved himself very capable.'

'Capable of what?' growled Malchus.

26

Credleigh turned from the window and smiled. 'Of undertaking the mission we have in mind.'

'Mission? What mission?' Malchus was glaring at Credleigh, although somehow it was Tummelwit who looked uncomfortable.

Credleigh began walking slowly around the room. 'We know very little about the Skentys: who and what they were. They had powers far greater than our own, and yet we have only a handful of their more minor artefacts, and precious few of those we understand. But it seems others may know more than we do, and their intentions may not be honourable. We need to be prepared for any eventualities. And more than anything, we need knowledge. We need to know about the Skentys and their powers. We need to know what we may be up against and how to counteract it.' By now he was standing directly behind Adam. 'In short, we need someone to find the Skentys.'

'What?' thundered Malchus. 'Find them how?'

'By going to the New World,' said Credleigh simply.

'The New World?' repeated Malchus incredulously. 'To look for legends of one-eyed lizards? Don't be stupid, man! The Skentys are long gone. You're not going to sail across the ocean and come back with some all-powerful god to save the Empire and usher in a new age of prosperity, you know!'

'Of course not, Malchus!' said Tummelwit as soothingly as he was able. 'But there must be relics, records even! We have to try!'

'And you want to send Adam. An apprentice illusionist who's never been outside of the Empire. You want to send him to the other side of the world to hack his way through uncharted jungle to find a lost city that may not even be there in the hope that some pictures on the wall will tell him everything we need to know.'

'As I said,' smiled Credleigh, 'Adam has shown himself to be very capable. An apprentice will attract far less attention than one of us. He can hire guides to get him through the jungle. And he needn't go alone.'

'You're sending someone with him?' snorted Malchus.

Credleigh took out a small ebony snuffbox and proceeded to place some snuff on his handkerchief. 'We believe Adam should choose his own company. Someone resourceful, loyal, and trustworthy, of course. Perhaps someone else who has already been of help to him in similar circumstances.' He snorted the snuff into each nostril very delicately.

'You mean Jana.' Adam had not spoken throughout this exchange, although everyone else had spoken about him.

'She would be a very useful travelling companion,' smiled Credleigh. 'Among other things, she has some archaeological and palaeontological expertise, which I am sure would be invaluable.'

'Why not just send a team of archaeologists?' asked Malchus. 'Do a much better job.'

'I don't think that would be wise!' cautioned Tummelwit. 'This needs to be very low key! Don't want to attract attention, and we don't really know who we can trust! Keep it amongst ourselves, yes?'

'Jana,' continued Credleigh before Malchus could protest that the girl wasn't exactly one of themselves, 'has already proved herself and knows about the Nexus. She would be ideal. But no-one else. You can enlist local help once you get to Nazca.' This was the first time he had spoken to Adam directly about the proposal. 'Without, of course, telling them of your real objective.'

'Damn fool idea,' snorted Malchus. 'Well he's not going. Come on, Adam, we're leaving.' He stood up.

'I am.'

Malchus stared at Adam. 'What?'

Adam looked up at him. 'I'm going, Malchus.'

'Don't be stupid.'

Adam smiled gently. 'You're all standing here talking about what I'll do. No-one's asked me yet. But it's my decision. Isn't it?' he looked across at Tummelwit.

The Chancellor nodded. 'Quite right, m'boy, of course it is!'

Adam turned back to Malchus. 'I want to do this. The last thing I said to Jana was I wanted to look for the Skentys. And she said take her with me. And now it's more than just my own curiosity. It's important.'

'But you're barely trained,' groaned Malchus. 'You haven't finished your apprenticeship yet.'

'He has completed most of his degree!' Tummelwit corrected him. 'And this level of work in the field could even negate the need for any exams!' The other wizards smiled at this, as it meant they wouldn't have to be bothered by setting any.

'But – ' Malchus sighed deeply. He had gone through all the same arguments trying to prevent Adam from going to the monastery. The boy had come back from that, admittedly within an inch of his life and at the expense of several others, but he'd arguably saved them from whatever had been in that cellar. And now he had a taste for adventure. And, worst of all, Adam couldn't let anything go. He always had to *know* things. It wasn't enough just to accept what he was told. He had to know why. And if you told him why, he'd just ask why the explanation was so. And here they were giving him the chance to go and find the answers to some of the world's greatest mysteries. How could he *not* go?

Adam saw the resignation in Malchus's eyes and turned again to Tummelwit. 'I'll do it, sir. And I'll take Jana with me. If she'll come.'

'How's he supposed to get there?' asked Malchus, sitting down again.

'Ah!' Tummelwit answered. 'Warden's area! Warden! You're on!' He looked around in bewilderment. The Warden wasn't there. 'Warden? Where the devil has he go to? Warden! Where are you man?'

'Aha,' came a voice from under the table. 'I'm, er, you see, I'm down here, Chancellor.'

Tummelwit pulled up the edge of the tablecloth and peered under the table. 'What're you doing down there?'

'Ah, just, er gathering these papers that I, erm, dropped.'

'That was ages ago!' spluttered Tummelwit. 'We've had time to get to the New World and back! Get yourself up here pronto and tell 'em about the arrangements!'

The dishevelled-looking Warden emerged from under the table, an untidy pile of papers in his arms. As he rose, some of them slipped off again. He was about to go back down to retrieve them, then hesitated, changed his mind, changed it again and was only relieved from his quandary by the Chancellor's hand grasping him firmly by the collar and sitting him in his chair. He glanced at Tummelwit, saw his beady stare and pulled himself together in much the way that headless chickens do. 'Ah yes,' he said. 'The, er, arrangements, um.' He leafed through the pile of papers he had left, and realised the ones he needed were on the floor. He briefly considered going to get them, decided against it and blinked several times before gathering at least a few of his thoughts and continuing. 'As you know,' he said, 'the last vestiges of the Skentys are believed to reside in Nazca, across the ocean, in the New World. At least there is evidence of their civilisation there, and that's the best clue we have. If nothing else, it may lead you on to somewhere else with more valuable evidence, or you may find the information we require right there. Of course, if it does lead you somewhere else, there would be certain – '

'Get on with it, man!' groaned Tummelwit.

'You're going to Nazca,' said the Warden quickly.

'How?' asked Malchus.

'We have arranged passage for you and a companion on a ship. The, er, the … ' He searched frantically through his notes but found nothing.

'*Venture!*' sighed Tummelwit.

'The *Venture*,' beamed the Warden. 'It sails from Anterwendt three weeks from today.'

'Should give you plenty of time to get there!' said the Chancellor. 'Well carry on, Warden! Don't keep us all waiting!'

The Warden smiled weakly. 'There is a letter of introduction for you to give to the captain. We have provided maps of the supposed locations of ancient Skentys sites … which may, er, be on the floor at the moment … ' He appeared to flirt briefly with the notion of making another attempt at retrieving them, but again thought better of it. 'The ship's captain will be able to give you an introduction to local guides and, er, yes, guides. We will also provide money for you to buy necessary equipment and, of course, food and any lodgings you require.'

'Bursar!' boomed Tummelwit, indicating that this was someone else's province. The Warden sighed in relief and looked pleadingly at the Chancellor, who raised his eyes to the ceiling and nodded curtly. The grateful Warden disappeared under the table once more.

The little moustachioed man smiled obsequiously. He had not spoken thus far, but had frequently worn expressions that suggested he thought the others were beneath contempt. Of course, Malchus did this all the time but the difference was that Melanin Psalter contrived to look as if they were all beneath *him* as well. It somehow occurred to Adam that this presumably meant the Bursar actually *was* the contempt everyone else was beneath.

'The – heh – ship's captain has already been paid for his – heh – services,' wheedled the little man in a voice that managed to sound both superior and toadying at the same time, 'so you will only need money for your own – heh – expenses.' Adam found himself transfixed, waiting for Psalter to twiddle his moustache. 'We have also – heh – arranged for your coach fare to Anterwendt – via Phelan, should you choose to enlist the services of your – heh – *friend* –' Adam was sure the word 'friend' was said in a vaguely disparaging manner. ' – as well as lodgings in both cities should that – heh – prove necessary.'

Adam frowned. 'You don't know when the ship's arriving?'

'We know the – heh – expected date of arrival but these things can be notoriously unpredictable. Ships can be delayed. The Warden has the address of your lodging house in Anterwendt.' He looked disdainfully at the empty chair and the sound of rustling papers from beneath the table. 'The College will be – heh – invoiced for however long you and your *companion* are required to stay.'

'And Phelan?' asked Malchus.

Psalter smiled at him in the way that only those with a seething hatred for each other can achieve. 'We are aware that you were assisted on your last – heh – escapade by an innkeeper there. We assumed this would be your hostel of choice should you require to stop there.' Adam nodded, sure that he would. Jana would not be able to leave her university studies at a moment's notice. Not this time, anyway. 'We have taken the liberty of writing to the – heh – proprietor and informing him of your possible arrival. He may bill us.'

'Bill us,' repeated Corban Torridon, speaking for the first time since his introduction. Everyone stared at him for a moment, Adam still wondering if he needed medical help, the others amazed he was actually keeping up with the conversation. Psalter looked slightly irritated but continued.

'You will therefore not need any money until you reach the – heh – New World.' At this point he slid the chest across the table towards Adam. 'For this reason – heh – the box is magically locked and will not open until your arrival at Nazca.'

'What?' Malchus exploded. 'You're sending the boy to the other side of the world to face who knows what dangers and you don't trust him with the money?'

'It's not a matter of trust, Malchus!' replied Tummelwit. 'Just precautions! Bandits and the like! You understand!'

'Yes I do!' seethed Malchus, but Adam put a hand on his arm.

'It's alright, Malchus.'

Malchus glared at him but receded. Psalter smiled nastily. Malchus gave him a black look. 'How will the box know when it's got there, eh?'

Psalter smiled again. 'I placed the enchantments myself.'

'Then you'd better take a crowbar,' Malchus growled to Adam spitefully, and was gratified to see Psalter glower at him.

'Hardly, Malchus, hardly!' protested Tummelwit. 'Now, I believe we've covered everything, so once the Warden has sorted out all his papers – everything alright down there? Good! – and given the appropriate ones to young Adam here, I think our business will be concluded! I'm sure you'll be anxious to get started and we wish you all the very best for this quite historic endeavour! Almost wish I was going meself, but I'm too old for that sort of thing now! Young man's game, eh? Good for you, Adam, well done!' He beamed across the table and Adam attempted to smile back. Behind him, Tapitlaw Credleigh finally sneezed, very delicately, and there was a thud from under the table as the Warden banged his head.

II. The Wonders of the West

*B*efore the ships came from Væringjar, they explored the seas to the far west and saw many wonders. In their own land they had seen men fasten boards to their feet, which made them swifter in the snow than birds on the wing, and they knew of a bog that turned wood to stone, and places where the sun shone through the night as bright as through the day.

But off to the west, in the seas of Thule and Frisland, they saw even greater marvels. There were whales who worked with the fishermen, driving the fish towards the land so they could be caught more easily. And there were great fences of ice that hedged in the sea so few escaped when they formed. Sometimes the sea itself turned into fields of thick ice, which no ship could sail through, and at others, great mountains of ice floated on its surface.

On the island of Thule there was an immense fire that raged constantly, though the entire land was covered in ice. It was hot enough to melt rock and stone and yet it did not melt the ice. Sometimes the fire raged so hard it caused earthquakes and caused the water in the springs to boil, sending hot water high into the sky.

But even more marvellous, the waters were infested with monsters. One such was the merman, a huge creature that towered out of the water. It had a human head on its broad shoulders, and above its eyebrows it wore a peaked helmet. But it had no hands and its body narrowed from the shoulders down. No-one ever saw whether its lower end was pointed or shaped like a fish's tail and no-one had ever been close enough to see whether its body had scales or skin like a man's. Whenever the merman appeared, sailors could be sure that storms would follow. Then the merman would turn and plunge into the sea. If it turned towards the ship, their lives would be lost, but if it turned away, they would survive no matter how severe the storm.

Its mate was the mermaid. From the waist up, it was like a woman, with long hair and large breasts. Its fingers were webbed like the toes of a swan, and below the waist it was shaped like a fish, with scales and tail fins. It had a large, terrifying face with a sloping forehead and wide mouth. Like its mate the merman, its appearance was always followed by storms.

The third monster was a huge fish or whale called the kraken, so large it was often mistaken for an island. When hungry it would belch up food to attract fish of all sizes. The monster would open its huge mouth and swallow the fish as they came close. It was so massive it was believed there were only two in the whole world and they never produced offspring.

But when the ships reached our islands, they found different monsters. And maybe they brought some with them.

3

Malchus had, of course, tried to persuade Adam to change his mind, but the old wizard knew it would be futile and had eventually given Adam some money he could use *before* he got to Nazca, as well as his most comprehensive book on the Skentys. The goodbye had been somewhat gruff, which Adam knew meant Malchus was probably upset but not showing it. He had muttered something about having to get a new apprentice now, but Adam knew he wouldn't, at least not for a while.

The coach journey to Phelan had been uneventful, and Adam had made straight for the University to find Jana. He was surprised to find a young man living in her room at the halls of residence, who said he didn't know her and suggested Adam ask at the Records Office. It took him almost an hour to find it in the endless corridors of the main university building but finally he found himself in a small room filled with filing cabinets and occupied by a woman with her hair tied in a tight bun. Adam knew what buns meant.

'What is the young lady reading?' asked the woman primly.

'Reading? What, now?' asked Adam, confused. 'I don't know. How will that help you find her?'

'What *degree* is she reading?' tutted the woman. 'Studying for?'

'Oh. Er, long name. Um, digging things up. Bones and stuff. Er ... '

'Archaeology and palaeontology,' she informed him, more than a touch impatiently.

'Yes, that's it,' agreed Adam as she opened one of the filing cabinets and began rifling through the folders within. After a few moments she stopped and tried another drawer, then two more before she finally turned to Adam.

'Are you sure about those subjects?'

Adam nodded. 'Yes. She was there when they found that dragon fossil last year.'

The woman frowned and tried a few more drawers. Then she returned to her desk. 'Well, I'm afraid there's no-one of that name at the University. Archaeology or otherwise. Sorry.'

Adam shook his head. 'Well, that can't be right. She had a room here and everything. I was in it!'

The woman gave him an appraising look. 'I could always try former students,' she muttered to herself in a tone that suggested she'd much rather not. She crossed to another filing cabinet and began looking through another drawer before suddenly stopping and looking up. 'Did you say dragon fossil?'

'Yes, that's right. The one in the cave.'

'Hmm.' The woman nodded to herself and tried a drawer at the bottom of the same cabinet. Finally she pulled out a folder and sat back down at her desk. 'Yes, here she is,' she said as she opened the folder and began reading its contents. 'Thought I'd heard the name somewhere. She *was* a student here – archaeology and palaeontology, as you say – '

'Actually you said it,' interrupted Adam.

She flashed him a warning glance before continuing. 'Until a few weeks ago when she was sent down – that means expelled – for breaking into a securely-guarded area and taking an unauthorised leave of absence. It was when you mentioned the dragon that I remembered. The securely-guarded area was the cave where the fossil was. It was the talk of the university for a few days.'

Adam was shocked to realise the 'leave of absence' referred to their journey to Kharesh after entering the dragon cave. 'So where is she now?' he stammered.

The woman shut the file and returned it to its drawer. 'We don't keep information on students after they leave the university. Especially not disgraced ones. She probably went back home, wherever that is. I'm afraid I can't be of any more help to you. Good day.'

Adam left the office in a daze. Jana had been expelled because of him. Then he remembered that *she* had been the one who had enlisted *his* help to get into the cave, and he didn't feel quite so bad. Still, he felt a little guilty as he trudged down to *The Magda*, the inn he had stayed at the last time he was here. The landlord, Udi Mensch, was delighted to see him and greeted him with a big bear hug – something physically dangerous from a man his size.

'Adam! Good to see you, lad. What are you doing back so soon? Come and sit down and I'll get you something to eat.' As he steered Adam towards a table he shouted a meal order through to someone in the kitchen. He then went behind the bar and returned with a bottle and two glasses. Adam had never drunk rum before, but Udi was an old sailor and Adam supposed this was meant to be a celebration of sorts. He tentatively sniffed the dark liquid and was surprised to discover that it smelled quite sweet. More confidently he took a sip – and felt his lungs cave in. He erupted into a coughing fit, and Udi laughed as he slapped Adam on the back, which at least cracked it back into place after the hug. 'That'll put hairs on yer chest,' Udi grinned, pouring two more glasses. Adam mused that there couldn't be many hairs left for his chest considering Udi was using so many of them in his beard. You could probably hide the entire lost Skentys civilisation in there if you wanted. He also had to keep reminding himself the eyepatch didn't mean Udi was a pirate.

'So what brings you back to Phelan? I got the letter saying you might be coming, but it didn't say why.'

It was fully thirty seconds before Adam was able to speak, and when he did it was in a hoarse wheeze. 'I came to find Jana,' he spluttered. 'I've got a proposition for her. But the University people said she'd been expelled and they didn't know where to find her.'

Udi smiled slyly. 'Is that so? Well, I've a feeling she'll turn up.'

There was a sudden cry from the direction of the kitchen. 'Adam!' He turned and saw Jana wearing an apron and carrying two plates towards them.

Adam stood up in surprise, and then was even more surprised to find that he hadn't stood up at all, the effects of the rum preventing his legs from doing anything much. However, a few seconds later it didn't matter as Jana had rushed over, dropped the plates on the table and pulled him bodily from his seat to give him a hug almost as tight as Udi's. He winced slightly as he remembered she was actually stronger than him but was still built the way girls were meant to be built.

She finally let him go and he collapsed back into the chair, failing in his attempt to make it look completely casual. 'I didn't expect to see you so soon. How are you? They expelled me from the university. Udi took me in and gave me a job. What are you doing here?' Ah yes. When Jana got excited there was no stopping her.

Udi laughed. 'Adam wants to propose to you,' he said with a mischievous twinkle.

'A proposition, Udi,' said Adam hurriedly.

'Sorry, proposition you. Same thing, isn't it?'

'Stop it, Udi,' scolded Jana. 'This is about the Skentys, isn't it? I told you to come and find me when you were ready to go looking for them.'

Udi looked impressed. 'I'm sure there'll be another plate of dumplings in that pot. Don't start without me.'

When Udi returned, Adam told them the whole story. Udi gave a long whistle when the tale was done.

'You've certainly got the taste for adventure, lad, I'll give you that. But abroad's very different. Most of the New World hasn't been charted yet, never mind built on. Lots of difficult country out there, and the heat won't be like anything you're used to. And as for the sea, take it from an old sailor: she's a treacherous mistress. Take you down to Davy Jones any chance she gets.'

'I know it'll be dangerous,' said Adam, 'but this is important. I have to go. And I'll have local guides and the ship's crew to look after me.'

'And me!' shrieked Jana.

'Now just a minute,' protested Udi. 'You've got a job here, I can't spare you.'

'Udi!' She looked at him imploringly. 'Udi, please. I have to go with him. I can't miss this.'

For a moment he looked at her sternly – then his face broke into a big grin. 'Course you can go. I don't own you. As if I could stop you anyway. Course, I'll be sad to lose you, but I knew you were only here till Adam came back to take you off to your certain death. You could probably do with some extra cash too, since you can't use the wizards' money till you get to Nazca.'

'Oh, Udi, thank you!' Jana threw her arms around the big man's neck and Adam wondered which of them would crush the other first.

It wasn't real, it was a dream. But that didn't stop it from *feeling* real. Even though he knew he was dreaming, every sensation felt as though it were really happening. The strange gaps and segues in the passage of time went completely unnoticed, and the surreal narrative seemed perfectly normal.

He was walking down a long staircase in darkness. The steps were wooden – except when they were made of stone, which happened occasionally. The air was cold and musty and his footsteps echoed as if he were in a cave. Even when he walked on the wooden steps. As he went down, the stairs seemed to get steeper and then they started to sway gently. Trying to keep his balance, he realised there was no handrail and he didn't know how far the stairs went down or where he would land if he fell. Or even if he would land at all.

He kept going, occasionally stopping as the stairs swayed a bit further than usual. He could hear a breeze now, and as he descended further, he could feel it on his face. At times he thought it sounded more like a whisper than a breeze, but then it would caress his skin and he knew it must be his imagination.

As the swaying continued, a creaking sound joined the breeze and it seemed to be in rhythm with the movement. At first he thought it must be the stairs that were creaking, but then he realised the sound was more distant. Just as he thought this, there was a sudden lurch and he almost fell, but a hand caught him and steadied him until he could stand alone. He looked but there was no-one there, and he realised its touch had been as cold as the breeze. And had someone whispered his name as it caught him?

He carried on downwards and, a few seconds later, reached the top. He emerged into sunlight and found himself on the deck of a ship. The crew was working hard, doing whatever it was they were doing, and singing a jaunty sea shanty. He couldn't work out where the accordion music was coming from until he looked up and saw the player sitting in the rigging. Above him flew a massive skull and crossbones. A pirate ship! He looked again at the crew as they all stopped work and turned to face him. Every one of them wore an eyepatch and some wore two. They were all grinning at him, some with knives between their teeth and some with no teeth at all. Most wore scarves tied over or around their heads, although a few had those pirate hats with the brims turned up at the front and with a little skull and crossbones painted in white. They either wore white shirts with sashes around their waists, or long coats, and more than seemed reasonable had wooden legs. Some had two, and as soon as he noticed this, they fell over using words he had never heard before. The one with the biggest beard stepped forward and said, 'Ha-haargh! Ye'll have to sail the ship alone, Cap'n. Ye're the only one here.'

And then he was. The pirates were all gone and he was alone on the deck. And it felt completely normal. And as the ship swayed, he almost lost his footing until an invisible hand steadied him and the breeze whispered his name.

Instinctively, he climbed up to the wheel and turned it. The ship came around much more quickly than he would have expected, and then he wished it hadn't. Right in front of it was another ship, much bigger than his and, he knew without actually seeing them, bristling with weapons, all of them trained on him. He could see figures lining the deck, and he picked up his telescope to get a better look. To his surprise, he saw a giant eye and wondered what kind of creatures he was facing, before realising the other ship's captain was looking back at him through his own telescope. He scanned around the deck and saw that everyone wore the uniform of the Imperial Navy. And they all had flippers instead of hands. Presumably in case they fell overboard and had to swim.

'Duck!'

And then he saw the big black thing hurtling towards him. Cannonball! He ducked and it slammed into the mast, shattering it. Then there were cannons firing from all over the Imperial ship, and cannonballs smashing into the side of his, turning it to matchwood.

He looked up to see who had warned him, and saw a man holding a duck. 'Quack,' said the man. 'Duck,' said the duck.

He ran for the stairs and leapt down them two at a time, the noise of the explosions receding into the darkness behind him. But each explosion rocked the steps more, until he lurched and fell headlong into the dark. Down and down he fell, the breeze still calling his name. He was falling and drowning, the water filling his lungs and slowing his descent. At first he struggled, but then he relaxed and realised it was actually quite pleasant. Fish came and nibbled at him, and it tickled until the shark bit his leg off, but a kindly octopus came and fitted him with a peg leg and he hardly felt a thing.

He kept sinking until another ship came into view. This one was a wreck and had been there for years by the looks of it. It didn't have the skull and crossbones, so it wasn't his, and there was no Imperial flag either. In fact, it was much smaller, more like a fishing boat. Its mast was broken in two and had fallen on top of the wheelhouse. Barnacles covered most of the hull, and the anchor was the dark orangey brown colour of rust. The water was the sort of vivid blue it always is in children's books, and small shoals of brightly coloured fish swam obligingly past to complete the picture. A large fish he didn't recognise, and which may not even have existed in real life, poked its nose out from a porthole. 'Fish,' it said.

He swam around the wreck until he saw an opening in the hull, and ventured inside. He found himself in a grotto much bigger than the boat, but this didn't seem strange to him. The ceiling seemed to be forty or fifty feet above his head, and had a hole where moonlight drifted in, even this far below the waves. All around the grotto were everyday objects like forks and pipes and mirrors, most of them once shiny but now long-tarnished. These sat on rocks and on ledges in the cavern – for it was now definitely a cavern and not a wreck at all – like some museum of the banal, or a shrine to small domestic objects.

One item stood out from the rest though. In the centre of the cavern, and dominating it, was a life-size statue of a man. Its back was to him, but he could see that it stood in a dynamic pose, one foot perched on a rock at knee-height, and one hand stretched out and pointing at something in front of it. As he moved closer, he saw the other hand was

41

raised to the face, stroking the chin. He looked to see what the figure was pointing at, and followed the outstretched finger to one of the ledges. On it sat a little glass dome filled with water, in which stood a model of a lighthouse. He picked it up, and without knowing why, shook it. Tiny particles of grit, which had formed the beach on which the lighthouse stood, swirled up in the water and floated back down in what looked like a miniature snowstorm.

He put it down and turned to look at the statue again. Before he could get a good look at the face, a shadow fell over him and he looked up to the hole in the ceiling. Something was passing overhead. A ship? He swam up to the hole and looked up along the shaft of moonlight to the surface. The underside of a large ship sailed lazily above him, scattering shoals of fish. He pulled himself up through the hole to get a better look.

'Quack,' said the man with the duck. 'Duck,' said the duck. Then everything went black.

And he didn't suddenly wake up, because people never really do. He stopped dreaming but carried on sleeping peacefully.

It was a dark and stormy night and a dark and stormy man guided a boat across the dark and stormy waters. It was a small boat, only big enough for one occupant, and surely too small to be out on the open ocean, but it moved swiftly and surely, negotiating the waves with ease. The boat had no sail, and yet it cut through the sea far more quickly than any vessel should have been able to. The occupant appeared to be rowing, but no oars could propel a boat at that speed. At least, no natural oars.

Had anyone been close enough, they would have seen that, beneath his hood, the oarsman had a dark and stormy visage, one that suggested dark and stormy deeds. And tonight was the darkest and stormiest deed of all.

The boat stopped. Despite its speed, it did not need time to slow down. It just stopped. There was a pause as the oarsman looked around to satisfy himself that this was the place. Then he started moving again, faster than ever. But this time the boat was sinking. The oarsman leaned forward, pushing his weight into it. He was deliberately sinking the boat. It was below the surface of the water now, but still moving. He brought it around in a tight circle – no boat should be able to perform such a manoeuvre – so it was heading back to the spot where he had stopped. Now he was leaning forward so heavily that the prow was pointing down at an angle. He was actually driving the boat into the water.

Within moments, his head sunk beneath the waves, still moving with the same phenomenal speed. And then the wind dropped and the water was still.

III. The Trows

W hen the farmer and his wife had gone to bed, they would not sleep, for they would lie awake in fear, listening for the sound of the latch being lifted on the locked door and of unwanted guests moving about in the kitchen. For night time was when the trows would come.

The trows were small, ugly creatures who lived under mounds known as howes. They were mischievous at best, malevolent at worst. Their walls were decorated with gold and silver, and only the finest food and drink was served at their banquets. Their greatest passions were music and dancing, and they would sometimes lure fiddlers into their mounds to play for them. They would keep the fiddler entertaining them for a whole night, but when he returned home he would discover, to his amazement, that a whole year had passed. However, he would be well rewarded for his playing, and would never want for money again.

The trows only ventured out at night, when their hatred of locked doors would bring them into the islanders' homes. If the householders were lucky, the hill folk would just warm themselves by the remains of the fire, and maybe steal some food or small objects that took their fancy. If the householders were unlucky, something far more precious would be stolen.

Trow children were weak and sickly, and so trows had a habit of stealing human babies and leaving their own unwanted offspring in their place. Whenever a child failed to thrive or was 'not normal', the family would be sure it was a trowie bairn and their own healthy child had been stolen away without their knowledge, despite all the precautions they would have taken to avoid such a tragedy. The unfortunate trowie bairn could then be safely ill-treated or neglected as punishment.

Sometimes the babies would be taken before they had even been brought into the world, the mothers being abducted while still pregnant, and kept to nurse the children. For this reason all care was taken to hide signs of pregnancy, so the trows would not know.

Trows were not the brightest of creatures. A clan of trows once decided to travel to a neighbouring island. They tied together as many ropes as they could muster and gathered on the cliff top. One of them tied an end of the rope to a rock, took the other end in his hand and made a magical leap across the water. Once safe on the opposite shore, he secured his end of the rope so it straddled the waves. The other trows began to climb on to the rope, and edge hand over hand along it. Soon, the last of the trows was hanging from the rope – but the first had not yet reached the other side. The weight of the entire clan caused the rope to snap and they all fell to their deaths in the sea below.

4

The Empire was a confederation of states and independent cities that had submitted themselves to the Emperor's laws in order to enjoy his protection and the various other benefits of membership, such as not being invaded. It was centuries since the Empire had invaded anywhere, but most of the provinces had joined in the bad old days.

Of course, 'the Empire' wasn't its full title. It was really the Great and Glorious Empire of (insert name of current ruler here), so it was currently the Great and Glorious Empire of Leopold II; but everyone called it just 'the Empire', if only for simplicity's sake. Well, everyone who lived there, that is. *Other* empires understandably resented this particular empire referring to itself as *the* Empire, as if it were the only one. In public they usually referred to it as 'the Empire of Leopold II'. How they referred to it behind its back was not a matter of record.

As well as Imperial law, laid down by the Emperor in Hapsdorf, each province had its own slightly different laws, and on the whole existed as an independent state unless it was politically expedient to do otherwise. Each of the provincial rulers was subject to the Emperor, but was equally eligible to succeed him, which inevitably resulted in politics.

The Principality of Niederland had no real ambition in that area or in political matters in general, its interests being more mercantile and cultural. Situated in the northwest of the Empire, bordering the Kingdom of Breton, the Principality's most important role was in controlling the Empire's major seaport, which was also Niederland's capital, Anterwendt. The Principality was actually governed from further west, in the city of Haagdatz, but Anterwendt had been the official capital ever since Niederland had existed.

Everyone knew that Niederland was flat, but Adam had always assumed this meant it just had smaller hills than everywhere else. It turned out to have no hills at all. It wasn't even wrinkled. Well, for most of the journey anyway. As the coach neared Anterwendt in the northwest, the landscape began to rise again. Not by much, but there were some hills, and as the road neared the coast, there were signs of distant cliffs. Admittedly not very high ones, but they counted.

The crisp spring air had a distinctive tinge to it. People say that sea air smells salty, but it doesn't. It smells of rotting seaweed. Adam had never smelled the sea before, but he thought it smelled like fish, and it was delicately laced through the background of Anterwendt. It wasn't unpleasant, which was a good thing because you couldn't escape it. Yet despite the aroma, the breeze – and there was definitely a breeze – felt fresh and invigorating. Adding to the effect was a distant rumbling crash, like baby thunder, which Adam knew must be the sound of the ocean, although he couldn't see it.

The other principal sound was a high-pitched screeching noise from above. Adam looked up and saw that the sky and the rooftops were filled with white birds. He'd seen pictures of gulls in books, but hadn't realised there were so many varieties. Some were white and pale grey, some had darker wings, and others black heads or pink legs instead of yellow. The real show-offs had distinctive red spots on their beaks. They were all much bigger than the pictures had suggested, and a hell of a lot noisier. The airborne ones seemed to float effortlessly, bobbing up and down without flapping their wings. Many of the chimney pots had nests on top of them, although Adam noticed that a few had strange grey cowls on top instead.

The buildings were different to any Adam had seen before. Instead of stone or more modern bricks, the walls were harled – covered over in tiny sharp stones to protect them against erosion from the salt thrown up by the sea. The harling gave the walls a rough texture that you could sand a brick on. There were other signs that this was a sea port. Some of the houses had coiled ropes hanging decoratively outside, and a few had lobster pots on the doorsteps. Inns had names like *The Ship* and

The Sailor's Rest, with brightly painted sailing vessels or white-bearded sea dogs on their signs. One had stained glass compasses in its windows, and another had an anchor propped up next to the door. The nautical theme carried over into the shops, which included more fish-mongers than Adam was used to, and where else would you find a sail maker? He kept expecting to hear sea shanties. He looked at Jana and saw that she was beaming. She liked this sort of thing. When he had first met her, she had kept pleading with him to show her some magic, and right now she was probably imagining pirates.

The coach dropped them off in the city square, and they soon found the lodging house Melanin Psalter had arranged for them. It was a seafront hotel called *The Stotfold,* and Adam was surprised to find that it was one of the larger and more expensive hotels in the city. He'd expected the nasty little man to provide something cheap and dingy, but presumably Chancellor Tummelwit had ensured otherwise.

The seafront provided three even more impressive sights. The most immediately arresting was the ocean itself. Adam had seen lakes and rivers, but he had never seen water that looked so alive. The waves lashed against the shore like they were trying to break it, continually retreating and then renewing the assault.

'Breathtaking, isn't it?' smiled Jana, relishing the feel of the wind in her hair.

'Have you seen this before?' he asked her.

'I was born in a seaside village. Nothing like this place but it does have the ocean.' She breathed in deeply. 'We left when I was seven, moved to a small town, but the sea never leaves you. It's in your bones.'

The grey water stretched away to the far horizon, and they could make out the silhouette of a boat in the distance. Adam realised there was no sign of the harbour and wondered where it was.

The second sight was the beach, something else Adam had never seen before. He had always imagined it to be something like a desert (not that he'd seen one of those either) and was therefore surprised at the reality. Where the waves rolled up to the shoreline was an expanse of wet sand. There was then a line of smooth, round stones followed by a necklace of some sort of plant life Adam didn't recognise. Even from a distance he could see it was a mixture of green, yellow and brown and had lumps all over it. Jana later explained that it was seaweed. This whole section of the beach was punctuated by rocks, many of which had a different, bright green plant coating them. Some of the rocks formed little basins with pools of water in them. This seemed to mark the highest point of the tide, because beyond this was a plain of dry, white sand, which eventually led to the dunes. Adam had thought sand dunes were just hills where the wind made the sand pile up, but these were clearly permanent features and were topped with a stiff, long grass and spiky yellow bushes. To the right, the sand eventually gave way to rocks while, to the left, the dunes became low cliffs and atop them was the third sight: a tall, gleaming white tower that Adam knew must be a lighthouse.

He looked out again at the boat in the distance. 'Is this where the ship will the ship arrive?'

'No!' laughed Jana. 'It's probably too rocky here. There'll be a harbour somewhere. Maybe across the other side of town. We'll go and look later.'

'Why not now?'

'Because,' she said slyly, 'I want something to eat. And it's on your wizard friends, so we can have the most expensive thing on the menu. Coming?'

Adam hesitated for just a moment. He shouldn't really but ... well, he was going to. If he protested, she'd just bully him into it anyway. He turned around and set off back into the hotel. Jana breathed the sea air deeply one more time and then followed him.

Four hundred miles away, another coach was arriving in another city. Hapsdorf was the capital of the Empire and its largest city. Although situated in the heart of the Grand Duchy of Nordland, in the interests of political fairness, Hapsdorf was an independent city-state ruled by the Emperor, while the province itself was governed from Castle Grünwald near the city of Wertenberg to the east. This did not stop Hapsdorf from being powerful, however. As well as the Emperor, it was home to the Empire's senior religious figure, the Grand Theoginist of the Church of Marius, and also to the High Palatine of the Northern Provinces, the most powerful administrative officer, both of whom sat on the Electoral Council. While hardly a democracy, the Empire was not governed by a single person. As an alliance of semi-independent states, it was ruled by all of them. Each province and city-state had its own ruler, all of whom sat on the Electoral Council, the Empire's governing body, and voted on decisions. A sort of government of the people, for the people by the people who had the biggest houses. There was only ever one actual election and it only happened when an Emperor or Empress died. All of the provincial and city-state rulers were eligible to succeed him or her, and the Council did the voting. This gave Hapsdorf another sphere of power because, when the new Emperor took office he moved to the capital and his province or city-state was inherited by his family, allowing Hapsdorf obvious influence in the Emperor's home state.

As well as the provincial Electors, there were several others who were not state rulers, and in some cases were not even of noble birth. These were the five religious leaders and the two Palatines, one for the northern provinces and the other for the south. These last two acted as the Emperor's representatives in the provinces, performing important administrative, legal and ceremonial roles. Neither the Palatines nor the religious leaders were eligible to become Emperor, but all were involved in choosing one.

The black coach that was now rattling along the streets in the direction of the Imperial Palace belonged to Lord Adolf Reitherman, High Palatine of the Southern Provinces and Sheriff of the League of Westmarch. Lord Reitherman was a man whose reputation preceded him and took the opportunity to spread vicious rumours before he got there. He was known as the Man in Black, and it was widely believed – especially by those who had never met him – that he was a dangerous man and not to be crossed. Those who actually *had* met him could never usually cite any specific ex-amples of his not-to-be-crossed-ness, but usually insisted that his unfailing politeness, tireless civic work and seeming ability to get on with anyone were merely a front for his true nature, and that the drinks he served at his regular parties for the working class pillars of the com-munity, whose opinions he trusted

51

more than those of the wealthy, were almost certainly spiked with hemlock. The fact that no-one had ever been poisoned at one of these parties was just confirmation of his deviousness. He did, after all, dress exclusively in black. Even his coach was black. Of course, most coaches were black, but that didn't prove anything.

Accompanying Lord Reitherman was his secretary, Albert Munster. The Palatine had been involved in the events at Kharesh and, after all of his adventures there, the main thing he had brought back with him was a newfound interest in what he called 'the singsong'. For much of the journey he had been trying, with extremely limited success, to introduce Albert to its delights. 'If I may say so, your Lordship, cream cheese seems a very impractical material for making hats out of and, while I can't profess to be an expert, I remain unconvinced as to the musical properties of kitchen utensils. Now perhaps we could return to the matter in hand. We're almost there.' His employer could, at times, be very easily distracted, and a large part of Albert's job revolved around keeping him focussed.

Lord Reitherman smiled thinly. 'You are quite right, of course, Albert. We have important and difficult work to do and I am wasting our time with frivolity. Please accept my apologies.'

Albert bowed his head modestly, but suspected his master was simply humouring him. Lord Reitherman was an astonishingly intelligent man and was usually several steps ahead of everyone else. He had probably considered all of the options and worked out a strategy between his front door and the coach, and was likely only wasting his time with frivolity in order to occupy his mind. Discussing and making plans would be more for Albert's benefit than anything else.

Albert pulled out the letter that was the reason for their journey. It read simply:

My dear Lord Reitherman,
It has come to my attention that you have neglected to keep me appraised of a possible item of interest under the terms of Edict 37. You are invited to visit me in Hapsdorf to discuss the matter in detail.
Sincerely,
Leopold II

When an Emperor uses the word 'invited', it's a polite way of saying 'summoned on pain of death or, if you really want to make something of it, on pain of pain.' In a similar vein, 'discuss the matter in detail' is Emperor-speak for 'explain yourself while a very big man holds dangerous implements near your politically sensitive areas'. The Emperor wasn't best pleased about something.

It had taken Albert a lot of careful research to find out what Edict 37 was, as it wasn't contained in any of the normal statute books. He had eventually learned it was something called a Private Edict, a law set by the Emperor personally and which only applied to certain people, usually the Electors, all of whom were notified individually. In other words a secret that the Emperor didn't want to be made public. Edict 37 ran as follows:

To all members of the Electoral Council,
PRIVATE EDICT NO. 37
All Electors are requested to report knowledge or rumour of any items which may be deemed of occult significance directly to my person and without delay. This does not apply to everyday magical objects but to anything that is known or held to have inherent power within the terms mentioned above. Even legends and folk tales are of interest.
Leopold II

Lord Reitherman had discovered that the Emperor had been accumulating such 'items of occult significance', and also that many religious relics and even local village charms had gone missing or been stolen. At the same time, the numbers of witch-finders had grown and their powers had increased. In fact, technically, witch-finders had no official powers. Nothing was written in the law regarding them, but somehow their authority was accepted and the one who had investigated the dragon fossil and followed Lord Reitherman's party to Kharesh had borne the Emperor's seal. It all looked deeply suspicious. Neither the Palatine nor Albert could work out why the Emperor would want to collect – let alone steal – occult artefacts, or why he would use witch-finders to do it. They weren't even sure what Lord

Reitherman had done, or rather failed to do, that had upset the Emperor so much. Considering the witch-finder had originally come to see the dragon fossil and decry the heretical notion that it might lend support to the new ideas about evolution, this seemed to be the obvious connection. Except Lord Reitherman had left for the March before the fossil was known to be anything other than an interesting archaeological discovery.

'I've been thinking about the timing of the Emperor's letter,' said Albert cautiously.

'Really?'

'The letter isn't dated, but judging by the date of its arrival, it must have been sent several days before anything unusual had been established about the fossil at all.'

Lord Reitherman stared at him in surprise. 'Do you know, Albert, I hadn't even considered that!' Albert allowed himself a pleased smile. 'So you're saying that not only could the Emperor not have expected me to know anything about the fossil's magical properties, but he couldn't even have known himself at the time the letter was sent.'

'Well, not by the usual channels,' said Albert carefully.

Lord Reitherman frowned. 'What do you mean?'

Albert looked nervous, but that wasn't unusual. 'The Emperor can't have been informed about the discovery until after it had been made. But what if such a discovery had been expected?'

Lord Reitherman leaned forward, his eyes even wider. 'Do you realise what you're saying, Albert?'

Albert's mouth went dry. 'I'm rather afraid I do, sir. But, if I may be so bold, do you?'

'You have a theory?'

Albert found himself leaning forward as well and, involuntarily, he was whispering. 'Lazlo Winter, the Court Magician, is Professor of Predictive Sciences at the Imperial College of Magic.'

There was a long pause as Albert let this sink in. Slowly, both men sat back in their seats. Eventually Lord Reitherman spoke.

'You're suggesting that Lazlo Winter predicted the discovery of the fossil and informed the Emperor, who sent the letter before the discovery was actually made?'

'I should say that I don't actually believe in astrology, sir, but I did some checking. While the letter must have been *sent* before the discovery was made, it *arrived* a day or two *after*. Had you been at home, it's quite likely we'd never have noticed the discrepancy.'

'So you think the letter may have been deliberately timed to arrive after the discovery had been made?'

'It's a theory, sir.'

'Indeed it is, Albert. A rather clever one at that.' Albert blushed. 'But let's not jump to conclusions yet. It's always possible that the Emperor isn't referring to the fossil at all.'

'Then what, sir?'

'I confess I don't know. But your theory does raise one rather worrying problem.'

'It does?'

Lord Reitherman looked at him very seriously. 'If you're correct about the timing of the letter, then the Emperor did not give me the opportunity to inform him. He assumed that I would not.'

Albert considered this. 'Why would he do that?'

'Indeed why?' The two men looked gravely at each other for a moment until, suddenly, Lord Reitherman's face fell. 'Because he knows, Albert. The Emperor knows that we suspect him!'

IV. The Sea-Trows

*T*he hill-trows might have been daft but they were down-right intelligent compared to their cousins the sea-trows. These used to live on the land too, but some long-forgotten feud with the hill-trows had caused them to be banished to the sea. They looked much like the hill-trows, but had longer arms and faces like monkeys beneath sharply sloping brows. Their hands and their flat, round feet were webbed, and their lank hair hung about them like seaweed. They liked to return to the shore, but their movements on land were clumsy, and they would be driven away by their hill-dwelling cousins.

It was said there were fallen angels, and those that fell on the land became the hill-trows, while those that fell in the sea became the sea-trows. But others said the ones that fell on the land became the fairy-folk, and those that fell in the sea became the selkies. The sea-trows certainly didn't seem very angelic.

Some believed they lived in their own kingdom at the bottom of the sea, where they breathed a special kind of air that was found nowhere else. When they wanted to visit the land, they had to put on the skin of some animal that could breathe in the sea. One shape they chose was a mermaid or merman, but their favourite was a seal, for in that form they could land on the rocks, cast off their skin to take on their own shape, and amuse themselves as they liked in the upper world.

In the water, the sea-trows would steal fish from the fisherman's line to eat for themselves, or if the fish weren't biting and the trows were particularly hungry, they would just take the bait. This was *dangerous, though, because they often became hooked or tangled in the line themselves, and would be hauled to the surface where the angry fisherman would surely punish them.*

They were not as evil as the hill-trows but oh, how they liked to play tricks on the islanders. Unfortunately, these usually backfired, leaving the slow-witted sea-trows bewildered as they became the victims of their own practical jokes. Foolish creatures!

5

The lobster was delicious, especially as neither of them had ever tasted it before, and even more so because someone else was paying for it. Jana particularly enjoyed saying 'Put it on the bill,' knowing someone else would be receiving that bill. She also enjoyed glancing furtively at the man eating soup at the corner table. Having led a relatively sheltered life, Adam assumed she was looking at the various paintings by local artists that adorned the walls. Most of them were landscapes, some of which Adam already recognised as local, while others were of boats or depictions of local life. A few showed animals and birds, with seals being popular, and one even had a scene of mermaids frolicking in the water. They shared the space with other maritime decorations such as nets, lobster pots and a large brass ship's bell above the bar. This shared pride of place with a very long painting of what looked like a storm at sea. It was just as you'd want a seaside hotel to be.

The landlord, Matheeus, was welcoming and efficient. His wife, Ceasg, was quiet and wore lots of shawls and skirts and layers of clothes that Adam wouldn't have known the name of, as if she was trying to hide in amongst them all. She had an unusual accent that Adam couldn't place.

These thoughts were interrupted by Jana suddenly achieving the not inconsiderable feat of shrieking and whispering at the same time. 'He's coming over!'

'What? Who?'

'Don't look! Shh!' She then gave the strangest laugh Adam had ever heard. He gave her a quizzical look. 'You just said something really funny,' she glowered at him.

'Did I? Whe– ow!'

'*Shh!*'

'You just kic– ow! Stop doing that.'

Suddenly Jana was smiling sweetly at him and Adam realised the man from the corner table was at his elbow.

'Excuse me,' said the man in the guttural Niederland accent. 'I hope I'm not intruding, but you seem to have just arrived, and I wondered if I might buy you both a drink to make you feel welcome.'

'That's very kind of you,' beamed Jana.

'My name's Ben,' said the stranger when he returned with the drinks. Jana had pulled over a chair from a nearby table, and Adam completely failed to notice that it was a little closer to her than to him.

'I'm Jana and that's Adam,' she said as their new acquaintance sat down. A little closer to Jana than to Adam.

'You don't sound like Niederlanders,' he ventured.

'No, we're from Oldenberg. Well, Adam is. I'm originally from Nordland but I've been studying in Phelan.'

'Really? I sat my zoology degree there. What are you studying?'

'Palaeontology.' She deliberately missed out the bit about having been thrown out of the university.

He smiled. 'You study old animals, I'm interested in new ones.' She laughed. Just a little too much.

Ceasg came to clear away the plates.

'When are you due?' Jana asked her with a smile.

Ceasg looked suddenly worried. 'I don't know what you mean,' she said, not looking Jana in the eye. Adam thought that whatever it was, her accent didn't sound like a Niederlander accent.

'You're having a baby, aren't you?' asked Jana.

'Sh!' said Ceasg urgently. She glanced around to see if anyone had heard, before whispering, 'No-one's supposed to know. Please don't tell anyone. It's *dangerous*.'

'Dangerous?' asked Jana, confused. 'How?'

'They might steal it! *Please* promise you won't tell anyone. Please!'

'Alright,' said Jana placatingly. 'I promise.'

Ceasg looked expectantly at Adam and Ben until they agreed too. 'Thank you,' she said with obvious relief and hurried off. Jana and Adam looked at Ben in bemusement.

'Local superstition,' he explained. 'Where Ceasg comes from, you're supposed to conceal a pregnancy in case the fairy folk hear about it and come steal the baby.' He turned to Adam. 'What about you? Are you a student as well?'

'Yes. Wolfsburg, sort of.'

Ben thought for a moment. 'Imperial College of Magic? You're a wizard?' He sounded impressed.

'He doesn't like to brag about it,' explained Jana, and Adam felt for a moment that she sounded proud of him. Ben seemed to notice it too.

'What do you do now?' Jana asked Ben, apparently fascinated.

'I'm interested in an unfashionable branch of zoology that I like to refer to as cryptozoology.'

Adam's brow creased. 'You study animals in tombs? Ow!'

Jana was smiling sweetly again and Ben suppressed a smile. 'It means hidden animals. I look for species whose existence conventional science prefers to dismiss.'

Jana's smile was suddenly replaced by a look of astonishment. 'Ben *Heuvelmans*? *Doctor* Ben Heuvelmans?'

He nodded modestly. 'I'm flattered that you've even heard of me.'

Adam wondered why she was blushing. 'I read your book. Your father rediscovered the chimaera when everyone else believed it was extinct. You've been mentioned in some of our lectures – ' Her voice faltered.

Ben laughed. 'Not, I imagine, in a very positive manner. Many scientists consider what I do something of a joke.'

'I don't,' said Jana, her enthusiasm recovered. Adam was again reminded of her childlike wonder at his magical abilities. 'And since the dragon, no-one else can either. Did you come and investigate it?'

'Ah, the Phelan Dragon. No, I'm afraid I was already busy here but one of my colleagues went. Unfortunately, despite the very many reliable eyewitness accounts, there was no physical evidence so the dragon has to remain unverified. We were particularly sad that they closed off the cave system. We would have loved to explore that. Did you see it yourselves?'

'No, we were away at the time,' said Adam guardedly, well aware that they had met their own share of strange creatures during their time at Kharesh. The chimaera may already have been known to survive, but this one was far away from its usual hunting grounds; and everyone was sworn to secrecy about the were-rabbit. 'So you look for extinct animals?' he asked.

'Sometimes. It's always seemed possible that some might have survived in remote corners of the world – and not-so-remote ones if your dragon is anything to go by. Mostly I chase legends and folk tales. Creatures people have always believed to exist, but science hasn't yet classified. And we also like wild animals that are outside their usual range, like the recent rumours of the March Cat.' Adam and Jana exchanged careful looks but said nothing. 'The world's full of areas we haven't even begun to explore – the jungles, deserts, remote mountain ranges. There must still be places we haven't even discovered yet. Perhaps entire continents. Even in populated areas like the Empire there are mountains and forests, and who knows what's living in the depths of the oceans? We're discovering new species all the time, and as you say, occasionally rediscovering some we thought had been lost forever. It makes sense that some of those animals would already be known locally or have made their way into legends. My job is to look for them.'

'What are you looking for here?' asked Jana, who was still smiling just a bit too much.

'Believe it or not, mermaids.'

'Mermaids? You don't belie– ' She stopped herself again, and this time Adam knew exactly why she blushed. He took a drink to cover his smirk and then realised his glass was empty.

Ben looked amused rather than offended. 'That's the whole point. There have been stories of mermaids all over the world for centuries, and yet people say they don't believe in them. But still we keep hearing of sightings.'

'Here?' asked Jana incredulously.

He grinned 'Right here. Fishing communities are the most likely places. Fisherfolk are often quite superstitious, so they're more open to believing in things that others dismiss. But they also spend their lives at sea. If anyone's going to see a mermaid – and believe what he sees – it's a fisherman.'

'And have you seen one yet?' asked Jana, her enthusiasm mounting again. 'I mean an actual mermaid?'

Ben smiled, still amused at her. 'Not yet, but I live in hope.'

'So what *have* you seen?' asked Adam, genuinely interested.

Ben stood up. 'Let me get those drinks and I'll tell you.'

Anterwendt had grown out of four communities, which had merged into one. The original town of Anterwendt had been inland at one of the turns of the River Anter, a small tributary of the Reisch, while the farming and fishing hamlet of Stotfold had stood where their hotel was now, on the coast to the east of the river. The town's access to the sea, via a small lake, had gradually silted up, and a new harbour had been built at the mouth of the river. Cottages were built next to it to attract new fishermen, and this brought immigrants from the far off Orknejar islands, thus establishing the Seatown. Soon a mercantile quarter sprang up in the area between the two hamlets and became known as Antermond. Eventually, the new town spread up the hill until it met Anterwendt and they became the modern city. The last major development had been the arrival, five years ago, of the Imperial Navy, who had set up a small training base with its own docks and barracks just east of Stotfold.

Ben had offered to show them around, and Jana had leapt at the suggestion. Adam wanted to visit the harbour in order to find out if the *Venture* was here yet and when it would sail. Considering Ben's profession, Adam had decided to tell him where they were going and, as expected, he was very interested and not a little excited.

'The College of Magic is mounting an expedition to look for the Skentys? I'd do anything to be going with you. If only Augsburg would find the money.' It turned out he was now based at the University of Augsburg, whose zoology department was forward-thinking enough to see merit in his radical branch of the subject. 'Promise you'll get in touch with me when you get back and tell me all about it.' Despite his obvious envy, he seemed genuinely pleased that someone was making the journey. He proved to be very good company, and soon Adam thought it only fair that they tell him they had actually met the March Cat, whilst being careful not to say anything about what had gone on at the monastery.

'You actually saw it? It was real?' He was disappointed to hear of the animal's death and the fact that there was, again, no physical evidence, but he was glad to have its existence confirmed, and planned to write a letter to Augsburg that evening recommending someone be sent to the March as soon as possible. 'So you've seen the March Cat, just missed the Phelan Dragon and now you're going off to find the Skentys. You two are amazing. Maybe if you stick around you'll bring me good luck and I'll see a mermaid.' Jana smiled happily at this suggestion and Adam wondered why.

They arrived at the harbour, which turned out to be two linked harbours at right angles to one another. The one on the right was full of fishing boats, most of which were painted black or brown, but occasionally blue or red, and one was even yellow. There seemed to be no activity here, and Ben explained that it only got really busy when the boats came in to land their catch and sell it at the weekly fish market. At the moment, all of the boats were either out at sea or their crews were resting for a few days.

The other harbour contained some larger vessels, a few of which could properly be termed ships. This was the merchant harbour and was much busier, with goods being loaded and unloaded, and all the bustle Adam and Jana had expected from a city port. The *Venture* was easy to spot. It was a big three-masted sailing ship, one of the largest and most impressive there. Goods were being loaded on, and Adam managed to find the ship's First Mate and confirm that passage had been booked for himself and Jana. The wizards had told him the ship was due to sail tomorrow, but it now transpired there was a delay due to an illness in the captain's family, and it would likely be the best part of a week before the ship sailed. The Mate already had the details of Adam's hotel should there be any change. When Adam returned to the other two and told them of the delay, Jana was surprisingly pleased, actually clapping her hands in joy.

'We can stay and help you find your mermaid!' she squealed to Ben.

Adam had never heard Jana squeal before. He'd seen her get excited but squealing was new. 'I thought you didn't believe in mermaids.'

She glared at him and Ben laughed. 'You should be careful she doesn't kick you again.' Jana turned bright red. 'Well, I'll be going mermaid watching later today,' Ben continued. 'You're more than welcome to join me if you like.'

'I'd love to,' enthused Jana, and Adam noticed that she didn't ask if he was coming too.

Ben did though. 'Adam?'

Adam still wasn't sure. 'People here have really seen mermaids?'

'I guess you're not convinced,' smiled Ben. 'But people in Phelan really saw a dragon, and you really saw the March Cat.'

'Yes,' conceded Adam, 'but those had already been proven to exist. Mermaids are just folk tales, aren't they?'

'It's my job to find out. But there have been sightings of mermaids here for centuries, and some of them quite recently. And people here think they're more than just folk tales.' He could see that Adam was still sceptical. 'Tell you what. Why don't I take you down to the museum and you can see for yourself.'

'See what?'

Ben just smiled enigmatically. 'You'll see.'

As they turned away from the harbour, something caught Adam's eye. 'What's that?' He pointed out to sea. A huge ship had rounded the headland and anchored itself on the open water. Its clean white sails bore the image of a double-headed eagle – the Imperial coat of arms.

The First Mate of the *Venture* was still nearby and came over to see what had caught their attention. He let out a long whistle. 'That's a man-of-war. Armed to the teeth, that one. The Navy doesn't keep anything that size here. It's just a training base.'

'Why are they sending a warship?' asked Ben. 'Are we expecting trouble of some sort?'

'Not that I've heard,' said the Mate. 'Don't know what it's doing here.'

'There's a rowing boat,' said Jana. As they squinted, they could see the smaller boat alongside the ship. Its occupants were dropping things into the water.

'Marker buoys,' explained the Mate. 'Looks like they're cordoning themselves off.'

'Why would they do that?' asked Adam.

'To stop anyone getting too close.'

'Not other warships then,' said Adam. 'They'd just fire at them, wouldn't they?'

''Sright. They wouldn't respect a cordon in battle.'

'Then the ship's not here for defence,' said Ben.

'No,' mused the Mate. 'Doesn't look like it. It's civilians they want to keep away.'

'Do you think they've found something out there?' asked Jana.

'Maybe. Maybe not. We'll probably never get to find out. And if you're going out there you'd best steer clear of them. They won't take kindly to anyone poking their noses in.'

Jana pouted at him, and Adam *did* know what this look meant. It meant trouble. Jana hated a mystery – or rather she loved a mystery but hated not knowing the answer. She wouldn't easily let something like this go, and a bunch of heavily-armed sailors with cannons pointed at her would be more of a challenge than a serious obstacle as far as she was concerned. Time to batten down the hatches.

V. The Fairy Reel

A fiddler was walking over a hill one night when he heard the sound of music in the distance. He looked around to see where it was coming from, until he realised, to his astonishment, that the music came from **inside** the hill.

The tune was so catchy he couldn't help but tap his foot to it. He listened intently until he could remember the music, and then he picked up his fiddle and started playing along. Suddenly a little head appeared out of the hill and stared at him. It was a trow.

Quick as a flash, the trow grabbed the fiddler and pulled him inside the hill. He found himself in a large chamber, although the ceiling was so low that he bumped his head when he stood up. The walls were decorated with gold, silver and precious gemstones, and there were tables laden with the finest food and ale. There were perhaps thirty or forty trows there, some playing fiddles and whistles, some dancing wildly and some eating and laughing. They applauded when they saw the man, and encouraged him to take up his fiddle and join in with their revelry. He did so, and soon he was lost in the wild music as it ran around his head and his fingers and his feet.

Many reels they played, none of which he had ever heard before but all of which he quickly picked up and was able to play along with. More than once he was dragged up to dance, and he was plied with delicious food and ale that made his head spin. He lost track of how long he spent with the trows, but it was a miraculous evening he knew he would never forget.

When he was finally allowed to leave – not that he'd been desperate to go, for he'd had one of the best nights of his life – he found himself back on the hill, and the air was silent. There was no music to be heard, and he half wondered if it had all been a dream. However, when he put his hand in his pocket, he found it full of gold coins, each one of them shiny and new.

Marvelling at what had happened to him, he headed for home. But what a shock he got when he came to his house. The roof was off, the walls were crumbling and the floor was overgrown with weeds. The place was a ruin, and none of his belongings were there.

He went to the neighbours' houses, but they were all strangers to him, and he couldn't find a soul he knew. Everyone told him the house had been a ruin since before they were born. He found the village's oldest inhabitant, but even he had no memory of anyone ever living in the ruined house. But he did remember his granny telling him a tale that the man who had lived there when she was a child had vanished one day never to be seen again. Everyone had believed he'd been spirited away by the hill-folk.

The fiddler was devastated and never fully recovered from the shock. He went back to the hill and called on the trows to come out and give him his life back, but they never answered. He spent the rest of his days sitting in that ruined house playing his fiddle and teaching anyone who cared to stop and spend time with him to sing or play those tunes he learned from the trows. Some of them are still remembered, and to this day they are called the fairy reels.

6

The Imperial Palace was, naturally, the largest building in the Empire. Strictly, it was a complex of buildings, but the central one was still bigger than some small towns. It was, of course, more than just a house for the Emperor. It was also servants' quarters and administrative offices and stables and barracks and lots more besides. But more than any of that, it was status. A palace *had* to be huge, and this one had to be huger than all the rest. It had to inspire awe from the moment you saw it – and that moment should be quite some time before you actually arrived at it. Lord Reitherman had seen it many times before, and took it very much in his stride, but Albert never failed to be impressed.

It was a long, curved, white building with lots of grand arches and pillars. A dramatic statue of a horse and rider reared up in the forecourt just in front of the steps that swept up to the main door, above which was a carved relief of the Imperial crest. Various depictions of the same double-headed eagle could be seen throughout the palace on tapestries, shields, paintings and even on some of the furniture. It was usually either a black bird on a scarlet background or a majestic gold one on rich purple, but these weren't the only colours. Sometimes the bird appeared on its own, but there were many variations, some more complex than others. A common one had it fronted by a shield on which were all of the crests of the Empire's provinces and ruling families. Many also bore the Imperial motto, *planto diligo non bellum,* which translated roughly as 'let others wage war while you marry'. Lord Reitherman explained this as an exhortation to dominate the world by

69

marrying into other royal families and inheriting territory rather than taking it by force. However, Albert often remarked that 'let others wage war while you marry' didn't sound like much of a choice to him.

Lord Reitherman would not be able to see the Emperor immediately. He would first have to announce his arrival and then wait to be granted an audience. A footman had conducted them to a withdrawing room where they had waited for the Lord Chamberlain to greet them. He had looked preoccupied and had held the Palatine's gaze slightly longer than usual, but he haddn't said anything out of the ordinary. This formality over with, the Chamberlain had left to inform the Emperor of their presence. They knew from experience this could prove to be a long wait. However, it wasn't to be entirely uneventful. After half an hour or so, the door opened and another man came in. He looked quite similar to Lord Reitherman: thin, grey-haired and dressed mostly in black, but he wasn't as tall and his mouth drooped permanently at the corners. Albert recognised him, with some distaste, as Lord Albrecht von Pfullendorf, High Palatine of the Northern Provinces.

'Adolf,' he said in a voice that sounded so sincere it could only be insincere. 'I had heard that you were coming. How pleasing to see you. And you have brought Alfred with you.' He smiled weakly at Albert, who blanched.

Lord Reitherman rose politely to greet him. 'Albrecht. Good day to you. My secretary's name is Albert, as I'm sure you recall now.'

'Ah, of course,' Von Pfullendorf acknowledged.

'It shouldn't be too difficult for you to remember as it's so close to your own,' continued Lord Reitherman affably, retaking his seat and indicating for von Pfullendorf to join them.

'Alas, I can't sit and enjoy your company,' von Pfullendorf said, his face looking far more upset than was really necessary. 'I'm very busy at the moment, no time for leisure. I'm sure you understand.'

'Pressing matters of state,' agreed Lord Reitherman.

However, von Pfullendorf didn't seem in much of a hurry to leave. 'I hear you have been summoned,' he said gravely. He lowered his voice to almost a whisper. 'The rumour is that the Emperor is displeased about something, although you did not hear it from me. Now I wonder what could have upset him so.'

'Perhaps he is dismayed that I am not as good at my job as you are,' ventured Lord Reitherman with a twinkle.

There was a moment's pause before von Pfullendorf reacted. 'What? Oh, yes. I see. Very good. Aha. Aha, ahaha. Yes, very droll, Adolf. I'm sure you won't need such wit when you have your audience. Well, you must excuse me. Lots to do.'

'Pressing matters of state,' smiled Lord Reitherman. 'I'm sure we'll find time to chat before I leave.'

'Oh, I do hope so,' replied von Pfullendorf. 'Until then, Adolf. Alfred.' And he left.

Albert turned to his master. 'Why do you humour that insufferable man, sir?'

Lord Reitherman winked at him. 'Because, Albert, I'm a politician. And because it's much more fun when he doesn't realise I'm being just as nasty back to him.'

The museum was housed in the building of the Fishermens' Mission, a charity run by the Church of Lothar for fishermen and their families. However, as Ben quietly pointed out, its main beneficiaries were actually their widows. The Mission was run by Father Langstok, a friendly, cheerful man who held an evening service once a week in the upstairs room. The museum was downstairs along with a small soup kitchen. Most of the exhibits were related to the history of fishing, and included various items of fishing equipment, including oilskins, nets, lamps, parts of boats and the ubiquitous lobster pots. There was also some information on different species of fish and seabirds, including the many types of gulls Adam had noticed since they had arrived in the city. But the thing that caught his attention the most was a long, horizontal painting of a storm at sea. Underneath was a small plaque, which read, 'The Stotfold disaster.'

'It's the same as the one at the hotel,' he said. 'Is it meant to be something important?'

Father Langstok came over and stood beside them. 'The Stotfold disaster is the shadow that hangs over everyone who lives in Anterwendt.

The fishermen risk their lives every time they take their boats out. They always say that you should respect the sea because it doesn't respect you.' He paused to allow the meaning to sink in before continuing. 'It doesn't happen often, mercifully, mainly because people here do respect the sea, but occasionally there's a tragedy and a boat is lost. You can't go around worrying about it or letting it weigh you down all the time, but it's still what everyone in every fishing port has to live with every day. There aren't many people here who haven't either lost a family member, or at least known someone who has. It's just life here.'

'So the Stotfold disaster was a ship being lost?'

'They're boats, not ships,' corrected Father Langstok gently. 'Ships are bigger. Don't worry, it's a common enough mistake. And the Stotfold disaster wasn't just one. It was almost a hundred years ago, when Stotfold was still a separate village. Three boats – the entire fishing fleet in those days – went out: The *Colleen*, the *Sapphire* and the *Speedwell*. It was a fair, mild morning, but during the afternoon a storm blew up. It overwhelmed all three boats and their crews were drowned. Twenty one men and boys.' He paused again before continuing. 'There have been bigger disasters in other places with greater loss of life, but Stotfold didn't just lose its entire fishing fleet that day.' He had remained looking up at the painting all the way through this narrative, but now he turned to look directly at them. 'Every able-bodied man and youth was on those boats. The village lost its entire working male population in a single afternoon. Only young boys and the elderly remained.' Jana gasped. 'They left seventeen widows and forty two children,' concluded the father sadly.

Adam's reaction to these sorts of things was always more intellectual than emotional. 'Is that why the Seatowners came? To replace the fishing population?'

Father Langstok smiled at him. 'That's right. The parish council actively sought crews to come here, even offering a bounty to the first crews who came. They weren't expecting them to come from so far afield, but that didn't matter as long as they came. And it's why this Mission was first set up, to help the widows and their families. It started just as a collection, and then a benevolent fund, and eventually became what you see today. I minister to the fishermen and their families, we keep a fund for them, and we set up the museum as a sort of tribute, so people might understand what it's like. The soup kitchen is used mostly by retired fishermen, as well as visitors to the museum.'

'It's also Father Langstok's job to inform families when men are lost at sea,' added Ben.

'The least enjoyable of my responsibilities, but also, thankfully, one of the less frequent.'

'It's not exactly your responsibilities that we're interested in today, Father,' said Ben, a hint of playfulness in his voice.

'Oh? Really?' Father Langstok sounded a little too innocent.

'We're here for your ... secular activities.'

'Oh, I see.' The priest was still playing along, but there was a twinkle in his eye. 'Then you'd better come with me.' He produced a set of keys and walked to the far wall, where there wasn't, as far as Adam and Jana could see, a door or lock of any kind. He inserted a key into a knot in the wood and turned. The door that wasn't there opened slightly.

Jana gasped. 'How did you – ?'

Father Langstok smiled mischievously. 'Illusion, my dear.' He looked directly at Adam. 'Are you familiar with the concept of illusion?'

Adam returned him an appreciative nod. Where Jana loved to be amazed – and frequently was – Adam viewed this sort of thing with more of a professional eye, and tended to look for the mechanism rather than the wonder. In this case, he found nothing unusual about a particularly well disguised door. The mechanism that really interested him was how Father Langstok had known he was an illusionist.

The priest pushed on the door a little, but then stopped and looked back at them. 'Are you sure you're ready for what's inside?' The playful tone had left his voice and now he sounded grave. Jana's wide eyed expression showed that she'd fallen for it.

'Ready for what?'

Father Langstok lowered his voice almost to a whisper. His face was deadly serious. 'To see the mermaid.'

There was an electrifying pause. 'What, a *real* mermaid?' Jana's eyes almost popped out of her head, but Adam knew a performance when he saw one. Father Langstok just smiled quizzically and waved them through the door.

It took a moment for their eyes to adjust to the gloom. They were in a musty room filled with tables and cabinets, laid out in such a way that there was only one route through it. There were paintings and wood-cuts of mermaids dotted around the walls, and fishing nets adorned with dried starfish, shells, crabs and lobsters hung from the ceiling, along with lobster pots and mobiles made from threaded shells and sea urchins, all arranged so that anyone walking through the room couldn't avoid being brushed by them. Adam thought it was a little tacky, but Jana looked around with wide eyes, taken in by the contrived atmosphere. Apparently she was fully expecting to see a real mermaid. She barely noticed the door closing softly behind them, but Adam did.

She picked up a book lying open at a woodcut of what looked like a hairy man sitting in a pile of fish. 'Look at this,' she said and started reading aloud from the book. ' "One day around 1204 the Stotfold fishermen caught something unusually heavy in their nets. As they struggled to pull their nets back on board their boats they saw some-thing large tangled up with the rest of their catch. They were sorely amazed when they – " '

'Sorely amazed?' interrupted Adam scornfully.

'Shush. It's old. "They were sorely amazed when they finally landed the catch for there, in the bottom of their boat, was a man gazing in anger at them. He was described as being naked and with a hairy body, as having a long straggly beard and with the top of his head being completely bald. Overtures to speak with him failed so the fishermen bound him and took him back to shore with them. The merman was taken to Anterwendt Castle where – " '

'Merman? It doesn't sound like a merman.'

'How would you know?'

'And I'm not sure that Anterwendt *has* a Castle.'

'Shut up!' She continued reading. ' " – where the castle custodian, Bartholomew de Gladville, kept him prisoner. He and the gaolers tried on divers occasions to question this merman but the creature uttered only grunts and other sounds. They observed that when he was fed raw fish he would squeeze the water out of them into his hands and then drink it. Bartholomew de Gladville grew vexed at the creature's silence

74

and he had the merman tortured by hanging him upside down by his ankles but still he did not talk.

"Bartholomew de Gladville then took him to the nearby church but it was plain that this meant nothing to the creature.

"One day, some weeks after he had first been captured, the merman was taken to the harbour that he might swim. Nets were hung across the entrance that he might be set free in the water but without escaping. Yet he made straight for the nets and easily swam under them and escaped out to sea, leaping out of the water in joy. He spent a little time that day frolicking in sight of the harbour but then dived under the waves and was never seen again." ' Jana looked up from the book. 'What do you think of that?'

'I think Bartholomew de Gladville isn't a Niederlander name,' said Adam 'and there wasn't a harbour here that long ago. I think they borrowed the story from somewhere else, and that monkeys must be better swimmers than I thought.'

Jana made a face and put the book down. As she moved on to the next table, Adam picked up the book and examined it. Most of the pages were stuck together so the only one that could be opened was the tale of the hairy merman. The cover was leather-bound, but had no title or inscription. He suspected it wasn't a real book at all, but something mocked up for the exhibition.

Jana was already reading from another 'book'. ' "In the year 1430, after a violent tempest, which broke down the dykes in Niederland and flooded the low lands, some girls of the town of Ijedam in West-Fryslan, going in a boat to milk their cows, observed a mermaid in shallow water and embarrassed in the mud. They took it into their boat and brought it into Ijedam, dressed it in female attire, and taught it to spin and obey a mistress. It supped with them, but never could be taught to speak. It was afterwards brought to Haerlem, where it lived for several years, though still showing a strong inclination for water. It was given a religious burial." ' She looked expectantly at Adam.

'Did the cows have a boat too?' he asked.

'Oh, you're impossible!' she pouted. 'Well look at this.' She held up a comb carved from some sort of shell or bone. Adam thought it had seen better days.

'It's a comb,' he observed.

She read the card on the table. ' "Mermaids shop at the Anterwend weekly market where they buy tortoiseshell combs. They come by a covered road on the sea bed." ' She looked at him defiantly.

'It's a comb.'

She scowled at him. 'Don't you believe anything you don't see with your own eyes?'

'I thought you didn't believe in them either.'

She looked down, embarrassed. 'I'm ... willing to be open-minded,' she said evasively, before picking up a scroll from the next table. It had a woodcut of something that looked like a cross between a seal and a hippopotamus, and was labelled '1517 See-wyf, Breton. A monster caught near the island of Borné in the Department of Amboine. It was 59 inches long, and in proportion as an eel. It lived on land, in a vat full of water, during four days seven hours. From time to time it uttered little cries like those of a mouse. It would not eat, though it was offered small fish, shells, crabs, lobsters, &c. After its death, some excrement was discovered in the vat, like the secretion of a cat. The copy from which I have taken the representation for this work is thus coloured: hair, the hue of kelp; body, olive tint; webbed olive between the fingers, which each four joints; the fringe round the waist orange with a blue border; the fins green, face slate-grey; delicate row of pink hairs runs the length of the tail.'

'None of these are much like mermaids,' said Adam. 'If you're going to make up mermaid stories at least make them what people expect. This isn't convincing anyone.'

'Surely that just makes them more plausible,' said Jana. 'Why would anyone make this up and *not* make it like people expect?'

'You're saying it must be true because it's so implausible?' asked Adam. 'Is this some new kind of reasoning they're teaching in universities now?'

She stuck her tongue out at him and continued around the exhibition. There was a carving of a more traditional mermaid that came from a village church, and a piece of dried-out scaly skin that could have come from almost any species of large fish, or possibly even a lizard. The exhibition ended at a second door next to the first, and in between them was a cabinet with front-opening double doors. On top was a sign, which read:

Herein lies the Haerlem mermaid, which was taught to spin but never learned to speak. The sight is not for the faint of heart but if you dare then open the doors and gaze upon its form.

'I thought the Haerlem mermaid was buried,' snorted Adam.

'Then they must have dug it up,' sighed Jana. She put her hands on the doorknobs. 'Ready?'

He raised his eyes heavenward. 'Go on then.'

She pulled the doors open and they peered inside.

It was not what they expected.

The carcass wasn't anyone's idea of a mermaid. It vaguely adhered to the half-human/half-fish principle, but filtered through a madman's nightmare. It was too small for a start, being more the size of a large baby. The tail was certainly fish, but the top half could not reasonably be described as human. True, it had a head, a torso and two arms in all the right places and correctly proportioned, but the fingers ended in claws and the head was bulbous, with large, staring eyes, no obvious ears and little sharp teeth in the mouth. It was topped with straggly long hair, and the whole thing had a leathery, mummified quality. It would be hard to imagine even the loneliest sailor falling in love with that monstrosity.

After overcoming his initial repulsion, Adam bent down for a closer look. Jana did the same but with a horrified fascination. 'Just ... just *look* at it!' she breathed.

'It's sewn together,' said Adam. 'It's got to be.'

'From what?' she asked incredulously.

'A fish and ...' he thought for a moment, 'a monkey probably. At least I hope it's a monkey.'

She looked at him in annoyance. 'You just won't believe, will you? Even when you see it with your own eyes.'

Adam stood up. 'You're suddenly a bit *too* willing to believe. It's obviously a sick hoax, just like the rest of this place. It's a freak show to scare the tourists, that's all.' He opened the second door and walked through it. After another look at the carcass, Jana closed the cabinet and followed him.

Father Langstok and Ben were waiting for them and there was another, older man sitting at a table eating a bowl of soup. He looked up at them, chuckled to himself and then returned his attention to the bowl, dunking a piece of bread in it.

'Well?' asked Father Langstok, again just a little too innocently.

'It was fascinating,' replied Jana, still wide-eyed.

The priest turned to Adam. 'And what's your considered opinion? Were you impressed by our mermaid?'

Adam noted the deliberate wording and remembered what the Father had said to him before they had gone through the door: *Are you familiar with the concept of illusion?* Instinctively he turned to look behind himself and saw that the exit door had closed silently and was as invisible as the entrance. He turned back and saw the gleam in the Father's eyes, and his annoyance faded a little. It was all illusion. He shouldn't be angry with the illusionist, and if he was honest, it was really Jana's gullibility that had irritated him, and now even that seemed churlish. Without willing victims the exhibition would serve no purpose. He had been annoyed at Jana failing to use her intelligence to see through the illusion, but he himself was an illusionist. He had seen the exhibition as exploitative, but if that were the case then what did it say about him? He met Father Langstok's gaze with respect but not entirely warmth. 'It was very instructive.'

'Did you learn anything from it?'

'I'm still considering that.'

Father Langstok smiled in that way that all clergymen do. 'Food for thought then.'

Sensing the atmosphere, Ben decided to intervene. 'Why don't you think about it while we go mermaid watching?'

Jana's eyes lit up, and for a moment Adam thought she was going to clap her hands with excitement.

'You two go on,' he said. 'I've seen enough mermaids for one day.'

Ben looked from Adam to Father Langstok and back again. 'Are you sure?' he asked with a note of concern.

Before Adam could answer, Jana was dragging Ben to the door. 'He's sure. Come and catch me a mermaid.' And they were gone.

Adam turned back to the priest. 'So what was it really?'

78

Father Langstok shrugged. 'It was a mermaid.'

Adam sat down at the nearest table with forced casualness. He wasn't going anywhere. 'One illusionist to another.'

Father Langstok smiled broadly and sat down too. 'I knew you wouldn't be taken in.'

'So what was it? Tell me it wasn't ever human.'

Father Langstok looked disturbed at the idea. 'Heavens, no. Sailors bring them back from the Orient as souvenirs. I believe they're made by Nihonese fishermen mostly, to supplement their income. These sorts of exhibitions are very popular over there, I'm told, and their idea of mermaids is somewhat different to our own. They call them Ningyo.'

'What does that mean?'

There was only the slightest hesitation before Father Langstok replied, 'I believe it means "mermaid." ' His face was deadpan. The man at the other table sniggered into his soup. Father Langstok continued. 'As far as I can tell, this one's made of a catfish tail and the torso of a monkey, probably with a few other bits of fur and bone attached. The workmanship is remarkable. I've studied it very closely and you really can't see the joins.' He paused for a moment before adding, 'Which I suppose must be a disappointment to you, because you like to see the joins, don't you?'

Adam looked at him suspiciously, but the priest's demeanour remained purely amiable.

'Your friend Jana,' Father Langstok continued. 'She's excited by the possibility of seeing a real mermaid. And perhaps other things too.' The comment sailed over Adam's head. 'But you're more interested in people. In *why* they believe in such things. You want to understand, to see how things work. Things or people. She enjoys being taken in by the illusion, but you want to know how it was done. Which is odd considering she's the scientist.'

There it was again. How did he *know?* And why was he looking all innocent, as if challenging Adam to work it out? And then he realised. 'Ben told you while we were in the exhibition.'

Father Langstok looked pleased. 'Smoke and mirrors,' he beamed.

Adam frowned again. 'But you knew I was an illusionist before we went in.'

'It takes one to know one.' Seeing Adam's expression he added, 'Oh, I don't mean to say that I have any magical training, but I recognised the showman in you. The way you reacted to the hidden door. And all the questions you asked were rather analytical, trying to piece things together, but they also suggested that you make it your business to understand people's motives. Something else we have in common. My job is very much about trying to understand people.'

'And he's damn good at it,' piped up the soup-eater in an accent Adam didn't recognise, but which sounded similar to Ceasg's, although not exactly the same. 'Too damn good sometimes.'

'If you don't like it, Pilot,' laughed Father Langstok, 'you shouldn't be so transparent.'

'I wouldna be if I kent what it meant.'

Father Langstok winked conspiratorially at Adam. 'He knows exactly what it means, and a lot of other things besides. He's not the country bumpkin he likes to make out.' The old man chuckled. 'Adam, this is Pilot. I think you'll find him far more interesting than I am.'

'Oh aye? Why's that then?' asked the old man.

'Pilot's one of those retired fishermen I was talking about. And he's a Seatowner. If you want to find out what makes the locals tick – why they're gullible enough to believe in fairy tales – you'll want to get to know them. Pilot, would you be so good as to take Adam on a tour of the Seatown? Introduce him to some people?'

'A tour?' scoffed Pilot. 'It's no big enough for a tour. But I'll tak you for a walk if you like, let you meet some fowk.'

Seeing Adam's frown, Father Langstok leaned a little closer and pretended to whisper. 'They have their own dialect. It takes a bit of getting used to.'

'Dinna be sae patronising, Faither. That's another big word I ken. I'll use a few mair if you like.'

'No need for that, Pilot. I'm still a priest, remember?'

'Aye, and no nearly so holy as you mak oot. A man that's got a monkey-fish in his back room knows a few choice words I'm sure. Now, let me finish my soup in peace and then I'll tak this lad and show him the sichts. Though I micht hae to mak them baith up.'

VI. Lukki Minnie

Young Willie was out playing on the hill one day, rolling a bannock his mammie had baked for him down the slope and chasing after it. Suddenly the bannock disappeared. Willie walked cautiously to the spot where it had vanished and saw, hidden in the grass, a hole. It was too big to be a rabbit hole, and in fact was just big enough for a boy his size to squeeze through. So, being a boy his size, and this being exactly the sort of thing that boys his size liked to do, he squeezed through it.

As soon as he did, he felt something grab him by the shoulders and pull him in. He struggled against it but it was too strong, and soon he found himself lying on the floor of a small cave. A peat fire smoked away in the centre of the cave with a wee dog sleeping by it, and standing grinning at him in the flickering light was Lukki Minnie.

Lukki Minnie was a trow, but far uglier and far more malevolent than any other. So malicious was she that she was known and feared all over the islands. This was not a good place for a boy Willie's size to be. There was nowhere for him to run and no-one to hear his calls. He was trapped!

Lukki Minnie grabbed him and stuffed him into a sack, which she hung near the fire. He could feel the heat and smell the peat smoke, and he knew she was going to eat him.

Shortly, he heard Lukki Minnie scrambling out through the hole, probably to fetch some vegetables. This was his chance. He took out his pocket knife and cut a hole in the sack. He fell to the ground with a bump, and it took him a few minutes to recover his wits.

When he had come to his senses, he hauled himself out through the hole – but he was barely halfway out when he heard Lukki Minnie coming back. Quickly, he dropped back down to the cave and grabbed the wee dog. He stuffed it in the sack along with the plates that Lukki Minnie had set out to eat him off. He hung the sack up again and hid in the darkness.

Lukki Minnie came back through the hole, her pockets filled with tatties and carrots stolen from a nearby garden. 'Ah'm gonnae eat ye noo,' she called out, 'but first ah'm gonnae saften ye up a wee bit, mak ye all tender like.' She took out a big stick and started beating the sack with it.

When she heard the plates smashing, she called out, 'Ah can hear yer bones brakkin'.'

When she heard the dog yelping, she called out, 'Ah can hear ye howlin' in pain.'

Willie was so pleased with his trick that he forgot himself and burst out laughing. In a flash Lukki Minnie whirled around and saw him. 'Ah'll get ye for this!'

Willie darted up through the hole and ran for his life, but Lukki Minnie wasn't far behind. 'Ah'm gonnae get ye,' she screamed.

It was dark now, and as Willie reached the bottom of the hill, he remembered to jump the stream at the bottom. When she saw him, Lukki Minnie did the same, but trows' legs are short and she came down with a splash in the water. The strong current swept her away, still cursing.

She was never seen again, but sometimes when the wind churns the water up into a white froth, people say, 'Lukki Minnie's still in there churnin' the butter.'

7

A fter another hour and a half, during which they had at least been brought lunch, Lord Reitherman and Albert were granted their audience with the Emperor. The throne room was, of course, the size of a small village, so that large state occasions could be accommodated and foreign dignitaries could be awed. The walls were hung with portraits of past Emperors, and where there weren't paintings could be seen intricate wood panelling. Around the edges of the room were plinths with busts of those emperors who had lived before canvas had been invented, and there was even a life-size statue of one on horseback. The sheer height of the walls naturally drew the eye upwards, showing off the equally detailed ceiling. Some of the ceiling panels were paintings of country scenes, and others supported elaborate candle chandeliers. The floor was lavishly carpeted and strewn with rugs, some of which were just animals opened out so that you could see them from all angles at the same time. Somehow the snarling maws didn't look quite as frightening as intended when the beasts were so much flatter. Ornate chairs and tables were placed strategically around the room, giving the impression they were there for a purpose – either business or for the leisure of those who were allowed to be at leisure in the Emperor's presence – rather than just scattered for the sake of having furniture. The most impressive piece of furnishing sat at the far end of the room. Made of gold (and, being the Emperor's, it was probably real gold and not just painted wood) was the throne, set on a dais beneath the most elaborate chandelier. And yet this was not what dominated the room because, behind the throne, was the largest painting of all. Twelve feet high, it was a full length portrait of the current Emperor in military uniform. If those foreign dignitaries weren't already impressed, then this told them they were in the presence of a giant and they'd better marry him now before he waged war on them.

Sitting on the throne was the Emperor himself. In his mid-fifties, Leopold II looked like both the regal statesman of modern politics and the warrior king of a bygone age. He was wrapped in a huge fur cloak that could easily have given one of the rugs a decent fight in its day. At his shoulder stood the Court wizard, Lazlo Winter, a man so rugged he made other men question their own sexuality. They were flanked by two soldiers, and another two stood at the main doors. A smaller door at the back of the hall formed the Emperor's private entrance.

'Ah, my Lord Palatine,' smiled the Emperor grimly. 'You're here at last. And you've brought your lackey with you.'

Lord Reitherman bowed and smiled warmly back, but inside he was on his guard. The Emperor was not usually so rude, and Winter did not normally attend private audiences. 'My liege, I came as soon as I received your letter. I had been away on Imperial business in the March.'

'Save your excuses, Lord Reitherman.' That was something else out of place. He usually addressed the Palatine by his first name. 'You're here now, let's get it over with. What do you have to say for yourself?'

Lord Reitherman was nonplussed. He had expected to be told directly of what he was accused. 'Sire, if perhaps you could tell me what I have done to offend – '

'You got the letter.' Lord Reitherman waited for the Emperor to elaborate, but apparently this was explanation enough. He chose his words carefully.

'The letter said that I had failed to inform you of a matter of interest under the terms of Edict 37.' The Emperor remained silent, and his expression gave nothing away. Lord Reitherman continued, wondering if he was being invited to dig his own grave. 'Before leaving for the March, I was unaware of any such item.' The Emperor continued to gaze at him impassively. 'On my return, I heard about the events surrounding the dragon fossil, but your letter had already arrived.' Still no response. He had no choice but to take the gamble. 'Given the timing of the letter, however, I can not believe that this is the item to which you referred.'

The Emperor sat up slightly, his brow furrowed. 'Timing? What d'you mean timing?' Lazlo Winter bent down and whispered in his ear but the Emperor waved him away irritably and pulled the fur closer around himself.

Lord Reitherman took a breath. He had to go on now. 'Well, the letter was sent before the fossil had even been discovered, so naturally – '

The Emperor stood up suddenly. The fur fell open revealing his military uniform. He only ever wore that on state occasions or in time of war. He pulled the fur closed again and glowered at Lord Reitherman. 'Be careful of what you are saying, my Lord Palatine.' And he turned and swept out through the private door.

Lord Reitherman and Albert stood and stared, unsure of what had just happened. They turned to look at Lazlo Winter, who leaned towards them slightly. 'The audience is over, Lord Reitherman. Good day to you.' And he too left by the private door.

Lord Reitherman turned to stare at his secretary. 'Well, I hope that you are more enlightened than I, Albert.'

The rowing boat bobbed gently on the water, which sparkled in the sun like hundreds of tiny mirrors. The sea was calm and a greenish-grey colour, the sky was clear and the sun was warm on their backs. It was a perfect afternoon.

'Do you just sit here, then?' asked Jana.

Ben looked worried. 'You're bored. I'm sorry, I'll – '

'No!' laughed Jana. 'I'm not bored at all. It's very peaceful. I just wondered what you actually do when you're out here. I mean, are you just *hoping* you might see a mermaid or is there a plan?'

'This is the plan. We just wait and watch.'

Two gulls circled each other in the air above them, cawing gently to each other.

'Why here then? Are we more likely to see something here than anywhere else?'

'I don't know. We're here because I spend a week at each part of the coastline before moving on to the next. I've only been here two days.'

She shook her hair to let the breeze catch it, partly because it felt good and partly for his benefit. 'What if they don't come in to the coast? What if they live further out to sea?'

'There's the problem,' he agreed. 'I only have this rowing boat, and it's not safe to go too far out in it. Occasionally I go out with one of the fishing boats, but I can't be as methodical that way. I have to go where they go. And the university won't fund a dedicated research ship.'

'So you get to spend your days sitting out here sunbathing.' She lay back and closed her eyes, basking in the warmth.

'I'm working!' he protested. 'I watch, I record, I catal–' Then he saw the slight smirk on her lips. 'Well, I am,' he said mock petulantly.

They sat in silence, the only sounds the lapping of the waves on the side of the boat, the gentle breeze and the occasional distant screech of a gull. Eventually, Jana said, 'Shouldn't you be underwater?'

'What?' He was jerked back to reality and realised that, rather than watching for mermaids, he hadn't stopped looking at her faintly smiling lips. They were very red.

She didn't open her eyes. 'Mermaids live underwater, but you're up here waiting on the off-chance that one'll come to the surface right in front of you. If you want to find something, you should go looking for it, not wait for it to come to you.'

'That sounds sensible, but I think I can see the flaw in your carefully constructed argument,' he said.

'What's that then?' Her smile widened a little, knowing what he was going to say.

'Underwater is, well, under the water.'

'Can't get anything past you,' she mocked.

'Breathing might be a problem,' he pointed out.

'Do you really need to?' she asked.

'It might be a short search if I didn't.'

'So negative,' she tutted. 'You'll never accomplish anything with an attitude like that.'

'No, but I might live longer.'

'Well, if you're not prepared to make some sacrifices.'

'I'll give you sacrifice.' He dipped his hand in the water and splashed her. Drops of water trickled down her raven locks.

'Hey!' She jumped, and the boat rocked alarmingly. She froze in fear, waiting for it to settle.

Ben just laughed at her. 'We almost got to try out your plan.'

She sat up carefully. 'It might not be as stupid a plan as you think.'

'It couldn't be nearly as stupid as I think,' he joked.

'Adam's a wizard. Maybe he could make it so you *don't* need to breathe underwater.'

Ben frowned. 'Can he do that?'

'I don't know, but we can ask him.'

'And then what? I swim underwater looking for mermaids?'

'Well why not?' She leaned forward enthusiastically. 'You'd have a much better chance of actually finding them, wouldn't you?'

He didn't answer, and then he realised it was because he was too busy looking at her mouth again. And wondering if she'd grabbed his hands in her excitement or for some other reason. Then she noticed and awkwardly let go of him. They both sat back and didn't know where to look.

'Well, I guess we can ask him,' said Ben. Awkwardly.

The gulls flew off in different directions.

Pilot had led Adam past the harbour and along the seafront, which was studded with shops, and at the far end, a restaurant. From here Adam could see another beach, different to the one overlooked by the hotel. Pilot said they were called the East Beach and the West Beach. This one, the East Beach, was largely separated from the rest of the land by the mouth of the River Anter, which emptied into the sea here. Spanning the river and connecting the city to the beach was a long, rickety wooden bridge, and at the inland end of the bridge was the Seatown.

Whereas the rest of the city was made up of sturdy buildings on organised streets, the Seatown was a scattered collection of low cottages with no real streets at all. It was like a hamlet the city had crept up on. Adam noticed that most of the chimneys had those same odd cowl-like things on top of them, like the ones he'd seen on first arriving in the city, and he asked Pilot what they were.

'Grannies,' was the answer. Adam looked again and realised they did resemble old women with shawls pulled up over their heads.

'What are they for?'

'They suck the smoke up so yer lum disnae reek.'

'Pardon?'

Pilot chuckled. 'They mak sure the smoke goes up the chimney instead o' doon.'

Pilot, it turned out, was a nickname from the days when he'd had a second job as the harbour pilot, bringing some of the larger merchant vessels into the harbour. It was common practice for captains to hire someone who knew the local waters and the harbour itself to do the job, and Pilot had been the licensed, well, pilot for Anterwendt until his retirement two years ago.

At the far edge of the hamlet were a few small allotments and fields of crops, and beyond those was a fair sized barn. Standing apart from everything, on a small hillock, was a large standing stone with a great hole through its middle.

One of the cottages had a sign above the door proclaiming it to be Mary Player's. Adam thought it looked like a shop sign, and this was confirmed when Pilot led him through the door and a little bell above it tinkled. Inside, the front of the cottage had been turned into a small grocer's, with a counter running the length of the room and all the food on shelves behind it. An old woman emerged from a curtained doorway behind the counter and beamed when she saw Pilot.

'What can I get for ye, Pilot?' It was that same accent again.

'A cup o' tea an' a chat,' answered the old fisherman. 'This is Adam. He wants to ken if ye believe in mermaids.'

'Mermaids?' Her eyes twinkled humorously. 'Been up at the Mission, have ye?'

'Aye. Adam's friends wi' young Ben.'

Mary Player lifted the hinged section of the counter and waved them through. On the other side of the curtain was a comfortable parlour, and Adam realised that the shop was just the front room of Mary's house. Mary went through another door and came back with a teapot, cups, a jug of milk, plates and a yellow fruit cake. Tea was a relatively recent phenomenon in the Empire, having been brought back from Zhongguo by merchants, but it had spread quickly and now it was even more popular than coffee. Mary poured them all a cup and cut three slices off the cake.

'Tea brak?' she asked, offering the plate to Adam. He'd never heard of it, but he knew cake when he saw it and didn't need to be asked twice. It turned out to be lighter than the fruit cakes he was used to and very tasty. Pilot and Mary took a piece each.

'So you want to hear some mermaid stories, do ye?' asked Mary.

'Um, not really,' said Adam. 'I was just a bit surprised that people were so willing to believe in them.'

'Were you now?' huffed Mary in mock indignation. 'An' what's wrong wi' believing in mermaids, might I ask?' She winked surreptitiously at Pilot, but Adam wasn't taken in.

'Why does everyone here keep making fun of me?' he asked. 'You all keep acting like you're having some big joke at my expense.'

Mary gave him an appraising look and then beamed. 'I like this one, Pilot,' she said. 'He's got a good head on his shoulders.'

'That's what Faither Langstok thocht,' agreed Pilot.

'So why *did* you come?' Mary asked Adam.

'To be honest,' he replied, 'I was being polite.'

Mary and Pilot both burst out laughing.

'He wisnae that impressed wi' the museum, but I think the Faither recognised a kindred spirit.'

'Bit of a people-watcher are you?' smiled Mary.

'I suppose,' said Adam dubiously. 'Understanding people is kind of what I do.'

'And what *do* you do?'

'Wizard,' said Pilot. 'Illusionist.'

'Ah.' Mary nodded in understanding. 'So you're here to observe us, are you? Work out why we're silly enough to believe in superstitious nonsense like mermaids?'

Adam felt embarrassed. 'Um, look, this wasn't my idea. I don't want to upset anyone. Maybe I should go.'

'Dinna be daft,' smiled Mary. 'Young Ben's here all the time believin''

89

every piece o' nonsense we tell him. Faither Langstok must think a healthy dose o' scepticism micht be a good idea.'

'An' there's aye the quine,' added Pilot. Adam stared blankly at him. Pilot sighed. 'There's also the girl,' he translated.

'A quine is there?' smiled Mary mischievously.

'She swallowed the whole museum hook, line and sinker,' said Pilot. 'I think Adam would like to bring her tae her senses.'

'Oh, I see,' said Mary. 'Weel, we'll just hae to get ye to meet some o' the locals, listen to their stories and then ye can mak yer ain mind up. An' we'll start wi' ma mither. My mother,' she added, after a pause, by way of translation.

She stood up and led them through the cottage to the only other room. The curtains were drawn and it took Adam's eyes a few moments to adjust to the darkness.

'Are ye wakened, mither?' called Mary softly.

'Aye, ahm wakened,' replied a croaking voice.

Adam now saw that the room contained two beds, and in one lay a very old woman wearing a bedcap.

'We've visitors,' said Mary.

'Visitors? Who is't?'

'It's Pilot. And this is Adam. Adam, this is ma mither, Willemena.'

'Pleased to meet you, Adam,' said the old woman, a little more formally. 'Did ye mak them a cup o' tea?'

'Aye, I gave them a cup o' tea,' said Mary. 'And some tea brak.'

'Good girl.'

Adam stifled a smile.

'Do ye remember,' said Pilot, now making an effort to tone down his dialect, 'when Faither Langstok telt ye aboot the Stotfold disaster?'

'Yes.'

'An' how only the women and young children were left in the village?'

'Yes.'

'Willemena was one o' the children.'

Adam stared. 'Really?'

'Aye,' said Willemena. 'I'd just been born a few weeks before it happened. An' now I'm the last one left.'

'Then you're not a Seatowner,' Adam realised.

'I *married* a Seatowner. And I've lived here more than eighty years, so I'm as much a Seatowner as any of them.' There was a hint of defiance in her tone, as if she'd had that argument before. 'My faither was on the *Sapphire*,' she continued, 'and my uncle was on the *Colleen*. Of course, I was too young to mind any of it, but a'body kens the story.'

They chatted for over an hour as she told them stories from her long life, and then Pilot took Adam to meet various other Seatowners, most of whom offered them tea and cake. As it turned out, none of them had much to say about mermaids, although they all seemed to find it amusing that Pilot had brought Adam to ask them about it. Despite this, they were all very friendly and happy to pass the time of day with a complete stranger. Some told him their life stories, some told him bits of history or folklore, and others just gossiped in the way that people do. Everyone had their own recommendations for places he should visit during his stay, and a few of the older ones warned him not to go near the caves under the lighthouse because Green Goon would get him. It turned out that none of them could actually remember who or what Green Goon was, and Pilot said it was just something they told to children because the caves were dangerous at high tide. It had been an interesting day, but Adam still didn't know why he was there.

It had rained while they had been in the last house, and as they left, Pilot pointed upwards. A rainbow brightened the sky, and its end seemed to fall somewhere in the city. 'There's a brig for a boy bairn.'

'You know I don't understand any of what you say.'

Pilot chuckled. 'There's a bridge for a boy child,' he translated. 'A rainbow's a sign that a baby boy'll be born in the next month.' He winked. 'A piece o' local folklore for you.'

For a second Adam thought of Ceasg but then dismissed the superstition. 'Kind of handy when you already know that Ceasg's pregnant.'

'Whisht!' said Pilot. 'Naebody's supposed to ken.'

'And you've got a fifty-fifty chance of it being a boy.'

'Nae flies on you, eh? It's just an old saying, nothing to get worked up aboot. If it is a boy I'll no gloat.'

'Pilot, why did Father Langstok really send me here? None of those people had anything to say about mermaids.'

'Aye, that was the point,' replied Pilot.

'What? What's that supposed to mean?'

Pilot continued gazing at the rainbow. 'The museum's no in the Seatoon. It's no us that's obsessed wi' mermaids.'

Adam stopped dead. Father Langstok had sent him not to find out what the Seatowners had to say about mermaids, but to learn that they had *nothing* to say about mermaids. 'Then who?'

'A'body else,' replied Pilot. He sighed when he saw Adam's blank face. 'Everyone else. We'll have to teach you to talk proper.'

'Everyone else is obsessed with mermaids?'

'Anither piece o' local folklore,' grunted Pilot. 'The Anterwendters like to believe that the Seatooners are all *descended* from mermaids.'

VII. The Hellihowe Hogboon

Once, nearly every mound had a hogboon. Some said they were the spirits of the dead staying to watch over the family farm. Others said they were a kind of sea-trow that had taken up residence on the land and was much friendlier towards humans than its kin. But while it could be a benevolent guardian, it would also take offence at any lack of courtesy shown to its knowe. If children played nearby or cattle grazed on the mound, this would incur the hogboon's wrath – and woe betide anyone who tried to break into the mound looking for treasure.

To appease the hogboon, regular offerings of the farm's produce had to be made, especially during the Yule festivities. The first milk from a cow that had calved, the first ale to be brewed, sacrifices of chickens; all were put through a hole in the top of the knowe. In return, the hogboon would protect the farm and do chores in the dead of night. The farmer would sometimes wake to find the corn ground or the cows milked, and there was one woman well known for leaving her spinning wheel on her mound overnight whenever it failed to run properly, and in the morning it would be running freely. But if the offering was neglected, tools would go missing or livestock would fall sick as the hogboon took its revenge.

A hogboon once lived near a farm at Hellihowe. The young farmer kent all aboot hogboons and that it was a blessing to have one – as long as you treated it with the proper respect. And so he always remembered to leave offerings of milk or ale or bread, whilst being careful never to disturb the mound. And as long as the hogboon re-

93

ceived his share, the farm was prosperous and the farmer lived a contented life.

Eventually the farmer took himself a wife, and she took over the domestic chores of the household. But she came from the mainland and knew nothing of hogboons and their ways. She was tidy and frugal, and so she never threw away food or drink, and she scraped all of the pots clean before they were put away, and so there was nothing for the hogboon.

The guardian was more than a little put out, and soon the farm's fortunes withered. The milk turned sour, the bread burned, the animals ran loose, the pots fell from the shelf with a clatter and the roof sprang leaks. The farmer would spend all day mending a wall, only to find the stones scattered the next day. Items would go missing just when they were most needed, and nothing ever seemed to work.

The couple were at the end of their tether. They could not even do anything to earn the hogboon's forgiveness, for they had only burned bread and sour milk to offer. Eventually they could take no more and agreed that the only course of action was for them to move house. The farmer went to the Laird and came home to his anxiously waiting wife with the news that they had been granted a lease on the other side of the island, far from the vengeful hogboon's knowe.

For the next few weeks they remained silent about their plan, for they could not risk the hogboon overhearing and taking action to stop them. They did not even make preparations until moving day arrived, and then they quickly and quietly packed all of their possessions and loaded them on to their ponies. The farmer led the first pony, carrying a butter churn, while his wife carried a small chest.

It was a fine summer's morning, and with the warm sun on their backs and little fluffy clouds in the sky, every step away from the knowe made them feel happier and more relaxed. They began to chat about the new life they would be starting and to make excited plans. They might even start a family.

As lunchtime approached, they arrived at their new farm. It was a pretty wee croft with a nice tract of land and not a mound in sight! The farmer put down the churn and threw his arms around his wife in glee and relief.

'We've escaped!' he cried.

Immediately, the lid flew off the churn and an ugly head popped out and grinned at them both.

'It's a fine new house ye've found for us, farmer,' said the hogboon.

8

J ana and Ben had gone back to the hotel. As they arrived, they
found there was a commotion inside. A small crowd had gathered
around Ceasg, who was arguing with Matheeus and another man
they hadn't seen before.

'Oh dear,' sighed Ben. 'It's Ceasg again.'

'Again?' repeated Jana.

'She's ... not well, if you know what I mean.'

'I want to swim!' screeched Ceasg. 'Why won't you let me go swimming?' She actually stamped her foot.

'You can swim any time you like,' said Matheeus reasonably. 'No-one
is stopping you from swimming.'

'But I need my skin. You know I can't swim without my skin!'

'Her skin?' whispered Jana.

'I told you,' said Ben, 'she's not well. Most of the time she's alright,
but now and again she takes turns like this and starts demanding her
skin so she can go swimming.'

'Does anyone know what she means?'

The other man turned and addressed her. 'Ceasg believes herself to
be a mermaid.'

'I ... I didn't mean to intrude,' stammered Jana.

'You were naturally curious,' smiled the man. 'And concerned for the
lady's welfare, which is commendable. And it's my job to reassure you
about her welfare and to take care of it. Doctor Vleerman.' He bowed
slightly.

Ben introduced Jana, as Doctor Vleerman opened his bag and took out a small bottle.

'What does she mean about skin?' asked Jana.

'Some old superstition,' answered the doctor. 'She believes that she has to shed her skin to walk on land but she needs it to return to the ocean. I will give her something to calm her down.'

Jana frowned. That didn't quite sound right but she said nothing for now.

The doctor poured a small amount of yellow liquid into a spoon and turned back to Ceasg. 'Here you are, Ceasg. Take this and you'll feel much better.'

'I want my skin!' pleaded Ceasg.

'Take this and then we'll talk about it,' said the doctor soothingly.

'What is it?' she asked suspiciously.

'It's your tincture.'

That seemed to placate her and she willingly drank the liquid. The effect was immediate. Her body visibly relaxed, her breathing slowed and her brow uncreased. 'Thank you,' she nodded. 'Thank you.'

'Take her through, Matheeus,' said Doctor Vleerman, 'and I'll join you in a moment.'

Matheeus led Ceasg through to their private rooms while the doctor packed the bottle back into his bag.

Jana still looked doubtful. 'That didn't smell like valerian,' she said.

'You're right,' confirmed Vleerman. 'Valerian has a distinctive odour and a calming nature, but Ceasg is an unusual case and I gave her something more appropriate to her condition.'

'What did you give her?' asked Jana.

Vleerman closed his bag. 'Fish oil.'

'Fish oil? What good will that do her? She needs medicine.'

'Not human medicine.'

'Not human?'

Had Adam been there, he would have known before she spoke that Jana was about to explode, but her tone of voice told everyone that they probably wanted to be somewhere else right now. Ben was quick enough to act, and he took her by the arm and steered her towards the door, making excuses about being late for meeting someone. Once they were far enough down the street he stopped and waited to see what would happen.

'What the hell did he mean "not human?" ' fumed Jana.

'Maybe he just meant that, because she doesn't *think* she's human, she'd feel happier with the fish oil. Maybe it helps her feel closer to the ocean or something.'

Jana didn't answer for a moment. There was some sense to what he said but she still didn't like it. 'There's something else wrong with his story,' she said eventually. 'I've heard of mermaids shedding their *tails* to walk on land, but do they shed their *skins?*'

'Most people aren't folklore experts,' said Ben. 'And there are other legends she's probably confusing.'

'Is this what Father Langstok meant about the people here believing in mermaids?'

'Ceasg's a bit different,' he answered, 'but her condition's probably influenced by the strength of local beliefs. Not that I'm a doctor.'

'Neither's Vleerman if you ask me.' Another thought struck her. 'Ceasg's an unusual name. It doesn't sound local.'

'It's not,' agreed Ben. 'It's an Orknejar name. She's a Seatowner.'

'The Emperor's behaviour is rather disturbing, Albert.' The Palatine and his secretary had withdrawn to their official chambers in the palace, unsure whether they would be summoned to another audience.

'I should say so, sir. He's always been a formidable man, of course, but he's never acted quite like that before.'

'You saw what he was wearing under that cloak?'

'His military uniform,' nodded Albert. 'That might be the most worrying thing of all.'

'You think so?'

'It makes me worry that he might have war in mind.'

'Indeed,' mused Lord Reitherman, 'but it was his manner that disturbed me the most. He was like a different man.'

'Or a very ill one,' ventured Albert.

'The cloak, you mean?' Lord Reitherman steepled his fingers as he often did when he was deep in thought.

'And why was Lazlo Winter there?' continued Albert.

'It does seem to fit with your theory, although he seems to be even more deeply involved than we had guessed.'

There was a knock at the door. Albert went to open it and almost yelped when he saw who was standing in the corridor. He stood aside and Lazlo Winter strode in.

'Professor Winter,' said Lord Reitherman, standing to welcome him.

'Lord Reitherman.' The wizard bowed politely.

'Do sit down. Can we get you some refreshment?'

Winter shook his head and sat. He looked over his shoulder to make sure that Albert had shut the door before he spoke. 'I don't have much time. I have to get back before the Emperor knows I've gone.'

'You're here against his wishes?' The Palatine exchanged a wary glance with Albert.

'I'm here to warn you, my lord,' continued Winter. 'You should tread carefully in case you find yourself on dangerous ground. Don't try to involve yourself in matters that are none of your concern.'

'To what matters are you referring?' asked the Palatine.

'I'm sure you already know,' answered Winter, 'and it would be unwise for me to be more explicit.'

'Unwise? Then am I to take it that your warning is a friendly one rather than a threat?'

Winter stood up. 'I have to go now before I'm missed. But Hapsdorf can be a dangerous place. You would be safer back in Phelan.' He walked to the door but stopped before he reached it. 'What did you make of the voice in the cellar?'

Lord Reitherman gave him an appraising look. 'I assume you're referring to the monastery at Kharesh.' Winter did not respond but held his gaze. 'I didn't encounter it myself. My knowledge of it is entirely second hand, I'm afraid.'

Winter considered this for a moment, then he turned and was gone. Albert closed the door and returned to sit with his master.

'This day gets more peculiar by the hour,' mused Lord Reitherman.

Adam and Pilot had parted company, and Adam had wandered about the city until he had come to the square. A market had set up there and he idly had a look around.

There was quite a variety of stalls, ranging from food to clothes and much more besides. The stall that had caught his eye sold a mixture of books and antiques. Books were always of interest, and antique shops sometimes concealed interesting artefacts, so he happily rummaged through what was on offer.

He was flicking through a history of Anterwendt when a sheet of folded parchment fell out. As he retrieved it, a woman came and stood beside him. She picked up an ornate hand mirror and studied it. She seemed to be admiring her own reflection.

Adam opened the parchment. It was a map, labelled in spindly writing he could barely read. He was about to ask the stallholder about it when the woman caught the man's attention first. Adam didn't hear her speak, but the stallholder was telling her the price of the mirror, and she had also found a tortoiseshell comb.

Suddenly Adam's foot felt wet. He looked down and saw that the hem of the woman's dress was wet and had brushed against him. He stepped away from her, and waited for her to finish her transaction. She handed over a silver coin and left with her new possessions. Every step she took seemed to be very precise.

Adam called the stallholder over and showed him the map. 'Any idea what this is? It was in this book.'

The stallholder looked at it carefully. 'Well, well,' he said. 'Didn't know I had this.'

'What is it?'

'Frisland,' said the man as if that explained everything.

'What's Frisland?'

'Old legend,' said the stallholder. 'Mythical island supposed to be somewhere off the Niederland coast. Used to appear on old maps until people eventually accepted that it didn't exist. No real market for a map like that. You can have it if you buy the book.'

Adam thought Ben might be interested in the map, so he bought the book and continued to wander around the market, accepting free samples of cheese and trying on hats he had no intention of buying.

As he wondered why anyone needed such elaborately decorated pottery, he realised he could hear music approaching in the distance. Other people had heard it too, and soon everyone was looking up the street to see what was coming.

By now it was clear that a crowd was accompanying the music, and soon children came running and dancing into the square. Whatever was coming had attracted an audience as it had wound its way through the city streets.

The music was close now, and as the crowd spilled into the square, Adam could see that a procession was coming behind them. At its head were two of the oddest figures he had ever seen. The first was a short man in a striped suit that was far too big for him. A spotted pink handkerchief cascaded out of the breast pocket and a garish yellow necktie clashed horribly with it. The man's face was completely white, save for a huge red smile painted over his mouth, and a bulbous red nose. The most bizarre aspect of his appearance was his bright red hair, which was attached to an obviously false bald pate.

His taller companion was far more soberly dressed in a black frock coat and battered top hat with two long black ribbons hanging from the back, giving him the appearance of an undertaker. The only signs of colour anywhere on his clothes were four coloured spots at the corners of his black bow tie. He also wore white kid gloves. His face was white too, except for a silver tear under his eye and a blood red gash painted over his lips, that turned up on one side in a cruel leer, and down at the other in a scowl. In his hands he carried a small silver horn with a leather bulb on the end.

Adam had seen pictures of clowns before, but he'd always understood they were meant to be funny. These two looked positively menacing.

Behind them came a brightly coloured carnival. There was a band of minstrels, followed by stilt walkers, tumblers, jugglers and fire eaters. Then came three decorated ponies, prancing in time together. Most of the carnival was taken up with brightly covered caravans, some with gaudy signs on the side advertising attractions like trapeze artists and knife throwers, others with their covers lifted to reveal exotic caged animals. One had pictures of the clowns on its side.

Several performers walked alongside the procession giving out hand-bills. Adam took one and read it. It proclaimed *'The Most Spectacular Show in the World! Death-defying Acrobatics! Fantastic Beasts from all corners of the Globe! The most Horrifying Sights you will ever see! Fun for all the Family! Children Half Price!'*

The parade headed off through the other side of the square, and Adam glumly wondered which part was meant to be fun.

Lazlo Winter's question about Kharesh had preyed on the minds of Lord Reitherman and Albert. Was that what this was really about? They had decided they needed to find out as much as they could about it, and Albert had been sent to the Hall of Records to research the monastery, while the Palatine went to the Hapsdorf University library to see if its occult section contained references that might relate to the mysterious voice in the cellar.

After several hours of diligent work, Albert walked back to the palace through the darkened streets. Some of the taverns were starting to empty, and a few drunks were staggering in what they hoped might be the direction of home.

As Albert turned a corner, someone lurched out from a doorway. Albert jumped and let out a squeal (although he left that bit out when he told anyone the story after). The man fell flat on his face. Albert hesitated and then stepped around him and continued on his way.

He didn't hear the man silently spring up again, creep up behind him and cosh him. Now it was Albert's turn to fall flat on his face.

Adam had returned to the hotel and had dinner with Jana and Ben. They had told each other about the rest of their respective days, and Adam had given Ben the map. Ben had looked it over and proclaimed it a fake.

'Maps with Frisland on usually show it much further west, out in the ocean. It was eventually identified with a real island. Whoever drew this map confused it with the Niederland region of Friesland and drew it in the wrong place.'

After dinner, Jana had suggested going for a walk on the beach. When Adam agreed, her smile froze for a second before she said, 'Off you go then, have a good time' and ushered him out while she and Ben stayed behind. Adam had thought it was odd, but he often thought that about Jana, and he set off alone.

He walked idly along the sand, listening to the sound of the waves and watching the sea sparkle in the moonlight. He was fascinated by the way the sand felt under his feet, and in a different way, by how it felt inside his boots.

As he drew nearer to the lighthouse, a line of high rocks blocked his way so that he had to scramble over them. As he did, he saw something on the other side and stopped. A shadow was hauling itself out of the water and up on to the beach. Adam watched for a few minutes, trying to work out what it was. Finally he realised it was something else he had seen pictures of in books. It was a seal.

Once it was fully out of the water, it rested for a moment. Then, to Adam's astonishment, it detached its back flippers and started to peel off its skin! Adam ducked as the creature hung its skin on the other side of the rocks to let it dry.

Adam waited for a few moments before tentatively raising his head again for another look. His hand touched something and he ducked again. It had been the sealskin. He recovered his composure and risked another look. Now he could see what had emerged from the sealskin.

It was a naked woman.

In the dead of night, when everyone was asleep and there was not a sound except for Jana's snoring, there was a scratching at the front door of the hotel. After a few minutes, the door handle rattled gently, but the door was locked. There was a pause and what sounded like whispering outside. Then the bolt slid itself back and the door pushed open just a little. Hairy fingers slid around, it and a large eye peered in from the darkness.

'Gisa peedie keek,' said a slow, reedy voice.

Then they slipped in and the door closed behind them.

VIII. A Close Tongue Keeps A Safe Head

*L*ong ago, a boatman met a dark stranger and entered into a bargain he would live to regret. It was at the Lammas Fair they met, while the boatman was looking for a present to bring home to his young daughter. The stranger wore a dark cloak with the hood pulled up about his head, so only his coal-black eyes could be seen glowering out from it.

'Will you take a cow to one of the northern isles?' he asked as he approached the boatman.

'That would depend on the price,' replied the boatman.

'The price would be twice the usual fare,' was the stranger's answer.

The boatman needed no more persuading and quickly asked the time and place.

'The time's now and the place is lead me to your boat,' said the stranger gruffly.

The boatman was a little taken aback to be required to sail immediately, but the fare was too good to argue, and he knew he could bring his daughter a much better present to compensate for his absence. 'You'd better fetch your cow then.'

They walked to the boat with the cow in tow, and when they reached it, to the boatman's amazement, the stranger hoisted the cow up on to his shoulders and lifted it on to the boat. When he had set it down again he turned to the astonished boatman and asked, 'What are you *waiting for? Time's wasting.'*

Throughout the voyage, the stranger proved to be a man of few words, save for every time they approached an island, when he would order the bemused boatman to pass it to the east.

At last, the boatman could contain his curiosity no longer and he asked, 'Just where is it that we're heading, that's to the east of every island that we pass?'

The stranger glared at him and then tapped the side of his nose. 'A close tongue keeps a safe head.' And he would say no more.

As they passed the northernmost island, the boat was enveloped in a thick fog that made it impossible to see more than a few feet ahead. The boatman was beginning to wonder if he would ever find his way back out when the fog suddenly cleared and the sunlight fell on a beautiful green land the boatman had never seen before. There was the sound of sweet singing and, to his consternation, he could hear some of the words:

' ... and one of us will very soon
Wed a human husband by light of moon ... '

Quickly, the boatman said in a loud voice, 'Are we nearly there yet, for my wife and daughter will be wondering where I've got to.'

Abruptly, the singing stopped and was replaced by wailing and screaming, which quickly faded into the distance.

'You must be blindfolded ere we go any further,' said the stranger.

'Why?' asked the boatman.

'Because I'm the one that's paying,' was the only answer, so the boatman submitted and pulled the boat ashore blindfold. He heard the stranger lift his cow on to the land, and then heard a clinking thud, which he took to be a bag of coins being dropped in the bottom of the boat. Then the stranger helped him to push the boat back to the water and guided him to sit in it. 'I'll turn you to face back home,' said the stranger.

But the boatman felt the direction of the turn and knew that the stranger was turning the boat withershins, against the direction of the sun, which was terrible bad luck. Angrily, he tore off his blindfold but immediately the fog descended and the mysterious island was lost to him. When the mist had finally cleared, his own island lay off to starboard. He looked at the bag of coins and saw that it was much larger than he had expected. Had the stranger paid him even more than promised? But when he opened it, he saw he had been paid only what had been agreed and the reason for the bag's great size was that the coins were all copper. Then he realised who the stranger must have been, for everyone knew that a Finman could not bear to part with silver.

A year passed and the boatman was once more at the Lammas Fair, looking for a present for his daughter, when he saw a familiar figure. 'Well, I never thought to see you again,' he said to the Finman.

The Finman glared at him. 'Did you see me?' he growled. 'You'll never say again that you've seen me.' And with that, he took a box of powder from his pocket and blew some into the boatman's eyes. And from that day and for the rest of his life, the boatman never was able to say that he had seen the Finman again – or anything else for that matter – for he was blind, and remained so to the end of his days.

9

Jana was woken by the sound of screaming. She ran out of her room to see what was happening, and was greeted by a small crowd in the hallway. They were gathered around the doorway leading to Matheeus and Ceasg's private rooms. She quickly found Ben and Adam. 'What's going on? I heard screaming.'

'Ceasg's gone into labour,' Ben told her. 'Matheeus has sent somone for the doctor.'

'Then let's hope she has the baby before he gets here,' muttered Jana.

There was a pushing behind them, and they turned to see three old women coming through the front door. One of them was Mary Player.

'It's the spae-wives,' breathed Ben.

'The who?' asked Jana.

'It's what the Seatowners call their wise women. They're here to help with the birth.'

All three greeted Ben as they passed and Mary smiled at Adam too. They went through into the private area, and shortly there was the sound of low voices, one of them male. The male voice became raised and the women sounded placatory. Eventually the argument subsided and the voices became soothing. Ceasg's distressed shrieks began to calm until they became soft moans. Mary came out and beckoned Ben.

'Hot water and towels, if you wouldn't mind, young Ben.'

Ben grabbed Jana's arm and they headed off to find the kitchen. Mary went back through the doorway, closing it behind her. A few minutes later, Jana and Ben went through with a basin and towels and then came out again.

'Matheeus doesn't look too happy that they're there,' Jana told Adam, 'but Ceasg seems to want them.'

'She's a Seatowner, he isn't,' explained Ben. 'Different traditions. But the spae-wives have delivered a lot of babies and are very highly respected in the Seatown. They've sometimes even been called out by non-Seatowners.'

The front door of the hotel opened and Doctor Vleerman came in. He pushed past the crowd and strode through the doorway into the private rooms. There were raised voices again, and this time some of it could be made out.

'What are these women doing here?' asked Vleerman in annoyance.

The replies were unclear but they started with Matheeus trying to explain in a conciliatory way, before the spae-wives gave their own, more forthright explanation.

It quickly turned into an argument and Vleerman's voice could sporadically be heard above it all. ' ... get them out of here ... medieval profession ... witchcraft ... '

Ceasg's voice called out in protest, and then Matheeus sounded conciliatory again. After a few minutes, the spae-wives came out looking very disgruntled.

'Stupid, arrogant man!' huffed Mary.

Ceasg's cries became more distressed again, and the spae-wives all shook their heads in a mixture of sadness and anger. They then busied themselves with dispersing the crowd.

'It'll probably last a few hours,' Mary told them, 'and it's not a show, so away ye go an' give them some peace if you don't mind.'

Reluctantly, people started to drift away and Adam, Jana and Ben got dressed and went to the dining room for breakfast.

'I've lost one of my ear-rings,' said Jana as they sat down.

'Have you checked under your bed?' asked Ben.

'I've looked everywhere.'

'Maybe you dropped it outside somewhere,' suggested Adam.

'I took them both off last night and put them on the chair,' replied Jana. 'I don't understand where they can have gone.'

'It'll turn up,' said Ben. 'I was thinking of going for a look at the circus. Anyone want to come?'

Adam wasn't at all surprised when Jana practically jumped up and down with excitement. 'That sounds like fun. Let's all go.'

Adam wasn't particularly enthusiastic, but it would be easier to endure the tacky sideshows than to listen to Jana tell him he was being boring, so he agreed.

'If we do that this morning' suggested Ben, 'then I can go mermaid watching in the afternoon.'

They finished their breakfast and headed out. The spae-wives were still in the hallway, and Mary shook her head slightly as they passed. Ceasg's screams were still as loud.

Albert woke up in the suite in the palace. Lord Reitherman was sitting by his bedside. 'Albert,' he smiled. 'Glad to have you back with us.'

'What happened?' asked Albert groggily. His head throbbed.

'It appears that you were attacked. A watchman found you lying unconscious in the street. Luckily someone at the watch house recognised you and they brought you here.'

'The streets aren't safe these days,' groaned Albert.

Lord Reitherman's face was grave. 'I'm not sure this was just a simple mugging, Albert.'

'Why not?' Suddenly a thought struck him. 'My research!' He tried to sit bolt upright, but quickly lay down again when the pain coursed through his head.

'No papers were found on you,' said Lord Reitherman. 'Whoever attacked you seems to have taken it, I'm afraid.'

'Why would they take it? What use could it be to anyone else?'

'I suspect the point was rather to ensure that it would be of no use to *us*,' said the Palatine.

'Then that must mean we're on the right track,' said Albert painfully.

'And that this business is as dangerous as we feared. I'm sorry you had to pay such a heavy price, Albert.'

Albert waved a hand. 'I knew what I was getting into, sir. But you do realise what this implies.'

Lord Reitherman nodded sombrely. 'That Lazlo Winter should ask us about Kharesh, and then your research on it should be stolen can only suggest his involvement.'

'It's always possible, sir, that someone overheard our conversation and then followed me. The theft may have been more opportunistic.'

'It's possible,' agreed Lord Reitherman. 'But it would still have to be someone in the palace.'

'Exactly,' said Albert. 'But there is a third possibility.'

'There is?'

Albert tried to sit up, more slowly this time. 'What if Lazlo Winter *wanted* us to do the research? And then stole it for himself.'

The Palatine smiled slightly. 'You have a devious mind, Albert. But what could we discover that he couldn't for himself?'

'Perhaps he couldn't risk being seen doing the research. Or perhaps he wanted us to find something out and then removed the evidence.'

Lord Reitherman considered this. 'I wonder,' he mused.

'I can remember most of what I'd written, sir.' said Albert.

'Good for you, Albert,' smiled the Palatine. 'You can tell me all about it when you're feeling better.'

The circus had set up on a large grassy area known as the playing fields. A large, round, brightly coloured tent dominated the field and was surrounded by smaller ones, stalls, animal pens and the caravans Adam had seen yesterday. The big top was closed just now, but the sideshows were all open for business. Everywhere, the animal smells were mixed with the aroma of food, and Ben bought a bag of roasted chestnuts to share. Signs advertised attractions such as 'The Smallest Man in the World' and 'Jonas the Giant'. There was a freak show promising joined twins, a skeleton woman and a fat lady, and someone biting the heads off live rats. Barkers encouraged people to try their hand at horseshoe pitching, archery or, for the really brave, a bout in the boxing tent. A puppet show attracted children, and the animals included lions, camels and even performing fleas. Ben had a go at the coconut shy and won a doll, which he gave to Jana who, for some reason that Adam couldn't work out, blushed. As they walked around the rigged games and caged animals, Adam wondered again how this was supposed to be fun.

''Allo,' said a voice behind them.

''Allo,' said another voice behind them.

They turned around to be faced with the two clowns Adam had seen leading the parade.

'My name,' said the short clown with the red hair, 'is Coco the Clown. But you can call me *Mr* Coco.' There was an emphasis on the word 'Mr' that suggested it would be a sensible idea to obey. 'And this,' Mr Coco continued, 'is my associate Mr Wobbly.'

The undertaker-clown squeezed the bulb on the end of his horn twice. *Toot toot.*

'We would like to welcome you to the Most Spectacular Show in the World,' went on Mr Coco.

'No we wouldn't,' said Mr Wobbly. 'Not really. But it's our job so we 'ave to.'

'That's right,' said Mr Coco. 'We don't actually like welcoming people at all. In fact, we'd much rather chase you off by throwing custard pies at you, but for some reason people seem to find that amusing, which isn't the intended effect at all, is it Mr Wobbly?'

Mr Wobbly tooted his horn again. *Toot toot.* 'No it's not, Mr Coco. The intended effect is to make you all run away in fear of your lives. I reckon we need to rethink our choice of weaponry. Hedgehogs might get the message across.'

Jana and Ben laughed. The clowns gave them a hard stare.

'See?' said Mr Coco. 'That's exactly the sort of thing we're talking about. We wish people would take us more seriously.'

'Well, we don't so much *wish*, Mr Coco,' said Mr Wobbly, 'as insist on pain of a spike rammed right up your – '

'Anyway,' interrupted Mr Coco, 'it is our happy duty – '

'No it isn't, Mr Coco, it's our *miserable* duty and we're not going to enjoy it no matter what they say.'

' – our miserable duty to offer you these free tickets to the show at the end of the week.'

Jana and Ben looked delighted, but Adam was immediately suspicious. 'Free? Why?'

'Oh stop it,' Jana scolded him. 'They do this sort of thing all the time. Give out a few free tickets to encourage more people to come.'

'Wouldn't it make more sense to make them for tonight's show then?' persisted Adam. 'If they want more people to come.'

'They'll give them out for all the shows,' insisted Jana.

'But – '

'Do you want the bloody tickets or not?' asked Mr Coco.

'Yes please,' said Jana, smiling sweetly.

The clowns handed her the tickets. Mr Coco gave Adam another hard stare before speaking again. 'Now, Mr Wobbly – '

Toot toot.

' – and I are off to tease the monkeys.'

'I told you before,' said Mr Wobbly as the clowns walked away, 'they're not monkeys, they're children.'

Jana and Ben laughed.

'Stop laughing!' came Mr Coco's voice from the distance.

They now noticed that they had stopped in front of the entrance to the freak show tent. A man covered in tattoos grinned at them.

'Dare you step inside?' he asked enigmatically. 'The most horrifying sights you will ever see!'

They read the sign again. Balloon-headed baby. Heads off live rats.

'It sounds horrible,' grimaced Jana.

The man grinned. 'It is.' He held up a jar full of live insects, carefully selected one and put it in his mouth. They all stared in horror. He looked apologetic. 'Oh, I'm sorry.' He offered the jar to them and laughed when they recoiled. 'Well, if I can't tempt you to a snack, can I at least tempt you to a visual feast?'

'Aren't you just exploiting those poor people?' Jana challenged him.

The man looked offended. 'These are all talented, hard working performers who choose to make their living this way. But if you want to satisfy yourself as to their welfare ... ' He waved them in.

'I'm not paying to see that,' insisted Jana, but he just smiled again.

'The clowns gave you free tickets.'

'To the show at the end of the week,' said Ben.

'Those tickets give you a free pass to all the other attractions too,' explained the tattooed man. When they still hesitated, he added reasonably, 'You can't call it exploitative if you haven't seen it. If you still think the same after you've been in, then feel free to tell everyone.'

He's good, thought Adam. He's spotted Jana's weakness and damn well exploited *that*. She won't back down from that sort of challenge.

He was right. Jana narrowed her eyes at the tattooed man and then marched in, dragging Ben with her. Adam rolled his eyes and followed them. 'How do these people make any money?' he muttered.

Inside was a series of linked tents with a corridor running between them. Signs stood outside each entrance announcing what was inside. The first proclaimed 'Prince Randian the Human Caterpillar'. Jana steeled herself and then walked in. Adam and Ben followed.

On the sandy floor of the tent was a dark-skinned man. He had no arms or legs and wore a tight-fitting woollen garment that covered his torso. He was wriggling around like a caterpillar. He winked as they entered, wriggled over to a wooden box, bent his head into it and came out with a stylus in his mouth. He put his head to the ground and wrote 'Hello' with the stylus.

Jana stared in horror. 'He shouldn't have to do this.'

Prince Randian dropped the stylus. 'Hey, it's a living,' he grinned. 'And you can buy my paintings at some of the other stalls.'

Jana didn't know what to say. 'Paintings?' she blurted.

'What, you think a guy with no arms can't paint?' he asked. 'Don't go bringing your prejudice in here.'

'No!' stammered Jana. 'I didn't mean ... '

Prince Randian gave her a black look and then smiled winningly. 'I'm just having fun with you. You're *supposed* to be amazed that I can do stuff. They are good paintings though. Hey, how about I paint you?'

'Me? I ... ' Jana was completely at a loss now.

'Not right now,' Randian continued. 'I'm working. But come back tomorrow morning and I'll do your portrait. You'll like it. It'll only take a couple of hours, I'm a fast worker.'

Jana knew she couldn't refuse. 'Alright,' she said weakly. 'Tomorrow.'

'See you, then,' grinned Prince Randian.

Jana was unusually subdued as they passed through the rest of the tents. The smallest man in the world was indeed very small, the skeleton woman was alarmingly thin and the fat lady looked equally unhealthy, although both appeared to be happy. Lionel the dog-faced boy proved to be a man whose entire face and body were covered in long hair, but who belayed his animal appearance by showing himself to be cultured and elegant and fluent in five languages. He recited a lengthy poem, changing language every few verses. The joined twins were no less talented, one playing the lute and singing while the other accompanied on flageolet, and the Great Lentini's third leg had to be seen to be believed. Jana refused to visit the rat-biting woman, and the balloon-headed baby, thankfully, was no longer a part of the show.

The next entrance had a sign that made them all look twice. It read 'The Feejee Mermaid' and had a picture of two typical fish-tailed women. This was not at all representative of what was inside though. Under a glass dome was a grotesque creature similar to the one in Father Langstok's museum.

None of them knew what to say. Eventually Jana said, 'See?'

'See what?' asked Adam.

'They've got one too. They *must* be real.'

'Remind me what kind of science it is they teach you at this university of yours,' mocked Adam.

'Tell him, Ben!'

'Even Father Langstok thinks it's a fake,' Adam said.

'Ben!'

'I don't think I want to be in the middle of you two arguing,' Ben laughed. 'How about we just move on, hm?'

Adam gladly followed him out. Jana lingered slightly, gazing at the mermaid, before joining them. There was only one more entrance left. The sign outside it proclaimed 'The Worst Horror of Them All!' They stepped through and were disappointed to find just an empty tent.

'Where is it?' asked Jana. 'What are we supposed to be seeing?'

'Maybe it's on its break,' said Adam disinterestedly. He was starting to get a headache and just wanted to leave.

They stood for a full minute, looking around the empty space, trying to see what they were missing. Eventually they gave up and turned to leave. Suddenly Ben laughed and pointed above the entrance. A small mirror was mounted there.

'So?' asked Jana.

Take a few steps back,' suggested Ben. They did. 'What do you see?'

'Just my own face.'

'The worst horror of them all,' he laughed.

Jana scowled and marched out. Adam thought of Father Langstok and shrugged resignedly.

Lord Reitherman walked towards the throne room deep in thought. He had finally been summoned again and had no idea what to expect. Should he bring up the attack on poor Albert? Was Lazlo Winter a friend or an enemy? Why was the Emperor behaving so oddly? And he still didn't know why he was here at all.

Albert was up and about, but was still in some pain and had been told to stay behind. They had not yet discussed their findings in case someone was spying on them.

Busts of former Emperors and the occasional Empress glowered at Lord Reitherman as he passed. He almost didn't notice the figure approaching him from the opposite direction.

'Adolf.'

It was von Pfullendorf.

'Albrecht.' Lord Reitherman forced a smile. 'How nice to see you.'

'I was so sorry to hear about poor Alfred,' said von Pfullendorf with far more sincerity than was believable.

'Albert,' Lord Reitherman corrected him.

'Of course,' oozed von Pfullendorf. 'I do hope he makes a swift recovery. How is he?'

'Oh, pulling through, pulling through.'

'That's good,' smiled von Pfullendorf. He made a show of looking over his shoulder to make sure that no-one was listening. 'I've just come from the Emperor.'

'Pressing matters of state?' ventured Lord Reitherman.

'*Most* pressing, most pressing indeed,' nodded von Pfullenforf with the gravest expression he could muster. 'The Khazar Ambassador will be meeting with him later today. I fear it is a conversation that should concern us all very greatly, *very* greatly.'

'Really? Why's that?' asked Lord Reitherman sharply, wondering whether von Pfullendorf was actually telling him something important.

'Oh, I've said too much already. You must excuse me,' said von Pfullendorf and hurried past him. 'Give my best to Alfred,' he called over his shoulder.

Lord Reitherman watched him leave. Was von Pfullendorf just scoring points as usual or was there really something important happening? Did that explain the Emperor's uniform? More worried than ever, he resumed his journey to the throne room.

He was admitted by the Lord Chamberlain. As he entered, he saw Lazlo Winter deep in conversation with the Emperor. The Chamberlain held up a hand to indicate that he should wait at the door. The conversation continued for a few minutes and at one point the Emperor appeared to become agitated before calming down again. Eventually they were finished, and the Chamberlain announced Lord Reitherman before withdrawing.

'My Lord Palatine,' growled the Emperor as Reitherman approached. 'I have a task for you.'

'I am at your service, Sire.'

'Of course you are. I'm Emperor.'

Lord Reitherman bowed uncomfortably.

'You are to go to Anterwendt,' continued the Emperor. 'There you'll make contact with a certain man and conclude a bargain that has been brokered with him. The Lord Chamberlain will give you an envelope with the details.'

'Might I ask who this man is and the nature of the bargain?'

'No you may not. You don't need to know.'

'Then how am I to make contact with him, my liege?' asked Lord Reitherman reasonably.

'He'll find you,' answered the Emperor. 'And he'll give you a piece of merchandise. You don't need to know what it is, but know this much, Lord Palatine. It is an artefact that comes under the terms of Edict 37. Return with it and you may regain my favour. Fail me and you will incur my wrath.'

A light came on in the Palatine's mind. Was this what it was all about? Had the letter just been a means of sending him on this errand

and putting him in his place? Was he simply doing the Emperor's dirty work? 'Forgive me, Sire,' he said, 'but if I don't know what the object I am being given is, how am I to know whether I have been given the correct one?'

'Stop questioning me, damn you!' The Emperor had stood up as he spoke and the fur cloak had fallen from his shoulders, revealing the full military uniform complete with ceremonial sword.

Winter leaned forward and whispered in the Emperor's ear. The Emperor considered for a moment and then sat down. Winter replaced the cloak around his shoulders.

'There is a carving of it in the envelope,' said the Emperor more quietly, and now Lord Reitherman could hear the tiredness in his voice. 'Go and do my bidding.' He reached out his arm and Winter helped him up. Without another word they turned and left, the Emperor leaning on Winter all the way.

His concern mounting, Lord Reitherman went back into the corridor, where the Chamberlain was waiting for him.

'I believe you have something for me,' said the Palatine.

The Chamberlain handed him a large envelope with the Emperor's wax seal on it. 'Good luck, Lord Reitherman,' he said and held out a hand. The Palatine shook it and the Chamberlain returned to the throne room. The Palatine walked away, and only when he was out of sight of the guards did he look at the piece of paper the Chamberlain had slipped into his hand. It had the word 'help' written on it.

IX. The Sorcerous Finfolk

W ho were the Finfolk, you ask? They were a race of dark, glowering sorcerers, feared and shunned by mortals. They were the best boatmen on the seas – and under them, for they lived on land and in water as they pleased. They sheltered the winter long in Finfolkaheem, their undersea city, but when summer returned, they would come ashore and live on the magical island of Hildaland.

The Finman looked for all the world like any other man, but he was tall, thin and dark and had a gloomy, serious countenance. His rowing skills were far better than any mortal and it was said he could row from Orknejar to Væringjar in seven strokes!

Finmen did not like humans trespassing in their territory, either on land or sea, and would take extreme measures against any who did. Humans would try to avoid them, but sometimes a fisherman could not help but stray into waters the Finfolk considered to be their own. Should a Finman catch a human fisherman in his waters, he would break the man's line so he could no longer make his living until he had repaired it. Sometimes the Finman might be even more vindictive and follow the poor fisherman back to shore. Once the mortal had gone home, the Finman would set his boat adrift, or break his oars, or worst of all, put a hole in his boat. The first two punishments would leave the man unable to fish and would be expensive to put right, but the third could cost a man his life. Not that the Finman would care about that. Far from it! It would just be one fewer mortal interfering where he had no business being.

123

But sometimes Finmen did have to tolerate mortals, for they had one true weakness: their lust for white metal. It was said a vengeful Finman could be shaken off by throwing a handful of silver over your shoulder, for he would always stop to pick it up; and all knew that Finfolk only ever paid their debts in copper coins, for they could not bear to part with silver ones. Sometimes their obsession with white metal would lead them to work for humans in order to receive payment. But such an arrangement would always be temporary, and it was more common for Finfolk to hire humans to do their bidding.

Sometimes, though, there would be no hiring involved. Sometimes the Finfolk would take humans and force them into lifelong servitude. But that's a story for another night.

10

There was smoke coming from the Seatown as they walked past it. Three great plumes rose into the sky side by side.

'Should we check that everything's alright?' asked Jana. 'It could be somebody's house.'

'I think it's fine,' Ben reassured her. 'Come and I'll show you.'

As they got closer, they could smell something like smoked fish, but stronger and more pungent. The smoke was some distance from the houses, presumably because of the smell. When they reached it, they found a group of women gathered around three large stone-lined pits. There were several big stones lying nearby. Adam recognised some of the women from his visit with Pilot. There was also a little girl a short distance off, singing away to herself and playing with an animal that they couldn't make out.

'Fit like, young Ben?' asked one of the women.

'I'm fine, Mae, how are you?'

'Nae so bad, nae so bad,' she smiled. 'An' it's nice to see you again, Adam. And who's this you've brought wi' you? Your girlfriend?' The women all laughed, and Adam, Jana and Ben all looked embarrassed.

'This is my friend Jana,' Adam managed at last.

'Adam and Jana were concerned about the smoke,' said Ben, hastily changing the subject.

'Oh, were you?' asked Mae sympathetically. 'Well there's nothing to worry aboot. We're just burnin' the kelp.'

'Burning the what?' asked Adam.

'Kelp,' repeated Jana. 'That's a kind of seaweed isn't it?'

125

'That's right,' smiled Mae.

'Why are you burning it?' asked Jana.

'Because the ash makes good fertiliser for the fields. An' it's good for makin' glass an' soap too. We sell maist o' it, for we're mostly fisher folk here. The farmers and the glass makers and the soap makers pay us good money.'

The little girl had moved closer now, and they could see that she was munching on an apple. She looked about six or seven. They could also see the animal more clearly.

'Is that an otter?' asked Adam in surprise.

'Oh, that's just Liban. Don't mind her,' said Mae. 'That otter follows her everywhere. No-one knows how she tamed it, but they're never oot o' each other's sicht.'

Liban responded to the sound of her name and skipped over to them with the otter in tow. She stood and gazed at Jana.

'Hello Liban,' smiled Jana. She noticed the girl had a string of tiny pearls around her neck.

Liban didn't react, but just kept looking her over intently. The otter sniffed around Adam's feet. He waited to be sure it wasn't going to bite him, and then risked stroking its back. It still didn't bite him, so he scratched its ears, which it seemed to like.

'What did you do to your leg?' asked Jana, noticing a bruise on Liban's calf. The girl didn't answer, but just kept looking at her.

'Och, she'll have fallen,' said Mae dismissively. 'She's always playing on the rocks or jumping off walls.'

Liban's eyes suddenly lit up. She had seen Jana's doll. She reached out a hand towards it. 'Ta,' she said, in the way parents say it to teach toddlers to say thank you, although she was clearly a few years older than that.

Jana looked anxious. 'Oh. No, Ben won this for me. It was a present.'

'Ta,' said Liban again and this time she sweetened it with a big smile.

'Liban!' scolded Mae harshly.

Liban's smile vanished and she took a hurried step back.

'Pay her nae heed,' Mae said to Jana. 'She's a trowie bairn.'

'A what?' asked Jana.

'She's a wee bit touched,' said Mae, whispering the last word.

'Touched?' repeated Jana.

Adam tensed as he sensed her hackles rising. The otter licked his hand. It tickled.

Jana took a deep breath and looked appealingly at Ben. 'Do you mind?'

Ben smiled and shook his head.

Jana held out the doll. 'Here you go, Liban.'

Liban's eyes widened. She stepped forward again and glanced at Mae before tentatively taking the doll. Once she was sure nothing was going to happen, she smiled and kissed the doll. 'Draatsie,' she called. The otter scampered to her heels and Liban took a few steps away. Then she turned and ran back, gave Jana a hug and skipped happily away, singing in between bites of apple.

'You shoulna ha' done that,' tutted Mae.

'Why not?' asked Jana with a dangerous edge to her voice. 'Because she's *touched?*'

Mae appeared oblivious, and said to one of the younger women, 'Maisie, go and tell the men the fires are goin' weel enough noo.'

As the woman left, a crow landed a few feet away and started pecking at a fallen scrap of Liban's apple. Some of the women whispered to each other and giggled. They nudged Mae and nodded at Jana.

'What?' asked Jana suspiciously.

'Ye have to startle the crow,' said Mae.

'Why? It's not doing me any harm.'

'If you startle a crow, whitever way it flies tells you where your future husband lives.'

Jana looked at her levelly. 'You're joking.'

'You'd better hurry before it goes itsel'.'

All the women were watching her expectantly.

'I'm not buying into your superstition,' said Jana through tightly clenched teeth.

'Suit yersel',' said Mae with a knowing smile.

There was an awkward silence. The crow pecked away at the apple.

'Well, maybe we should go,' said Jana innocently, standing up. The crew flew away. Startled. 'Oops,' said Jana, trying to look as if she wasn't watching it fly into the distance.

'Aye, that'll have just been an accident,' smirked Mae. 'Ye'll no have seen which way it went.'

'No, said Jana innocently. 'Didn't notice.'

'Stotfold,' said Mae without looking up. 'Not that you'll be bothered.'

'No. No I won't,' said Jana stiffly.

Adam and Ben stood up too, trying not to laugh. Adam tried especially hard because he had a better idea than Ben of what the consequences would be. Ben's laughter was mixed with some embarrassment, but Adam couldn't work out why. 'Goodbye, Mae' said Ben.

'Cheerio, young Ben,' said Mae.

As they walked away, the woman who had left earlier was coming back with three men. She was holding hands with the youngest. The other two were big men, although one was considerably bigger than the other, and also much hairier.

'Hello there, young Ben,' he said.

'Hello, old Ben,' said Ben.

Old Ben wasn't old at all, but he was older than young Ben, and Adam finally realised why all the Seatowners always made a point of calling *young* Ben 'young Ben'.

'Adam, Jana, this is Ben Varrey and his brother Donny,' said Ben. 'And that's Abgal, Maisie's intended.'

'Good to meet you both,' said Donny. Abgal nodded and smiled. 'Seen any mermaids yet?' smirked Donny and his companions all laughed.

'Just give me time, Donny.'

'Given you plenty o' time already.' Donny punched his arm. 'Ye're just embarrassing yerself now.'

'How many do you want me to get you?' asked Ben.

'Put me down for a dozen, then,' laughed Donny. 'None for Abgal, though, he's gettin' maried.'

'What about old Ben?' asked Jana, trying to join in the banter.

Donny's smile faded a little. 'None for him either. Liban wouldnae like it, eh?'

Old Ben grunted and the party carried on towards the kelp burning.

'What was that all about?' asked Jana.

'Old Ben's Liban's father,' explained young Ben. 'I guess she wouldn't take well to a new woman around the house.'

'Where's her mother?'

'She died, I think. They don't really talk about it.'

They walked back towards the town, and when they looked back a few minutes later, they saw the men covering the pits with the stones. Donny and Abgal were each lifting one at a time, but old Ben was effortlessly carrying one in each hand.

As they walked through the streets, they saw that there were posters for the circus everywhere, advertising the show times and also the other towns it would be visiting. There were several different designs showcasing different acts. The freak show performers were especially common, appealing to people's more ghoulish instincts, but there were also some that showed animals, or the more spectacular acts like the trapeze artists or the acrobats. But the one motif they all had in common was the disembodied heads of the Scary Clowns, which Adam was sure would put anyone off going.

When they got back to the hotel, the spae-wives were still there and Ceasg was still screaming. 'It's close now,' said Mary, but there was a note of worry in her voice.

'Has Vleerman let you in to see her?' asked Jana.

'She's asked for us a few times,' said one of the others, who Ben introduced as Murgen. 'He's let us in for a few minutes, when she's screamed until he gave in. But he aye throws us oot again.'

'But he's happy to send us for more water and fresh towels,' snorted the third woman, whose name was Baabie.

'Will she be alright?' asked Jana.

'It wouldna ha been so difficult a birth if he'd let us stay,' said Baabie.

Adam, Jana and Ben went to the dining room for lunch. Jana was unusually quiet as they ate, and the conversation was dominated by Ben telling a story about one of his colleagues investigating mermaid sightings in some far off islands in the south seas, where they called it a ri. The colleague had even seen it himself – a long dark shape in the water – and all the descriptions consistently agreed that it had light skin, long hair, breasts and hands. After several weeks of tracking, the story came to a sad end when a large sea animal had been pulled out of the water. It was a dead dugong. No hair, no breasts, and flukes instead of hands, but the locals insisted that this was the ri. It had a spear embedded in its carcass, and the locals blamed the villagers in the neighbouring bay.

Then Ben had to explain to them what a dugong was.

As they left to go back up to their rooms, Dr Vleerman came out, wiping his hands on a towel. He looked tired and very grave. He glanced at the spae-wives but didn't speak. A worried look passed between all three women and they rushed into the private rooms. There was a cry that sounded like Murgen's voice, and then Mary rushed out carrying the basin.

'Oh, Jana,' she said when she saw them. 'Would you be a dear and fetch me another basin of clean water and some more towels? The doctor hasn't bothered to clean up in here.'

Jana went to the kitchen, and when she came back with the water and towels, Mary ushered her straight in. Ceasg was lying in bed, sobbing softly with Murgen comforting her. Matheeus was sitting on a chair with his head in his hands. Baabie was holding the baby, wrapped in a shawl. Mary took the basin and towels from Jana and started cleaning. Jana stood uncertainly for a moment, and then decided to at least have a look at the baby. Baabie gave her a look that told her something was terribly wrong, and then turned towards her so Jana could see the baby. At first, she could see nothing untoward. The baby lay asleep in Baabie's arms. Then Baabie pulled the shawl down to expose the baby's legs.

Except they weren't legs. There was just a single limb where the legs had been fused together. The feet were still separate and splayed outward. It looked for all the world like a mermaid's tail.

X. The Mermaid and the Finwife

*T*he daughter of the Finfolk was a mermaid, a beautiful girl with snow-white skin, flowing locks of golden hair and a shining fish tail. She was more beautiful than any mortal woman, and she had a singing voice that could calm the stormy seas and would cast a spell over anyone who heard it – especially a man.

But her beauty would not last for ever, and if she remained with her own kind and married a Finman, that beauty would fade and she would grow uglier with each passing year. In the first seven years of marriage, she would lose her incomparable beauty. In the second seven years, she became no fairer than a mortal woman. And in the third seven years, she would turn into an ugly Finwife.

The only way she could avoid such a fate was to marry a mortal man. Then she would lose her fish tail, become a mortal woman and remain beautiful for the rest of her life.

For this reason, gaining a human husband became the mermaid's only goal in life, and she would sit on the rocks showing off her beauty and using her enchanting voice to bewitch mortal men and lure them into marriage.

If the mermaid failed to marry a mortal and was doomed to an existence as a Finwife, she would still spend much of her time among mortals, for the Finmen often sent their Finwives ashore to earn them white metal. The Finwife would make a living spinning and knitting, and also using her magic to cure disease in men and livestock. All the while, she would send silver coins back to her husband, as well as messages that were relayed through a black cat who had the power to transform itself into a fish.

But if the supply of white metal sent was too little for the Finman's tastes, he would pay the Finwife a visit and reward her with a terrible beating that would leave her laid up in her bed for days!

11

lbert and Lord Reitherman sat in the black coach as it left Hapsdorf behind. The Palatine had read the contents of the envelope and shared them with Albert, who shook his head in bemusement. The carving of the object they were to collect was entirely unfamiliar, and they were at a loss as to its purpose.

'What does it all mean, sir?'

'I wish I knew, Albert, I wish I knew.'

Albert took off his glasses to clean them. 'Do you think the Emperor intends to go to war with Khazar? I mean, the uniform, and the ambassador, and what Lord von Pfullendorf said. Perhaps the fleet is massing at Anterwendt.'

'It is possible,' mused Lord Reitherman, 'although I think the *Invincible* has a more immediate mission first.'

'But what has it all got to do with Edict 37?' wailed Albert. 'I can't abide all this intrigue.'

'Well,' replied the Palatine, 'now we are away from eavesdroppers, let's compare notes on our research and see if we can make any sense of it. What did you learn about Kharesh?'

Albert put his glasses back on. 'The village grew up around the monastery, which was founded around four hundred years ago by the Poor Knights of the Order of the Sanctuary.'

Lord Reitherman thought. 'Should I have heard of them?'

'They were disbanded a hundred years later. The order was originally formed during the religious wars in Arabaya. It was a monastic order, charged with protecting pilgrims from bandits, and with caring for the poor, sick and injured. But they were also military knights, and said to be the best fighters in the wars.'

'So they created the casualties and then sewed them back together,' said the Palatine.

'Aha, yes, sir, very droll,' said Albert. 'The knights took individual vows of poverty, but the order as a whole was very wealthy, due to donations and its business ventures.'

'Business ventures?'

'Banking, sir. They practically invented it. They used to look after the money of other knights going to the wars, and turned out to be rather good at it. They had a whole team of non-combatant members who just handled the business.'

'How enterprising,' said Lord Reitherman.

'But after the wars their popularity waned, and there had always been rumours about them – '

'Rumours?' asked Lord Reitherman.

'A bit vague, but they hinted at some sort of unsavoury practices. Anyway, then they fell foul of the King of Breton. He was heavily in debt to their bankers, and used the rumours to have charges levelled at them so he could get out of paying them back. There was a series of trials at which they were accused of heresy, apostasy, demon worship and sometimes worse. The order was disbanded, many were executed and others fled.'

'And where does Kharesh come in?'

'It had been founded after they returned from the wars. It wasn't their main base – that was in Breton and was seized after the trials – but when the authorities went to the monastery at Kharesh, they found only monks, and everyone in the March told them the knights had left years ago. They found nothing in the monastery to contradict that – no knightly trappings, no money, just a quiet religious order – so the monastery was left alone.'

The Palatine mulled over what Albert had just told him. 'You said demon worship.'

'Well, many believe the charges were falsified but considering what your friends encountered in the monastery ... '

'Indeed,' agreed the Palatine. 'Are there any details?'

'Testimonies varied widely, and they were all quite vague. The most common motifs were heads of one kind or another, but there was no real agreement. There was a word or a name that kept on cropping up though: Baphomet.'

The Palatine sat up sharply. 'Baphomet?'

'Do you recognise it, sir?'

The Palatine thought. 'It doesn't really seem to fit with what you've told me, but there was a Skentys myth I came across concerning twelve demons they created in their attempts to create the gods. The demons rebelled against them and fought a war. There are various stories about how they did it, but the Skentys destroyed them all in turn. Except one. One disappeared and was never caught. Its name was Bafihumet.'

'So if this demon really did escape from the Skentys,' suggested Albert, 'perhaps the Knights of the Sanctuary somehow harboured it in the monastery.'

'Perhaps,' agreed the Palatine. He closed his eyes and was silent for a few minutes. Eventually he opened them again. 'Any thoughts, Albert?'

'It occurs to me, sir,' offered Albert, 'that this would very much come under the aegis of Edict 37.'

Lord Reitherman smiled. 'I believe you may be right. Unfortunately, our avenues of research may be limited. The best occult library in the Empire is in the College of Magic, but we can't risk going there in case Lazlo Winter hears of it. Fortunately there is a man in Anterwendt itself who may be able to help us. We'll need to stop somewhere to pick up some ginger.'

Ben had taken Jana mermaid watching again, and she was discovering the mundane realities of his profession, as there was a drizzle and Ben refused to move the boat. The main reason was his systematic research method, but there was also the fact that Jana would be sitting there with wet hair.

Jana was still very preoccupied. 'Do you think the baby will be okay?'

'I've heard of that condition before,' Ben answered. 'It comes up from time to time in mermaid lore. I think it's very rare.'

'You didn't answer my question,' said Jana.

He took a breath. 'As far as I know, they usually die. There are all sorts of internal problems.'

'That's awful … '

'But there have been cases where they survived,' he added hurriedly. She looked at him hopefully. 'One or two,' he finished lamely.

Jana bowed her head again, and it occurred to Ben that this might be a good time to comfort her. Or maybe it would be completely inappropriate. Probably best not in case she took it the wrong way. Perhaps he should try and take her mind off it.

'Did you enjoy the circus?'

'The horror show, you mean.'

Ah. Maybe not the best topic. 'That tattoo man said they weren't being exploited. The caterpillar guy's going to paint you.'

'If he can paint, then why isn't he just making a living as an artist instead of letting people gawk at him because he looks different?'

'Well, he *is* being an artist. As well … '

'But he's still letting everyone treat him like a freak. And that dog guy's really clever. He could be a linguist or a translator. They should all just be living normal lives.'

'Well … well maybe they don't want to,' he said reasonably. 'Maybe they're happy.'

'And what about that poor girl Liban?' continued Jana. 'Did you hear the way they spoke about her?' She looked up and was annoyed to see that he was grinning. 'What?'

'You care about *everything*, don't you?'

'Well, what's wrong with that?'

'Nothing,' he smiled. 'Nothing at all.'

'Why did you want me to meet the Seatowners?'

Father Langstok looked up from cleaning the tables and smiled. 'Nice to see you again, Adam. How are you?'

'Confused,' said Adam. 'What is it that you want from me?'

Father Langstok continued cleaning. 'How did you get on with our fisher folk?'

'Can't you just answer a straight question?' said Adam in irritation. 'I met them, they gave me tea and cake. *Lots* of tea and cake, in fact. I think there might not be any left for a while.'

'They're very welcoming people,' agreed Father Langstok. 'They consider it bad manners not to give guests a cup of tea and a slice of tea brak. Even strangers.'

'You didn't send me there for the hospitality,' persisted Adam.

'Did you learn anything when you were there?' asked the priest.

'They're not particularly interested in mermaids, but Pilot says the Anterwendters believe the Seatowners are descended from mermaids.'

'That's true,' said Father Langstok. 'Although don't be deceived by the Seatowners' unwillingness to talk about it. Mermaid legends feature heavily in their traditions, although other strands of their folklore are more important. But the reason they avoid talking about mermaids is *because* some of the Anterwendters make such a big deal about it.'

'You didn't send me there to be educated either,' said Adam. 'You want something from me.'

'You like to get straight to the point, don't you?' smiled the priest. 'I still find it interesting that Jana's the scientist and you're the wizard.'

'And presumably that's why you want me. Because I'm a wizard.'

'An illusionist, yes,' said Father Langstok. 'You get into peoples' heads, change their perceptions. Sometimes even change their minds.'

'For goodness sake, Father, just tell me what you want!'

The priest wrung out his cloth and put it away. 'There's something I'd like to show you,' he said, 'if you can spare a few minutes.' Seeing Adam's expression he added, 'After that it'll all be clear. It's not far.'

Adam sighed heavily – heavily enough to ensure that the priest knew what it meant – and agreed. Father Langstok locked up the Mission and led him through the streets.

'Where are we going?' asked Adam.

'To the Church of Marius,' replied Father Langstok.

'Are Lotharans allowed into the Marian church?'

Father Langstok laughed. 'It's a church. Everyone's allowed in. They might have something to say if I tried to preach, but I'll promise not to.'

Father Langstok's definition of not far turned out to be a little different to Adam's, and the journey took them fifteen minutes. For the sake of making conversation on the way, Adam said, 'Did you know that the circus has its own mermaid? Like yours, I mean.'

'Does it really?' asked Father Langstok. 'I might have to pop down for a look. Here we are.'

The church of Marius was a large, imposing building. The door was open, although there was no sign of anyone inside. The interior was, typically, more ornate than a Lotharan church, with stained glass windows, elaborate carvings and more gold than Adam had ever seen in one room.

'Isn't it a bit risky leaving this place open with no-one here?'

'Indeed it is,' said a voice.

Adam looked around but could see no-one, until a man in priestly robes appeared in the pulpit. He had evidently been kneeling down.

'Francis,' he beamed at Father Langstok. 'What brings you here?'

'Hello, Nicolas,' said Father Langstok. 'I'm just showing Adam here around. Adam, this is Father van Bleric.'

'Sorry if I startled you,' said Father van Bleric. He held up a cloth. 'I was cleaning the floor. We had a break-in last night, and our intruders spilled some wine.'

'Oh dear, I'm sorry to hear that,' said Father Langstok. 'Was there any damage?'

'None that I can find,' answered Father van Bleric. 'In fact I'm still not sure how they got in because all the doors and windows are fine, and were still locked when I arrived this morning.'

'Well, that's a blessing,' said Father Langstok. 'Anything taken?'

'Only some blankets we were collecting for the poor. They drank some wine and ate some bread, but that's all as far as I can tell. They may just have been poor folk in need of food and warmth.'

'All this gold and they didn't take any?' asked Adam incredulously.

'I know,' agreed Father van Bleric. 'It's a mercy. It's a shame about the blankets, but they're more easily replaced, and I'm the only one who'll usually see the stain in the pulpit. Anyway, you two feel free to look around.'

'I particularly wanted to show Adam the mermaid chair.'

Mermaids again. What was it with this place and mermaids?

'Ah, a very fine piece of workmanship,' said Father van Bleric, leading them to a large wooden bench sitting in one of the side aisles. Its seat was covered with a dark blue cushion, embroidered with five golden fish. But the real point of interest was the chair's left side, which was decorated with an intricate carving of a mermaid holding up a mirror in one hand and a comb in the other. 'There's a story to go with the chair,' Father van Bleric told them. 'A beautiful woman used to come to the church to listen to the choir singing, but no-one knew who she was. One day a young man followed her after the service, and when she tried to run from him, she tripped and he saw that she had a mermaid's tale. Neither of them was seen again, and it was assumed he had joined her in the sea. But many believe he may have gone against his will.'

Father Langstok smiled as if he knew what was coming.

'In some legends,' continued Father van Bleric, 'mermaids are fallen angels who have no souls. The only way they can gain a soul is by marrying a human, and so they will stop at nothing to achieve this. The mermaids live in their undersea kingdom and drag unwary sailors down there and keep them prisoner. They can eat only living flesh, and so they capture sailors with their bewitching voices, or with a unique scent, or create storms to cause shipwrecks, and lull them to sleep and then tear them to pieces with their spiky green teeth.' He paused before adding, 'All nonsense, of course, but a little different to the legends you may have heard.'

'Um,' said Adam after a while, 'if mermaids are so evil, why do you have a carving of one in your church?'

Father van Bleric laughed. 'A very good question. They *are* just legends, and the chair has been here for some hundreds of years. But it does serve as a reminder not to give in to our lustful natures lest we endanger our immortal souls. And the mirror and comb in the carving warn us against the sin of pride.'

'Or it might just be nice to have a picture of a naked lady,' said Adam.

There was a pause as Father Langstok waited to see how his counterpart would react. Father van Bleric just laughed. 'Well, I just hope that's not the only reason my parishioners come,' he said.

139

After they had left, Adam said to Father Langstok, 'Okay, so they have a problem with mermaids. Which is a bit weird considering mermaids aren't real. But it still doesn't explain what you want from me.'

'The Anterwendters, and especially the Stotfolders – encouraged, I'm bound to say, by the Church of Marius – have generally negative legends about mermaids, seeing them as evil demons who cause shipwrecks and steal their souls or at least encourage sinful behaviour.'

'Yes – '

'And they believe that the Seatowners are descended from mermaids.'

Adam considered this. 'So you're saying the Stotfolders don't like the Seatowners.' Father Langstok inclined his head. 'Couldn't you have just said that?'

'I wanted you to understand,' explained the priest. 'And to meet the people for yourself.'

'And you want me to what, change their minds?'

'Oh, I realise it doesn't quite work like that,' said Father Langstok, 'but I sense a change coming. Nothing definite, but things like Ceasg's baby increase tensions. Someone like you could be useful in calming those tensions, should it become necessary.' He looked at Adam for a reaction. 'You're only here for a few days, so I'm not asking you for a long-term commitment. But if anything should happen during your stay, your assistance would be much appreciated.' He smiled in that winning way he had.

'And what is it you're expecting to happen?' asked Adam suspiciously.

'Hopefully nothing. But people can be … impetuous.'

'I think you probably overestimate my abilities. People do that. But,' Adam sighed inwardly, 'I'll help if I can.'

'Thank you, Adam,' said Father Langstok. 'Now, when are you going to show me this mermaid of the circus's?'

Jana and Ben walked back towards the hotel, laughing in the dusk.

'A special scent?' repeated Jana in disbelief. 'They lure sailors with their magical smell?'

'I guess so,' laughed Ben. 'Legends are a bit strange sometimes.'

'And what smell is it?' asked Jana. 'The smell of fish?' They both hooted. 'Mind you,' giggled Jana, 'you know what else smells of fish, don't you?' They both sniggered but then Jana suddenly stopped. 'Oh, hang on, though,' she said, 'I heard about some new theory that male animals can smell when females are in heat. Maybe it's a bit like that.'

'See?' grinned Ben. 'There's always some truth in old legends. Oh look, there's Adam.'

As Adam approached he noticed Jana and Ben took a hurried step away from each other. Had they just let go of each other's hands? That was a bit odd. And were they trying to pretend they hadn't just been laughing? Why were they doing that?

They walked into the hotel together and found the spae-wives still there. 'They'll be here for a few days,' explained Ben. 'It's their duty now to protect the baby.'

'From what?' asked Jana.

'From bein' stolen by trows,' replied Baabie, 'tho' it's too late for that if ye ask me.'

'What does that mean?' asked Jana, her hackles rising again.

'That's no a normal bairn,' answered Baabie. 'The trows have taken it an' left one o' their ain in its place. That daft doctor should've let us in.'

Adam and Ben quickly steered Jana into the dining room before an argument could start. 'How can they think something like that?' she fumed as they ate.

'It helps them come to terms with it,' explained Ben. 'Gives them someone to blame.'

Jana shook her head in despair. 'Yeah, that's what the baby needs.'

They heard a familiar voice out in the hall. 'Aye aye, Baabie. How's Ceasg and the bairn doin'?'

'Aye aye, Pilot. Baith holdin' up,' answered Baabie.

Pilot came into the dining room and looked around. He saw Adam, Jana and Ben and came over to their table. 'I thocht I'd find you three here,' he said. 'How d'ye fancy goin' fishin'?'

Ben sat up. 'Fishing? You mean on one of the boats?'

'I was speakin' to some o' the boys, and Donny says ye can come oot on the *Renown* tomorrow. The three o' ye if ye want. I'm goin' too. Havena been oot for ages.'

141

'I'm in,' said Ben immediately. 'It'll be a chance to check the waters further out.'

'That's what we thocht,' said Pilot. 'Donny says yer friends are welcome too.'

'I'm having my portrait painted,' said Jana, who didn't seem very enthusiastic anyway.

'What about you?' Ben asked Adam. 'Do you want to come out on a fishing boat for a day? It'll be an experience.'

'Alright,' said Adam dubiously, wondering why people kept pushing him to do strange things.

Later that night, Adam went for another moonlight walk on the beach – but not in the hope of seeing more naked ladies, oh my goodness no. He sat on a rock – the same rock as it happened, but that was just coincidence – and watched the waves lapping gently on the shore. Going out on a fishing boat didn't sound like the sort of 'experience' he'd have chosen, but he didn't have an excuse like Jana. What with that and Father Langstok asking him to solve the problems of an entire city, he wished the *Venture* would hurry up and leave.

A movement caught his eye, and he saw a silhouette pass by on the other side of the rocks. It wasn't a woman or a seal this time, but a man, who was carrying something wrapped in a blanket. He walked down to the shore and set the bundle down in the water. He gave it a push and watched it float out to sea. After a minute, he turned and walked back up the beach.

Adam sat for a few minutes looking at the moonlight reflected on the water, and wondering what the man had been up to. Once he'd given him time to get far enough away, Adam headed back to the hotel.

In the dead of night, two small figures crept along the corridors and through the locked doors. The door to Matheeus and Ceasg's room creaked slightly.

'Yin dower's wheeskin' agin,' said a reedy voice.

Large red eyes peered at Ceasg, asleep in bed. 'Don's deeskit oan dat koad.'

The other suddenly jumped and stifled a cry as a spider scuttled across the floor.

'Whisht yir beerin'!' whispered its companion.

'Yin ettercaps fleggit ma.'

The other spied a gap between two shelves and squeezed into it. After a moment it came back out. ''Sa dower ahint heer.'

Both squeezed through the gap to the door hidden behind the shelves. The one that had been frightened by the spider suddenly started brushing frantically at its face.

'Whitna ye claan at?' asked the other.

'Moosewab!' replied its companion, wiping the remaining cobweb from its face.

'Ye bulder. Yir cheust clarted.'

They climbed up the shelves until they reached the door. It was locked by a sturdy padlock. So they opened it. The shelves didn't allow it to open very far, but there was enough of a gap for them to squeeze through. Inside was a small overhead storage locker. There was only one object inside. It was a mottled grey material, folded in a neat pile. One of the intruders rummaged about in the folds and pulled out something black and whiskery. It was a nose. And then two eyes. A seal's head. The object was a perfectly preserved sealskin. Both pairs of eyes turned in amazement to Ceasg.

'Don's a selchie!'

That night he dreamed of the beach, and of waves crashing on the rocks. A tall, thin man carrying a doctor's bag walked down to the shoreline. Every footprint he left in the sand filled up with blood. Or possibly jam. 'Quack,' said the man. 'Duck,' said the duck.

The man walked waist deep into the water. Then a horse rose up underneath him. But it wasn't underneath him. It was part of him. The apparition turned around, and the man had become a legless one-eyed lizard merged into the top of a horse with no skin and flippers where there should have been legs. Luckily, that meant the thing could barely move once it was on the land, and so it flopped about comically, threatening no-one. Then it rained, and the horse part collapsed and slowly dissolved. 'Nay,' said the horse. 'Duck,' said the duck.

The one-eyed lizard tried to walk up the beach, but not having legs made it much harder. It used its hands to haul itself along the sand and do acrobatics, and the trail it left made a beautiful picture of a mermaid. At last it reached him and drew itself up on its knuckles, and when it opened its foul, black mouth, out came an almighty burp, and it at least had the good grace to look embarrassed.

And this time he did wake up suddenly, because someone was screaming. He ran out into the hallway to find a crowd gathered. Mary Player had her arm around Ceasg, who was sobbing uncontrollably.

'My baby!' she cried. 'They've taken my baby!'

XI. The Storm Witch

A young lass called Janet Forsyth loved a young man called Benjamin Garrioch. One night she had a terrible dream of a ship travelling on dry land, which everyone knows is an omen of death. She begged Benjamin not to put out to sea the next morning, but he heeded not her words, and sure enough, a thick mist wrapped around the boat, and when the mist cleared, the boat was gone.

Janet pined awfully for her lost love. She would go out in her father's boat, whatever the weather, to look for him, and whatever the weather, she would always come back safe and sound. This seemed unnatural to her neighbours, and they took to calling her the Storm Witch. They started blaming her for shipwrecks and drownings, saying that when she sang to herself at night, she was calling on Teran deep in the sea.

One day, during a terrible storm, a large ship was sighted, lurching on the waves. The islanders did nothing to help it, expecting it to be dashed on the rocks. But Janet went out in her wee boat and soon reached the ship. She climbed aboard, took the wheel and steered the ship to safety. The crew were very grateful, and the captain tried to reward her with white metal, but she rushed away, saying she only wished someone had done the same for her poor Ben.

But the islanders did not congratulate Janet. They took her actions as proof of her witchcraft, and they put her on trial. Witnesses were brought and testified that she had bewitched them. Robert Reid swore he'd been taken ill at sea, and that when he'd gone to Janet and *accused her of causing it, she'd thrown a bucket of salt water over him and he'd felt better the next day. No-one stood up for Janet and she was found guilty. She was sentenced to be hanged on Gallows Hill and her body burnt to ashes. 'Save me, Ben!' called Janet, and then she fainted. A navy sailor rushed to her aid but was pulled off, and she was taken down to the cells to await her fate.*

But next morning when they went to take her to her death, her cell was found empty, with the door wide open and the hangman and guards dead drunk.

Years later, an islander was in the city on the mainland and came across a shop with the name of Benjamin Garrioch above the door. He went in and found none other than Janet Forsyth behind the counter. She told him that Ben and his friends had been picked up in the fog by a navy ship, whose crew had press ganged them into service. The trial was the first time in two years that he'd been back. He'd rescued her and taken her to that ship she'd saved, whose captain was only too glad to return the favour.

But Janet wasn't the only Storm Witch. There is a natural seat in the cliff by the Muckle Water known as the Maiden's Chair. Here sat Scota Bess predicting the weather at sea. The local men took her for a witch and dragged her off to beat her with flails soaked in holy water. But when they buried her, her body rose to the surface again. Twice more they buried her, and twice more she rose to the surface. Then they threw her into the Muckle Water and covered her with boatloads of dirt. This created the only island in the Muckle Water and Scota Bess finally stayed buried.

12

The *Renown* ploughed through the waves much faster than Adam would have thought possible. Donny Varrey and his crew were friendly enough, and seemed amused at Adam's lack of maritime knowledge. They weren't unkind, though, and Ben said they'd treated him the same way on his first voyage.

Another fishing boat, the *Intrepid,* had put out that morning shortly before the *Renown*. Its six man crew were all Sotfolders, and Adam noticed that they weren't particularly friendly to Donny's crew, barely acknowledging them beyond giving them some dark looks. Another man who had been talking to them, called Pieter, had made some remarks about 'immigrants', and seemed to be trying to provoke a fight until he was dragged away to the inn by his friend.

Adam and Ben had felt a little awkward about leaving the hotel after last night's events, but what use could they be? The Watch had been summoned but had shown little interest, saying it was probably for the best considering the baby's condition. Jana had told them exactly what she thought of that, and Adam and Ben had been forced to restrain her in order to avoid even more events. Baabie and Murgen insisted the baby must have been stolen by trows because Matheeus and Doctor Vleerman had not allowed them to take the proper precautions, such as placing a knife in the baby's cot. When Adam had sensibly pointed out the danger of the baby cutting itself, Baabie had shaken her head and muttered something about 'all that learnin' an' nae common sense'.

They hadn't bothered going back to bed after that, because the boat was leaving before first light anyway. The sea wind was bracing to say the least, and the tossing of the waves churned Adam's stomach. Would it be like this all the way to Nazca?

After about an hour, the wind had dropped and the air had warmed up, while the sea had become almost unnaturally calm. Adam was standing looking over the side of the boat when Pilot came and stood behind him.

'Are you ready then, Adam?'

'Ready for what?'

'Takin' a turn steerin' the boat.'

'What?' Adam whirled around. He saw Ben a few feet away, grinning.

'They made me do it my first time too.'

'I've no idea how to drive a boat,' protested Adam.

'Then it's aboot time you learned,' said Pilot, putting his hand on Adam's back and steering him firmly but gently to the wheelhouse. 'I'll show ye what to do.'

Donny had the wheel at the moment but as they entered, he let go and left with a smirk.

'What if I sink the boat?' asked Adam.

'Ye'll no sink the boat, ye eejit. Ye're just steerin' it.'

'What if I steer it onto rocks?'

'Aye, that'd sink it,' agreed Pilot. 'Ye'd best no do that. Now will ye tak the wheel?'

Adam did nothing.

'I'm not takin' it,' said Pilot. 'If you don't, then it'll steer itsel' onto rocks wi'oot your help.'

Adam took the wheel and Pilot gave him directions. The most frequent of which was, 'Will ye just relax?' He steered the boat for about fifteen minutes and didn't sink it and no-one fell overboard or even jumped on purpose, and after a while he began to enjoy himself. Eventually Donny came back to take over, and Adam eagerly asked them both how he had done.

'No' bad for a first go,' smiled Donny.

Adam felt pleased and turned to Pilot for his opinion.

'You were just supposed to steer it,' said the old man, 'no write yer name wi' it.'

Donny and Pilot laughed as Adam's face fell.

The crew had by now cast out the huge net, and it was being towed along behind the boat. Then they set about making breakfast, which turned out to be much better than Adam had expected. As they ate, Ben took out the map Adam had found at the market.

'I've been doing some reading, and this may not be a fake after all.'

'Really?' asked Adam.

'Yes. It turns out that the earliest known map to include Frisland did place it much further east. Roughly where it is on your map. It probably refers to completely different islands, perhaps ones that are below the water level now, but it's an interesting puzzle. I know a guy in the geography department back in Augsburg who loves this stuff. I'll pass it on to him when I get back.' He took a sip of his coffee.

'Disappearing islands is it?' asked Donny. 'Maybe it's like Hildaland.'

'What's Hildaland?' asked Adam.

'Old Orknejar legend,' Donny told him. 'Home of the Finfolk.'

'Finfolk?'

'A race of evil sorcerers,' explained Ben. 'Sort of.'

'Hildaland was their magical island that mortals couldna see unless they knew the richt magic. In most stories it was surrounded by magical fog, but some said it sank below the waves and only rose up when they wanted it to. Maybe this Frisland o' yours is a bit like that.'

Ben looked thoughtful. 'There are stories of ghost islands all over the world,' he said.

'Surely that's just down to inaccurate maps or poor navigation or whatever,' said Adam.

'Probably ... ' Ben was looking at the map intently.

'And you said yourself about the water level rising.'

Ben spread the map on the table and they all leaned over it. 'Look at this map. Frisland isn't just some rock that could disappear if the sea level changed. It's got towns, and I'm sure I read once about it being at war with somewhere.'

'So it's a mistake on the map,' insisted Adam.

'What if there's another explanation?' Ben's eyes were alight.

'What are you thinkin', young Ben?' asked Donny.

'I'm thinking about Hildaland. A magical island of sorcerers that rose up out of the sea, and vanished again when they wanted to hide it. And there are similar stories all over the world. Lots of vanishing islands, some magical, some not.'

'Well, they're just folk tales,' said Adam.

Ben looked directly at him. 'What if they were Skentys colonies?'

He's as bad as Jana, thought Adam. 'You've got no evidence for that. You just made it up.'

'Skentys?' asked Donny. 'Is that *your* folklore?'

'Pretty much,' said Ben. 'But think about it, Adam. It would explain a lot. Ghost islands, the Finfolk, all sorts.'

'That doesn't make it true,' said Adam. 'It's just a wild guess.'

'It's a hypothesis,' Ben corrected him. 'An explanation that fits the facts, but which hasn't been tested yet.'

'What facts? Folklore isn't facts. Maps showing islands that we know don't exist aren't facts.'

Donny stood up and his crew followed suit. 'We'll leave the pair o' you to it,' said Donny, slapping Ben on the back as he passed. 'We've got to check the net.'

'Father Langstok's right about you, you know,' Ben said to Adam after the crew had gone. 'You're really much more of a scientist than you are a wizard.'

'What's that supposed to mean?' asked Adam, not sure whether he'd just been insulted.

'Oh, don't worry, it's a good thing. Science is about evidence, and testing theories and not believing everything you hear. It's about looking for explanations rather than just accepting things. Personally, I think magic and science aren't that far apart. Magic's just science we don't understand yet. The difference is just the people who practice it. Most wizards I've met just like being all mystical, and are happy enough that they can do magic without wondering how it works. But one day science will be able to explain magic, and people like you will be at the forefront of that.'

There were sudden shouts from above and then Donny's voice called, 'Young Ben, you'll want to see this.'

'What is it?' shouted Ben as they both leaped up.

'It's a merman.'

'You have to sit very still,' said Prince Randian for the third time.

'Sorry,' said Jana. 'I'm not good at still.'

'I noticed.'

Randian had been perched on a pedestal when she arrived. An easel was set to one side of it, along with a stand on which sat his wooden box. His painting materials were laid out next to it. He chatted away throughout the sitting, despite the brushes being in his mouth, and had evidently had a lot of practice at it, as he managed to sound perfectly intelligible the whole time. Jana presumed he had learned it from a ventriloquist during his time with the circus.

'Why do you do this?' she asked.

'I like painting,' he said.

'I mean the freak show. Why do you let people gawp at you? Like you're ... well ... '

'A freak?'

She didn't answer.

'You think what we do here is demeaning.'

'Well, isn't it?' she asked.

'Look,' he said, 'I'm a bit short in the arm and leg department. Which makes me a bit short altogether. And you feel sorry for me, which is all very nice of you. And I could feel sorry for me too, or I could pull myself together – well, not pull, but you know what I mean – and make the most of what I've got. So here I am. Star of my own show, a bit of painting on the side. What's wrong with that? And here I'm accepted for what I am. People would stare at me anyway, but here they do it on my terms. And pay for the privilege. Well, most of them. You're staring for free.' Jana looked embarrassed, which had been the intention. 'At least I'm not all hairy like that dog guy,' he concluded. Jana looked shocked and he burst out laughing. 'You've got a lot to learn.'

'I might be hairy but at least I can pick my own nose,' came a voice through the tent wall. 'Now imagine the sign I'm making with my fingers that you can't, stumpy.'

Randian chuckled.

Jana didn't know where to look. Eventually she managed, 'You could just do the painting and not do, well, this.'

'Why would I do that? I *love* being in the show. You think we're being exploited, don't you? But by who? I'm not some pathetic monster who's chained up at night by the evil circus owner, who feeds us mouldy bread and water while he coins it in. We all get an equal cut of the freak show admissions, same as the big top performers get an equal cut of the main show takings. And I keep the money from selling my paintings. And I get to spend my life travelling, performing, meeting interesting weirdos like you, and I do it all with friends who are just like me. Except they're not, cos there's no-one just like me. But they understand me and accept me.'

'No we don't,' came the voice through the wall, 'we hate you and think you're a mutant.'

'Shut up, dog breath.'

'Fancy a drink later? We can get legless.'

'Yeah, it'll put hairs on your chest.'

Something over Jana's shoulder caught Randian's eye. She turned to see what he was looking at, and caught a glimpse of the Scary Clowns walking past the entrance. Mr Coco's hair was now red and he wore a bowler hat.

'Where are you two going?' called Randian.

The clowns walked back into the doorway. Backwards. Mr Coco was carrying a fishing rod. Mr Wobbly had a net on a pole.

'We,' said Mr Coco, 'are going fishing.'

'Fishing,' said Mr Wobbly.

'You two fish?' asked Randian in surprise.

'We do today,' said Mr Coco.

'Today,' agreed Mr Wobbly.

'What are you hoping to catch?' asked Jana.

Mr Coco gave her a withering look. 'Fish,' he said at length.

'Fish. Yeah,' said Mr Wobbly.

'Any particular kind?' asked Randian.

'There are different kinds?' replied Mr Coco in evident surprise. 'That may complicate things.'

'Complicate,' said Mr Wobbly.

Jana sniggered.

Mr Coco sighed. 'You still seem to be under the impression that clowns are funny,' he complained.

'Funny,' repeated Mr Wobbly.

'For your information – Mr Wobbly,' – *toot toot* – 'will you please stop doing that!'

'Sorry Mr Coco. I just wanted to be part of the conversation.'

Jana was doubled up with laughter.

'Any more of that, young lady,' said Mr Coco sternly, 'and we'll be back with the quick-setting whitewash and the shaved monkey.' And with that they left.

Randian waited a full minute before he said, 'I can't paint you while you're rolling around on the floor.'

Adam and Ben stared in awe at the apparition in front of the boat. It was hard to be sure, but it seemed to be some distance away, which made it indistinct. Despite this, it wasn't what Adam would have expected a merman to look like. It was huge for a start, towering out of the water. It was roughly man-shaped, with a pointed head, broad shoulders and a tapering body. It bobbed a little and appeared to be watching them.

'That's a merman?' asked Adam.

'Sailors from Væringjar have described them just like this,' breathed Ben, not taking his eyes off it, 'but I've never actually seen one before. It's beautiful.'

'Means there's going to be a storm,' growled Donny.

'Aye,' agreed Pilot. 'There's always a storm after a merman appears.'

Then they heard the noise.

It was unlike anything Adam had ever heard before. Ethereal, magical, it swooped and sighed like some giant horn, utterly unmelodic but somehow hauntingly beautiful nonetheless.

'That's a mermaid singing,' said Donny, his voice full of dread.

'*That's* mermaid song?' asked Adam in amazement.

Ben just smiled knowingly.

The merman suddenly pitched forward and disappeared, although Adam was sure he caught a distant glimpse of fluked tail.

'Probably a whale,' said Ben.

'What?' Adam was confused. 'I thought you said it was a merman.'

'That's what the old Væringjar sailors believed, but it's really just a mirage. When the hot air starts to turn to a storm, it can cause an illusion in the water that distorts the shape of objects. This one must have been a whale poking its head above the water. You'd never have made out a dolphin's tail at that distance.' He gave Adam a sidelong look. 'Science,' he said smugly.

'What about the singing?'

'Whalesong. Whales make all sorts of noises,' he added in reply to Adam's blank stare. 'Only a few kinds make the singing though. That was probably a humpback.'

There was a rumble of thunder overhead.

'Best turn back,' said Donny, and ran to the wheelhouse while the crew started to pull the net back in.

'Best hold on, boys,' warned Pilot. 'Could get a wee bit rough.'

As Donny brought the boat about, Adam felt the first big spots of rain. Soon after, the wind began to whip up, and then the boat began to lurch as the waves surged.

'You two alright?' Pilot called to Adam and Ben. Adam nodded and Ben waved. Then the boat lurched again and he fell over the side.

Closer to shore, the sea was calmer. A little rowing boat bobbed up and down on the water, and its occupants bobbed up and down with it. Mr Coco's fishing rod hung over the side, and Mr Coco hung on to the end of it while Mr Wobbly kept a tight hold of the oars. It was safe to say that water was not their natural milieu.

'Is it entirely necessary for there to be so much of it?' asked Mr Coco testily. He did not look happy. Even more so than usual, that is.

'I think there has to be for the boat to work properly,' suggested Mr Wobbly. 'Rowin' across sand's much harder.'

'Did you bring the picnic?' asked Mr Coco.

'Course I did.' He took a checked cloth from his pocket, and with a flourish, laid it on the floor of the boat. From a different pocket, he took small silver salt and pepper shakers and put them on the cloth. He lifted his top hat, and under it were two small plates balanced on his head, which he also put on the cloth. He put his gloved hand up to his mouth, and from it he produced a hard boiled egg, which he handed to Mr Coco. He then produced another egg, which he kept for himself. He continued to do this until they had four eggs each.

The clowns peeled and seasoned their eggs in silence, and began to eat them. After a few bites, Mr Coco asked, 'Weren't there sandwiches?'

'Oh yeah,' said Mr Wobbly. 'I almost forgot.' He leaned across, put his hand next to Mr Coco's ear and produced a sandwich from it.

'What kind is it?' asked Mr Coco.

Mr Wobbly checked. 'Egg.'

'Next time you might want to try a bit more variety,' said Mr Coco.

'If you leave it long enough it might turn into chicken,' suggested Mr Wobbly optimistically.

'I think I might get hungry before then. I'll have the egg.'

Mr Wobbly handed him the sandwich and went on to produce three more in the same manner, one from each of the three remaining ears on the boat, giving one to Mr Coco and keeping the rest for himself.

'Anything to drink?' asked Mr Coco after a while.

Mr Wobbly reached into his pockets and produced two cups and saucers, which he placed on the cloth. Then he raised his hat again, and this time there was a small teapot perched on his head. He lifted it down and replaced the hat.

'Whadda you fancy?' he asked.

'Cocoa,' said Mr Coco.

Mr Wobbly poured hot cocoa into Mr Coco's cup.

'What are you having?' asked Mr Coco.

'Beer,' said Mr Wobbly, pouring it from the same teapot.

As they ate and drank in silence, a spot of rain landed in Mr Coco's cocoa. Then another bounced off the end of his red nose. They both looked up to the sky and held out the palms of their hands in the way people do to check whether it's raining when they already know.

'It's raining,' said Mr Wobbly.

'I'd noticed,' said Mr Coco.

'Maybe that's why there's so much water,' guessed Mr Wobbly.

'Having all that water both above us and below us is a sign of bad planning,' said Mr Coco.

'We're getting wet,' pointed out Mr Wobbly.

Mr Coco took out a tiny umbrella. It was smaller than his hat. He held it between them so that neither was actually under it at all, and they ate their sandwiches, drank their drinks and continued to get wet.

Then something pulled on the fishing line. Mr Coco grabbed it and started pulling. 'Quick, Mr Wobbly,' – *toot toot* – 'the net!'

Mr Wobbly dipped the net into the water and tried to get it under whatever was pulling on the line. The boat rocked as they struggled to land their catch, and several times one or other of them almost fell in, but was only saved by the other grabbing their coat tails and heaving them back. At least twice this almost resulted in the boat capsizing in the other direction.

Finally Mr Wobbly got the thing in his net and started to lift it out of the water. It struggled, though, and didn't make it easy. Mr Coco grabbed the checked cloth, sending crockery flying, and as the net was finally raised out of the water, he bundled their catch into it and tied the corners in a knot. Whatever was inside continued to struggle but the knots held firm.

The clowns nodded to each other and shook hands. Then they sat down and took an oar each. They started to row, but as they were facing in opposite directions, the boat just went around in circles. Eventually, Mr Coco slapped Mr Wobbly's hands and took his oar from him. Mr Coco started rowing towards the shore while Mr Wobbly sat glumly watching the struggling checked cloth. And occasionally hitting it with a mallet to make it stop.

The first thing he noticed was the cold. The water was freezing and numbed his muscles almost instantly. Everything was a murky bluish-grey. His body instinctively tried to swim for the surface, but his

156

muscles were too cold and he hadn't the strength, and just seemed to be going further down instead.

Panic set in and he screamed. Water flowed into his lungs. He had a brief moment of clarity and closed his mouth, trying to conserve what air he had left. He tried again to push for the surface, but his hands and feet just waved helplessly in the water.

His chest felt like it would burst, and his spine felt like it was being crushed. He had to let the air out. He knew that he shouldn't, that it was all he had left and there would be no more coming in, but it was becoming too painful not to. It was unbearable.

And then it wasn't. The pain seemed to ease. He thought of his family and how they would cope with the loss. He relaxed and breathed. And took in more water. But this time there was no panic, no pain. It was almost pleasant.

Suddenly he wasn't alone in the water. There was a woman with him. A beautiful woman. Kissing him. No, not kissing. She was breathing air into his lungs. There wasn't much room and she seemed to realise this. She put her hand in his mouth and forced him to be sick. He was disgusted and wanted to apologise but immediately she kissed him again and breathed more air into his lungs, holding his nose and then firmly closing his mouth when she was finished. She put her arms around him and swam upwards. At some point he looked down and realised that she didn't have legs.

Then he felt hands grab him and pull him up. Moments later he was lying on the deck coughing up water.

'Thocht we'd lost you there, young Ben,' said Pilot anxiously. The whole crew was standing looking down at him, and Adam was sitting cradling his head.

'You were under a long time,' said Donny. 'It's a miracle you came back up at all.'

'There was a woman,' spluttered Ben. 'Saved me.'

The fishermen all glanced at each other uneasily.

'What woman?' asked Adam.

Ben grinned stupidly. 'She was a mermaid. An actual real live mermaid.' He giggled.

The fishermen all peered at the sea around them, hoping not to catch a confirming sight. 'That's terrible bad luck, that,' muttered Donny. 'Mermaids are always bad luck.'

'Not for me,' grinned Ben.

'Rescuing you's bad luck too,' said Pilot. 'The sea'll aye have its prey, and if any man deprives it then he'll have to tak the victim's place.'

'Then maybe it's a good job it was a mermaid that did the rescuin',' suggested Donny.

'Aye,' said Pilot thoughtfully. 'Aye. That'll do.'

'Let's get out of here,' ordered Donny roughly.

The crew all busied themselves with manning the boat. The wind had started to whip up, and it was raining. The storm was almost on them, but the *Renown* was a fast boat and they were managing to stay just ahead of it.

There was a sudden cry from one of the crew. 'Vessel to starboard!'

Everyone ran to the side of the boat, and Ben was by now sufficiently recovered to join them. In the distance was another fishing boat, tossing alarmingly on the waves. The storm had overtaken it and it was clearly in trouble.

'That's the *Intrepid*,' said Donny. His voice was hollow.

The waves surged beneath the *Intrepid* and tossed it like a toy. Pilot put a hand on Donny's arm.

'Donny, we have to keep goin'. If we stay and watch, we'll be sunk.'

Donny tore his eyes from the other boat and nodded grimly. 'Back to work lads.' Then to Pilot, 'Keep an eye on the *Intrepid*.'

'Aye aye,' said Pilot, and the crew went back to bringing the *Renown* to safety. Adam and Ben stood beside Pilot, watching the stricken *Intrepid*. Another surge obscured it from their view for a second, but when the wave went down and the boat became visible again, it was the wrong way up. 'She's capsized,' said Pilot quietly. 'Don't tell the others yet. They need to concentrate on saving us.'

Adam and Ben nodded dumbly and watched the upturned boat receding into the distance.

XII. The Wee Mermaid

A mermaid lived at the bottom of the sea, and she was young, and she was pretty and she had the most beautiful singing voice you ever heard, but she was not happy, for she longed to see the world above the ocean. She was fascinated by the things that drifted down from shipwrecks, and above all, she desperately wanted to live in the human world.

One evening, a ship sailed overhead, and she rushed up to the surface to watch it. There were men on board, but she only saw one of them, for he was the most handsome creature she had ever seen, and she instantly fell in love with him. She watched from a distance so they would not see her, but she sang for him and she did not mind if he heard.

Suddenly the men on the ship cried out in fear, for a terrible storm had blown up, and the ship was being battered by strong winds and lashed by the waves. The mermaid was in fear for their lives, but most of all for the one she loved.

Then the mast broke and the ship sank, and the men all cried out as they fell into the water. Many were drowned, but the wee mermaid caught hold of her love and took him safely to shore, where she left him on the sand, for she did not want him to see her mermaid's tale and be repulsed.

Now she wanted more than ever to be a part of the human world, so she went to the Storm Witch and asked for her help. She knew how dangerous this was, for the Storm Witch did not help anyone out of the goodness of her heart. How could she when she **had** no goodness in her heart? She would exact a terrible price, but the mermaid did not care, for any price would be worth it to live in the human world and see her love again.

'Yes, I can help you,' smiled the Storm Witch. 'I can change your tail into legs so you can walk upon the land like the humans do. But every step you take will feel like walking on broken glass or sharpened swords. And you will have to pay me.'

'What payment do you want?' asked the mermaid fearfully.

'I want your voice,' said the Storm Witch gleefully. 'Your beautiful singing voice.'

'But how will I speak to him if I have no voice?' asked the mermaid.

'You will speak to him with your beauty,' smiled the Storm Witch.

'But how can I give you my voice?' asked the mermaid.

'I will cut out your tongue,' smiled the Storm Witch. 'And know this too. Once I have given you legs, you will never be able to regain your tail and return to the sea. Once you walk upon the land, you must remain there, whether your man loves you or not.'

The mermaid wept, for it was a terrible price to pay, but then she thought of living in the human world and being with her love, and she agreed to the bargain. So the Storm Witch cut out her tongue, and separated her tail and turned it into legs, and when the mermaid walked on land, every step was like walking on broken glass or sharpened swords. And though she could no longer sing, and every step was agony, she learned to dance instead, and became the most graceful dancer you ever saw.

And she found her love, and he was entranced by her beauty and her graceful dancing, even though she could not speak or sing. But he loved another, and the mermaid's heart broke, and it was far more painful than walking on broken glass or sharpened swords.

Then the Storm Witch came to her and she brought a knife. 'Take this knife and kill the one you love,' said the Storm Witch. 'Let the blood drip on your feet and you will become a mermaid again, and be able to return to the sea.'

In her despair, the mermaid agreed, but when she reached out her hand to take the knife, the Storm Witch snatched it away. 'There is a price if you want this second service from me,' she laughed. 'You must *give me your beautiful long hair.'*

The mermaid did not care about the cost any more, and so she willingly cut off her hair and gave it to the Storm Witch in exchange for the knife. But when she saw her love lying asleep beside his new wife, she could not bring herself to harm him. Instead, she threw away the knife and threw herself into the sea. And because she was no longer a mermaid, she drowned.

13

That's amazing!'

Jana looked at her portrait in awe. It wasn't large – it would have taken far too long to paint a large portrait – but it was an excellent likeness, and Randian had a style that made it compelling to look at. She clapped her hands in joy.

Randian wrapped the canvas in a sheet and gave it to her. 'I don't do framing,' he said, 'but you'll be able to find someone who can frame it if you want.'

'Thank you, Randian,' said Jana. 'You're very talented.' She leaned across and kissed him on the cheek.

'Well,' he said, blushing. 'We don't get that very often. Usually it's funny looks and snide comments and clutching the children to their breast.' Despite the joking, he seemed genuinely touched.

The tattooed man poked his head around the door. 'Randy, you seen anyone strange hanging around?'

'Yeah. All of us. Why?'

'No, I mean strangers. The mermaid's gone.' He disappeared again.

Randian looked at Jana. 'Would you mind carrying me through? I don't do quick.'

They rushed through to the area where the mermaid had been yesterday. Its pedestal was empty, and the glass dome sat on the floor.

'Why would anyone steal it?' asked the tattooed man, baffled. 'I mean, it's hideous.'

'It spoke highly of you too,' said Lionel, who was already standing there. 'In fact, it was thnking of asking you out.'

163

'Not to worry,' came the voice of Mr Coco behind them. They all turned to see the Scary Clowns walk in. Mr Wobbly was carrying a sack that was struggling against him. 'We've got a replacement,' said Mr Coco. 'A live one.'

'You've got a live mermaid?' asked Jana in amazement. 'Or is this another of your jokes?'

'Jokes?' repeated Mr Coco in irritation. '*Jokes?* We do not tell jokes. And if you laugh at that, Mr Wobbly' – *toot toot* – 'will be forced to fetch the bucket.'

Jana kept a straight face and waited to see what would happen next.

'You've seriously got a live mermaid in there?' asked the tattooed man sceptically..

'Well we certainly haven't *comically* got a live mermaid in there,' said Mr Wobbly.

Mr Coco gave him a hard stare. 'I don't think you should talk without asking me first, Mr Wobbly.'

Toot – The second toot didn't come. Mr Wobbly looked at Mr Coco questioningly.

'Tooting is permitted,' confirmed Mr Coco.

– *toot*.

'Just open the bag,' sighed Lionel.

Mr Coco signalled to Mr Wobbly, who unceremoniously dumped the bag on the floor. It continued to struggle, but the creature inside didn't manage to find its way out. Mr Wobbly sighed and picked it up again. He turned it upside down and shook until his catch came tumbling out.

They all stared at it.

'I'm pretty sure that's not a mermaid,' said Randian. 'It's got legs for a start.'

It did indeed have legs. Short spindly ones that matched its longer but just as spindly arms. Its round head, with its small, yellow face and green teeth, did look a little like the missing mermaid, in that they were both quite monkey-like, but there was certainly no fish tail. Its large, round, red eyes darted around, it wrung its brown woollen mitten-clad hands, and its skinny chest heaved in terror under its dark grey jacket. It backed away and put the pedestal between itself and its captors.

'I think we may have made a mistake, Mr Wobbly.'

Toot toot.

The not-mermaid jumped in alarm.

'What the hell is it?' asked the tattooed man.

'Whatever it is, it's terrified,' said Jana. 'Let it go.'

'She's right,' agreed Randian. 'Let the poor thing go.'

The tattooed man walked to the edge of the tent and lifted a flap. He made sure that the creature had seen it, then walked to the entrance. He motioned to everyone else, and they all joined him at the entrance, putting more distance between them and the creature. It stared at them for a few seconds, and then slowly backed towards the edge of the tent, never taking its eyes off them. Once it was there, it felt around behind itself until its fingers found the canvas and lifted it. With one last look to make sure no-one was going to lunge at it, the creature dived under the flap and was gone.

'Shame,' said the tattooed man. 'People would definitely have paid to gawp at that.'

The *Renown* had managed to outrun the storm and make it back to port. Donny had let Pilot take the boat into the harbour, and the mood had been sombre. They secured the boat, and then everyone walked in silence up to the Mission, where they found Father Langstok looking less composed than usual.

'Hello, lads,' he said, smiling but looking worried at the same time. 'You've caught me at a bad time, I'm afraid. It seems there was a break-in last night, although there are no signs of forced entry. But believe it or not, the only thing they took was the mummified mermaid in the museum. Why would anyone want to steal – ' He noticed their expressions and stopped. 'What's happened?'

'The *Intrepid* went doon,' Pilot told him. 'We saw it.'

Father Langstok stared at them and then sat down heavily at the nearest table. 'Oh no,' he said, shaking his head sadly. 'Oh, that's terrible.' He looked up at them. 'You weren't able to rescue anyone?'

'We were too far away,' said Donny, 'and there was a storm coming.'

'I think Donny might ha' tried if we'd let him,' said Pilot, 'but we'd never ha' got there in time, and we'd just have ended up joining them.'

'Of course,' nodded Father Langstok. 'There's no need to explain.' He took a deep breath and stood up. 'I'll have to go and tell the family.'

'Family?' repeated Adam. 'There were six men on that boat.'

Father Langstok nodded sadly. 'That would be tragic enough in itself but the *Intrepid* was very much a family business. Its captain was Marten Terhorst. The first mate was his brother and two of the crew were Marten's sons. The other two were married to his daughters. That's all the men in one family killed in a single day. This could be the worst tragedy since the Stotfold disaster.'

Jana had left her portrait at the hotel and gone for a walk on the beach. Randian had given her lots to think about, and she still wasn't sure whether she was comfortable with the idea of the freak show, although she certainly saw its performers in a different light now. She was also still worried about Ceasg and her baby, especially as the Watch seemed so disinterested.

As she walked, she saw the lighthouse looming ahead of her, and the entrance to the caves below it. She stood and gazed up at the white needle of the lighthouse on the headland.

'Boo!'

She whirled around and saw Liban laughing at her.

'Where did you spring from?' smiled Jana as Draatsie scampered up to sniff her ankles.

Liban held up the doll and then hugged it tight.

'Aah, you love her, don't you?' said Jana as she bent down to stroke Draatsie's back.

'Liban!' The girl looked worried at the sound of the male voice, and stood staring at her feet. A figure came over the high rocks and Jana realised that it was Ben Varrey.

'Sorry Daddy,' said Liban quietly, although he was not yet near enough to hear her.

'Liban!' he shouted again as he approached them. 'I told you not to go running off.'

'Sorry Daddy.'

'If ye're not careful, Green Goon'll get you.'

Liban looked fearfully at the caves and repeated, 'Green Goon.'

As Ben Varrey reached them, Jana said, 'She's okay. No harm done.'

He glanced at her and muttered, 'Aye,' before turning back to the girl. 'Don't you go running off like that again,' he scolded and he smacked her hard across the backs of her legs.

Liban burst into tears. 'Sorry Daddy, sorry Daddy,' she squealed.

'Hey!' snapped Jana, instinctively putting an arm around Liban. 'Don't hit her.'

Ben Varrey glared at her. 'Don't tell me how to raise my own – ' He stopped for a second before finishing, 'how to raise a daughter.'

Jana stood up and was about to challenge him further when another voice shouted, 'Ben! Ben! Are you there?'

Ben Varrey turned as Abgal came scrambling over the rocks. 'What is it, Abgal?'

'It's your horse, Ben,' panted Abgal as he reached them. 'It's sick.'

'What kind o' sick?' asked Ben Varrey.

'Foamin' at the mouth an' lyin' on its side. Adaro's is the same.' Ben looked grave. 'And there's more,' continued Abgal.

'What?' asked Ben Varrey, dread in his voice.

'The barley in Tam's field's all mildew.'

Ben Varrey's face turned white. 'Mortasheen!' he breathed. 'Here?'

'The kelp was burned just yesterday,' Abgal reminded him.

'We've always burned kelp here,' protested Ben Varrey. 'Nothing's ever happened before.'

'Aye, well, we'd best get back,' said Abgal.

Ben Varrey nodded grimly, and they both ran off the way they had come. Jana stared after them and then felt a tugging at her leg. They'd left Liban! They'd just run off without her. 'Hey!' she shouted, but they were already too far away. 'Don't worry,' Jana reassured the girl, 'I'll get you home.' She picked her up and then turned for one last look at the caves. They'd have to wait for another day she supposed. Hang on, though. Was that something moving? She took a step forward and immediately felt Liban go rigid in her arms. She looked down and saw that the girl was staring wide eyed at the caves.

167

'Green Goon,' she whispered.

Jana looked at the caves again. There was definitely something moving in there. Something ... green ...

Liban tugged frantically at her sleeve. 'Green Goon,' she said urgently. 'Green Goon!'

It was obvious she was scared, so Jana turned around, and after checking that Draatsie was following, headed back the other way. Liban turned to peer over Jana's shoulder.

'Green Goon,' she whispered again. 'Green Goon.'

By the time Father Langstok returned, about an hour later, looking tired and sad, Mae was sitting in the Mission with the others. 'Hello, Mae,' sighed the Father. 'You've heard?'

'Aye, Father.' She took his hand as he sat down. 'Isn't it awful? And today of all days too.'

'What's today?' asked Adam.

'Maisie and Abgal are gettin' married the day after tomorrow,' explained Mae. 'It canna be put off, but it'll look awfully insensitive.'

'How's the family?' asked Pilot.

'Devastated,' said Father Langstok. 'Just devastated.'

There was silence for a few minutes, before Mae felt she could bring up the other thing. 'There's trouble at the Seatown too.'

'What trouble?' asked Donny?

She looked at him with something like fear in her eyes. 'It's mortasheen, Donny.'

He stared at her in disbelief. 'Mortasheen? It can't be.'

'All the horses are sick and the crops are failing.'

The fishermen all shook their heads numbly as they tried to take in this latest disaster.

'What's mortasheen?' Adam whispered to Ben.

'It's a disease that kills the horses and the crops. From an old Orknejar legend about a demon called the Nuckleavee. It's the most feared monster in their folklore, and it hates the smell of burning kelp. It takes its revenge by spreading mortasheen.'

'But if they believe that, then why do they keep burning the seaweed?'

'We thought we were safe from it here,' said Donny. 'We're far away from the islands, and we've been doing it for near a hundred years. Why should it follow us now?'

Before Adam could voice his scepticism, the door opened and Jana walked in carrying Liban, with Draatsie trailing behind them. When Liban saw Donny, she scrambled down and ran over to him, jumping up to sit on his knee. Although he was obviously distracted, Jana noticed that Donny seemed more affectionate towards his niece than her father was.

'I heard about the shipwreck,' said Jana with obvious concern, as Draatsie scampered over to investigate Adam's ankles. 'Everyone's talking about it. Are you all okay?'

'Aye,' said Pilot, 'though young Ben's lucky to be back on dry land He fell overboard.'

Jana looked worried, even though he was clearly sitting right in front of her, very much alive. 'You fell in? Are you alright?'

Despite the tragic atmosphere he managed a grin. 'I was saved by a mermaid. A real live mermaid.'

'No-one else saw it,' argued Adam. 'He was probably seeing things from all the drowning.'

'He was under a long time,' reasoned Pilot. '*Something* brought him back up.'

Adam almost felt betrayed. 'I thought you didn't believe in mermaids.'

'I never said we didna believe in them. I said we werna obsessed.'

'Rescued by a mermaid were you?'

No-one had noticed the man standing in the doorway, but the anger in his voice, and the smell of alcohol, told them they'd better start noticing him now.

'Pieter,' said Father Langstok soothingly. 'This isn't the time.'

'My quarrel's not with you, Father,' said the man. 'Don't get involved.'

'I know you're upset, Pieter,' continued the Father. 'We all are, but casting blame won't help.'

'Marten's boat didn't come back. Theirs did. And they had mermaids helping them. I heard them say it.'

169

'Pieter – '

'Shut up, Father!' His vehemence sent the tension up another few degrees. Liban went rigid and clung to Donny's arm. 'Mermaids bring the storms, they were saved by mermaids, they made it back but my friends didn't. Because we're not descended from them.'

'This is silly, Pieter,' said the Father. 'You've had a bit too much to drink and – '

'You're always taking their side,' spat Pieter. 'Well we won't stand for it any more.'

He suddenly turned and marched out. Everyone let out the breath they'd been involuntarily holding.

'I really thought he was going to do something foolish,' said Father Langstok.

The window exploded in a shower of glass, as a large stone landed inches from Draatsie's tail, sending the otter scurrying for cover behind Adam's legs. Liban screamed and followed her. Donny leaped up and ran to the door, but immediately ducked back in and slammed it shut a fraction of a second before it resounded with a loud thud, followed by two more.

'He's no on his own,' said Donny, bolting the door. 'There's four or five o' them oot there.'

Another window shattered as another stone came flying through it. Everyone instinctively ducked under the tables. Liban hugged Draatsie for dear life. Then the air was full of breaking glass, thuds and stones. None of them saw it because they all had their eyes screwed shut, but the noise was terrifying. The onslaught only lasted a few seconds, but it felt like a lifetime, probably because there was so much danger of it being the end of someone's.

Then it all stopped and there was silence. For several minutes everyone stayed exactly where they were, worried in case it began again. Eventually Donny slid over to the wall and risked a look through what was left of the nearest window. His body visibly relaxed and he stood up.

'They're gone,' he confirmed. 'Everyone alright?'

They all stood up and dusted themselves down. All except Liban, who stayed cowering under the chairs. Jana bent down and gently coaxed her out. 'Come on, Liban. It's alright. The bad man's gone now. We'll look after you.'

Liban hesitated, and then finally took Jana's hand and crawled out. As she did, Jana noticed that the little girl's blouse had fallen off her shoulder, revealing a large purple bruise. 'Liban's hurt!' she called.

Everyone picked their way carefully through the broken glass as they came over to see.

'One of the stones must have hit her,' fumed Jana, carefully sitting Liban on a table that was free of glass. 'Wait till I get my hands on him.'

Adam noticed Donny and Mae exchange uneasy glances, before Mae said, 'She might just have fallen. It mightna ha' been a stone at all.'

Jana was about to snap back at her, but Father Langstok tactfully intervened. 'Jana, would you be a dear and go into the kitchen and boil up some water for tea and coffee? We'll need it while we tidy up this mess. You'll also be able to get a damp cloth to put on poor Liban's shoulder so it doesn't swell.'

Jana took a deep breath and did as she was asked. As the others looked around at the devastation, the sounds of water being poured into a kettle could be heard.

'Please everyone be very careful,' warned Father Langstok, as he handed out brooms and people gingerly began picking up stones. Jana came back with a damp cloth and placed it on Liban's shoulder. The girl winced a little, but it didn't seem to be causing her too much pain.

They worked for a few minutes, until the sound of light bubbling filtered through from the kitchen. Mae looked up sharply at the noise.

'Ye havena left that water boiling alone have ye?'

'It'll be fine,' said Jana. 'It won't come fully to the boil for a few minutes yet.'

'That's no the point!' shrieked Mae, far more urgently than seemed necessary. 'It's terrible bad luck.'

'Why?' snorted Jana.

'If ye leave water boiling alone, you're sure to lose your sweetheart,' said Mae firmly.

Jana shook her head dismissively. Adam didn't notice the direction her eyes darted in but Father Langstok did and allowed himself the tiniest of smiles.

'I'll go and watch it if it'll make you happy,' grumbled Jana. 'It's probably nearly ready anyway.'

Father Langstok's smile widened just a little as she stomped back into the kitchen.

Rain was starting to fall on the coast as the storm moved closer to land. Along the beach, past the lighthouse, she came out of the water. She swam into the shallows and then stood upright. Her skirt was gathered around her feet to form something that almost resembled a tail. She rearranged it to free her legs, and revealed a beautifully embroidered petticoat underneath. From a pocket, she took a mirror and a tortoise-shell comb. She looked at her reflection in the mirror as she combed her long hair, sifting the salt crystals from it. Once satisfied, she pulled her hair back and used the comb to fix it in place. She put the mirror back in her pocket and walked on to the beach.

Every step was very precise. Because every step was like walking on broken glass or sharpened swords.

XIII. Tammas and the Nuckelavee

*O*f all the sea creatures held in check by the Mither o' the Sea, none was as feared as the Nuckleavee, a beast spoken of only in whispers of terror; a creature so malevolent that his sole purpose was to plague the islanders – a purpose from which he never shirked. Only the power of the Mither o' the Sea kept him off the land in summer, and his fear of fresh water kept him in hiding during the rain and snow of winter, but at other times, he wandered the land searching for mortals to torment.

The Nuckleavee was blamed for all sorts of disasters and ailments – perhaps more than he was truly the cause of, but most often the blame would be deserved. If crops failed, or cattle died or the islanders were struck by injury or sickness, the Nuckleavee would be held responsible and would gladly take the blame. But his deadliest curse was the terror of mortasheen.

The islanders collected kelp from the seashore to spread over the fields and to sell to the soap makers and the glass makers. But before it could be used, the seaweed had to be burned, and the odour it created caused great offence to the Nuckleavee. The stench of the smoke drove him into a terrible rage that could only be sated by taking his cruellest revenge. He would gallop around the island afflicting the horses with a deadly disease called mortasheen. Once it had taken hold, it would spread across the island, and then to the other islands, until every horse was struck down and would soon be dead. Only then would Nuckleavee's revenge be complete and its anger dampened for a time.

173

Few ever encountered Nuckleavee and lived to tell the tale, but one such was Tammas, who was out late one night walking along the path next to the seashore. The stars were out, and the moon glimmered on the surface of the freshwater loch that ran along the other side of the path. As he walked, Tammas saw a large shape ahead in the distance. At first he was scared in case it was some evil thing, but as it drew closer, he saw that it was only a horse and rider, and so he relaxed and whistled a tune to make himself feel brave.

But when the creature came nearer still, he realised with dread his mistake, for the apparition that approached was none other than the Nuckleavee! It was indeed in the shape of a horse and rider, but they had merged into one sickening monster. The lower half was just like a huge horse, but with great flippers attached at the fetlocks. The horse had but one eye, burning bright red like a flame, and the breath came noisy and hot from its nostrils like steam from a kettle. The rider did not sit on the horse, but simply grew out of its back, with no legs and with great long arms that hung almost to the ground. The head was like a man's but much larger, and with that same single red eye, and a gaping wide mouth from which spewed a foul black reek. But the most horrible of all was its skin – for it had none! Horse and rider were completely skinless, just a mass of raw flesh. Thick black blood, black as tar, could be seen trickling through yellow veins, and thick grey-white sinews stretched and writhed with every movement.

Tammas dared not flee, for he knew it was dangerous to turn your back on anything evil, and besides, he could not outrun it. As it came closer still, he backed towards the loch, knowing there was nowhere to go. And then, at last, the creature's lower head drew level with his own, and as the maw gaped and the long arms reached out, the rank breath surged from the nostrils and into Tammas's.

The shock of the stench and the burning sensation made him take a step back, and his foot went into the loch, splashing freshwater on the beast's legs. It neighed loud enough to wake the dead, and shied back a little towards the shore. Without a moment's hesitation, Tammas ran for his life. In a flash the Nuckleavee bellowed like a storm at sea, and Tammas heard the galloping hooves chasing after him.

And gaining.

Tammas thought he was done for, but then he saw his chance. Just ahead of him was a stream that drained the loch into the sea. If he could cross the freshwater, the Nuckleavee could not follow and he would be safe. He could feel the sweaty breath on his back, and a finger scraped at his bonnet, but at last he reached the stream and leaped over it.

For a terrible moment he felt his head go cold and thought he had been struck, but then he heard the unearthly cry of rage, and realised his pursuer had given up the chase. Panting great deep breaths, Tammas turned and saw, still on the opposite bank, the Nuckleavee pacing up and down and angrily tearing up the bonnet. As he fell into exhausted unconsciousness on the safe side, Tammas's last thought was that the bonnet had been expensive, but Tammases were priceless.

14

dam, Jana and Ben walked idly along the sea front, catching up on the day's events. Ben had given Jana a more detailed account of the abortive fishing trip and his rescue by the mermaid. The last was particularly detailed and effusive, until Jana had become annoyed and changed the subject. Adam was surprised at her sudden lack of enthusiasm for all things mermaid, but hoped it would last.

She had told them about her portrait sitting, and the Scary Clowns' mermaid hunt and its unexpected trophy. She had expected Ben to show more interest in the strange monkey-like creature, but he was still too caught up in his mermaid adventure. He had at least responded to her report of the movement in the caves, but to her irritation, it was just to be dismissive, saying that Green Goon was barely a legend at all, but rather a vague bogeyman with no known story attached to it.

Annoyed at Ben's offhand manner, Jana stopped and gazed out to sea at the Imperial warship. 'Why's it just sitting there?' she wondered. 'What's it doing? What's it waiting for?'

'I hate to tell you this,' said Adam, 'because I'm going to have to put up with you long after we leave here, but we'll probably never find out. They obviously want to keep people away,' he added as she scowled at him, 'so it's not very likely they'll be telling anyone what they're here for.' He knew better than to conclude with any suggestion that she try to forget about it. Instead he said, 'If you try and find out, they'll probably execute you for spying or something.'

As they walked on, Jana said, 'I wonder if there's any news about Ceasg's baby.'

'Why would anyone steal a baby?' asked Adam. 'I mean, what would they do with it?'

'It's about as strange as everything else in this place,' said Jana. 'The warship, whatever the clowns caught, Green Goon.' She flashed a look at Ben, but he didn't seem to notice.

'I know,' agreed Adam. 'The stolen mermaid things, the woman on the beach, the man the next night.'

Jana frowned at him. 'What man and woman on the beach?'

'The ones I saw.'

'What are you talking about, Adam?'

'Didn't I tell you?'

Jana stopped. 'No, Adam,' she sighed. 'You *never* tell me. Not until it's too late. Usually when we're about to die because of the important thing you didn't tell me because you hadn't decided what it meant yet.'

It didn't even occur to Adam to defend himself. Instead he just told her about the naked woman on the beach.

'A seal that turned into a woman?' repeated Jana incredulously. 'You must have mistaken it in the dark.'

'I know, but it was still pretty strange. I mean, she was naked.'

'Skinny dipping,' shrugged Jana.

'No. She took her clothes off after she got *out* of the water.'

'And hung them up to dry. She wasn't expecting anyone to be watching,' she said reprovingly.

'I didn't know she was going to do that!' said Adam defensively.

'Wait a minute though,' said Jana. 'You said it was like she took her *skin* off.'

'Well, that was when I thought she was a seal. She definitely had skin when I saw her naked. Otherwise it would have been a very different experience. I mostly couldn't see her cos of hiding behind the rock,' he finished defensively.

She shook her head at him despairingly. 'I was thinking about Ceasg. Remember what she said earlier that day. When Ben and I saw her with Vleerman that first time. She said she wanted her *skin* so she could go swimming.'

'It wasn't Ceasg I saw.'

'No, but Vleerman said the skin thing was about her believing she was a mermaid. Ben, didn't you say something about it being confused with some other legends?'

But Ben wasn't listening. He was just gazing out to sea, lost in his own thoughts. Jana scowled and turned back to Adam.

'What about the man you saw the next night?'

'It was at the same spot,' said Adam.

Jana smirked. 'You went back to the same spot the next night?'

'Well,' blustered Adam, 'I've never seen … a beach before. It's all new to me.'

'I'll bet it is,' she laughed. 'Anyway, the man.'

'He was putting something into the water. Something wrapped in a blanket. I couldn't see what it was.'

'How big?' asked Jana suspiciously.

'Not very.'

'About the size of a baby perhaps?'

'Well, I suppose – ' He stopped and stared at her. 'No. You can't think that.'

'Ceasg's baby went missing the same night. I bet it was Vleerman you saw, disposing of it because it was deformed. Not human as far as he's concerned.'

Adam could see the anger building in her. 'He never said the baby wasn't human.'

'No, but we all saw his face when it was born.'

'Jana, we don't know that it was him on the beach, and we don't know what he put in the water. You're making all of this up.'

She took a deep breath to calm herself down. 'Maybe,' she said at last. But she said it in a way that told Adam she was far from convinced. 'Let's get back to the hotel. After lunch I'm going back to those caves.'

Adam tapped Ben on the shoulder. 'Come on, Ben.'

Ben turned his head to look at him but didn't move. Jana made a face and turned sharply on her heel. 'Oh just leave him,' she said and marched off.

Adam gave Ben's arm a gentle pull, and this time he responded. They walked slowly after Jana.

Baabie was sitting in the hotel lobby knitting. A black cat lay purring at her ankles and eyed them suspiciously as they entered.

'How's Ceasg?' asked Jana as Baabie smiled in welcome.

'She's hardly been out of her room all day,' sighed Baabie. 'She won't eat anything, and Matheeus is at the end of his tether wi' her. Mary and Murgen have been helping out around the hotel so he'll not throw us out.' She leaned forward conspiratorially. 'Maybe if someone closer to her own age had a wee word with her ... '

Jana smiled sympathetically and nodded. She turned to Adam. 'Take him up to his room and make him lie down or something. I'll catch up with you later.'

After Adam and Ben had left, Baabie asked innocently, 'Things not going well with you and your young man?'

'He's not my young man,' said Jana stiffly. She knocked on the door to the private rooms, but there was no answer. Baabie gave her an encouraging nod, and she opened the door. 'Ceasg? It's Jana. Can I come in?' It was dark but she could see Ceasg's silhouette sitting on the edge of the bed. Jana walked over and sat beside her. 'How are you doing?'

'Have they found Lorelei yet?' asked Ceasg in a hollow voice.

'Is that your baby's name?' asked Jana. 'It's a lovely name.'

'Why did they take her, Jana?'

Jana took Ceasg's hand. 'I don't know, Ceasg. I wish I did.'

'Do you think it's because of her tail?'

Jana hesitated. 'I don't think it's a tail, Ceasg,' she said carefully. 'I think her legs – '

'It's a tail,' said Ceasg matter-of-factly.

Jana bit her lip. 'Is this because you think you're a mermaid?'

For the first time, Ceasg looked directly at her. 'I'm not a mermaid. Who told you that?'

Jana was taken aback. 'Well ... I ... All that stuff about your skin. So you could swim.'

'Yes. My selkie skin. I'm a selkie.'

180

'What's a selkie?'

'I'm a seal-person. I can change into a seal when I put my skin on, and I become human when I take it off.'

Ah, thought Jana, much more rational. 'And you've lost your skin?'

'No, Matheeus has it.'

'Matheeus?'

'If a human takes your skin, you can't return to the sea. You have to stay on land. Men take selkies' skins and hide them so that they'll marry them.'

Jana tried to pick her way through the fantasy. 'Are you saying that Matheeus holds you here against your will?'

'He's a good man. He takes care of me. But the pull of the sea's strong. If I could get my skin, I'd go back to the sea.'

'And you don't know where he's hidden it.'

Ceasg pointed to the shelves. 'It's in a locker behind there. It's padlocked and I can't get into it. But I know it's there.'

Jana wasn't sure what to say, and was spared from having to say anything by a commotion outside. The door burst open and Ben stood there with Adam and Baabie trying to drag him out.

'Jana!' said Ben breathlessly. 'You've got to come and see this!'

'Ben!' snapped Jana angrily.

'I'm sorry,' said Adam. 'I tried to stop him.'

Ben broke free and grabbed Jana's arm. 'Come and see.'

She tried to pull away but he wouldn't let go. 'Ben, stop it. This is Ceasg's bedr— '

'I know, but this is important. Come upstairs.'

Realising he wasn't going to leave until she did, Jana apologised to Ceasg and allowed herself to be led upstairs. They stopped at the door to Ben's room.

'You have to be quiet,' said Ben. 'She's still nervous and we don't want to frighten her.'

'Her?' repeated Jana with a warning note to her voice.

Ben slowly opened the door and stepped in. He beckoned Jana and Adam to follow. Jana took a breath and walked through the door. Inside, standing by the window, was a woman. A beautiful young woman with long golden hair and huge blue eyes. And quite clearly legs and not a tail of any sort at all. She wore a simple green dress that was parted at the skirt to reveal a petticoat elaborately embroidered in gold and silver thread. Ben walked to her and took her hands. That gesture and the way they looked at each other said it all.

'This is Serena,' said Ben dreamily. 'She's the one who rescued me. She's my mermaid.'

Jana turned and ran out.

Adam recognised her reaction. He'd seen her behave this way once before in Kharesh. It wasn't fear or anger. He didn't know why, but she was upset. And he knew that he had no idea how to comfort her, but it was still his job to try, because he was her friend and no-one else was going to do it. So he followed her. He caught the door to her room before it closed behind her, and he went in.

Jana stood in the middle of the room with her back to him, breathing heavily. Adam knew this was her trying not to burst into tears. 'Are you alright?' he asked.

She didn't turn around. 'I thought … me and Ben … and now he drags me upstairs to meet *another woman*.'

'Another woman?' asked Adam, confused. And then the penny dropped. 'You mean … you and Ben?'

Jana turned, and he saw the tears trickling down her face. 'Oh Adam, you're hopeless,' she said. And because she knew just how hopeless he was, she walked over and made him hug her. And then she wept until he was really uncomfortable.

The storm had gradually built throughout the day, and by evening the rain was horizontal. Donny had spent the day at the Mission, helping Father Langstok board up the windows until the glassmaker could come. The others had gone back to the Seatown to see how bad the horses and crops were, but Donny had insisted on staying. Pilot had offered to take Liban and drop her off home, but Donny had refused and no-one had argued with him. She and Draatsie had managed to amuse themselves in the way children and otters always can. By the time Donny had finished the windows, the rain had started and he had decided to wait it out in the hope it would pass. Instead, it had grown heavier and the wind had grown stronger. Eventually, he realised that he and Liban would have to brave the storm and go home. They had wrapped up as best they could and set out into the weather, with Liban clinging to Donny as he carried her. Draatsie had quickly scurried off on her own.

As they passed the harbour, Donny glanced across at the *Renown* and thought he saw movement. Someone was crouched near the boat, apparently doing something to the hull.

'Hey!' Donny shouted.

The figure jerked up and stood motionless, caught out.

'What do you think you're doing?' called Donny. There was no response and the figure still didn't move. Warily, Donny walked towards whoever it was. As he got closer, he saw the man's face and his heart sank. It was Pieter Fredericks.

'Well look who it is,' slurred Pieter. He had a bottle in his hand. The other hand was behind his back.

'What are you doing to my boat, Pieter?' asked Donny.

Pieter took a swig from the bottle and then brought his other hand out in an uncoordinated swing. Donny took a hurried step back as he saw the knife in it.

Pieter looked surprised, but then he looked at the knife and laughed. 'You think I'm gonna stab you?' He looked towards the boat, and following his gaze, Donny saw where one of the mooring ropes had started to fray. He relaxed just a little.

'I think you'd better go home, Pieter.'

Pieter took another swig. 'I don' thing so. I'm not goin' stab you, but I am gonna beat seven bells out you.' He didn't put down the knife.

'Come on, Pieter. I've got my niece with me.'

'Then put her down.' He took a step forward and Donny backed away. Liban was shaking in his arms.

'You don't want to do this.'

'Yeah do. Don' tell me what I want.'

'For heaven's sake, Pieter,' pleaded Donny, 'I've got Liban.'

As he spoke he saw Pieter bunch the hand with the knife in it into a fist. He probably didn't even realise the knife was still there, because he was aiming to punch, not stab, but that didn't make it any less danger-ous. The harbour path was narrow, and if Donny dived left he'd end up in the water. As the fist and blade swung wildly towards him, he had no choice but to dive to the right, battering his head against the harbour wall. He heard Liban scream as the impact forced him to drop her. Luckily she fell on top of him and wasn't hurt, but Donny was stunned. He felt her cling even more tightly to him, and looked up to see Pieter looming over them, a vicious leer on his face. He took another swig and realised the bottle was empty. He looked at it in irritation, before changing his grip on it and raising it like a club.

'Sorry Daddy sorry Daddy sorry Daddy!' screamed Liban.

Donny tried to turn his body over to shield her from the blow, but it never came. He heard the smash of glass and looked up to see that Pieter had dropped the bottle and was staring in disbelief out to sea.

'What the hell?'

Donny struggled into a sitting position, still holding Liban, and then managed to get to his feet. He looked over the wall to see what had distracted Pieter.

There was a boat approaching the harbour. It had no lights, but was clearly a fishing boat. The reason it had stunned Pieter so much was that it was approaching at a ferocious speed. No boat should be able to move that fast. It was going to crash into the harbour wall.

Checking to see that Pieter was still watching the boat, Donny care-fully backed away, putting distance between himself and both Pieter and the oncoming vessel. But then he stopped and stared in amaze-ment. The boat had suddenly changed course. Again it was a man-oeuvre that should have been impossible for a boat of that size, but now it was heading straight for the harbour entrance. It was still going at the same speed, though, and would now crash into the inner wall instead, if it didn't hit one of the moored boats first.

Donny had managed to get back to the road, so he and Liban were out of harm's way, but now he stood and watched to see what would happen. He daren't call Pieter to safety in case he attacked them again, but the boat was headed for the other end of the harbour anyway.

It came speeding through the entrance, a great plume of spray soak-ing Pieter, and although it now looked like it would manage to miss the other boats, it couldn't help but plough headlong into the inner wall adjacent to the street.

And then it stopped.

It was just a few inches from the wall when, impossibly, it stopped dead. Its prow pointed directly at the wall, and it was too dark to see whether there was anyone in the wheelhouse, while there was no sign of anyone on the deck. It just sat there, dark and silent.

Slowly, Pieter staggered his way around the harbour and back to the road. He had completely lost interest in Donny, though, and his eyes never left the boat. Cautiously, Donny moved to get a closer view. Even Liban had stopped shaking, and stared wide-eyed at the strange boat.

It was mostly black, with a red line and two white ones running around the hull. It was covered in barnacles, and had signs of extensive damage. In fact, it barely looked seaworthy. It also looked quite old, not just in condition, but also in design. It was similar to modern boats, but not quite the same, and looked more like the sort they used fifty years ago or more.

And then Donny saw the name painted on the prow, and he realised why. It was a name from much more than fifty years ago. More like a hundred. It was a name everyone in Anterwendt knew. One of three they all knew from an early age and never forgot. Three names from paintings all over the city, such as the ones in the Stotfold hotel and the Mission. Its companions were the *Colleen* and the *Speedwell*, two of the boats from the Stotfold disaster. And this boat sitting in the harbour was the third. It was old and damaged and barnacle-encrusted from having sunk a hundred years ago and lain at the bottom of the sea. The boat that had arrived so impossibly, and now sat there so ominously, was the *Sapphire*.

XIV. The Goodman o' Wastness

A goodman lived in Wastness, and a more handsome lad you never did see. He was strong, ran a successful farm, and all the local girls hoped they'd be the one he'd choose for a wife. But the goodman was not interested in marriage, saying he had trials enough without being tried by a wife too! Nor did he listen to the old women when they told him that one day he'd be smitten by a woman whether he liked it or not.

One day the goodman was down at the beach collecting lugworms for bait when he saw a group of people, some lying on the rocks sunning themselves, others playing in the water. As he drew closer, he saw that every last one of them was naked, and there were sealskins carelessly strewn on the sand nearby. It was then he realised they must be selkies.

For the fun of it, he crept up on them until he was close, and then suddenly ran at them with a great shout. With a terrible fright the selkies snatched up their enchanted sealskins and ran headlong into the water. But one, in her rush, forgot to grab her skin, and the goodman snatched it up before she realised.

When the goodman looked out to sea, he saw that all but one had taken on their seal form and were looking at him with their sad brown eyes. Pleased with his prize, the goodman tucked the sealskin under his arm and headed for home.

But as he went, he heard a sobbing behind him. Turning, he saw a young woman at his heels. She held out her arms and begged him to return her skin, for she could not return to her own kind without it.

The goodman was not unkind, and he had only taken the skin for sport, but when he saw the tears fall from those big brown eyes, he could not bring himself to give the skin back, for he was instantly smitten and could not bear to let the selkie woman leave him. Instead, he declared his love to her and asked her to marry him. Realising he would not return her precious skin, the selkie reluctantly agreed, for she could see that he loved her and would make a devoted husband.

And so they married, and although she always longed to return to the sea, the selkie was not unhappy, for the goodman indeed loved her and treated her well. She bore him seven fine children, four boys and three girls, and everyone agreed there were no more beautiful children anywhere in the islands.

But although all seemed happy, whenever the goodman went out, his selkie wife would search the house high and low, looking for her skin, for the pull of the sea was too great. One day, when the goodman and the four boys were out fishing, the selkie wife sent the two eldest daughters into the village to buy bread. The youngest girl stayed behind because she had skinned her knee climbing on the rocks. As usual, the selkie hunted for her skin, but though she searched every inch of the house, she could not find it.

The little girl, sitting by the fire, had been watching her mother. 'Mammie, what are you lookin' for? she asked.

'I'm looking for a bonnie skin to mak' a bandage for that knee o' yours,' replied the selkie.

'But I ken where there's a skin, Mammie. One day when you were out and Daddy thocht I wis asleep, he took it oot o' the chimney an' looked at it for a while, an' then he put it back.'

The selkie ran to the chimney and felt around with her hand. With a cry of joy she pulled out the skin. She kissed the girl, and bade her goodbye and ran down to the sea. She threw on the skin and dived into the water, never again to return.

The goodman often walked along the shore hoping to see his lost wife, but all he ever saw were seals playing out in the water, and whenever they saw him they swam away.

15

Crowds had been gathering at the harbour all morning. No-one had been brave enough to get too close to the ghost ship, and a couple of unenthusiastic watchmen had been sent to make sure they didn't. No-one was quite sure why, except it was usually the Watch's responsibility to see that the general public didn't do things.

There had been no sign of Jana, nor Ben and his supposed mermaid at breakfast, and Adam had let them all sleep. When he'd left Jana yesterday evening, he'd seen Ben arranging a room for Serena, but had not spoken to him because he had no idea what to say. He had woken early, gone down to breakfast alone, and found Mary Player serving. She had told him about the night's events, and he had wandered down to see what was going on. Now he stood amongst the crowd, staring at the ancient boat and wondering what he was supposed to make of it.

'These are very strange times,' said a voice at his shoulder.

Without turning, Adam said, 'But I'm sure you appreciate the showmanship, Father.'

Father Langstok laughed. 'Indeed. It was an impressive entrance. I wish I'd been there to see it.'

'Are you sure you didn't arrange it?' asked Adam drily.

'This is a bit beyond my resources. Unfortunately.' Adam smiled. 'By the way, you still haven't taken me to the circus.'

'You know they don't have their mermaid any more?'

'Neither do I. Which is interesting. But I'm sure there must still be lots to see.'

'Then we'll have to go sometime,' said Adam. He took a deep breath.'
'Speaking of mermaids ... '

As he told the Father about the previous evening's events, they both failed to notice the coach drawing up behind them. It sat for a few minutes, politely waiting for Adam to finish his tale, before a cultured voice said, 'What's everyone looking at?'

They both turned and Adam's look of surprise turned into a still surprised grin. 'Lord Reitherman! What are you doing here?'

'I might ask you the same question,' smiled the Palatine warmly. 'We're both a long way from home. Are you alone or is Jana with you?'

'She's back at our hotel,' said Adam. 'We're waiting for a ship to the New World.'

'Really?' The Palatine sounded impressed. 'We obviously have some catching up to do. Perhaps we can do it over dinner this evening. Are you both free?'

'Well I am. Not sure about Jana. She's, um, not feeling too well. I'll have to ask her. Where are you staying?'

'Ah,' said the Palatine, 'perhaps you can help us with that. Our journey was somewhat last minute, so we haven't made any arrangements. You mentioned a hotel?'

'Don't you have some official place where you stay on these sorts of visits?' asked Adam.

'Oh, you know me,' answered the Palatine breezily. 'I don't really go in for all that ceremony. I much prefer to be where the real people are. Besides,' he confessed, 'Anterwendt isn't strictly in my jurisdiction. My presence here is a little unusual. So if there's room at your hotel, I'm sure it'll suit us very nicely.' He looked at Father Langstok. 'Perhaps you'd introduce me to your friend.'

'This is Father Langstok from the Fishermen's Mission.'

'I'm very pleased to meet you, Father. You're welcome to join us for dinner too.'

Father Langstok smiled in greeting. 'Well, that's most generous, your lordship. Am I right in thinking that you're the Lord Reitherman who's Palatine of the southern provinces?'

'I'm afraid so, but please don't hold it against me,' smiled the Palatine. 'Now, what's so fascinating about those fishing boats?'

Adam was about to explain, when there was an excited murmur from the crowd. He and Father Langstok turned to see what was happening. A hatch had opened on the deck of the *Sapphire*. For several minutes the crowd stood in excited anticipation, waiting for someone to emerge. And for several minutes no-one did. The hatch sat upright, but there was no other movement, and no sound from below. Gradually the crowd became restless, and the murmur increased in volume.

Then finally, after an agonising eternity, a tall figure climbed up on to the deck. He was dressed from head to foot in charcoal grey, and his face was obscured by a cowl. He wore possibly a coat, or a cloak, or perhaps both, but it was hard to make out exactly what all the layers were, or exactly how large he was underneath them. He could have concealed a lost civilisation under there. He walked slowly to the prow of the boat and placed his hands firmly on the rail. Then he looked around at the assembled crowd. 'What're ye all gawkin' at?' he barked.

The crowd fell silent. When it became clear that the stranger wasn't going to say any more, there were a few whispers and nudges, until someone finally plucked up the courage to speak. 'Who are you?' It was Pieter Fredericks.

The man on the deck raised his hands and pulled back his cowl, revealing a thin, stern face. He fixed his steely gaze on Pieter. 'My name's mind your own business,' he snarled. 'This is a free harbour and I have business here. *Private* business.'

The crowd muttered. Pieter asked, 'Where did you get that boat?'

'Salvage,' answered the stranger. 'That makes it legally mine, and if anyone touches it, they'll have me to answer to.' And with that, he turned and went back down below, closing the hatch behind him.

The crowd chattered excitedly, wondering what to make of this, and gradually they began to disperse, still discussing the stranger. Adam turned back to the Palatine, and saw that he was staring pensively at the boat.

'I wonder what that was all about,' said Father Langstok, looking shrewdly at the Palatine.

'I wonder,' repeated the Palatine, lost in thought. Suddenly he sat upright and smiled. 'Well, I mustn't stay here blocking the street. Perhaps you'd be good enough to give my driver directions to the hotel.'

Ben and Serena were eating breakfast. Mary Player brought more bread, and apologised for the lack of milk, but the cows hadn't given much this morning.

'Not havin' yer breakfast wi' Jana today?' she asked Ben pointedly.

'I haven't seen her,' replied Ben, not taking his eyes off Serena.

'No, ye haven't, have ye?'

She saw Jana appear at the door and then stop as she saw Ben and Serena. She hovered uncertainly, and then turned away. Mary went after her.

'Would ye like your breakfast brought up to your room?'

'I'm not really hungry,' lied Jana.

'That'll be why ye came to the dining room,' said Mary.

Jana gave her a black look but didn't reply.

'I could put something nasty in his porridge,' suggested Mary. 'No-one'd ever know it was me.'

Jana almost smiled. 'I thought ... ' she said helplessly.

'So did we all,' soothed Mary. 'But young Ben's so caught up wi' mermaids, that actually finding one changes everything for him an' he canna see past it.'

'She's not a mermaid,' said Jana disdainfully. 'She's got legs.'

'Mermaids sometimes tak' legs on the land,' reasoned Mary. 'Anyway, *he* thinks she's a mermaid, and that's what counts.'

'How can they just change their tails into legs?' snorted Jana. 'It's impossible.'

'Maybe you should tak' a closer look at those legs,' suggested Mary conspiratorially.

'Why?'

'Just.'

There was the sound of the front door opening, and Mary peered over Jana's shoulder. 'Who's this?'

Jana turned to see a familiar figure. 'Lord Reitherman!'

'Jana, how delightful to see you again. I don't think you've met my secretary Albert.'

By the time introductions had been effected, and the new guests had taken their luggage to their rooms, Ben and Serena had left the dining room, and so Adam, Jana, Albert and the Palatine all had breakfast together. Adam didn't mention that this was his second breakfast, and Mary just winked at him as she brought the toast. Adam and Jana explained about their mission to the New World, and the various things that had happened since they arrived in Anterwendt, although they glossed over Jana's feelings for Ben. The Palatine was vague about his reasons for being in the city, saying only that it was a minor Imperial matter, and he also kept his concerns about the Emperor quiet, but he did tell them about Lazlo Winter's mysterious warning and their researches into Baphomet. He also surprised them by taking an interest in Ben and Serena, and asking to meet them some time. However, he was astute enough not to suggest Ben and his mermaid join them all for dinner that night.

Once they'd finished swapping stories, the Palatine steepled his fingers in thought. 'You've certainly unearthed some intriguing mysteries while you've been here. Perhaps we can pool our resources and be of help to one another. Albert and I have some errands to run today, but I'd be rather interested to see Father Langstok's exhibition later on. Jana, you expressed an interest in visiting the caves. Adam's seen some unusual things on that beach, so perhaps you should satisfy your curiosity. Do be careful though. Get one of the locals to advise you regarding tides and so on. Meanwhile, I wonder why your friend Mary suggested looking at Serena's legs. Adam, I know you have an appointment with the Father to visit the circus, but perhaps you could make the time to find a discrete way of investigating that avenue.'

'What about the *Sapphire?*' asked Adam.

'Would you allow Albert and myself to look into that? Good. That's all settled then. We can all swap notes over dinner. This is rather fun, isn't it?' He beamed happily, although Albert didn't look as if he was having quite as much fun.

Once they had all gone their separate ways, Albert ventured, 'Sir, am I right in thinking that you believe the man on the boat to be connected to our mission?'

'It's possible, Albert, it's possible.'

193

'And do you really think that mermaids come under the terms of Edict 37?'

The Palatine smiled. 'How well you know me, Albert.'

'But mermaids, sir? They're hardly occult.'

'Even legends and folk tales are of interest, Albert,' said the Palatine, quoting Edict 37. 'And there are a lot of legends and folk tales here.'

In a booth in a darkened corner of the Poulsard Inn, Pieter Fredericks sat nursing a glass of beer.

'You must've heard them wrong.'

'I swear,' said the man sitting opposite him. 'That's what they said.'

Pieter rubbed his chin and looked again at the door to the snug, where the man from the *Sapphire* had taken up residence half an hour earlier. He had walked in and glared at everyone until they had stopped looking at him. Then he'd ordered a bottle of whisky, and upset the barman by paying with a handful of small change, before walking into the snug and shutting the door. He had not come out or made a sound since, and no matter how hard Pieter stared, he could not see through the frosted glass.

'Pieter!'

Pieter jolted out of his reverie and turned his attention back to his companion. 'Yes, I'm listening.'

'It's the same mermaid that saved Heuvelmans,' insisted Rutger. 'It must be.'

'If the mermaids are coming ashore ... ' mused Pieter.

'The *Intrepid* was just the start. They could be planning anything.'

Pieter sat in silence for a moment, and then nodded slowly. 'We have to get that mermaid.'

A face appeared at his shoulder from the next booth. A white face with a red nose.

'Did someone say something about a mermaid?' asked Mr Coco.

Ben and Serena weren't in the hotel, but Murgen had heard Ben say something about going to the beach. She didn't know which one, so Adam decided he would take a detour to the East Beach before calling on Father Langstok. Jana was going to the West Beach to investigate the caves, and while not ideal given the circumstances, at least one of them stood the chance of fulfilling the unusual task of looking at Serena's legs.

Adam stood on the promenade, looking out towards the beach. He could see two figures walking around the dunes. One seemed to be walking a little awkwardly, and he thought again of Serena's legs. The figures stopped and appeared to kiss.

A flash away to the left distracted his attention. He looked out to sea and saw the Imperial ship. Sure enough, there was another flash and then another, both from the man-of-war. After a pause, there was an answering flash from the direction of the harbour. A final flash came from the ship and then no more.

Adam wondered who might be signalling to the Navy, but then he returned his attention to the beach. He walked down to the bridge, skirting the Seatown to avoid being waylaid.

The bridge looked old and weathered, the weather in question being a violent storm in the middle of an earthquake. The entire structure was made of wood, and several of the planks looked loose or rotten. And it was very long.

It creaked as Adam put his foot on it. Creaking. Not a good sign. Creaking was what wood did before it splintered. And your foot went through it. And then there would be one leg dangling and groin-aching embarrassment. Or possibly both feet and salty drowning.

But the Seatowners came across here all the time to collect kelp, didn't they? And Ben and Serena had crossed it without incident. None of which would be at all comforting when he plummeted to a watery grave with bits of wood sticking out of his nether regions. And into, which was probably worse.

And so over he went, *creak, creak, creak,* slowly and carefully with white knuckles gripping the handrail, *creak, creak, creak,* a little bit of him praying to gods he didn't believe in, and another little bit of him trying to control his bladder.

And eventually, after what seemed like a very long time and probably was, the speed he'd been going, he was halfway there and only had the same amount left to go, knowing he'd have to do it all again on the way back. By the time he finally got to the far end, he was beginning to feel there was something wrong with *his* legs, never mind Serena's.

He still found walking on sand slightly odd. It wasn't solid beneath your feet, but then it was. You sort of took a step, sunk a bit and then stopped, resulting in a lurching gait that must have looked comical to anyone watching. Well, anyone who wasn't also on the sand. Maybe that was why one of the figures had been walking awkwardly.

He'd lost sight of Ben and Serena, and had to lurch his way around to the seaward side of the dunes before he saw their footprints stretching along the sand, down to the sea, and then back up towards the dunes before disappearing. They must be up in the dunes somewhere. That was a shame, because he'd discovered from his West Beach excursions that walking on the wet sand near the water was much easier, because the sand was somehow more solid, for reasons he couldn't fathom but were probably caused by science. If Jana had heard him say that, she'd have given him a stern lecture on how, actually, science was caused by the reasons, and not the other way around.

Adam started to climb the dunes, which proved to be even more hilarious than walking horizontally, because now he was trying to go upwards while the sand kept giving way downwards. It was like trying to climb a hill of custard. That kept getting into your boots. Ever since he'd arrived in Anterwendt, his boots had been full of sand, no matter how much he cleaned them out, and washing his feet didn't seem to have much effect either.

Somehow he managed to get halfway up the dune, and then hauled himself the rest of the way by reaching up and grabbing the thick, spiky grass that grew on the top. Several times it pricked his hands and other parts, sometimes drawing spots of blood.

Finally he stood on the top of the dunes and looked around. And saw Ben and Serena down at the bottom on the other side, heading back to the bridge!

Using every swear word he could muster, he ran down the dune. Well, he ran approximately three steps and then fell the rest of the way.

Well, he fell the length of his body and then tumbled head over heels until the sand at the bottom failed to break his fall, and then the sand underneath it succeeded. Suddenly sand seemed much more solid, just when it could cause pain.

Bruised, sore and covered in more pink pricks of blood where the grass had found his remaining hitherto untouched regions, he groggily realised that no amount of washing would now ever get the sand out of his crevices. He looked up from where he had come to an undignified halt, and saw Ben and Serena staring at him in surprise.

It was little comfort to realise that he could now get a good view of Serena's legs without arousing suspicion.

Jana stared at the cave entrance. What was it with her and caves?

The opening was set into a horseshoe-shaped wall of rock that formed part of the low cliff on which stood the lighthouse. The sand sloped from the entrance down to the beach. To the left, the cliff gave way to an even lower row of dunes, which stretched away from the beach into grassland.

She thought about everything that had happened on this stretch of beach so far. There was the legend of Green Goon, which didn't seem to be much of a legend at all, but just a name to frighten children. And to keep them away from the caves, which seemed reasonable considering they were so close to the tide line. But they were still a little *higher* than the tide line, which meant they didn't flood. So it would be safe for someone or something to hide in there. And she was sure she'd seen movement when she was here with Liban.

So was it Adam's seal woman? Did she come out of the water and go into the cave? Adam hadn't seen where she'd gone – he'd been too busy hiding behind the rocks. But a seal that changed into a woman was ridiculous, wasn't it?

As for the man throwing the bundle into the sea, he hadn't come from the cave, but from somewhere inland. Come to think of it, where *had* he come from? She looked at the grassland and wondered where it led to. He must have come from that direction. Once she'd finished in the caves, she'd explore that way.

But first the caves. She peered at the hole in the rock, but could see nothing. No movement, no green. Just a dark hole in the rock. The horseshoe shielded it from the sun, so that even in daylight it was hard to see more than a few inches in. Gingerly, she walked up the slope, wondering why she felt the need to move gingerly, and just what ginger had to do with anything anyway.

Now she stood just a few feet from the entrance. Still she couldn't really see anything. She took a breath and walked the extra few feet until she was just inside. It was too dark for her eyes to adjust and make anything much out, so she lit the lantern she had borrowed from the hotel. There was no sound of anything being surprised within, and nothing leaped from the darkness and ripped her throat out, so she assumed that if anything really was living here, then it wasn't at home.

She moved the lantern in an arc, so it could illuminate the whole area. It was enough to tell her what she needed to know. The remains of a fire lay a few yards further in. Whoever had lit it presumably knew enough to keep the smoke from getting outside, as no-one had noticed and made it the talk of the town. There was nothing else except a large pile of seaweed. *Green* seaweed. And a few footprints and marks where something might have been dragged across the sand. Curiously, there were no tracks outside. The occupants had been careful to cover up their presence. Whoever they were.

Jana thought of the strange creature the Scary Clowns had captured, and wondered whether this was its lair. Was it Green Goon? Was there something to the legend after all?

She held the lantern higher to see how far the caves stretched. It turned out they were not so much caves as cave. Just one. It didn't stretch back far at all. It wasn't a cave system, just a hollow in the rock. Big enough for shelter but not much else. Certainly nothing was hiding deeper inside, and there was nothing else to be seen here. She doused her lantern and left.

The beach was empty as far as she could see. No-one waiting to confront her. She took a deep breath of sea air, and climbed up the dunes and on to the grassland. It was the same coarse grass that topped the dunes, but not as spiky, and it gradually gave way to softer grass. There was a rough path worn from regular use. This seemed to be the sensible route to follow. Of course, the man could have come a different way without using any path, but she could always come back if this proved unfruitful.

She had only been walking for a few minutes when she saw the road. The path looked like it headed towards it, and the road looked like it went towards Anterwendt in one direction and past the lighthouse in the other. Probably it continued along the coast, perhaps to the naval base, and most likely there was a branch that led directly to the lighthouse itself. The path stretched in the direction of Anterwendt and she could now see that there was a solitary house in the distance, on the outskirts of the city. The man must surely have come from there.

She strode purposefully towards it. There was no sign of anyone else on the grassland or on the road, and as she approached the house, it too seemed quiet. It looked a little like a farmhouse, but there was no farmland, only a small garden and some outhouses. One of them might have been big enough to stable a horse. There was a washing line with clothes on it, although there was an odd gap as if an item was missing. As she drew closer, she saw there was a sign on the gate. It gave the name of the occupant.

With a nod of satisfaction she turned away from Doctor Vleerman's house and headed back to the beach.

XV. Ursilla's Children and the Great Selkie o' Suleskerry

*U*rsilla was the daughter of the laird of one of the oldest families in the islands. She was a handsome woman, but was not one to wait for men to come courting her. She would rather do the choosing herself, and her eye fell on a young barn-man who worked on the estate. But she knew her father would be black affronted and might disinherit her, so she kept her passion hid-den in her own breast, and treated the barn-man the same as any of the other servants, while she bided her time and kept a close eye on him.

When her father died – and her inheritance was safe – she told the barn-man of her love for him and commanded him to marry her, and they made their oath at the Odin Stane. The gentry were appalled that she should marry a servant, but she ignored them and made a good wife to her husband, managing the house well, and, it was said, man-aging her husband and the estate too.

But Ursilla was not happy. Her husband did not love her back, and had only married her because he had been ordered to. He was too gallant to say anything, and he never once treated her badly, but it was not a good match and Ursilla was unsatisfied and lonely. But she was too proud to admit it, for she did not like to show weakness and the gentry would only mock her even more, so she decided to find another way to ease her sadness.

She went down to the shore and sat on the rock of Suleskerry, and at high tide she shed seven tears into the sea. It was said they were the only tears she ever cried. And in answer to her tears, a great grey selkie swam up to her.

'What is it that you want with me?' he asked. She told him what was in her heart, and he agreed to return at spring tide, for that was when he could take human form. And he left, singing 'I am a man upon the land, I am a selkie in the sea, and when I'm far frae every strand, my dwelling is in Suleskerry.'

And at spring time he came, and many times after that, and when Ursilla's bairns were born, every one of them had selkie paws – webbed hands and webbed feet. She clipped the webs so they would not be seen, and she clipped them many times after to prevent them from growing back, and over time they hardened into crusts on the palms of the hands and the soles of the feet. To this day the descendants of Ursilla still have a horny growth on their hands and feet.

Eventually the selkie man stopped coming and left Ursilla with her children. But seven years later, Ursilla went and sat on the rock of Suleskerry, and her selkie lover returned with a gift of a golden chain for the oldest boy. He vanished below the waves once more, but another seven years later, they met once again at Suleskerry. The boy was now fourteen and this time, when the father left, the boy went with him.

A year later, Ursilla's husband came home with a present for her. It was a golden chain, and when she saw it, she knew it for the one the selkie had given her son. 'Where did you get it?' she asked.

'It's the strangest thing,' he told her, 'for I was oot hunting and I shot two grey seals, one great and one small. And the wee seal had this golden chain strung aroon its neck, and I thocht it'd mak a fine present for you.'

And Ursilla wept for only the second time in her life.

16

Albert hadn't expected a pharmacy. He'd assumed it would be a wing of a large townhouse, or even a separate building of its own. A small shop was something of a disappointment. The bell even tinkled as they opened the door. He was always impressed by the ones that didn't tinkle again as the door closed.

It was a fairly big pharmacy. Not one of those narrow ones with a single row of shelves behind a counter, but rather a spacious shop with shelves on every wall, all filled with jars and vials and bowls of various coloured things. And proper chemicals, with nary a bat's wing or tiger's unmentionables in sight. This was a pharmacy that had left superstition behind and embraced science with a manly hug.

A man came through from a back room. He was wearing one of those long, curly white wigs that had recently become all the rage in places that cared about, or indeed even knew, what the rage actually was. He seemed to be completely bald underneath, and yet somehow managed to look dignified rather than as comical as a bald man in a silly wig should, by rights, look. He also looked relatively well-off, judging by his red silk housecoat and stylish cravat. He had the kind of intelligent face that could carry off holding a lizard in a bottle – which he was currently doing – without looking at all disturbing.

'Ah, gentlemen, forgive me,' he said, indicating the bottle. 'I was just doing some private research into Hemidactylus turcicus here. A hobby of mine. How may I help you?'

'My name is Adolf Reitherman,' said the Palatine, 'and this is Albert Munster. Are you Albertus Seba?'

'That is correct,' said the man. He looked at the Palatine quizzically. '*Lord* Adolf Reitherman? The Palatine?'

He nodded modestly. 'I didn't think I'd be recognised so far north.'

'Are you hoping to remain incognito?' asked Seba.

'Not particularly. I'm just surprised. But then you're a highly educated man, and your knowledge is what we've come here for, if you would be so good as to avail us.'

'Not my pharmacological knowledge, I presume.'

'Indeed,' smiled the Palatine. 'I believe you sometimes accept spices as payment.'

Albert produced a paper parcel. 'We brought ginger.'

Seba took the parcel and he was gracious enough not to examine it. 'Most kind. In fact, I don't charge for viewings of my collection, or for the knowledge I have gained from it. I normally accept spices as payment for delivering medicines to certain wealthy patrons. Nevertheless, it would be remiss of me to turn down such a valuable com-modity, especially as you are already expecting to part with it and, considering your station, can easily afford it. I'm sure you understand.'

'Oh, of course,' said the Palatine. 'Consider it a gift.'

'Very generous. Thank you. Now, was there something particular that you wanted to see?'

'Do you have anything on the Skentys?' asked the Palatine.

Seba gave a short laugh. 'I'm afraid to say that no-one has anything on the Skentys. Nothing reliable at any rate.'

'What about the name Baphomet?' pressed the Palatine. 'Does that mean anything to you?'

'Ah!' This appeared to explain everything. 'You've been reading Klauber's *Myths & Legends*. There's a copy in the Imperial collection. He mistakenly attributes the legend of Baphomet to the Skentys.'

'You mean it isn't?' asked Albert.

'Well, it may be, but that can't be substantiated. It's a Nazcan legend.'

Albert looked confused. 'Isn't that the same thing?'

'Again, possibly, but it can't be substantiated. The Nazcans are the people who currently inhabit the continent of Nazca. They have their own mythology and religion, which may or may not have originated with the Skentys. The legend of Baphomet comes from them.'

204

'I think it's clear that we've come to the right man,' said the Palatine.

Seba smiled appreciatively. 'Come this way and we'll see what we can find for you.' He led them through the door behind the counter and into a short corridor. There was a door either side and a staircase at the far end. 'Do you want to go straight to your enquiry, or have you time for a tour of the full collection?'

'Oh, we'd be fascinated to view the entire collection,' said the Palatine enthusiastically, 'wouldn't we, Albert?'

'Oh. Yes,' replied Albert uncertainly.

Seba smiled appreciatively and opened the left-hand door. 'Most of the collection is natural history,' he explained, waving them through. 'Exotic animals and plants. I pay sailors and ships' doctors to bring them back for me.'

The room was not huge, but somehow, in spite of the sheer number of objects within, managed to be spacious. To the right were two large bookcases, each filled with leather-bound volumes stacked on top of one another, or with their spines uppermost to prevent dust from getting on the pages. A few rolled scrolls lay here too. Glancing at the books revealed them to be bestiaries, accounts of travellers' encounters with various exotic creatures, and other animal-related works. One was Dr Durant's controversial *Genesis of the Species*.

On top of the bookcases were corals and dried sponges. The vaulted ceiling was decorated with all sorts of seashells, and preserved fish and other sea creatures, such as crabs, urchins and starfish. The wall opposite the books was occupied by a row of pull-down cabinet doors, one of which was opened to reveal pigeonholes filled with teeth, and claws, and feathers and insects. Below were cupboard doors, and again one was open, revealing shelves with covered jars and specimen boxes. Above the cabinets was a mantel, on which stood an array of stuffed birds, and behind these were glass cases, some filled with butterflies, and others with small fossils. Opposite the entrance was a tall window with open shutters, and on the wall either side hung two large turtle shells, each different from the other, as well as a variety of horns, antlers and tusks. One of these was several feet long and formed an intricate spiral along its entire length.

'Surely that's not meant to be a unicorn's horn?' asked Albert.

'Actually it's a tusk from a particular type of whale found only in the frozen north,' said Seba.

Suspended from the ceiling by ropes were various larger specimens, including lizards, a crocodile and several animals that neither Albert nor the Palatine recognised. The largest looked like a dolphin, but with a head like a seal with heavy jowls.

'A dugong from the south seas,' explained Seba when he saw them looking at it. 'Naturalists are still unsure how to classify it. Please feel free to browse.'

They spent some time looking around, reading the informative labels and opening the cabinets, two of which turned to be filled entirely with a multitude of insects. Seba told them about armadillos, and puffer fish, and how the crocodile was from the New World and wasn't a crocodile at all, but a possibly related animal called an alligator.

In amongst the hanging creatures, the Palatine spotted something that caught his eye. 'Is that a Feejee mermaid?'

'Ah, you're familiar with them then,' said Seba appreciatively. 'A fake of course but expertly made. I've never been able to find the joins.'

'I believe Father Langstok has one in his museum,' said the Palatine.

'Indeed. It's as fine an example as my own. The circus has one too. Three in the city all at once! And oh how I'd like to preserve some of their performers for my anatomical room. Unethical, of course,' he smirked, seeing Albert's worried look.

After about half an hour, during which Albert had found the whole experience to be much more absorbing than he had expected, Seba led them across to the opposite room, which was a similar arrangement but filled with plants. Being a keen gardener, Albert found this room particularly riveting, although he was rather bemused by the fern-like plant that was labelled *The Vegetable Lamb of Tartary*.

'Er, vegetable lamb?' asked Albert. 'Is that like a roast-with-carrots-and-sprouts plant, ahaha?'

Seba chuckled. 'It's a fanciful idea from the east, where some believed in a plant that grew sheep as its fruit. Ridiculous, of course. It was probably a way of explaining cotton or perhaps this fern, whose bulb looks almost lamb-shaped if you turn it upside down and squint in a darkened room.'

Many of the books here had pressed flowers between their pages, while the pigeonholes contained carefully-labelled stones, and phials of variously coloured mineral salts and soil samples, and the cupboards were filled with larger rocks and dried vegetables.

One particular book held Albert's attention for several minutes, and the Palatine smiled to himself as his secretary devoured it.

When they had finished here, Seba led them upstairs to a third room. This one contained a mixture of artefacts that had either been made by humans, or once been them. The centrepiece was a complete human skeleton, hung on a stand so that visitors could walk all around it and examine it from every angle. Many of the books here were medical or anatomical texts, but there were also accounts of foreign civilisations, as well as biographies and works of literature. Some books were in languages and even alphabets that were unfamiliar to Albert, although he suspected his master was probably conversant in at least some of them. Carvings and sculptures from all over the world were littered around the room, and the walls were adorned with swords, spears, clubs and an array of tools and musical instruments. A Nazcan feather headdress sat next to an elaborate suit of Nihonese armour, and there were several other costumes from various exotic lands. Among the items hanging from the ceiling was a long canvas-covered object that was pointed at both ends and curved underneath. A large hole in the centre of the flat surface revealed it to be hollow.

'No-one's entirely sure what it is,' Seba told them, 'but my guess is that it's a boat of some kind. The canvas is certainly waterproof. The pilot would presumably sit in the hole, and perhaps use oars.'

There were also examples of modern technology: a metal bird that sang and flapped its wings; a miniature clockwork monk who walked in a square, beat his chest and raised a holy book to his lips and kissed it; a machine with a metal duck on top that ate grain and then appeared to defecate; and three Nihonese dolls, who jerkily bowed and served tea.

One of these was a full-size leather replica of a man. 'Made over a thousand years ago by Yan Shi the Artificer, for the Emperor Mu,' explained Seba. 'It's said that it walked and danced and sang in perfect tune. But when it had finished its performance, it winked and made advances towards the ladies of the royal court, which angered the Emperor, who threatened to have Yan Shi executed on the spot. In mortal fear, Yan Shi took the thing apart, showing it to be nothing more than leather and wood held together by glue and lacquer. The Emperor examined it and found it to have a complete set of internal organs overlaid by muscles, bones, skin, hair and teeth, all of them artificial. When the heart was removed, the mouth could no longer speak. When the liver was taken away, the eyes no longer saw. And when the kidneys were extracted, the legs lost their power of locomotion. The Emperor was delighted, and allowed Yan Shi to live. Many have examined the artifice over the centuries, and it is exactly as described, with all the organs and so on, but no-one has ever been able to make it work.'

'Well, it's just a story, surely,' said Albert.

'Oh, probably,' agreed Seba, 'but a good one. And it's intriguing to think that it *might* be true.' He looked over the bookshelf and selected one of the books. 'Now, I think this is what you're interested in. The Books of Chilam Balam. Nazcan miscellanies of traditional knowledge. Or at least a translation of them. And the accuracy of that translation is questionable, I'm afraid. Our knowledge of the Nazcans is still very limited. There are actually several cultures there, and most of our interaction with them has involved stealing their gold and killing them when they asked for it back. Not the best way to learn about people, but some have made the effort. Anyway, that means there's a fair amount of guesswork involved, but the legend of Baphomet – the precise name's open to question, by the way – comes from here.'

'And it mentions the Skentys?' asked Albert.

'Not as such,' said Seba. 'Nazcan mythology is quite complex, and each culture has its own traditions. Klauber – the book you read – has interpreted some of their myths as referring to the Skentys. And, to be fair, it's a valid interpretation – but by no means the only one. The word "Skentys" doesn't appear in any known Nazcan language, and the descriptions of their gods don't match our descriptions of the Skentys.'

'But the name "Baphomet" *is* derived from Nazca?'

'That's right. It appears in one legend and one legend only. That we know of, anyway.'

'How close is Klauber's version to the original?'

'The Chilam Balam tells the story of Tiki Tupaca, the creator of all things.' He showed them a picture in the book of an elaborate gold figure. 'But the first things he created were the Runa Waris, giants carved from stone. They built temples to worship Tiki Tupaca, but they became disobedient and he destroyed them in a great flood. When the bodies were counted, though, one was missing. That giant was called Bafihumet or Baphomet or other variations.'

'How did Klauber turn that story into Skentys?' asked Albert. 'His story is about the Skentys trying to create the gods.'

'He was influenced by other strands of Nazcan mythology,' explained Seba. 'Such as the Tzitzimimeh – goddesses of the stars among other things – who fell from the heavens. Some have misinterpreted them as star demons, and their queen wore a cloak that made her invisible, which might fit with the disembodied voice your friends encountered in Kharesh.'

The Palatine gave him a suspicious look. 'You've heard about that?'

Seba smiled mysteriously. 'Oh, I hear about most of these sorts of things. It's my business to.'

'Then you knew why we were here before we told you.'

'I suspected,' said Seba with deliberate false modesty.

'Does that mean you already knew about the connection between the Nazcan myths and the Knights of the Sanctuary?' asked Albert.

'Oh yes. Of course, someone could just have appropriated the name, but the events at Kharesh are suggestive. You obviously agree, otherwise you wouldn't be here. Anyway, Klauber has noticed similar elements in myths from various Nazcan cultures, and concluded that they must have a common origin in the Skentys.'

'Er, isn't that just forcing Nazcan mythology to fit in with *our* mythology?' asked Albert.

'Quite,' said Seba. 'Although, if we're right about the Skentys coming from Nazca, then it could be a valid interpretation. But that involves a lot of ifs and buts.'

'How could the Knights of the Sanctuary have come across the name Baphomet?' asked the Palatine. 'They were disbanded before we'd even discovered Nazca.'

'Very good,' beamed Seba. 'You're an intelligent pair, you two. It's possible the similarity of the names is just a coincidence. These things do happen. But it could lend credence to the idea that Baphomet was a real demon or whatever.'

'But, um, not a stone giant,' said Albert.

'Perhaps not, but who knows what powers a demon has? Perhaps it can transform itself. Or maybe the Runa Waris are just a corruption of the original story. Or maybe none of it's true at all.' He smiled. 'But there is one more clue worth considering.'

He paused so Albert was forced to ask, 'What's that?'

'You'll be aware from your own researches that a recurrent motif in the accusations made against the Order of the Sanctuary was they worshipped heads of various descriptions.'

'Yes,' confirmed Albert.

'Well, a recurrent motif in Nazcan art and architecture is gigantic stone heads.'

XVI. How the Mermaid Got her Tail

*L*ong ago, a great queen was bathing in the sea. She was beautiful, with flowing red curls and big green eyes, and everyone agreed she was the most beautiful in the land. She was also a woman of high morals, and covered her modesty while bathing in the sea.

As she came out of the water, she spied a mermaid sitting on a rock and combing her hair. Now the mermaid had been created the most beautiful of creatures, perfect in form, and at this time had no tail. The queen was amazed at the mermaid's great beauty, and thought her the loveliest creature she had ever set eyes on. But she was also shocked to see the mermaid was naked, and so she sent her maids with a gown for the mermaid to put on.

The mermaid thanked them for their consideration, but said, 'I am a mermaid, queen of the sea, and I am not ashamed of my body. I wear no gown, or dress or cloak, and clothe myself only in my long hair.' And her voice when they heard it was so sweet as to be bewitching.

The queen was filled with jealousy, and worried that people would think the mermaid more beautiful than herself, especially if they were to see her in her nakedness. She raised a great clamour among the women of the land, saying it was a sin for one in the form of a woman to parade naked on the seashore. And what's more, they said the mermaid's beauty was so great, and her voice so sweet, that any man who saw or heard her would never again care for any woman but her. And they said her beauty and the sweetness of her voice could only come from magic and sorcery.

And so they beseeched their gods, or perhaps their sorcerers, to give the mermaid a punishment, and doom her to wear a tail. That way her beauty would always be tempered by the sight of her lower half, and her voice would forever be tinged with a note of sadness.

But when the men heard what had happened, they too beseeched the gods – or perhaps the sorcerers – and they saw to it that, should a man ever fall in love with a mermaid, she would have the power to lay aside her tail so she might marry him.

And so in this way, the mermaid got both her tail and the power to shed it for the love of a man.

17

As the beach came back into view, Jana saw there was someone lying sunbathing on the line of rocks. She was too far away to see who it was, but as she drew closer, they noticed her, and to her surprise, rolled off of the rocks and on to the sand. Then she realised her mistake: it wasn't a person but a seal. It dragged itself awkwardly across the sand to the water and swam away.

By the time it had gone, Jana had reached the rocks herself. She stood for a moment, thinking about what she had just seen, and about Ceasg's selkies. Could they be based on people making the same mistake? Then she thought about Adam's story of the naked woman in the night. In the darkness, perhaps he might also have mistaken a seal for a person, but he said it had shed its skin and put it on the rocks to dry. He'd touched it. And the detail of the woman being naked suggested he'd seen clearly enough to make out the ... bits.

She turned and walked up to the cave again. She gazed at the marks in the sand. Like something had been dragged. Or dragged itself. Then she looked at the pile of seaweed, and then back out along the beach. There was plenty of seaweed. Most of it lay along the high tide line, where it had been washed up. Some was lower down and there was also some in rock pools, all of which were between the tide line and the sea, but most of it was at the high water mark. There was none higher up. It didn't grow on the beach. It was only there because it had been washed up by the tide.

She turned back to the cave. It was well above the tide line. The sand was dry. The cave didn't flood because the tide didn't come this far. So how had the seaweed got here? She rolled up her sleeves and plunged her arms in. She rooted around for a minute, and then got annoyed because now her arms smelled and there had been nothing hidden under the pile, so it had been for no reason.

She went down to one of the rock pools to wash, and then walked back along the beach, her head full of thoughts. Most of them were there to stop her from thinking about Ben. As she turned all of the thoughts over in her mind, the one that came to the front was Ceasg's baby. Not the question of where it was – although that was certainly in there – but the matter of who had come to the birth. And more importantly, who hadn't.

'She, er... she doesn't say very much, does she?'

Serena looked down sadly.

'She can't speak at all,' explained Ben. 'I'm not sure why.'

'Then how do you know her name?' asked Adam.

'She wrote it down. That's the only thing she's written though.'

'Um, here's a thought,' ventured Adam. 'If she can't speak or write anything except her name, how do you know she's a mermaid?'

Serena looked up sharply and nodded vigorously, a look of urgency on her face.

'Ah,' said Adam. There was an awkward pause as he thought about how to put his next question. Eventually he gave up and just went for it. 'Have you, er, have you looked at her legs, Ben?'

Ben looked scandalised. 'What's that supposed to mean?'

But Serena leaped to her feet with a huge smile and pulled her skirt up higher than was decent, apparently eager to show them off. Clearly she was proud of them.

Ben stared, and Serena's expression changed when she saw his, to a mixture of worry and confusion. She looked at her legs and back to the two men's faces. This wasn't the reaction she'd expected.

Adam took her hand and gently pulled her back to a sitting position on the sand. She shook her head to show that she didn't understand what was wrong.

'You think your legs are beautiful, don't you?' Adam asked her.

She nodded, but this time uncertainly.

'Have you ever seen anyone else's legs?'

She thought for a moment and then shook her head slowly.

Adam rolled up the leg of his breeches and indicated for Ben to do the same. Serena stared at them both, and then at her own legs. Ben's leg was quite hairy. Adam's was less so, but they both had smooth, pinkish skin, just like the skin on their arms and faces. Serena's legs were very different. The skin was grey and hairless, and appeared to be thick and shiny. And the insides of both legs, and all over the feet, were covered in scars, as if they had healed after some terrible injury.

Serena looked from Adam to Ben and back again, her eyes pleading for an explanation.

'Have they always been like that?' Adam asked her.

She nodded.

'You were born that way?'

This time she shook her head.

'Then how can they always have been like that?'

Serena raised her hands and then dropped them again in frustration at not being able to communicate.

An idea struck Adam. 'I think we should take you to see a doctor.'

Pieter and Rutger watched the strange men with the white faces walk out of the inn. They waited until the door had closed behind the clowns before speaking.

'What d'you think?' asked Pieter.

'I think they're freaks and we should have nothing to do with them,' answered Rutger.

'They want what we want.'

'Why should they want what we want? They're not from here. They just want to use us to get what they really want.'

'If it helps us then who cares?' reasoned Pieter. 'Everybody wins.'

'And what are they going to do? Take one mermaid for their freak show? How does that help us?'

'They'll expose it!' There was a zealous fire burning in Pieter's eyes. 'Expose the Seatowners. Everyone'll see them for what they are.'

The door of the snug suddenly swung open, and the man from the *Sapphire* emerged, his voluminous clothes swirling around him like a hurricane. He walked straight to Pieter and Rutger, and glared at them with his cold eyes.

'And just what is it that they are?' he asked.

When Jana walked into the lobby of the hotel, she was surprised to see Adam talking to Doctor Vleerman. She took one look at the doctor and ran. Adam stared after her and shook his head in bemusement. She had behaved very oddly since they got here. Even odder than usual.

He led Vleerman up to Ben's room and knocked on the door.

'Ben, it's Adam. I've got the doctor.'

Ben opened the door and let them in. Serena sat on the bed looking nervous. Adam gave her an encouraging smile.

'Serena, this is Doctor Vleerman. He's here to help. Just like we talked about.'

'Hello, Serena,' smiled Vleerman. 'I'm just here to look at your legs. See if I can give you some answers. Maybe even help with the pain.'

Serena took a deep breath and nodded. She pulled up her skirt to show her scarred legs. Vleerman tried unsuccessfully to hide his surprise. He sat down on the end of the bed and stretched out his hand.

'I'm just going to touch the skin, very gently. You let me know if it hurts, alright?'

He waited for Serena to nod her consent, before gently pressing on her calf. He ran his hand up one leg and then the other, testing both the fleshy parts and feeling for the bones. Then he looked carefully at the scars. Finally he sat back and considered.

'I can see why you called me in,' he said at last. 'The scarring is consistent with the legs and feet having been separated at some point. They may have been fused together at birth, like Ceasg's baby, and surgically separated.'

'That's why she said her legs had always been like that but she wasn't born that way,' Adam explained to Ben. 'And why it's so painful for her to walk.'

'But it's never been done before,' continued Vleerman. 'It's a very dangerous procedure, with all sorts of complications. The likelihood of anyone surviving is very small. And I'd have heard about it. Everyone would. The surgeon would be famous.'

'Is there any other explanation?' asked Adam.

'Of course. The scarring could have been caused any number of other ways. And then there's the skin. And the flesh.' He looked directly to Ben. 'What does the skin look like to you?'

Ben avoided his gaze. 'You're the doctor.'

'Yes, but I think this is more your area of expertise than mine. Perhaps if you were to feel the flesh.'

'I don't need to.'

'No, I don't think you do. It looks like whale blubber to me.'

Ben sighed. 'More like dolphin,' he said. 'Or porpoise.'

'I'm surprised that you're so reluctant to accept it,' said Vleerman.

'What do you mean?'

'Doesn't this help your research? You believe that Serena's a mermaid. She doesn't have a fish's tail, but her legs do seem very similar to dolphin flesh.'

Ben looked at him sharply, realisation dawning.

'I'm sure you've read Dr Durant's book. If he's correct, wouldn't a dolphin's tail be more compatible with a human body than a fish's?'

Ben stared at him. 'Are you saying she had a dolphin tail that's been turned into legs?'

'If she has, I'd like to meet the surgeon. But it's certainly an interesting thought, isn't it?'

The part of Doctor Vleerman that Jana had taken one look at was not his face, but his left hand: no wedding ring. And there had been no women's clothes on the washing line, so there probably wasn't anyone else at his house. It would be empty.

It was only when she arrived back there that she realised she had no idea what she was planning on doing. She wasn't sure what she was looking for, and she certainly didn't know how to break in.

She stood hopelessly for a moment, before her eye landed on the outhouses. There were three: two small and one larger. Earlier, she had thought the large one might stable a horse, and when she looked through the window, she could indeed see riding tackle and straw, although the horse was not there.

She turned her attention to the other two outhouses. One was padlocked and the windows were dirty, but she could see enough to confirm that it was used as a shed, and was mainly full of gardening equipment. The other had curtains over its windows, and they were pulled tightly closed. Curtains in an outhouse? What didn't he want people to see?

And how could she be the one to see it? She didn't want to break windows or locks because, well, she was brought up better than that and would only get caught anyway. She didn't want to leave any tracks. Or sweeping up.

She tried the door, but it was solid and firmly locked. She turned her attention to the windows. There were two, one on each side. They weren't designed to open, only to allow light in. Which they weren't doing on account of the curtains. They were small, but she'd be able to squeeze through. She pressed at one of the frames, just to see. To her surprise, it moved slightly. She looked more closely, and realised the wood was rotten and some of the stonework had started to crumble. It probably wouldn't take much effort to push it out completely – but then it would fall inwards and smash.

She took a deep breath and pressed more firmly on one corner. Carefully, she worked up and down the one edge, trying to push it in just enough to create a gap.

Finally one appeared. It was tiny, but she pushed her fingers into it, trying to force them through. It was painful, because basically her hand was jammed in a window, but she persevered until she could crook her fingers around the other side. Now she had a grip on the window, and there was a chance she might be able to push it right in without it falling. At the same time, though, the window had a hold of her, and it was bloody sore! And if someone caught her here, she wouldn't be able to escape. And would look a bit silly.

Suddenly she stiffened as she heard the sound of hoofbeats on the main road. They were joined by a rattling that told her it was a coach. She waited nervously, but the noise faded into the distance.

She started to push on the bottom edge of the frame with her other hand. Now that one edge was free, it was easier to move the rest, but there was also more risk of it falling in, and there was no guarantee she'd be able to hold on to it. Or that her hand would hold up. Her fingers were going numb. She reached the corner and started working up the third edge.

Suddenly she pulled her hand back in pain. It was just a splinter, but it hurt and she reacted on reflex. The jerk caused her to push inwards before pulling away. It was enough to make the window come away completely, and it fell inwards. She tightened her grip with the other hand, but the numbness and the sudden weight made it hard to hold on. It was slipping. She tensed her body and kept stock still. The window was barely hanging from her fingers. Slowly she twisted her body so she could reach in with her other hand. She had to be careful, as any false move could cause her to drop it.

She stretched her arm, but couldn't quite reach. She'd have to lean further in, but keep her numb arm held up so she could reach the window. Despite the numbness, her muscles ached. And she realised she'd been holding her breath for longer than was comfortable. But now wasn't the time to breathe out. She edged her free arm further into the gap, and at last her fingers brushed against the frame. Not enough to get a grip, but enough to give her hope.

Her lungs ached now. She'd *have* to breathe out, but the movement could be enough to make her drop the window. Her numb arm was starting to shake. She couldn't last much longer.

She let the air burst out of her mouth. The window slipped, but the release of breath gave her the impetus to lunge forward and grab it with her other hand. She breathed heavily a few times and gripped on to the window for dear life. She tried to move her numb arm across to hold it with both hands, but she had lost all feeling and it wouldn't move. She made sure the grip she had was firm, and lowered the window carefully to the ground. With a huge sigh of relief, she let it go, stood up and tried to rub the feeling back into her arm. Once the needles and pins had stopped, she actually looked at her hand and saw all the blood. Ha! She'd need to get a doctor to look at that later.

After checking there was still no-one coming, she pulled the curtain aside and climbed through the hole, careful to avoid putting her foot through the glass and ruining an eternity of effort and agony. She didn't immediately look around. Her first priority was to place the window back into the hole, so that if Vleerman did return, he wouldn't notice anything amiss. It sat in the space well enough, but a decent gust of wind would blow it in now. As long as she was gone, it would just look like wear and tear. Wouldn't it?

She allowed herself to relax a little now, although not much, as she was still trespassing in someone's outhouse, having first vandalised it to get in. In fact, come to think of it, what the hell was she thinking? Breaking and entering? And she didn't even know what she was looking for!

Then she turned around and saw exactly what she was looking for.

XVII. Johnny Croy and his Mermaid Bride

*J*ohnny Croy was the handsomest, bravest young man in all the islands. Many a bonny lass cast her glance Johnny's way, but he never once paid attention.

One day, Johnny was down at the seashore gathering driftwood. The tide was out, and he was walking near the big rocks when he heard the most beautiful sound he had ever heard in his whole life. It was a woman's voice singing, but oh so sweetly, and a tune like no other he had ever had the good fortune to hear. He stood transfixed for a minute or two, before coming to his senses enough to seek out whoever was making such a delightful sound.

It must be coming from around the next rock, and so he crept up to the edge and peeped around. Sure enough, he saw a sight that made his heart leap. Sitting on a seaweed-covered rock was a mermaid, singing and combing her flowing golden hair. The sun sparkled on her locks, and she wore a long silver petticoat, with the train folded behind her like a tail.

In that moment, Johnny fell hopelessly in love, and swore by the Great Odin Stane that he would woo her though it should cost him his life. He crept carefully and quietly among the rocks, getting ever nearer, and occasionally glancing at her bonny face. And each glance made his heart burn more. And all the while she combed and she sang, unaware of her suitor.

At last he was only a few feet away, and then Johnny leaped forward, threw his arms around her and kissed her sweet mouth. For a moment she sat stunned. Then she leaped to her feet – for feet she had beneath that petticoat – lifted the folded tail and gave Johnny such a wallop with it that he fell flat on his back. She ran down to the sea and spread out her train in the water behind her.

Johnny scrambled to his feet and saw the fair maiden staring at him with fierce eyes, angry at being kissed so rudely – but not so much at being kissed at all, for that kiss had left its mark, and as she watched him, love was growing in her heart. What's more, she knew that if she were to win the love of a mortal man, she could keep her beauty for ever and not turn into an ugly Finwife.

A glint in the sand caught Johnny's eye, and he looked down and saw the mermaid had dropped her golden comb as she fled. He picked it up and held it aloft, calling out, 'Thanks, fair maiden, for leaving me this love token.'

Seeing it, the mermaid gave a bitter cry. 'Alas! Oh, won't you give me back my golden comb? To lose it means dreadful shame for me, and I shall forever be known among the Finfolk as the lass that lost her comb.'

'I shall return it when you come and live on the land with me as my bride,' retorted Johnny, 'for I can never love another now that I have seen you.'

'But I can not live on your cold land, with its black rain, and its white snow, and its hot sun and its reeking fires that would shrivel my skin in a week. No, you must come away with me! I'll make you a chief among the Finfolk. You'll live in a crystal palace where rain never falls, wind never blows and sun never burns. There we shall be happy forever.'

'I cannot live under the sea,' replied Johnny, 'but if you'd only come and live with me, you shall bide in a stately home with plenty of cows and sheep, and you shall be mistress of all. Come with me, my Gem-de-Lovely.'

And so they stood there for I know not how long, each offering temptations to the other. And all the while their love grew stronger. But at last, Gem-de-Lovely saw people coming in the distance, and she bade him farewell and swam out to sea. Johnny watched her go, the sun sparkling on her golden tresses, and once she was out of sight, he turned and headed for home with a heavy heart, still carrying the golden comb.

Johnny's mither was a spae-wife, and when he told her what had happened she chided, 'Ye're a fool, Johnny Croy, to fall in love with a mermaid when you could have any lass on the land. But men are fools the whole world over. If ye must have this sea lass, then ye must keep that comb as a treasured possession, for it gies ye power o'er her. If ye're wise, ye'll cast it intae the sea and forget aboot her. She may mak for a bright summer, but it'll end wi' a woeful winter. But I ken ye'll go yer own road and end up in the quagmire. I'll only be able to save one. If only it wis you, my son.'

Johnny locked up the comb safely and went about his work, always thinking of his Gem-de-Lovely. Then one night, after tossing and turning and only falling into a doze near daybreak, he was wakened by the sound of singing. It was the same voice he had heard that day on the shore, and when he sat up, there was his Gem-de-Lovely sitting at the foot of his bed, every bit as beautiful as he remembered.

'My bonny Johnny,' she said, 'I've come to ask again if you'll give me my golden comb and come away with me to live in that crystal palace under the sea.'

'You know I cannot,' he said, 'but unless you stay with me now, my heart will surely break.'

'Then I'll mak you a fair offer,' said she. 'I will bide here with you and be your wife. I'll stay here for seven years, if you'll swear that, when that time is up, you'll come with me and all that is mine, and we'll go to live with my people under the sea.'

At that, Johnny leaped out of bed, fell to his knees and swore to keep the bargain. And so she fell into his arms, and they kissed and cuddled so much it would make you sick.

And so they married, and Gem-de-Lovely covered her ears as the priest prayed, for her folk have no souls. But all said that she was the bonniest bride they ever did see, and her face shone gold, and her dress shone silver, and the string of pearls around her neck shone the brightest white.

She made a loving wife to Johnny. She baked the best bread, brewed the strongest beer, and all agreed she was the best spinner for miles around. And she was also the best mother, for she and Johnny were blessed with seven of the bonniest bairns, each one weaned on Granny Croy's knee. And for seven years they were happy.

But all must come to its end, and as the seven years drew to a close, the Croys began preparations for a long sea voyage. Gem-de-Lovely was brisk and busy, but with a distant look in her eye, while Johnny was quiet and preoccupied.

On the eve of the last day of those seven years, the day when Johnny and his family were due to depart, Granny Croy rose at midnight and went to the fireplace. She took with her a piece of iron that had been blessed by the priest, and she heated it in the embers until it glowed. Then she crept to the cradle of the youngest bairn and held that piece of iron to its bare bum, and the bairn howled like a demon!

The morning came, and Gem-de-Lovely walked down to the boat, as beautiful and as regal as ever. There on the beach stood her Johnny and the six oldest bairns. And there was Granny Croy, sitting on a rock with a tear in her eye. But the baby was not there, so Gem-de-Lovely sent the servants to bring him. Off they went, but soon they came back, saying try as they might, they could not lift the cradle nor the babe from it.

A cloud passed over Gem-de-Lovely's face, and she ran up to the house herself. Sure enough, when she tried to lift the cradle it would not move. So she pulled back the blanket and tried to lift the baby out, but the moment she touched him, her hands and her arms burned as if they were on fire. She screamed and ran back to the boat, with tears filling her bonny blue eyes.

And there was Granny Croy, still sitting on the rock, and still with a tear in her eye too, but also with a half smile upon her lips.

With heavy hearts and heads hung low, Johnny and Gem-de-Lovely and the other six bairns boarded the boat and sailed away. And as they sailed, Gem-de-Lovely sang a lament for her lost baby, and all who heard it said it was the saddest and yet most beautiful song they had ever heard. And Johnny and his fair wife and their six eldest bairns were never seen again.

18

Water lapped against the sides of the launch as it rowed out towards the *Invincible*. Albert Munster wasn't very happy on water, but the Palatine seemed unperturbed. Albert had to shade his eyes against the glare on the surface of the waves.

The signal they had sent earlier, by catching the sun's reflection in Lord Reitherman's shaving mirror, had summoned a boat from the Imperial ship, which had waited for them at the naval base where, they noticed, the fleet was apparently *not* massing for the moment.

The launch pulled up alongside the ship, and one of the two sailors stood up and grabbed hold of a piece of rope. With a gulp, Albert realised this was a rope ladder and they were expected to climb it.

A veil shall be drawn over exactly how it was that Albert Munster reached the deck of the *Invincible,* but it became a legend in the Imperial Navy for many years after, although the three sailors directly involved would never speak of it for the rest of their lives.

The Palatine, of course, climbed the ladder gracefully, and acted as if Albert had done the same.

The Captain was a well-built man with a beard that could have thatched a roof. He knew enough not to salute civilians but make them feel as if he had. 'Welcome aboard, your Lordship,' he said. 'Welcome aboard, sir,' he repeated to Albert, who suddenly felt as if the rope ladder incident had never happened. 'If you'll come this way, sirs, I'll show you the turtle.'

'The turtle?' asked the Palatine.

'Yes, sir. The turtle.'

'I'm afraid, Captain, that you have us at an advantage. We were told to rendezvous with you but we were not told why. You'll have to explain why we need to see a turtle.'

'Not *a* turtle, sir. *The* turtle.'

'The fact that it's a specific animal doesn't leave us any the wiser,' said the Palatine. 'Perhaps you should show us before we make ourselves look any more foolish. Or rather *my*self, as Albert has wisely said nothing on the matter.'

The Captain smiled. 'This way, sir.' He led them to a large hatchway in the middle of the deck. He nodded to the nearby sailors and they lifted the cover, revealing the hold below. The Palatine and Albert looked down and they saw the turtle and finally understood.

'Oh please no,' whimpered Albert.

Jana stared in horror at the row of jars. There were twelve of them sitting in a line on a table. Next to them lay a leather-bound journal. Each jar contained a baby suspended in some sort of liquid. Well, not so much a baby as a foetus, each one at a different stage of development. The two that were the most fully developed had their legs and feet fused together, just like Ceasg's missing baby, although neither of these was Lorelei. They looked like mermaids. The other ten were all at much earlier stages of development, so that several were barely recognisable as human at all.

She opened the journal and flicked through a few pages. It contained notes and drawings of more foetuses. No, not *more* foetuses. They were drawings of the ones in the jars, each carefully labelled and annotated. There were several pages on the subject of babies with fused legs, under the heading 'Sirenomelia or Mermaid Syndrome'. The drawings of the other ten foetuses all drew attention to ridges or flaps in the areas that would have eventually developed into their necks, had they survived. Jana had not noticed these at first, but now she looked again, and they were present in each of the ten. She looked back at the drawings and saw that in each case the ridges were labelled 'gills?' Did

Vleerman really think these were mermaid foetuses? What the hell was he up to? And had he taken Lorelei as part of his creepy research? But if he had, why would he throw her into the sea instead of preserving her in one of his ghoulish jars?

She spent a few minutes reading the journal and then, after satisfying herself there was nothing else of interest in the outhouse, she carefully removed the window and climbed back out. Once she was outside, she reached back in, and with a very painful stretch, lifted the window back up to the hole. It was more difficult to replace from the outside, and it took her several minutes.

Just as she was sure she'd done it, a voice behind her said, 'What do you think you're doing?'

She let go of the window and it smashed to the floor.

'This is a really bad idea, Pieter.'

Rutger and Pieter stood on the promenade, staring intently across at the Seatown. Plumes of smoke curled up from some of the chimneys, but not from the kelp-burning pits, which had been inactive since the advent of mortasheen.

'It's a great idea,' disagreed Pieter. 'We've got all of them looking after our interests.'

'And what happens when they find out that we've been playing them off against each other?'

'By then we'll have what we want.'

'But *they* won't!' Rutger grabbed Pieter's arm and pulled him around so they were facing each other. 'They're dangerous.'

'The stranger's dangerous,' said Pieter. 'We give the mermaid to him. The other two are just circus clowns. What are they going to do? Throw pies at us?'

Rutger looked doubtfully at the two complimentary tickets Mr Coco had pressed into his hand before leaving. 'I'm not so sure. There's something scary about them.'

'That's just part of their act.'

'And they've got all of the circus people behind them.'

'Stop worrying, Rutger.' Pieter clapped him on the back reassuringly. 'It'll be fine.'

Rutger didn't look convinced. 'So what's the plan?'

'Get your best clothes ready, Rutger. We're going to a wedding.'

The turtle, it turned out, was actually the *Turtle*, a submersible craft that looked more like an egg than a turtle. It was made of wood waterproofed with tar, and had a stubby tower at the top, inset with six round windows. To Albert's relief, there was only room for one person, and that person was the Palatine. The Emperor's orders were very strict that only Lord Reitherman should see whatever lay at the bottom of the sea.

After half an hour of instruction in its operation, the Palatine was sealed inside the *Turtle,* and it was winched out of the hold and lowered into the sea. He instantly felt the temperature drop. Once underwater, the natural light disappeared, but the interior of the vessel was illuminated by a piece of cork smeared with foxfire. This allowed the Palatine to see the controls, which consisted of a valve to allow water into the bilge tank, causing the vessel to dive, and two hand-cranked propellers for horizontal propulsion and steering. The glow from the foxfire also allowed him to see a few feet out of the windows, but beyond that was murky darkness.

He descended in silence. Sometimes curious fish swam up to the windows and stared in at him before darting away, but most avoided the strange object. Occasionally something larger swam past, but all he could see were vague impressions that called to mind dolphins or porpoises. Once he saw a squid, but it quickly lost itself in a cloud of ink and disappeared.

The Captain had impressed on him that he had only thirty minutes of air, so there would be very little time for him to achieve his objective. He had to hope the *Invincible's* coordinates were accurate.

As the *Turtle* dived deeper and the temperature got colder, he saw a faint light in the distance. That must be it. He steered the submersible towards it. As he got closer, more of the larger shapes swam by, but always keeping their distance. However, the closer he got to the light, the further he could see, and gradually the shapes became clearer.

They weren't dolphins.

He could now see the source of the light. It wasn't often that Lord Reitherman was amazed, but he stared at the spectacle before him in stunned stupefaction. Things were beginning to make sense.

The not-dolphins were all watching him from a distance, but still did not approach. He wondered whether he had enough time to move in closer. He had been counting all the way, and was now at twelve minutes, which only left him three before he would have to head back. No-one had mentioned whether the return journey would take the same length of time as the descent, and he wondered whether going upwards might take more effort, and therefore more time.

Suddenly the light went out. He had been warned this might happen. The phosphorescence from the foxfire sometimes failed when the temperature got too low. The light from outside was enough for him to see the controls, but once he moved away from it, he would have to complete his ascent in darkness.

Reluctantly, the Palatine grabbed the hand pump that expelled water from the bilge tank, and propelled the *Turtle* upwards. After a few minutes, he had left the light behind and was in pitch darkness, still marvelling at what he had seen. Unable to steer visually, he hoped the vessel would go straight up and not veer off course. Or hit the bottom of the ship.

Dr Vleerman unlocked the door and waved Jana inside. 'I find it easier this way,' he said. 'I tend to break fewer windows.' There was no hint of a smile.

'What are you going to do with me?' asked Jana nervously. 'I'll be able to escape through the window. Cos it isn't there.'

'You think I'm going to lock you in here? What kind of person do you think I am?'

'The kind who keeps babies in jars.' Jana shuddered at the grotesque line-up in front of them.

'I assume you read the journal while you were breaking in. So you'll understand that this is important medical research.'

'It's a horror show.'

'Very scientific,' snorted Vleerman. 'You saw Ceasg's baby. My research could be very helpful to her.'

'By pickling her in a jar?'

'Sirenomelia is a very rare medical condition. Perhaps one baby in a hundred thousand is born with it. Lorelei is the fifth to be born in Anterwendt in the last ten years. All of the mothers were Seatowners.'

Jana looked at the two in the jars. 'What happened to the other two?' she managed.

'Both died within hours of birth and were buried in the cemetery. These two were miscarried and expelled naturally. The church's somewhat unenlightened attitude doesn't allow miscarried or stillborn babies to be buried in consecrated ground. I was prevailed upon to dispose of the remains, and took it upon myself to study them in order to help future cases. I know you think that compassion isn't in my nature,' he continued, seeing Jana's surprise, 'but that is the whole point of the medical profession.'

'What about the others?'

'Some of those were miscarriages too. Others I believe came from either abortions, or from mothers who died during pregnancy. Most aren't local, but were donated by other doctors to assist with a related branch of my research.'

'You think they have gills.'

'You did read the journal,' he smiled. 'But no, they're not actually gills. They're merely folds of skin that bear a superficial resemblance to gills, and disappear during foetal development. Certainly I know of no humans ever being born with gills.'

'Then what's your interest?'

'Are you familiar with Doctor Durant's evolutionary theories?'

Remembering her adventures in Kharesh, Jana nodded.

'Then you'll know that in our proposed evolutionary chain, Durant believes we had ancestors with gills. My own theory is that these skin folds may be a vestigial remnant of those gills.'

By now Jana's scientific curiosity had been aroused. 'And you think that somehow relates to the high incidence of – sirenomelia is it – in the Seatowners?'

'Well, it might help explain the local belief that the Seatowners are descended from mermaids. I certainly don't believe it myself, and I'm firmly of the opinion that sirenomelia is a purely medical condition, with no real connection to actual mermaids, if such things exist. However, I saw something today … ' He tailed off.

'What?'

'Serena. Huevelmans's friend who claims to be a genuine mermaid.'

'Yes, I know who she is,' said Jana hotly.

'Her legs,' Vleerman continued. 'They appear to be made not of normal human flesh, but of blubber, like a dolphin. And they show scarring, as if they had been surgically separated. Of course, it's impossible for all sorts of reasons, but I still don't know quite what to make of it. Except, if Durant is correct, it would make more sense for a mermaid to have a dolphin's tail than a fish's one.'

'Are you saying she's really a mermaid?' asked Jana incredulously.

'I don't know what I'm saying,' confessed Vleerman. 'But there's something here I don't understand. Yet.'

Jana was impressed by the last word. He was determined to solve the mystery. But then she remembered why she had come here in the first place. 'What did you do with Lorelei?'

'What do you mean?' He saw the look in her eye and realised what she was suggesting. 'You think *I* took the baby? Why?' He looked at the jars and stared at her in horror. 'You think I would steal a baby for research? That's monstrous!'

'Adam saw a man on the beach putting what looked like a baby into the sea. He came from the direction of your house.'

Vleerman was obviously appalled at the accusation. 'Whoever your friend saw, it wasn't me. I'm a physician. I save lives, I don't take them. And you don't even know that it *was* a baby. I pray to all the gods that it wasn't. Who would do such a thing?'

Jana considered. If Vleerman had taken Lorelei for his research, why would he put her in the sea? It made no sense. And she was beginning to realise her initial impression of him had been wrong. 'I'm sorry,' she said at last. 'I've been unfair to you.'

'I was genuinely trying to help Ceasg with the fish oil,' he said. 'I don't think she's inhuman, but her condition is purely in her own mind. No medicine can help her, but she believes the fish oil helps, and if it calms her, then it's all I can prescribe. It's better than leaving her in her distress. Surely you see that.'

Jana nodded. 'I understand. I'm sorry.' She looked at the broken window lying on the floor. 'What are you going to do with me?'

Vleerman smiled mischievously. 'By rights I should turn you over to the Watch for breaking and entering. But the Watch here is next to useless, and you thought you were exposing a public menace. I think we can put this misunderstanding behind us.'

Jana smiled back at him, realising she had made an unlikely friend.

He looked at the remains of the window. 'The frame was rotten anyway. I'd been meaning to get it fixed. You can help me cover up the jars before I fetch the glazier. By the way, do you know what happened to my shirt?'

Jana was confused by the question for a moment, until she remembered the space on the washing line. 'It was gone when I got here.'

'A shame. I liked that shirt.'

'There's a lot of sawdust,' observed Father Langstok, as he and Adam walked around the sideshows. 'I wonder what they need it for.' He took another bite of his honeyed apple. 'I might have to take up beekeeping.'

They had passed through the animal enclosures where, as children and adults had teased the lion to make it roar, then jumped back in fright, Adam had thought it looked a bit pitiful caged up while people made fun of it. He got some small satisfaction at the monkey cage, when one of its residents threw its own faeces at the boy who had kept holding out an orange and then snatching it away whenever the monkey reached for it.

The performing fleas hadn't been very amusing either, because the fleas themselves were far too small to see, and watching a miniature seesaw go up and down on its own, or a tiny Ferris wheel turning unaided, was surprisingly unimpressive, especially when Father Langstok explained there were really no fleas at all but just clockwork and magnets and clever illusion. He chuckled at the ingenuity and seemed disappointed Adam didn't enjoy it too.

Adam realised he was only here because Father Langstok had asked that he take him, and even then it had originally been to see something that was no longer there. Adam didn't actually *want* to be here. There was nothing about it that he liked. Caged animals, the freak show, the weird clowns – they were all a bit, well, tacky. But it was the flea circus that really summed it up. Father Langstok liked the showmanship and the pulling the wool over people's eyes, and he assumed Adam must like them too. But illusionism wasn't the same as performance and parlour tricks. They were poles apart. And Jana wasn't much better, just seeing magic as something to get childishly excited about. But Ben had said Adam was more like a scientist, and magic was just science that hadn't been explained yet. The more he thought about it, the more it made sense.

If he hadn't been so lost in those thoughts, he might have seen the clowns coming and been able to avoid them before they got too close. Instead, they were right on him, and no doubt going to subject him to one of their routines.

''Allo,' said Mr Coco.

''Allo,' said Mr Wobbly.

'My name,' began Mr Coco, 'is Coco the clown but you –'

'Yes, I know who you are,' interrupted Adam irritably. 'I've seen this bit before.'

'But *he* hasn't,' said Mr Coco indignantly, indicating Father Langstok.

'Ah, you must be the famous Scary Clowns I've heard so much about,' beamed Father Langstok. 'Mr Coco and Mr Wobbly, isn't it?'

The horn tooted a little uncertainly.

'Well ... yes,' said Mr Coco nonplussed. 'It sounds better when we say it though.'

'At least he knows who we are,' reasoned Mr Wobbly. 'Our reputation has procecded us.'

'It's *pre*ceded, you doughnut,' scolded Mr Coco.

'I like doughnuts,' smiled Mr Wobbly happily. ''Specially wiv jam in.

233

Or custard. Them's good too. Ooh!' Suddenly his eyes lit up. 'Mr Coco, I've just had a brainwave.'

'Oh dear,' sighed Mr Coco, shaking his head. 'It's the monkey army all over again.'

'No, no, this is a good one,' insisted Mr Wobbly.

'Go on then,' said Mr Coco, with a complete lack of enthusiasm. 'Amaze me.'

'Well,' said Mr Wobbly excitedly, 'you put custard and jam in the *same* doughnut – and then you've got – ' he paused for effect and grinned, 'a *trifle* doughnut!'

Mr Coco stared at him. 'Mr Wobbly,' – *toot toot* – 'that is brilliant!'

It's possible that Mr Wobbly blushed, but you'd never tell under all that white make-up.

'That is pure genius,' said Mr Coco.

'Told ya,' beamed Mr Wobbly. Well, it was more of a sneer than a beam, because that was the best he could manage, but he was obviously pleased with himself.

'Of course,' continued Mr Coco as they began to walk away, lost in their dreams of trifle doughnuts, 'you'd never have managed it without my influence.'

'Very entertaining,' laughed Father Langstok, finishing the last of his honeyed apple.

Adam said nothing, because he knew it would only lead to questions about why he didn't like the clowns, and he couldn't really be bothered. He realised they were outside the freak show, as a stilt walker went past. They had no free passes this time, but Father Langstok had no hesitation in buying tickets for both of them.

There were more people here today, and a small crowd had gathered in Prince Randian's tent, where Randian was playing noughts and crosses in the sawdust with anyone who cared to challenge him. Adam noticed that Father Langstok showed no reaction at all to Randian's lack of limbs. It was as if he didn't even notice.

The Father waited patiently until it was his turn to play, and he happily sat on the floor and drew in the sawdust with his finger.

'Where are you prince of?' he asked innocently as he contemplated his next move.

'Somewhere very far away,' replied Randian. 'You wouldn't have heard of it.'

Father Langstok smiled knowingly. 'You're probably right.' Then he drew a line through the three crosses he had made.

'Hey,' said Randian mock indignantly. 'I'm a cripple. You're supposed to let me win.'

'Oh, I don't think you're a cripple at all,' said Father Langstok as he stood up, 'and I wouldn't insult you by deliberately losing.'

Randian winked at him appreciatively. 'Good answer, Father. We should play poker sometime.'

'A man of the cloth playing poker?' Father Langstok looked scandalised but his eyes twinkled.

'You're right,' said Randian. 'I wouldn't be safe, would I?'

They passed through the other tents, with Father Langstok particularly enjoying the musical rendition by the joined twins. He held a conversation in Bretonnian with Lionel and then tried him with another language Adam didn't recognise.

'Palare la carny?'

Lionel looked impressed. 'Bona, godly homie, bona.'

They went on in this fashion for a few minutes, obviously having fun, and more than once Lionel looked scandalised by something Father Langstok had said. After they had finished, they explained to Adam that they were speaking Polari, the secret language of carnival people.

'I'm too shocked to tell you some of the things the Father was talking about,' laughed Lionel, 'but if anyone understood it, he'd be defrocked.'

They both laughed at some joke that went over Adam's head.

'Lionel tells me the circus performers come from all over the world,' Father Langstok said. 'He himself is from Moravia, many of the acrobats come from Khazar, and there's even a family of trapeze artists from Zhongguo. And of course,' he added with his customary twinkle, 'Prince Randian is prince of somewhere we've never heard of, but Lionel says the New World's full of places we've never heard of.'

'Hey!' came an indignant voice through the walls of the tent. 'Professional secrets, eh?'

'You wriggle around on the floor and lie about where you come from,' shouted back Lionel. 'What's professional about that?'

'At least I shave once in a while.'

'You rub your face on a block of sandpaper. Don't go getting yourself airs and graces.'

'Hairs and graces? You can speak.'

'Yes, I can speak. Five languages, as a matter of fact.'

'Swearing in Bretonnian doesn't count as speaking a language.'

'How would you know? You can't even speak one properly.'

Father Langstok eventually bade Lionel goodbye and led Adam back into the corridor, but suddenly his eyes lit up and he bypassed the remaining entrances, walking straight to the Feejee Mermaid sign.

'It's not there any more,' said Adam, catching up with him. 'It was stolen, remember?'

'Yes, I know,' replied the Father sadly. 'I just wanted to look at the sign.' He gazed at it admiringly for a few minutes, before walking into the tent anyway. Shaking his head, Adam followed.

The pedestal was still there and the Father looked at it carefully before glancing around the tent.

'It would have been so nice to see it,' he said at last, and then left. His eyes were drawn immediately to the sign for 'The Worst Horror of Them All!' His face brightened again, and he walked in without a moment's hesitation.

Adam did hesitate before following. He wasn't sure why. When he entered the tent, he noticed Father Langstok's reaction to the empty space was very different to his own, Jana's and Ben's the other day. There was no look of disappointment or feeling of being cheated. Instead he was clearly trying to work out what it was he was supposed to be seeing. Adam stood in the entrance and watched him. His head was getting sore and he felt a little queasy.

Suddenly Father Langstok looked up and chuckled. 'Ah, of course!' He had seen the mirror. 'Very good. Very good indeed. Excellent showmanship.' He looked at Adam and his expression changed to concern. 'Are you alright?'

'Yes, fine,' said Adam. And then he fainted.

XVIII. The Trowie Bairn

*T*here was a man whose wife was pregnant and due to give birth any day. The spae-wife came to make the house ready and chased the husband out, saying he'd only be in the way and this was women's business. So he took his fishing rod and headed off to the Craigs for some peace and quiet.

But on the way he saw a group of small figures scurrying in the direction of his croft. They were trows, and fear gripped him because he knew what they must be planning. The birth of a bairn was a dangerous time if the precautions were neglected, so he dropped his rod and ran helter-skelter back home as fast as he could.

When he arrived, he slammed the door shut and put the key in the lock, being careful to leave it unlocked, because everyone knew that locked doors anger trows.

The spae-wife sat poking the fire and tutting at his presence, but he ignored her and carried on with his precautions. He rummaged in his trunk until he found the holy book, which he placed next to the door. Then he took a knife from the kitchen and laid it in the baby's crib. Satisfied with his work, he told the spae-wife not to let her patient go past the fire. The spae-wife gave him a look of disdain. As if she would have forgotten any of the precautions!

The spae-wife still wanted him out, so he left, but this time he was only going as far as the neighbour's house, so he would be close if there should be any trouble. But he'd only got as far as the stile when the trows arrived. They realised at once that he had prevented them from getting their prize and, angered, they took all power from him, so with just one leg over the stile, he found he could go no further and was stuck there.

And there he stood, unable to move, for hour upon hour until the spae-wife came out, shook her head at him and freed him.

At first he thought all was well, but the baby soon took to crying and never stopped for eight days. And then it slept, almost lifeless, for another eight days. And then it was hungry and wouldn't stop eating for the next eight days, until they fretted that the older it got, the more the bairn would eat, and they'd never have enough to feed it. But no matter how much it ate, the child was sickly and stupid, and everyone said it didn't look like their child at all.

There could be no doubt that despite all the precautions, the trows had achieved their goal and stolen the baby, replacing it with one of their own: a trowie bairn. And so they consulted the spae-wife to find out what they should do.

Her advice was clear, and they followed it to the letter. First they beat the child with a switch until it howled loudly. Then they held it so near the fire it screamed in pain. And then they set the cradle outside of the house, beyond the shadow of the lintel, and went to their bed.

In the morning, the husband went outside and he found the changeling was no more. All that was left was a pale image huddled lifeless in the little cradle. Their own child was never returned, but at least they were free of the trowie bairn.

19

The hotel was quiet when Jana got back. Baabie was sitting in the corridor knitting, while Mary and Murgen were working in the kitchen. Presumably they had stayed around this long to help out because Ceasg was still confining herself to her room, but Jana had started to wonder where Matheeus was.

She found a chair and sat next to Baabie. 'Where are Ceasg's family?' she asked.

Baabie didn't look up from her knitting. There was a slight pause before she answered, and when she did, her voice was very measured. 'Matheeus is probably oot the back somewhere.'

'I didn't mean Matheeus. Although now that you mention it, he doesn't seem to have been around much lately. I meant her parents, brothers and sisters or whatever. She's just had a baby – and lost her – and none of them's turned up. Where are they?'

Baabie didn't answer.

'Ceasg's a Seatowner so her family are local. They should be here.'

Baabie sighed slightly. 'She's no exactly a Seatowner by birth.'

'What does that mean?'

Baabie still stared intently at her knitting. 'Ye'll have noticed that Ceasg's a wee bit ... different. No quite right in the head. Talks aboot bein' a selkie and suchlike.' She paused for Jana to answer, but when there was no response, she resigned herself to carrying on. 'She disnae ken her own name half the time. She's a poor soul and no mistake. She was found on the West Beach. She'd been living in the cave under the lighthouse. I don't know how long. Naebody kent where she came from and she couldna remember hersel. Matheeus took her in. We all agreed to say she was a Seatowner. Most folk fae the rest of the town wouldna ken if it was a lie or no. And most o' the time neither does Ceasg.'

Jana thought about the remains of the fire she'd seen in the cave. Had Ceasg been back there? But surely she'd have been seen leaving the hotel. At least one of the spae-wives had been sitting outside her door since the birth, and it didn't seem likely that she'd have come down while she was pregnant.

Then she thought – reluctantly – about Serena, who'd appeared from nowhere and believed she was a mermaid. Was it too much of a co-incidence? But now she was thinking about Serena and Ben and how much it hurt. She bit her lip to stop it from quivering, but Baabie no-ticed straight away.

'Men are daft, m'dear,' she said kindly. 'They don't know what's good for them, and they just want whatever looks shiniest at the time.' Her tone made it sound as if there might be some feeling behind that re-mark. She patted Jana's arm. 'It's still raw now, but it'll get better.'

Jana felt a tear roll down her cheek and got annoyed with herself. To avoid looking Baabie in the eye, she looked at the knitting and saw it was a baby's jacket. She looked up again and saw the desperate hope in Baabie's expression.

There was a voice in his head. A familiar voice, although he couldn't remember where from.

I knew you'd come. I've been waiting for you. Come with us. Run away and join the circus.

Slowly he opened his eyes, and immediately wished he hadn't. The light hurt, and everything was blurry, and swayed in a way that made him feel sick. He closed and reopened his eyes a few times, until every-thing stopped moving and the brightness was less painful. Now he could see there was a ring of concerned faces gazing down at him. Father Langstok was there, as were Prince Randian, the tattooed man and Lionel. Then he jumped as he saw the Scary Clowns. There was a guy with no arms or legs, and another who looked like a werewolf, but the ones who made him jump were the two covered in make-up. They might be in a freak show, but it was the clowns who were weird.

'How are you feeling, Adam?' asked Father Langstok.

Adam tried to sit up and his head swam. The tattooed man caught him as he fell back, and helped him into a sitting position, supporting his back once he was up. 'My head hurts. I think. It's hard to be sure. Does anyone know where it is?'

'He'll be alright,' smiled Randian.

'Any idea what happened?' asked Lionel.

'Saw his own face in the mirror probably,' Randian joked. 'That'd make anyone come over all faint.'

'What, after seeing all of us?' said Lionel.

'Speak for yourself, beardy. My wife thinks I'm handsome.'

'Hand*less*, you mean.'

'You're just jealous cos you're not getting any. Anyway, it's either that or he's just a big girl.'

'Don't let Jana hear you say that.' Adam tried to stand, and the tattooed man helped him to his feet. And then caught him when he fell down again.

'Had you been feeling ill?' asked Father Langstok. 'Maybe we should fetch a doctor.'

'I had a sudden headache.' Adam's brow creased. 'Come to think of it, I had one the last time I was here too.' He looked around the tent but there was nothing to see. Except the mirror. The worst horror of them all. He wondered ...

'Who actually runs the circus?' he asked. 'I mean who's in charge?'

Randian frowned. 'Well, we're all in it together,' he said uncertainly.

'Aren't the clowns in charge?' asked Lionel. 'They're the ringmasters.'

'I think they decide where we go too,' added the tattooed man. 'I'm pretty sure they decided to come here.'

'Yeah, but we're more of a collective aren't we?' said Randian. But he sounded more like he was hoping someone would confirm it for him.

'We all just do our own thing,' agreed Lionel. 'We have our own jobs, our own responsibilities.'

Adam looked around the circle of people staring down at him. They weren't sure who ran their own circus. And oddly, the clowns had remained silent on the question of their own role.

'*Do* you run things?' Adam asked them.

There was a pause before Mr Coco answered, 'We may have taken on an administrative function. From time to time.'

'Bookings, advertising, itnerarararies,' added Mr Wobbly, getting lost among the syllables.

'Someone has to,' concluded Mr Coco.

'So is it your circus?'

'No.' This time the response was surprisingly quick. But it was followed by an awkward pause, before Mr Coco said, 'It's everyone's circus. A collective, like they said.'

'So you're not in charge,' Adam pressed.

'Not as such, no.' An uncomfortable edge was creeping into Mr Coco's voice. 'We make certain decisions because that's our job, but everyone's ... ' he searched for the words, 'master of their own fate. They do their own thing. Let it all hang out,' he concluded, with less certainty than usual.

'Sometimes we 'ave to 'ave a chat with 'em about that,' added Mr Wobbly, 'cos it frightens the old ladies.'

'How did the circus first start?' asked Adam.

'Before our time,' said Randian. 'It's been around for about forty years. Someone *was* in charge back then. BD Burnheim. Great showman, so they say. Started with the mermaid and other stuff like it, expanded into the freak show, and eventually added the circus. Huge in its day, very famous. When he died, everyone just sort of kept going, I think. No-one really took over. It's been that way since long before any of us joined.'

'And when did you two join?' said Adam to the clowns. But while everyone's attention had been on Randian, they must have slipped out.

He looked again at the mirror. The worst horror of them all ...

Now that he had his mermaid, Ben had stopped looking. He didn't go out in the boat any more. He didn't search for evidence. He didn't even lecture people on folklore. It wasn't just that he had the evidence in front of him. It was more like he was under some sort of spell. Not just infatuation or even love. He walked around in a daze, barely aware of anything except his mermaid.

Even Doctor Vleerman's theory about Serena's legs didn't seem to arouse his scientific curiosity. A few days ago he'd have been ploughing his way through any medical research Vleerman could have provided, and he would have been discussing it at length with Adam and Jana. Especially Jana. Why wasn't he discussing it at length with Jana?

'You're staring.'

Jana jerked her head up and saw Mary putting her soup on the table. 'I wasn't!'

'No, of course you weren't,' smiled Mary. 'And when you're eatin' your soup you'll try and make it a wee bit less obvious.' She patted Jana's arm and returned to the kitchen.

Jana raised a spoonful of soup towards her lips and tried not to stare. Tried really hard. For longer than was absolutely necessary. They were holding hands. And gazing into each other's eyes. And he was brushing her hair off her forehead. He'd never brushed Jana's hair off her forehead. Which was a good thing because that was soppy and girly and –

'Are you going to eat that or just let it dribble all down your shirt?'

Jana jerked in surprise and dropped the spoon. The splash made a pattern on her, complimenting the one that had already dribbled there. She banged her fist on the table in frustration and looked at Adam as he sat down.

'I wasn't staring,' she said hotly.

'No?' He used his finger to mop up some of the soup that now adorned the table, and licked it.

'No,' she said firmly. Then, more quietly, 'I was gazing. It's different.'

Adam nodded sagely, having no idea of what the difference was. 'I know I'm not very good at this stuff, but I at least know that you're upset, and it's because of them, and it's really not doing you any good. And *because* I'm not very good at this stuff, I have no idea what I'm supposed to do about it but, well, I am your friend, so if you tell me what I should do, I'll try and do it. Cos I don't like you being upset.'

She looked him in the eye and a tear trickled out of hers, but she managed a weak smile at the same time. 'Maybe you're not so hopeless

243

after all.' She squeezed his hand gratefully. 'Just keep me occupied so I don't think about it too much. And sometimes just give me a hug for no particular reason.'

'Will that make it better?'

'No but it'll help. A bit.'

Adam nodded, even though he still wasn't entirely comfortable with the hugging part. But distraction he was good at. He'd sat exams in distraction.

'So where did you run off to earlier?' he asked.

Jana glanced around to make sure no-one was listening, and then she leaned forward conspiratorially. She opened her mouth to speak but realised Adam hadn't leaned forward conspiratorially too. Shaking her head, she grabbed him and pulled him closer, and told him about her encounter with Doctor Vleerman. 'I don't think it was him you saw on the beach,' she concluded.

'You've changed your opinion,' said Adam in wonder. 'You're ... you're not admitting that you were *wrong* are you?'

'Shut up! I tested a hypothesis and the evidence disproved it. That's how science works.'

He tried not to smirk at her, but didn't try too hard because he wanted her to see him trying not to smirk at her. She did and scowled back. But then she broke into a smile. He was distracting her and she knew it.

'So who was it then?' asked Adam, returning to the subject. 'And what were they doing?'

'You're sure it was a man?'

'Pretty sure.'

Jana leaned close again and almost whispered. 'Have you seen Matheeus lately?'

Adam looked at her in shock. 'You think he'd drown his own baby?'

'I don't know what to think,' sighed Jana sitting back. 'We still don't even know for sure it *was* the baby. It might have been a cabbage for all we know.'

'But you can't stand not knowing, can you?' Adam grinned at her again. 'You never can.'

'I know, I know. I turn everything into a mystery so I can solve it. But there really is a missing baby. And the local Watch don't seem to be doing anything about it.'

'There's definitely something going on here,' agreed Adam, trying not to glance at Ben and Serena kissing. But Jana caught his gaze.

'And those two are part of it somehow,' she sighed. 'It's alright,' she added, seeing Adam's concern at failing to distract her. 'I can't avoid them for ever. And, despite my personal involvement almost certainly clouding my judgement, it is weird the way he's been acting since she showed up.'

'It's not just you,' Adam confirmed. 'It's almost like he's under some kind of spell.'

'Like a love potion you mean?' asked Jana, her enthusiasm for magic undiminished.

'Maybe. Although the priest I met with Father Langstok said something about mermaids bewitching sailors. What was it?'

'A special scent!'

'Yeah, that's right. How did you know?'

'Ben talked about it too. It reminded me of some research I'd read about animals being able to smell when others are in heat.'

'You mean they can smell sex?' asked Adam.

'Well, something like that. Maybe mermaids have something similar that makes them, I don't know, irresistible or something.'

'You think she's really a mermaid then?'

Jana shrugged.

'But why only Ben?' Adam continued. 'If she has some magic smell, why isn't everyone affected? Why not me or anyone else?'

'Maybe something happened when she rescued him. I don't know. Maybe some chemical transfer.' She didn't say how this transfer might have occurred, but even Adam could guess, and knew it would hurt her to say it.

'Will ye both be comin' to the wedding tonight?'

They both looked up in shock. Mary had returned to clear away Jana's plate. She gave a disapproving look when she saw that Jana had hardly touched her soup. Then she registered the look in both their eyes. Realising what they were thinking, Mary gave Jana a reassuring smile. 'Abgal and Maisie's wedding.'

Jana practically deflated with relief. 'Oh, right. I thought the wedding was tomorrow.'

'The marriage is tomorrow but tonight's the fit-washin' night.'

'The what?'

'Fit-washin'. They wash the bride and groom's feet.'

Jana turned her nose up. 'That sounds ... hygienic. Why would they want to do that?'

'It's tradition. And a bit o' fun for the lassies. Ye'd both be welcome.'

'I'm not really the traditional type,' muttered Jana. 'Anyway, we've got a dinner appointment tonight.'

'Well, if you change your mind, I'm sure there'd be time for both. Are you having anything to eat, Adam?'

'That soup looks good,' he said hopefully.

'I'll get you a fresh bowl.' She bustled off with the uneaten soup.

Jana looked across at Ben and Serena again. 'I'm going for a walk. You coming?'

She got up and took a step towards the door, before turning back to look at Adam enquiringly. He realised the question had been rhetorical and he was expected to follow. Looking longingly towards the kitchen, from which emanated the appetising smell of soup, he gave a resigned sigh and didn't dare disobey.

The Palatine had been silent as they rowed back to the shore, and Albert knew better than to ask questions. Even when they had returned to their coach he had said nothing, and eventually Albert had asked the coachman to drive along the seafront until the Palatine was ready to tell them what he wanted to do.

They drove past the lighthouse and into Anterwendt. They passed the hotel, wound through the streets and skirted the square, turned right at the harbour and headed along the promenade. The Palatine leaned out of the window and looked intently at the *Sapphire* as they passed it. Then he sat back and lost himself in his thoughts once more.

As the river came in sight, the Palatine suddenly knocked on the ceiling, signalling the driver to stop. He peered out of the window.

'That, I presume, is the Seatown. Source of the local mermaid legends and site of the mysterious crop and horse blight. Mortasheen I believe it was called. Shall we go and take a look?'

Albert was used to his master's sudden whims, and followed Lord Reitherman as he slipped from the coach and strode towards the Seatown. Albert gave the driver a knowing look as they left.

The Palatine took deep breaths of the sea air as they walked, and used the word 'bracing' a little too often for Albert's liking. The secretary breathed more modestly, and was fairly sure he could manage without being braced.

As they walked among the cottages, the Palatine looked carefully at them all, even glancing in the windows when he could. 'Do you see all the mermaids, Albert?'

'Er, no, sir. I don't see any at all. Not a single one I'm afraid. Perhaps I'm not – '

'Exactly, Albert. Not a single one. This isn't mermaid country. They may have old legends, but that's all they are. Mermaids aren't important to these people at all.'

'Then why – '

'But agriculture is. Even though fishing is their bread and butter – if you'll excuse the rather garbled metaphor – *actual* bread and butter are important too.' He pointed to a far corner of the hamlet. 'That field would appear to be where the bread comes from.'

Albert peered at it. 'I don't think so, sir. That's barley.'

The Palatine smiled mysteriously. 'Well done, Albert. I stand corrected by your superior knowledge. I had indeed thought that it was wheat or corn. Barley is, of course, used mainly for animal fodder, soups and making alcohol. However, if you'll forgive me, I believe these people originated in a culture where they make something called barley bread. Either way, the crop is very important to them.'

As they walked towards the small field, a man came from one of the cottages to meet them.

'Can I help ye, gentlemen?' he asked.

'Do forgive the intrusion. My name is Adolf Reitherman, this is Albert Munster. We are friends of Adam and Jana, with whom I believe you may be acquainted.'

'Oh aye? Well, they call me Pilot, and if ye're a friend o' theirs then ye must be a good sort. Will ye have a cuppa and some tea brak?'

'That sounds delightful,' grinned the Palatine, 'and we'd love to take you up on it later, but we'd heard from Adam that you might be having a problem. Something I believe you call mortasheen?'

Pilot looked grave. 'Aye. Weel. No doot a'body's heard by noo.'

'There's a slight chance that we may be able to provide some assistance. Would it be an imposition if we were to take a look?'

'I doot onybody can help, but you're welcome to try. An' even if ye fail, ye'll still get that cuppa.'

He led them to the field, and Albert knelt down to examine the barley. Pilot and the Palatine stood and watched. Albert briefly looked at the stalks and heads, but quickly turned his attention to the leaves. Even then he only gave the upper leaves a cursory glance before moving to the lower ones. To Pilot it almost looked as if he knew what to look for.

There were small patches of a fluffy greyish-white growth on the upper surfaces of the leaves. Some had tiny black spots on them. He scraped one patch with his fingernail, and it came off easily. He turned some of the leaves over, and saw they were turning yellow rather than the green of the upper sides. He nodded slowly.

'What do you think, Albert?'

'It's powdery mildew, sir. No mistake. I sometimes get it on my cabbages.'

'You looked like you were expecting it,' observed Pilot.

'Well, it's the right sort of climate for it,' explained Albert. 'Cool and wet. The islands your ancestors come from even more so. And barley is one of the plants it commonly affects. So I knew what to look for, yes, but it's not really what I was expecting.'

'Why not?' asked Pilot.

'Because, from what I've been told, this mortasheen that blights the crops on your islands is devastating. Powdery mildew reduces the yield and affects the taste, but it doesn't decimate the crops. But more than that, it shouldn't affect the horses.'

'Perhaps whatever is affecting the horses is unrelated,' suggested the Palatine.

'I suppose that's possible, sir, but again it doesn't fit with the historical mortasheen.'

'Maybe this isn't a case of mortasheen.'

'Maybe. But it's a strange coincidence, don't you think?'

'Would it help to see the horses?' asked Pilot.

'I'm no vet,' said Albert, getting up and rubbing off his hands, 'but I'm willing to take a look. And I'd like to spend some more time examining the barley. I might find something else.'

'Stay as long as you like, Albert,' said the Palatine. 'This is your area of expertise and I can be of little use to you I fear. I'm going to pay that visit to Father Langstok. I'll come back here when I'm finished. It's not far to the Mission, so I'll walk and leave the coach at your disposal.'

Once he had gone, Pilot took Albert to see the horses. There were only two in the whole Seatown, and both were stabled in the barn not far from the barley field. Before Pilot had opened the door, Albert could hear that the horses were distressed. Once they were inside, he saw the bay horse was frantically rubbing its side against the barn wall, trying to scratch an itch. The black one stood tossing its head from side to side in a rhythmic pattern.

'They're baith mad,' said Pilot.

'So I see,' said Albert. 'Can I get closer to them? I mean, is it safe?'

'They still seem to accept people so far.'

As if in answer, the black horse took a step towards them. It limped. Albert tentatively approached and placed his hand on the horse's side. It did not react. Albert nodded and withdrew his hand.

'It's hot. And lame.'

'The other one's been scratchin' at that same itch for hours,' said Pilot. 'It's a shame to look at.'

Albert looked thoughtful. 'Lame already,' he mused.

'What do ye mean 'already'?' asked Pilot. 'You do know what it is.'

'Not yet. Not for certain. But this is more like what I was expecting.'

'So what is it?'

Albert shook his head. 'It still doesn't make sense. I need to go back out to the field.'

249

The Palatine walked carefully around the museum, taking in every detail with fascinated interest. The secret door had delighted him, and now he was enthusiastically examining each exhibit with an appraising eye. He chuckled at the story of Bartholomew de Gladville, which he read twice, pored over the woodcut of the Borné See-wyf, and carefully examined the empty cabinet that had once housed the Haerlem mermaid. But what captured his attention the most was the tortoise-shell comb, or rather the card accompanying it. He read and reread the brief legend, and then stood lost in thought for several minutes. Finally, he replaced the card exactly as he had found it, and left by the second door.

Seeing Father Langstok's expectant face, he gave him a broad smile. 'Most impressive, Father. And very entertaining. Such a pity your star exhibit was stolen. Who would do such a thing?'

'Presumably whoever stole the one from the circus too,' said Father Langstok sadly.

'Are you aware there is another in the private collection of Albertus Seba, the apothecary?'

Father Langstok brightened a little. 'Why no, I didn't know that. I should very much like to see it, if it were at all possible.'

'Easily arranged,' smiled the Palatine. 'I'll take you to meet him sometime if you like.'

'Oh, that's most kind of you,' said Father Langstok happily. 'I'm sure there'll be lots of fascinating items there.'

'Indeed,' agreed the Palatine. 'My own visit was a little brief, but I should love to go back for a longer one. Now, do you by any chance have some charts of the local waters?'

'Why yes. I have some for the fishing museum. They're not on display at the moment, but I can easily get them for you. They're historical, so they may be a little out of date, I'm afraid.'

'That's quite alright. Better, in fact.'

Father Langstok raked around in a cupboard for a few minutes, and eventually emerged with some rolled up papers. He spread them out on a table and the Palatine pored over them, his brow deeply furrowed.

'What is it that you're looking for?' asked Father Langstok.

'I'm not entirely sure. It may not be here at all, or may appear to be something else entirely. Tell me, Father, are there any local stories of people seeing mysterious lights at sea?'

'Not that I know of. Why?'

'Are you aware of any underground cave systems or channels?'

'Nothing of that sort, I'm afraid.'

'Not even in legends?'

'I don't think so.'

'And the lighthouse caves only extend a short distance?'

'There's really only one. It's a long time since I was last there, but I did explore it in my younger, more adventurous days, and it was rather disappointing.'

The Palatine scanned the charts again. 'Then perhaps I'm wrong. But how else ... ?' He thought silently for a few minutes, and then suddenly looked directly at Father Langstok. 'Or perhaps it's someone else who's wrong!'

Father Langstok looked back at him in bemusement. 'I'm sorry?'

The Palatine was already heading for the door. 'No need, Father. No need. I'll see you at dinner tonight,' he called as he left. 'And thank you! You've been a great help.'

Never happier than when he was in amongst the flowers and vegetables of his little garden in Phelan, Albert was on his knees in the middle of the barley, sleeves rolled up, hands dirty, relishing the challenge. The leaves here didn't show any of the signs of powdery mildew the ones around the edge did. But the ears showed signs of something else. Some of them were black, and there were blobs of a sticky, white substance dripping down them. The barley a little further out had the same white droplets but not the black ears. The powdery mildew was only at the edges.

Albert slowly became aware he was not alone. He glanced behind himself and saw a little girl standing watching him very seriously. She held a doll, and an otter was capering about her feet. When she saw Albert looking at her, the girl gave him a winning smile.

Albert smiled back. They shouldn't be here, the girl and the otter. In fact no-one should. He'd seen all he needed to. He shuffled around on his hands and knees until he was facing the girl. She giggled.

'Do you know the way out of here?' Albert asked her. 'You see, I'm lost and I don't think I can get out on my own.' The field was barely twenty feet square, and Albert was taller than the barley anyway, although the girl wasn't.

She nodded and held out her hand to him. Albert took it but didn't stand up. Instead he allowed her to lead him out on his hands and knees. As he emerged, he found himself looking at two pairs of boots. He scanned up the legs of the first pair, and saw Pilot looking down at him with a mixture of anxiety and amusement.

Albert didn't need to look up the second trouser leg. He'd know his master's boots anywhere.

The Palatine reached down a hand and helped Albert to his feet. The girl kept hold of his other hand and joined in. Once Albert was properly stood up, the Palatine let go but the girl held on to her new friend.

'Liban, you can let him go now,' said Pilot kindly.

'No she can't,' answered Albert. 'I might fall over.' He winked at her and she giggled.

'I see you made use of the coach,' observed the Palatine. 'It's not where it was parked when I left. Another visit to Albertus Seba?'

'Yes, sir. I needed to have another look at that book I was reading the first time. Crops aren't really my area, so I needed to check.'

'Quite right, Albert, quite right. And have you drawn any conclusions?'

'I'm rather afraid I have, sir.'

'Then you know what it is?' asked Pilot.

'Remember, I'm not an expert, but I'm fairly certain.'

'Not powdery mildew, I take it,' said the Palatine.

'It is on the edge. But only the edge. Almost as if it was there to hide the real problem.' He was unsurprised when the Palatine nodded at this suggestion, but Pilot also picked up on it.

'Hide? Then it *is* deliberate. It *is* mortasheen.'

'Mortasheen may be your name for it, but it's not supernatural. In fact it's quite common. It's ergot.'

'What's ergot?'

'A common disease of crops. The barley in the middle of the field is at an advanced stage, and it's spreading outwards. The recent storm will have encouraged it.'

'And the horses?' asked the Palatine.

'They must have eaten some of the diseased crops. Ergotism can be deadly to animals. And to people. The horses show some of the symptoms mentioned in the book. They won't recover, I'm afraid, and neither will the barley. It'll have to be burned to stop anyone else being poisoned.'

'So mortasheen's a common disease that's written aboot in books?' asked Pilot, slowly coming to terms with the new information.

'It looks like it, yes,' confirmed Albert.

'Not sent by the Nuckleavee?'

'Did anyone actually see this Nuckleavee?' asked the Palatine.

'Well, we all just assumed. The barley was all mildew, the horses were sick.'

'And people attribute it to a demon because they don't understand it.'

'But you said it was deliberate,' insisted Pilot.

'Well, it could just be a coincidence, but it is rather odd that all the barley around the edges of the field has a completely different disease. And a much less harmful one. If I hadn't gone deeper into the field I'd never have known, and it all would have stayed a mystery.'

'But who would do such a thing?' asked Pilot. 'And why?'

'Indeed,' said the Palatine. 'Perhaps someone who *wanted* you to believe it was the Nuckleavee. Someone who wanted to frighten you.'

'And someone who knew how to cause the diseases in the first place,' added Albert.

'There seems to be a lot to untangle here,' said the Palatine. 'We'll do our best to find you some answers, Pilot. In the meantime, I suggest you get on with burning that barley.'

253

As Adam and Jana walked idly along the harbour, the Palatine's coach drew up alongside them and stopped. The door opened and Lord Reitherman leaned out.

'Hop in Jana. Quickly, please. You're welcome to join us, Adam, but it's Jana I particularly need.'

They both jumped in and the coach sped off out of the city.

'Where are we going?' asked Jana, recognising the road.

'I need you to show me the cave.' He wouldn't say any more.

The coach dropped them off near Dr Vleerman's house, and Jana led them along the path to the beach. As they approached the cave, the Palatine stopped to look up at the lighthouse. He also glanced out to sea, raising an eyebrow as the sun played along the surface. Then he marched up the slope to the cave entrance. He had brought a lantern from the coach, and lit it now so they could see. Everything was as Jana remembered it except ...

'The seaweed looks different. Like it's been moved.'

'I expected as much,' nodded the Palatine. 'The fire's been lit recently too. Strange that the occupant's never here when people come calling.'

'I think they might have been the first time I came,' said Jana. 'When Liban wouldn't let me go in. I saw movement.'

'Let's have a closer look in that seaweed, shall we?' suggested the Palatine, rolling up his sleeves.

'I already did,' Jana reminded him. 'There was nothing there.'

'Perhaps not. But perhaps it's back now. Or perhaps you didn't know what you were looking for. Or,' he grabbed a handful of seaweed and moved it to one side, 'perhaps both.'

The others followed his lead and began reducing the pile. It was not long before they confirmed this time, there was definitely something hidden beneath it. It was made of – or at least covered with – some sort of canvas, and as they uncovered more, it proved to be about six feet long and pointed at both ends, with a large hole in the middle of the top surface.

Albert recognised it immediately. 'It's like that boat in Herr Seba's collection.'

'Indeed,' nodded the Palatine. 'And look.' He moved more seaweed to reveal what looked like a double-headed oar. 'This would appear to confirm Herr Seba's conjecture. The owner must have been out in it when you came before,' he said to Jana.

'I'll tell you something else,' said Adam, running his hand along the canvas. 'I think this is made of the same stuff as that sealskin I touched the other night.'

'Yes, that would make sense,' nodded the Palatine. 'It may actually *be* sealskin. Naturally waterproof, although possibly bolstered with some pitch.'

'You knew this would be here?' Jana asked him.

'Actually no. I was looking for something else, although I suspected there may have been more hidden here.'

'So what were you looking for?'

'Help me move the boat and I might be able to show you.'

They dragged the unusual boat to one side, and underneath there was a hole. The Palatine shone the lantern down it, revealing a set of rough steps. It was difficult to tell whether they were natural or artificial.

'I believe we may have found the covered road used by mermaids to enter Anterwendt unobserved.'

'How come no-one knows about this?' asked Jana. 'It's easy to find.'

'Green Goon,' said Adam. 'Keeps everyone away.'

'Shall we investigate?' smiled the Palatine.

'What if whoever's been living here is down there?' asked Jana.

'Unlikely. They might have dragged the boat over the hole once they were down there, but they couldn't then have covered it with seaweed.'

'Then how do they use the steps at all?'

'Perhaps they don't. But if they do and we meet them, then it'll be another mystery solved. Coming? Stay close, we've only one lantern.'

The steps went down just far enough to allow them all to walk up-right in the underground passage, which then sloped down towards the sea. The further they walked, the colder and damper it became, and there were sounds of water dripping from the rock, which felt slimy to the touch.

They didn't get far. The Palatine's boot kicked something on the ground in front of him. He lowered the lantern to see what it was.

It was a body.

'Ah. Something I hadn't bargained for,' said the Palatine grimly.

They all knelt down for a closer look. The Palatine reached out and turned the unfortunate man over so they could see his face.

'Well, we did solve a mystery after all,' breathed Jana. 'It's Matheeus.'

XIX. The Girl who was Loved by the Trows

*T*here was once a girl whose mother had been taken by the trows when the girl was born. She grew up to be a bonny, bonny lass with big green eyes, full red lips and long, golden hair that fell in waves about her shoulders. Such hair had never been seen in all the islands, and no girl ever wore their hair as free as she did, but whenever she tried to tie it up, it always worked loose and fell about her again. Everyone marvelled at that hair, at the way it shone in the sunlight and out of it, and all thocht it was the bonniest hair they had ever seen in all their days.

The girl was a sweet singer, and she often wandered aboot singing to herself soft airs, lilting melodies and sad laments. People stopped and listened as she passed, and young men lost their hearts, and everyone whispered that her singing was a fairy gift, and her golden hair must be 'the blessing o' them that loves her,' for they believed she was under the special care of the trows.

But a witch was jealous of the girl's golden hair and wanted it for herself. One day, when the girl laid herself down among the hay and sang herself to sleep, the witch crept in with a knife, and cut off her lovely tresses and ran off with them. When the girl awoke and found her hair shorn, she wailed in distress at her loss. She hud to walk home and endure everyone's looks and questions, and she never recovered from her shame. She pined away, the song vanished from her

257

lips and so did the smile, and eventually she lay dead – and still in her teens.

But then, miracle of miracles, her hair began to grow again! And it was restored to its former length before ever the coffin lid was closed.

But the witch never prospered from her terrible act. The trows, who had indeed loved and watched over their bonny lass, cursed her. Her mind became ravelled, she wandered around trowie haunts and was plagued day and night by visions of evil creatures. Whenever she tried to sleep, the trows would wake her with unearthly noises or frightening dreams, so she could never find rest. It went on that way for the rest of her life, until she reached old age, when she was spirited away altogether and never seen again.

20

The Palatine had immediately taken charge of the situation. He had explained that the Anterwendt City Watch was privately rather than state run, and therefore not always reliable if there was no profit to be made. This explained why they had shown little interest in the disappearance of Lorelei. The Palatine had suggested asking Captain Hofstadt of the *Invincible* to investigate the matter instead. He admitted he had an ulterior motive behind this, as he wanted to keep the existence of the passage from the general public for now. He asked his companions to keep it to themselves, and would not explain why, beyond saying it related to the matter of Imperial business he was in Anterwendt to conduct and he wasn't at liberty to discuss it.

Albert was sent in the coach to the naval base to arrange for Captain Hofstadt's arrival, and Jana offered to go to the hotel to inform Ceasg of her husband's death.

As they waited, the Palatine said to Adam, 'Ideally I'd like to post a guard here, to ensure no-one else discovers the passage, but that would deprive us of discovering whoever has been using the cave. We'll have to trust to the legend of Green Goon continuing to keep people away.'

It was half an hour before Captain Hofstadt arrived with the ship's surgeon, who confirmed Matheeus had probably been dead for a couple of days, and that his neck was broken. While foul play was a possibility, there was no evidence of violence, and it was more likely he had slipped on the wet floor.

'Then who covered the entrance?' asked Adam.

No-one had an answer to this, but it was agreed they needed to find the cave's occupant as soon as possible.

Albert suddenly ran out of the cave, stood outside looking upwards for a moment and then ran back in. 'I think I know a way we can keep watch without being seen,' he said excitedly. 'As I understand it, the lighthouse is unmanned, except when it's needed. I think we could see anyone approaching the cave from up there.'

'Capital, Albert!' beamed the Palatine. 'You seem to be unstoppable today.'

Albert blushed.

'They keep a set of keys to the lighthouse at the base, your Lordship,' said Captain Hofstadt.

'Excellent. That avoids any of the locals finding out. I suggest we remove the body and cover the passage entrance. We should also brush our footprints from the sand, so our quarry doesn't know we've been here. Assuming they haven't already seen us. The deceased can be taken back into town for burial. Captain, if you could requisition the keys, perhaps Adam would investigate the lighthouse.'

Matheeus's body was wrapped in a tarpaulin the surgeon had brought, and was loaded on to the coach. The strange boat was replaced and covered with seaweed, and the sand leading up to the cave was brushed clean of footprints. Then the coach headed towards the naval base to fetch the keys.

Two pairs of red eyes watched the activity.

'Thiyve rood yin tang intae a rookel agin.'

'Noo wur in furt.'

It had been agreed that Jana would just say Matheeus had been found in the cave, and there would be no mention of the passage. On the way to the hotel, she'd been annoyed to find herself wondering how she would feel if something happened to Ben. She held her breath to keep from crying, and was shocked to realise that a part of her was thinking the swine would deserve it! She tried to shake the thought out of her head, but she couldn't think about how much it hurt without wanting to hurt *him*. And all she wanted to think about was how much it hurt.

She'd had to take a moment to compose herself before going into the hotel. When she'd told the spae-wives what had happened, Mary had shrieked, Murgen had sat down in shock and Baabie had turned grey and shaken her head in disbelief. None of them stopped her when she walked through the door to the private rooms.

Taking a deep breath, she knocked on Ceasg's door and went in. It was lighter than the last time Jana had been in here, and the curtains were open. Ceasg was sitting on the chair knitting. She looked up and smiled when she saw Jana.

'Hello, Jana. It's nice of you to come and see me. Will you sit down?'

Jana sat on the end of the bed and steeled herself for what she had to say. Ceasg saw her expression.

'What is it?' There was a note of panic in her voice. 'Has something happened? Is it Lorelei?'

'No, Ceasg. It's not Lorelei.' Ceasg relaxed just a little. 'It's Matheeus.'

Ceasg frowned, only slightly. 'I haven't seen Matheeus for a while. Do you know where he's been? Is he back now?'

Jana's throat was dry as she forced the words out. 'Ceasg, I've … I've got some terrible news … '

Ceasg leaned forward and put a hand on Jana's leg. 'It's alright, Jana. You can tell me. We're friends, aren't we?'

She was comforting her! Jana was about to deliver the worst possible news, and had given Ceasg enough of a clue to realise what it was, and Ceasg was comforting her. Was she really so naive?

Jana gently took Ceasg's hand in hers. 'Ceasg, Matheeus is dead. His body was found on the beach. In the cave. We think he slipped and broke his neck.'

She looked hard at Ceasg's eyes for a reaction, but the first thing those eyes did was dart towards the cupboard. The one where she believed Matheeus had locked up her skin. Matheeus's death meant freedom to her.

It was only for a second, and then Ceasg returned her gaze to meet Jana's. 'That's so sad. His mother and father will be so upset. They live in Haerlem, you know.'

261

What a strange reaction, thought Jana. But she also thought, *so Matheeus wasn't an Anterwendter, which may explain why he was happy to marry a Seatowner*. And it occurred to her that the Haerlem mermaid was the one stolen from the Mission. And then she couldn't help herself from thinking, *Ceasg used to live in the cave, and I'd been wondering if she was the one who'd been there recently. Was that strange boat how she arrived there? Did* she *kill Matheeus?*

'Ceasg?'

'Yes, Jana?' Her face looked completely innocent.

'Have you been to the cave recently?'

'Oh, no-one goes to the cave. Green Goon might get them.'

Completely innocent. 'You do know that Green Goon's just a story to frighten children.'

'Of course,' said Ceasg matter-of-factly. 'Because the caves are dangerous at high tide.'

She was obviously reciting it by rote – she knew there was really only one cave – but it was only when Ceasg, who used to live in the cave, said it that it hit Jana. *Because the caves are dangerous at high tide.* That was the reason the adults gave for why they really wanted children to stay away from the cave. Except Jana had been there, and one of the first things she had noticed was the tide didn't come as high as the cave. Not even high enough to cut it off and leave someone trapped there. There was another reason for people shunning the cave – perhaps one forgotten now and replaced with the lies about high tide and Green Goon. And it had to be the passage. The Palatine had said they'd found the covered road used by mermaids to enter the city unobserved. And the Anterwendters didn't like mermaids. Even the Seatowners were superstitious of them. So where did that passage lead?

And now there was another secret Jana wanted to know.

A short track led from the main road to the lighthouse. It didn't look very well travelled, suggesting the lighthouse was infrequently visited.

It was a tall, whitewashed needle with a glass dome at the top, exactly as you expected lighthouses to be. There were no outbuildings, just the pillar of the lighthouse itself, punctuated by windows at intervals, and a single door at its base.

Adam lifted the heavy keyring and selected the one that looked as though it would fit the lock. It didn't, and he had to try three keys before realising the first one did fit after all. He tried to turn it, but it was stiff. Presumably it hadn't been used for some time. Even the storm apparently hadn't merited the use of the light.

It took a few minutes before the key consented to turn, and Adam hurt his wrist in the attempt. He shook his hand in the way people with sore wrists inexplicably do, and then wished he hadn't, in the way people who have just shaken their sore wrists and made them hurt even more, invariably do.

He pushed at the door but it was stiff. Perhaps it had swollen and was stuck in the frame, or dropped on its hinges and was catching on the floor, but it wouldn't budge. He tried lifting it by the handle and then put his shoulder to it. It moved about an inch and then stopped. He gathered his breath and tried again. Another inch. Gritting his teeth, he kept at it, lifting and pushing, lifting and pushing, until eventually there was enough of a gap to let him in.

It was, of course, dark inside, but Captain Hofstadt had shown the foresight to provide a lantern. Adam lit it and swung it into the darkness. Straight away he saw the floor was covered in dust.

And footprints.

A trail of small, child-sized footprints led up the stairs. But that door couldn't have been opened for months at least. He went back outside, and quickly walked around the base of the lighthouse, but there was no other entrance, no cracks in the wall a child might squeeze through, and the windows were all too high for even an adult to reach. And they couldn't be old footprints, because they'd have been covered over with more layers of dust by now. How could a child have got in here?

He shone the light around the chamber at the bottom, which turned out to be a store room. Taking a deep breath, he put a foot on the stair and began the spiral ascent. Normally, he didn't like spiral stairs, as he always felt like he might fall off, but this one had walls on either side, with occasional doors up the outer wall. He tried the keys in the first door, and it opened into a small kitchen-cum-dining room. There were a table and chairs, a small stove and some cupboards. Despite not being in regular use now, clearly the lighthouse had been designed for permanent occupants at one time. Again, the room was dusty, but there were signs someone had been in here recently. The dust on the table had been disturbed, and there were marks on the floor where the chairs had been moved.

Adam continued upstairs to the second door. He tried every key in the lock three times, but although one fitted, none would turn, and the door was firmly locked. After trying for a few minutes, he gave up and carried on to the third door. This opened easily into another dusty room, which contained a desk and chair with charts and a ledger. The last entry was almost five years ago. The lighthouse had apparently been out of use for a long time. But someone had been inside very recently. Someone very small.

He climbed the last of the stairs, and emerged on to a railed gallery that went right around the top of the lighthouse. In the centre was the lamp, surrounded by glass panels reinforced with metal bars. Another door underneath the lamp led to a small room, with a stack of boxes of what looked like thick, rolled candle wicks and some kegs, which Adam assumed contained oil for the lamp. There was also a small staircase up to the lamp itself.

It was still daylight, so Adam set the lamp down, leaned over the railing and looked out to sea. The waves were calm and a few long-necked black birds he didn't recognise sat idly on the water as the sun sparkled off it. Up this high, there was a bit of a breeze, and a few gulls circled noisily. Something leaped out of the sea and splashed back down again – one of those small whales. Dolphins, was it?

He looked down at the clifftop at the back of the lighthouse. It was all short grass and there was a large mound, which gave way to the edge of the cliff. A few daisies grew in irregular patches, and here and there dandelions and dock leaves.

He walked around the gallery until he was over the beach. He couldn't actually see the cave entrance, but he could see the approach to it. Anyone entering or leaving the cave would easily be seen from here. But there was the likelihood they would see their observer too.

His eye was caught by a thick plume of smoke from the direction of the Seatown. They must be burning the barley, and he wondered about the fate of the two horses.

The breeze became stronger and the gulls' calls louder. For a few seconds it almost sounded like there was one somewhere inside the lighthouse, but it was probably just a trick of the wind. Their shrieks reminded him of babies crying. He put that out of his head, picked up the lantern and headed back around the gallery to the stairs, thinking about how to watch the cave without being seen. On the way down, he tried the middle door again, but to no avail. Compared to the noise above, the inside of the lighthouse was silent.

As he got to the bottom of the stairs, he noticed his own footprints now sat alongside the small ones. A thought struck him, and he used his feet to kick the dust off the second step so that it fell on the bottom one, forming a new layer. Then he went outside and extinguished the lantern. It was just as much effort to close the main door as it had been to open it, and he had to pause for breath before walking back along the track to the road.

The sun was beginning to set as Ben and Serena walked back across the bridge from the East Beach. They were so wrapped up in each other and, frankly, in each other's lips, they didn't notice the two figures coming the opposite way until they met in the middle of the bridge. Even then, they only became aware of them when one spoke.

'Fine evening, Ben.' There was no friendliness in Pieter's voice.

'Oh, hi Pieter,' replied Ben. 'Rutger. Didn't see you there. Have you met Serena?'

It didn't occur to him that the two fishermen were completely block-ing their way across the bridge.

'Serena is it?' asked Pieter. 'No, we haven't met.' He smiled at her, a leering smile that made her clutch Ben's arm and pull closer to him. 'But we have heard about her, haven't we Rutger?'

'What? Oh, yeah,' said Rutger nervously.

'People say she's a real live mermaid. Is that true, love? Are you a real live mermaid then?'

Serena edged slightly behind Ben, who finally began to realise something was wrong.

'What's up, love?' pressed Pieter when he got no answer. 'Sea Witch got your tongue?' He sniggered at his own stupid joke.

'Can you let us past, Pieter?' asked Ben.

'Now that's not very polite,' said Pieter in mock offence. 'We're just trying to have a nice conversation, and you don't want to give us the time of day. What, we not good enough for the like of you?'

'Come on, Pieter. You're frightening her.'

'Oh, we are sorry, aren't we Rutger?' said Pieter mockingly. Rutger smiled weakly. 'We don't want to frighten the mermaid, do we? She might sink our boats if we start doing that.'

'Everything alright, lads?'

No-one had noticed Ben and Donny Varrey, with Liban and Draatsie in tow, approaching behind Pieter and Rutger. The two Anterwendters shuffled nervously.

'Yeah, everything's fine, Ben,' said Pieter carefully. 'We'll just let you get past.'

He pulled Rutger to one side to make space for the newcomers to pass. Without taking his eyes off of Pieter and Rutger, Ben Varrey deliberately stood to one side himself.

'We'll just let young Ben and his lassie get through first.' He nodded to the couple. Serena needed no more encouragement and pulled Ben through the gap. She kept pulling once they were past, and they practically ran towards the Seatown.

'Well, we should be going too,' said Pieter and took a step in the same direction. But Ben Varrey put his arm around Pieter's shoulder and wheeled him back in the direction of the beach. Ben Varrey was a big man and Pieter didn't resist.

'Goin' for an evenin' stroll on the beach were you?' said Ben Varrey. 'I'll be glad o' the company.' Pieter and Rutger glanced nervously at Donny and Liban. 'It's getting dark, Donny,' said Ben. 'Take Liban back to the house.'

Donny looked at him uneasily, but didn't protest. 'Come on Liban.' They turned around and headed back to the Seatown. There was a look of relief on Liban's face as they left.

Ben Varrey put his other huge arm around Rutger's shoulder, and the three of them continued across the bridge towards the beach. Donny stopped for a moment and watched as the trio walked away. Liban reached up and took his hand.

'Sorry, Daddy,' she said quietly.

Across on the promenade, two figures watched the whole scene. They couldn't hear what had been said, but they could see Ben and Serena heading off alone, while Pieter and Rutger were steered towards the beach by the big hairy bloke.

'Well, that could have gone better,' said Mr Wobbly.

Mr Coco glared at him and walked away.

The restaurant on the sea front was called *The 1029*. The building had previously been a bakery, but had been disused for years, and when it was being renovated, the workmen had unearthed a foundation stone with those numbers inscribed on it. It was assumed this was the year it had originally been built, and Signor Guido, the Napoletan proprietor, had decided it would be an excellent name for his new business.

Unsurprisingly, the establishment specialised in seafood, but it was a much more sophisticated menu than the one at the hotel, and included a lot of Napoletan and Bretonnian dishes. In fact, it was a more sophisticated menu than Adam had seen anywhere before. He could tell by the prices. Thank goodness the Palatine was paying. Wasn't he?

Adam scanned the menu for something he recognised, but it was full of things he'd never heard of and couldn't pronounce. 'What are mowles mareenyer?' he asked.

Jana smiled indulgently and patted his arm. 'You'll love them,' she said. 'And try the escargots for a starter.'

The Palatine gave her a quizzical look before returning his attention to the menu. 'The calamari looks rather good. And I can never resist langoustine.'

'An excellent choice, signor,' nodded the waiter, who was also Napoletan. 'The langoustine has been particularly good this season.'

Albert seemed unsure that he should really be there. 'Um, everything is so expensive,' he fussed. 'Maybe I should go back to the hotel – '

'Not a bit of it, Albert,' insisted the Palatine. 'You are here as my guest, and very welcome too. If you'll allow me, I'd recommend the champignons condatina, followed by the roast loin of venison.'

'Venison?' spluttered Albert. 'Oh my! I've never had venison before.'

'Which is precisely why you should try it. What about you, Father?'

Father Langstok took off his glasses to wipe the steam from them. 'I'm not used to such rich food,' he said humbly. 'Which is why I'm going to make the most of your generosity and overindulge.'

'Capital!' laughed the Palatine heartily. 'Indulge away.'

'Well, I've always been partial to monkfish, and the lobster bisque sounds delicious. Thank you, your Lordship.'

'Not at all, Father. I'm glad to have you all here.'

Everyone's attention now tuned to Jana. 'Pasta sounds interesting,' she said. 'I'll try the – ' she checked the menu again, ' – spaghetti. Is that how you pronounce it?'

'Eccellente,' grinned the waiter. 'And for the starter?'

'Do you have any herring?'

The waiter was a little taken aback. 'We do not have a herring dish, but it is an ingredient of some dishes.'

'Would the chef be able to make me something with a salt herring?' She gave that sweet smile she always gave when she was trying to persuade someone to do something for her.

The waiter knew what she was doing, but he liked her cheek and knew the chef enjoyed the occasional special request. 'Signor Guido will make you a very nice herring, like no other you ever taste before.'

'And would you bring us two bottles of your very best wine?' asked the Palatine, 'one white, one red. I'll trust your judgement as to the best to accompany our meals.'

'Very good, signor. I bring you something very nice.'

Once the waiter had gone, Adam told them about his experience at the lighthouse. 'If anyone going into the cave looks up at the lighthouse, they'll see whoever's up in the gallery. I went down to the beach

268

to check. Don't worry, I wiped my footprints away.'

'What about the windows?' asked the Palatine. 'Do any of them overlook the cave?'

'They all do. The top one might just be high enough, although it's not a great angle'

'Then it'll have to do,' said the Palatine.

'Er, isn't there another option?' asked Father Langstok with that familiar twinkle in his eye.

'You appear to have something in mind,' said the Palatine.

'Well, our problem is that someone on the lighthouse gallery would be seen by anyone looking up from the cave entrance. So what we want is for them to be there without being seen.' He looked meaningfully at Adam.

Jana was the first to realise what he meant. 'Magic!' She clapped her hands in excitement. 'Adam's an illusionist. Not being seen is what he does. I've seen it. Well, sort of.'

'How about it, Adam?' asked the Palatine. 'Could you do it?'

'Not from that distance. I couldn't get inside their head.'

'That's a shame,' said the Palatine as the waiter brought the starters.

'Your calamari, escargot, the bisque, champignons, and for signorina, chef has prepared polenta and herring with sautéed mushrooms and a tapenade.'

'Thank you very much,' smiled Jana. 'It was kind of him to do that for me.'

'Is no trouble. Enjoy your food.'

As the waiter left, Adam gave Jana a questioning look, wondering why she had specifically asked for herring. Then he turned his attention to his own plate. It was a little metal tray with twelve shells on it. He assumed they were some kind of shellfish. Laid next to the tray were a set of tongs and a two-pronged fork. Presumably he had to hold the shells with the tongs and extract the escargot with the fork. He did so, and pulled out a grey scaly thing. It appeared slimy, not at all like the lobster. He looked uncertainly at the others, who were all watching him expectantly.

'Go on,' Jana encouraged him. 'Try it.'

He held it up and sniffed it. Garlic. And possibly wine. That didn't seem so bad. He steeled himself and put it in his mouth. It didn't taste like the lobster either. It had a strange, chewy texture he didn't recognise. It tasted mainly of garlic, and was that chicken? Hmm, that was alright. It was unusual but not unpalatable. They were all still watching him for some reason, so he nodded his approval and went for the second one. The others smiled to each other before attacking their own food.

As Jana took her first bite, her expression changed to a look of horror. They all followed her gaze to the door, which had just opened.

Ben and Serena were coming in.

Neither of them appeared to notice the group as they were led to a table in a far corner out of sight. Everyone looked warily at Jana. She stared icily in the direction the new arrivals had gone. Eat a salt herring, Baabie had told her with a glint in her eye, and your future husband will appear with a draught of cold water to quench your thirst. And, scientist that she was, Jana had done it. She'd given in to superstition because her head had been turned by a nice smile. And now that nice smile had walked in with someone else on his arm. Someone who apparently smelled better. Jana gritted her teeth and returned to eating her food. The others exchanged glances before doing the same. They all noticed when, just as Adam scratched his leg, she transferred her fork to her left hand so she could put her right below the table. They also noticed when Adam winced and then picked up his fork with a hand that now had four fresh scars on the back.

'The calamari is very nice,' said the Palatine conversationally. 'How are your mushrooms, Albert?'

'Oh, they're delicious, sir. Better than any I've tasted.'

'I am pleased.'

Ben Varrey was a hairy man. His long, unkempt hair covered his head like gorse. His beard was so bushy that his namesake could probably have found three undiscovered species nesting in it. His bushy eyebrows met in the middle, and his ears and nostrils sprouted unappealing growths. His lavishly carpeted chest, so thick it could have been plaited, had earned him the nickname 'Bear', while his equally hairy back, thicker than most men's chest hair, had earned him the screams of any women who had actually seen him bare. His arms and legs were like fir trees, so hairy that when he rolled up his sleeves or trouser legs, no-one noticed, and his hands and feet were covered in hair down to the knuckles. He could walk bare legged in the snow and still feel warm. If he stripped naked, he'd be shot and mounted on a wall. His hairy backside was the only proof that he wasn't in fact some undiscovered species of baboon. Even his internal organs were hairy. And most mornings his tongue was furry too.

He had walked Pieter and Rutger along the beach and back in uneasy silence. Uneasy, that was, for Pieter and Rutger, who spent most of the time wondering if they would end up buried like pirate treasure. But, apart from keeping a firm grip on both men's shoulders, Ben had done nothing to them except steer them to the end of the beach, and then turn them around and march them all the way back again.

As they reached the end of the dunes and were about to turn towards the bridge, Ben stopped, which inevitably meant Pieter and Rutger stopped too. Ben was looking intently at the sea. Then he looked up at the sky, scanning around as if looking for something before returning his gaze to the water.

Pieter and Rutger tried to see what had caught his attention. The sea was calm and motionless except for where the slight motion of the waves was illuminated by the moonlight. There was nothing remarkable or even interesting, although someone other than Pieter or Rutger might have found the light pretty.

They looked up at the sky but there was nothing there either. It was a bit overcast, so few stars were visible and the moon was hidden behind a cloud.

Oh.

They looked again at the patch of moonlight on the water and wondered where it was coming from.

As the waiter brought the main courses, the Palatine asked, 'How did you enjoy your escargot, Adam?'

'I wasn't sure at first, but it turned out to be quite nice.'

The waiter put the new plates on the table. 'For the lady, spaghetti carbonara. The langoustine for signor, the monkfish, your venison signor and the moules marinier.'

Adam looked at his plate in mild surprise. 'More shellsfish?'

The waiter frowned. 'More, signor? No. Shellfish, yes, but no-one else has had the shellfish.'

'But the escargot – '

'Ah, no signor. Escargot is lumache. Snails. Enjoy your meals.'

Even Jana managed to smile at the look of horror on Adam's face.

'Snails? I was eating *snails?*'

'But you said you enjoyed them,' the Palatine reminded him.

'Yes but ... ' He looked down at his main course, and looked back up at the Palatine with a pleading expression.

The Palatine chuckled. 'Don't worry, those are mussels. I'm sure you'll find them delicious.'

Jana was examining her spaghetti with a perplexed look. She lifted it with her fork to see how long it was. 'How do I ... ?' After a few attempts, she finally managed to wind some on to her fork and make it stay there long enough to get it to her mouth. Then she found her only option seemed to be to suck the strands until she got to the end. And they splashed sauce all over her face. There was a sudden tension as the others waited to see if she would explode. Instead, and in spite of herself, she laughed and everyone relaxed.

Adam did enjoy the mussels, even though they tasted pretty much like the snails. Albert seemed almost afraid to eat his venison, as if he was scared someone would come and arrest him for being so presumptuous, but once he started, his expression changed to one that could only be described as rapturous.

When they'd all finished and the plates were being cleared away, the Palatine asked, 'Anyone for dessert?'

Adam looked hopeful but Jana immediately said, 'Thank you, but we have an engagement to keep in the Seatown. We promised Mary we'd be there.'

'Did we?' asked Adam.

'Yes. Yes we did. But thank you very much, Lord Reitherman. This meal has been wonderful, and it was very kind of you to invite us. Sorry we have to leave so early.'

'Not at all, Jana, not at all. I have another engagement myself tonight, although I could still squeeze in something sweet first. What about anyone else? Father?'

'Oh, I'm very tempted,' smiled the Father, 'but if I gave in, then I'd have to do some sort of penance. But thank you for a lovely evening.'

The Palatine turned to Albert, who looked like he desperately wanted dessert but was still a little unsure about asking. 'Just you and me then, Albert. You really should try the tiramisu.'

Albert looked like he was in love.

As they walked towards the Seatown under the moonless sky, Adam asked Jana as casually as he could manage, 'So are you okay now?'

'I'm fine,' she answered, but something in her voice made him glance at her to check. There was a tear rolling down her cheek, and her mouth was tightly set.

'That's good,' said Adam, awkwardly. 'So where is it we're going?'

'That foot washing thing, remember?'

'I thought you weren't the traditional type.'

'Shut up.'

Adam knew he should probably do or say something helpful and comforting at this point, but he had no idea what, so he decided to do as he was told and shut up.

Mary hadn't actually told them where to go, but they followed the sound of giggling and soon found themselves at the door of Mary's shop. Mary answered the door and beamed at Jana.

'Ye made it after all! Good. We're just started.' Then she looked at Adam with a mock scowl. 'But you canna be here yet. It's too early for the menfolk. Ye'll have to go away an' come back.'

'But you said we should both – ' began Adam.

'Shut up, Adam'

Adam looked sharply at Jana and tried not to glare. He briefly wondered whether being hurt gave her the right to be so mean to him, and then he remembered that she was mean to him when she was happy too. He had the scars and bruises to prove it.

'The bridegroom and the other lads can't come in until nine o'clock,' explained Mary, 'so you'll have to go and find something else to do until then. Go on. Away wi' you.'

She ushered Jana inside and closed the door on Adam, who stood nonplussed for a moment before walking away with a forced casual gait.

Jana was taken into Mary's parlour, where Maisie was sitting on a stool next to a tub of water. Three young women sat around her on the floor, giggling and chatting. Mae sat in one of the chairs and in another was Mary's mother, Willemena, who had come through form the bedroom for the occasion.

'We're just startin',' Mary told Jana. 'Sit wi' the lassies and join in.'

'What am I supposed to do?' asked Jana uncertainly.

'Nothin' yet. We'll tell ye when it's your turn.'

Jana sat on the floor with the younger women, who smiled in welcome and made space for her.

'This is us,' said Mary to the whole company. 'On ye go, mither.'

Willemena looked theatrically around at them all before speaking. 'First of a', the bride's mither removes the bride's shoes and stockings.'

Mae knelt at Maisie's feet and carefully unbuckled the bride-to-be's shoes. She pulled them off, and ceremoniously placed them on the floor. Then she rolled down Maisie's stockings, folded them and placed them on top of the shoes.

'Now,' continued Willemena, 'the bride's feet must be pulled ower the water. In a sunwise direction, mind,' she added sharply as Mae grasped Maisie's bare feet and moved them slowly over the tub.

'An' noo the blessing,' said Willemena.

Mae gently patted Maisie's right foot while reciting, 'May the sun and the moon and the sea look favourably on this blissful union.' Then she patted the right foot and again said, 'May the sun and the moon and the sea look favourably on this blissful union.' Then she pushed Mae's feet downwards, immersing them in the water.

This apparently was the sign for the three younger women to dive forward, plunge their hands into the water and begin scrubbing Mae's feet, giggling and laughing as they did so. Mary gave Jana an encouraging nod, and with a shrug, Jana rolled up her sleeves and joined in. There was a lot of good-natured jostling, and Jana could feel the myriad hands scrabbling about at the base of the tub, as if searching for something.

Her own hand brushed against something metallic, and she picked it out and held it up to see what it was. There was a mixture of squeals and sharp intakes of breath from Mae and her friends as they saw the ring in Jana's hand. Jana looked questioningly at Mary but everyone else's head turned to Willemena for confirmation.

'Weel done, lass, weel done,' laughed the old woman. 'Ye've foond the ring. D'ye ken whit it means?'

'That someone won't have to explain to her husband how she lost it?'

'It means, lass, that you will be the next one here to marry! After Mae, of course.'

Jana stared at Willemena. Then she let the ring slip from her fingers back into the water.

There was an awkward silence, broken by Mary saying, 'Right! Meg – go and empty the tub. Shona – fetch the bucket o' sea water. Mairi – round up the menfolk. You've got one hour.' The three young women scurried off to do as they were told, and Mary turned to Jana with a warm smile. 'And Jana – you'll be having a cuppa and some tea brak.'

Without consciously trying, Adam had ended up back at the circus. He had wandered along aimlessly, or so he thought, his mind wandering with an equal lack of purpose, and somehow he found himself standing outside the entrance to the freak show. It was quiet here, although he could hear the sounds of the performance still in progress in the big top. The flap covering the entrance to the freak show had been pulled shut, but it was easy to lift it and slip inside.

He wasn't entirely sure why he was doing this, but some unconscious urge was directing him. He glanced into Prince Randian's tent, but it was deserted. The whole place seemed empty, the performers presumably either having retired to their caravans or involved in the show. The tents were much more unsettling in silent, empty darkness than they were when full of deformed freaks.

His feet took him, unsurprisingly, to the final tent – the Worst Horror of Them All. He hesitated at the entrance, remembering the last time he had been here. Then he steeled himself, took a deep breath and walked in.

Immediately, he felt his head beginning to throb, and a queasy feeling in the pit of his stomach. It was stronger this time. His head swam and he could sense consciousness slipping away. His instinct was to fight it, but somehow he knew this was the wrong thing to do, and he deliberately dropped to his knees and allowed himself to succumb.

He was surprisingly conscious in his unconsciousness. Although it shouldn't have surprised him, because it was exactly what he had expected. It was the way to communicate.

You came back.

'Yes. I came to talk to you.'

Have you come to join the circus?

'Are you in charge here?'

In charge of what?

'The circus people don't know you're here, but you still tell them what to do, don't you?'

I ... suggest. I influence their subconscious minds.

'Why did you talk to me then, if you don't talk directly to them?'

Guess.

'Because we've met before, haven't we? It is you, isn't it? The voice from the monastery. You're Baphomet.'

XX. The Dancing Giants

O ne dark night, a group of giants crossed the causeway from the mainland to the islands. They were ugly and fierce and brutal, and they all wore glowering expressions as they looked around to be sure no mortal had seen them. They stopped in a field and lay down their clubs and axes and other weapons. Then one opened his pack and pulled out, of all things, a battered fiddle, and he began to play.

As the music struck up, the fearsome giants all grinned stupidly, clasped each other's hands, and with whoops and shouts, began dancing. They whirled round and around in a circle, and the ground shook beneath their feet, and people on the other side of the island feared it was an earthquake.

All night they danced and skipped, and they were enjoying themselves so much that they didn't notice the red glow as the sun began to rise. The rays crept across the grass until they touched the skin of the dancing giants. And then the giants stopped dancing, for they had been turned to stone.

And there they stand to this day. The dancing giants became the Great Ring and the fiddler, standing outside the circle, became the first Odin Stane.

But one foggy Yule night, a traveller was sleeping near the causeway when he was woken by a feeling that the earth was trembling. He peered through the fog and saw a number of huge, dark shapes standing at the shore, bending forward for a drink. Scared of what they might be, he crept cautiously away. Once he was far enough from

277

them, he ran up the road, but as he passed the field where he knew the Great Ring to be, he stopped in amazement, for hard as he looked, he could not see a single stone through the fog. And ever since, it's said that each year on Yule night, all the standing stones on the islands move from their spots to the nearest water for a drink.

21

The tub of water had been taken outside, and two chairs carefully placed next to it, side by side, but with a small gap so the moon – which had come out from behind the clouds – could shine between them. Mae sat on one chair with her feet in the tub. Shona and Meg had both arrived back with buckets filled with water – Shona's from the sea and Meg's from the well. Mairi had not yet returned, but some of the menfolk were starting to turn up, most of them laughing and chatting excitedly. Jana noticed Adam was not among them, although Donny and Liban were.

Mary hadn't asked her what was wrong, but Jana was well aware that she didn't need to. They had just drunk tea, and eaten cake and chatted idly. Putting the world to rights, Mary had called it, and while nothing had changed and the world definitely wasn't any closer to being right than it had been before, Jana felt a little better. Maybe that was all Mary had meant.

Eventually Mairi came skipping back, dragging Abgal by the hand. Everyone cheered when they saw him, and Mae blushed a little. Mairi led him to the empty seat and made him sit down. Without having to be told, he took his shoes off and put his feet in the tub next to Mae's. Then Shona and Meg emptied their buckets into the tub, and Mae and Abgal both had their breath taken by how cold the water was.

Suddenly, a long shape scooted over to the tub, and with a cry of dismay, Liban ran over and grabbed Draatsie before she could climb into the water. There was general laughter, and Liban slunk back to Donny looking ashamed, and wagging a finger at the restrained otter.

This time there were no instructions from Mary. She simply nodded to Abgal, who scooped up some water in his hands and began washing Mae's hair.

The chatter had died down now, and everyone watched with something approaching reverence. Even Draatsie behaved. Evidently this was an important ceremony, almost verging on sacred, although Jana couldn't work out why. However, there was obviously something intimate and sensual about it for the bride- and groom-to-be, so perhaps that was the point.

Once Abgal had finished, it was Mae's turn to wash her fiancée's hair. This didn't take nearly as long because, well, his hair wasn't nearly as long as hers. Once she had finished, they were given a towel to dry each other off. Then, while they put each other's shoes back on, Shona took the tub over to a nearby hole in the ground and emptied the water into it. Mary stood over the hole and quietly muttered something Jana couldn't make out, before one of the older men took a shovel and filled in the hole, placing a sod of turf on top.

While this had been going on, Mairi had disappeared back inside, and now she came back out carrying a bowl with two spoons. She gave it to Abgal, and suddenly the excited chatter started up again. Apparently the serious part was over and more fun was about to begin.

Mary leaned close to Jana and whispered, 'That's the kissin' maet. Kissing food,' she explained to Jana's blank expression. 'Limpets boiled in milk and water. They have to eat it now. And do something else besides.'

Jana's heart sank as she realised why it was called the kissin' maet. To squeals from the young women, cheers from the men and laughter and clapping of hands from Liban, Mae and Abgal kissed. Then they each took a spoon and fed each other the limpets until the bowl was empty. Then they kissed again, to one more rousing cheer from the crowd. This seemed to signal the end of the ceremony, and the crowd started either drifting away, or coming and slapping the happy couple on their backs.

Mary looked sidelong at Jana and pouted. 'Maybe it wasna' such a good idea to bring you here,' she said. 'I thought a bit o' fun might cheer ye up, but I suppose ye didna want to see the kissin' and suchlike.

I should've taken a thought to masel'. I'm sorry.'

Jana didn't reply. She just gazed at the bowl and spoons left abandoned on the ground.

Mary looked around at the disappearing crowd. 'I didna see Adam. Where do you think he's got to?'

'Don't know,' said Jana quietly. 'I'll go an find him.'

Mary was about to say there was no need, but then realised there probably was very much a need, so she held her tongue and watched Jana walk away alone.

She was about to walk away herself when she heard an owl hooting nearby. She looked around, and saw it was sitting on the roof of the cottage. Her face fell. An owl on the rooftop could mean only one thing: there was to be a death.

His head full of thoughts he couldn't quite remember, Adam walked back towards the sea front. *Run away and join the circus.* He wasn't sure what it meant, or even where he had heard it. Things were a bit fuzzy. He'd been wandering near the circus, but couldn't recall having gone there. The last thing he remembered was something about snails.

For some reason his legs had taken him in this direction rather than back to the hotel, and he decided to follow them and see where they took him. A few figures were coming up from the Seatown, and as he drew closer, he saw it was Abgal and some of his friends.

'Hey, Adam!' called Abgal. They were all in very good spirits. 'Ye missed the ceremony. I think Jana's already away. We're going for a drink. Will ye come with us?'

'Ummm,' said Adam vaguely, 'thanks but I'm feeling a bit ... Should probably go to bed.'

'You alright?' asked Abgal. 'You look like you've had a few drinks already.'

'Just a bit tired. You go and enjoy yourselves.'

'Alright,' said Abgal, looking mildly concerned. 'You're coming tomorrow though, aren't you?'

'Tomorrow?'

'The wedding.'

'Oh. The wedding. Yeah. Yeah, I'll be there. See you tomorrow.'

They parted company, and Adam walked on towards the harbour. As he drew close, he saw two figures on the deck of the *Renown*. They were in shadow, but he recognised them both by their silhouettes, and stopped to watch. They were apparently deep in conversation, but he was too far away to hear anything. After a few minutes they shook hands, and then the tall thin one climbed down a rope ladder to the harbour wall, while the other stood and watched him leave, before pulling the ladder up. Adam drew further back into the shadows to avoid being seen, and watched the Palatine walk away.

Jana had pulled the chair over to the window and sat gazing out of the upper room of the lighthouse. She had to sit in darkness so as not to alert the cave's occupant, but that suited her. Right now she preferred the dark.

She could see the approach to the cave, but most of her attention was on the sea, rhythmically lapping against the shore, and then receding in preparation for another run up. In the distance, a patch of water was lit by what she presumed must be the moon outside of her limited field of vision. It almost glowed.

As she watched, a shadow leaped out of the lit patch of sea and then splashed back into the water. It had been too quick and too dark for her to see it clearly, but it must have been a dolphin or a porpoise.

Besides the sound of the waves, it was almost silent. The gulls were all asleep, night time being the only respite from their incessant shrieking. How did the locals put up with that all the time, day in, day out?

On her way up the stairs, she had noticed the childlike footprints, including some in the new layer of dust Adam had made, and she wondered if it had been Liban. But there were no Draatsie-sized pawprints accompanying them, and fear of Green Goon would probably keep Liban away from here anyway. But a lighthouse would be a wonderful playground for a child, and she wasn't surprised one had come here for an adventure. She would have done the same.

She kept watching the sea, hoping for another porpoise. Or another lifetime. Maybe it would be nice to *be* a porpoise, just swimming around and leaping out of the water, with no complications or worries, except for where the fish were.

There was a bang. From somewhere inside the lighthouse. Had she left the door open? But there was no wind, and it would take a hurricane to move that door. Had something fallen over? But what would cause it?

Nervously, she got up and looked around for a weapon. There might be something up in the lamp room, but all there was here was the ledger. It would have to do. She picked it up and cautiously opened the door. There was no sound, and so, after waiting to make sure no-one was lying in wait for her, she crept out and started down the stairs. She was sure the noise had come from below rather than above.

As she passed the locked door, she stopped to listen. Could she hear whispers? Almost as soon as she thought it, they stopped, and she wondered if it had been her imagination. She waited longer, but there was no more sound. And then there was, from further down. Someone was coming up the stairs.

Quickly, she flattened herself against the inside wall and raised the ledger above her head. She held her breath so as not to make a sound, and waited for the intruder. A shadow appeared on the wall as the footsteps got closer. The shadow loomed larger and larger, and the footsteps came closer and closer, until she knew they were just seconds away. She darted out and brought the ledger down hard.

'Oh hell, Adam, I'm sorry!'

'Ow.'

'Does it hurt?'

'Of course it hurts, you hit me with a – what *did* you hit me with? The log book. Why did you hit me with the log book, Jana?'

'I'm sorry, I didn't know it was you!'

'Why were you hitting *anyone* with the log book?'

'Well, I heard a noise and I ... '

'You acted like a crazy person, like you always do. There's gonna be a lump.'

'I'm really sorry. Really.'

'I know you are. I just wish sometimes you'd decide not to inflict the physical abuse on me, so you wouldn't have to be sorry at all.'

'What are you doing here?'

'I could ask you the same question. But I don't need to.'

'I'm keeping watch.'

'Yes,' said Adam, following her up to the top room, 'Lord Reitherman said that you'd come here to do that. And Mary told me about the foot washing thing. You came here to hide from everyone, didn't you?'

'Someone's got to keep watch for whoever's living in the cave,' she said quietly.

'I'll watch with you then.'

'There's only one chair.'

'That's alright. I was going to lie on the floor and moan softly for a while until the pain went away.'

She almost smiled. 'I really am sorry.'

'Is there a part of me left that you haven't injured in some way?' he asked, as he leaned his back against the wall next to the window and slid slowly down until he was sitting on the floor. Jana took up her position looking outwards again.

'Did you fall over something on your way in?' asked Jana.

'No, you hit me with a book, remember?'

'The banging.'

'What banging?'

'There was a bang when you came in. That's how I knew someone was there.'

'I didn't hear anything.'

'You mean it wasn't you?'

'No. Maybe a bird flew into the glass up above. That'd be why you heard it and I didn't.'

'Maybe. Come with me while I go and check.'

Adam closed his eyes. 'There's no-one up there. You go and I'll be unconscious for a few minutes.'

Jana hesitated, hoping he'd change his mind, but when he didn't, she picked up the ledger and went by herself. She was only gone a few minutes before he heard her come back.

'You were right, look.'

Adam opened his eyes to see whatever it was she wanted him to see. Lying on the book was a mottled grey-brown bird, a little bigger than his hand, not including the tail and the wings, which were spread awkwardly. Its eyes were closed and there was blood around its beak. At first he thought it might be a kestrel, but when Jana brought it closer, he realised it wasn't even a bird of prey.

'What is it?' he asked.

'I think it's a nightjar. It had flown into the glass around the lamp.'

'Why did you bring it down here?'

'To look after it, of course. It's still breathing.'

'And when you've nursed it back to health, we're going to have a bird flying around inside, desperate to get out. And it'll probably fly into the window.'

'Then we'll open the window. Just let me look after it.'

'You should be looking after me. At least its injuries were self-inflicted.'

She stuck her tongue out at him, and after laying the bird on the table, returned to her vigil.

'You'll still be going to the wedding tomorrow,' said Adam after a while.

'No. I won't be doing that,' she replied without looking at him.

'They'll be offended if you don't.'

'I'm sure they'll understand. I'm not in a weddingy mood any more.'

'I'll look after you.'

There was a silence, and he opened his eyes to see that she had turned to look at him, and her eyes were glistening.

'For all that you're completely hopeless, Adam' she said, 'sometimes you say exactly the right thing.'

'Then you'll come?'

'I'll think about it.' And she turned back to the window.

After a few moments she said, 'You probably shouldn't stay here if you're going to sleep. Not after that blow to the head. You should go back to the hotel and sleep in a proper bed.'

'I came to make sure you were okay.'

'I am, and it was sweet of you, and I'd appreciate your company if you were actually conscious, but being here won't do you any good. You should go back to the hotel and maybe see Doctor Vleerman in the morning.'

But Adam wasn't listening. At least not to Jana. There was another voice, whispering to him in his semi-conscious state.

Run away and join the circus.

Suddenly he sat bolt upright.

'What is it?' asked Jana.

Adam shook his head to clear it, trying to remember ... he didn't know what he was trying to remember. It had gone.

'You're right,' he said. 'I should go back to the hotel. See the doctor tomorrow. Will you be alright?'

'I'll be fine,' she smiled. 'I've got him to keep me company.' She nodded towards the table.

'A concussed bird.'

'It's no worse than a concussed you. Go. I'll be back in time for the wedding.'

Adam hauled himself to his feet, leaned against the wall for a minute until the room stopped spinning, and then walked unsteadily towards the door.

'Take care,' Jana called after him. 'Make sure you get back safely.'

And she kept gazing out of the window.

The harbour was silent as Donny Varrey walked past on his way home. The water was still, and so the boats were still too, not one of them swaying or creaking. He walked on by, oblivious to the fact that others were abroad this night.

Moments after he had passed, a dark shadow emerged from the hulk of the *Sapphire* and dropped on to the land. The figure looked around and then walked off up the hill.

The others waited a full five minutes to make sure the stranger was really gone. Then they emerged from the shadows and ran lightly, almost gracefully, over to the *Sapphire*. One cartwheeled instead of running. On reaching the boat, the cartwheeler jumped aboard and effortlessly shimmied up the mast, hanging off it with one arm and acting as a lookout. Another dived into the wheelhouse, while two more disappeared below. After about five minutes, they all emerged again and silently shook their heads. The lookout let go of the mast and dropped, only to be caught by two of the others, who then threw their companion upwards. The move was completed by the lookout landing upright on their shoulders with a flourish. Then he or she – it was hard to tell in the dark – jumped down, and they all swarmed off the boat and back into the shadows.

By now Donny had reached the Seatown and was almost back at his cottage. He passed his brother's on the way, and as he did he heard the sound of Liban sobbing and saying, 'Sorry Daddy, sorry Daddy,' over and over. He didn't stop, but he breathed heavier the rest of the way home, and didn't sleep any better than he did most other nights.

Her eyes grew heavier and Jana was finding it hard to stay awake. After a while, she slumped on the windowsill and her dreams were filled with porpoises leaping, whispering voices, babies crying and the sounds of fluttering and banging on the window.

She jerked awake. The nightjar had regained consciousness and was frantically flying around the room and into the window, trying to escape. Quickly she reached past it, ignoring its beak pecking at her hand, and fumbled with the window latch. Eventually, she managed to open it, and the bird flew out to freedom.

Breathing heavily, she pulled the window closed again and inspected her bleeding hand. She'd live. She was about to sit down again when something caught her eye. There was someone on the sand near the cave. The figure was hugging the rock wall, as if trying not to be seen. And carefully wiping out their footprints as they went.

Jana leapt up and ran to the door. Then she stopped, came back and grabbed the ledger, and ran down the stairs and outside. It would take too long to go down to the main road and back across the dunes, but the rocks were too high to just jump down. She decided to take a chance, and ran to the edge of the rocks, so she was directly above the cave mouth. Cautiously she looked over, and saw that the figure was facing away, still wiping out footprints. She could now see it was a woman. A naked woman. Presumably Adam's naked woman. Her lack of clothes might give Jana an advantage.

'Hello,' she called out.

The woman turned around with a start. She looked around wildly until she finally saw Jana above her.

'Um, hello,' said the woman. She had a distinct accent, not like the Seatowners or the Anterwendters, but there was still something familiar about it. She waited for Jana to speak again.

'A bit late to be out on the beach. With no clothes on. Isn't it?'

'I like to swim at night,' said the woman. 'No watching eyes.' She didn't seem at all uncomfortable in her nudity, and made no attempt to cover up. 'But you are out late too.'

'I was in the lighthouse.'

'Are you the keeper?'

'I am tonight. I'm Jana.'

'Merrow.'

'Have you been living in the cave?'

Merrow looked caught out. 'I knew someone had been in. The seaweed had been moved.'

'We found your boat.'

'Kayak.'

'What?'

'It is called a kayak,' Merrow explained.

'Does everyone use them where you come from?' asked Jana. Seeing Merrow's expression she added, 'Your accent isn't local.'

'You are right. I am from Væringjar.'

'We found the tunnel as well.'

'Is it a tunnel? I have not explored it. I was not sure it would be safe.'

'It wasn't for someone,' said Jana. 'We found a dead man in there.' Merrow looked shocked. 'Did you kill him?'

'*Maid?*' exclaimed Merrow in her own language. 'No, of course not! I did not know he was there.'

The reaction seemed to be genuine, and Jana considered herself a good judge of character. Then again, she'd been wrong about Doctor Vleerman.

'Maybe you should put some clothes on while I come down.'

Merrow seemed mildly amused at the request. 'My clothes are drying on the rocks, over there.'

Adam's naked woman had put her sealskin on the rocks to dry. Jana walked along the cliff until it met the dunes and it was safe enough for her to jump down. Then she made her way back to the beach. By the time she arrived, Merrow had dressed. She was wearing a one-piece garment that covered her entire body and even had a hood. It was made of some sort of animal skin. In fact it looked like ...

'It is sealskin,' Merrow confirmed when asked. 'It helps keep out the water. But after time it gets filled of water, and I have to take it off and let it dry.

The boat was covered in animal skin too. 'The – what did you call it, kayak?' Merrow nodded. 'That needs to dry too, doesn't it?'

'Of course.'

Jana thought about Adam's naked woman. The woman who had been a seal until she took her skin off. Adam had never actually seen a seal, except in pictures. In the darkness, it would be easy for him to mistake something he had never seen before. Had he taken a glass of wine with his meal? She couldn't remember, but it would contribute. Merrow's kayak was very light. She could paddle it right on to the beach and then haul it out of the water without having to get out of it, but she'd probably have to lean over the front to do it. So Adam would have seen her bent forward, with her hood up, with the back end behind her. Jana could see how he might have mistaken her for a seal. Then she'd got out of the kayak, which Adam had described as 'detaching her flippers.' And then she'd taken off her sealskin and put it on the rocks to dry. Adam had even touched it. What he'd seen wasn't one of Ceasg's selkies shedding its magic skin, it was a woman with a funny boat taking her clothes off.

And then she finally realised what was familiar about Merrow's accent. Ceasg's accent wasn't exactly like the true Seatowners. It was a mixture of Seatowner and, Jana now realised, Merrow's Væringjar. And now she thought about it, there was even a physical resemblance.

'You're Ceasg's sister, aren't you?'

'*Maid?*' exclaimed Merrow again. 'You know Ceasg? She is here?'

'I'm staying in her hotel.'

'She owns a hotel?'

'Well, her husband does. Did. He's the dead man.'

This was obviously a lot for Merrow to take in. 'We lost Ceasg a long time ago. Her kayak became, um, *piatseket*. What is your word? Separate. In a storm. I have been searching for her ever after. A sailor told me that a man here has a kayak, so I have been living in the cave and searching around the coast here for her.'

A sudden thought struck Jana. Merrow would stand out in her sealskin. 'Did you steal some clothes so you could walk around in the city?'

'No! You think I am a thief? I have not been in the city yet. I searched the beaches first, hoping I may see her. She is well?'

Jana hesitated. 'She … has some strange ideas,' she said carefully.

Merrow nodded. 'She always did have. Her mind was never strong. She can not manage on her own. But married? Really, I did not expect that. Are there any children?' Jana's face gave her away immediately. 'What? What is wrong?'

There was no point in hiding it. 'She had a baby a few days ago. But the baby was … There was something wrong with her. With her legs.'

'A baby girl?' asked Merrow breathlessly. But she is alright? She is alive?'

'I don't know,' admitted Jana. 'She disappeared. We don't know what happened to her.'

'Disappeared? You mean someone took her?'

'Probably. But, well, we don't really know.'

Merrow took a few moments to digest this, and then appeared to make a decision. 'Will you take me to Ceasg?'

Jana considered. She was fairly sure Merrow was genuine. She nodded. 'In the morning.'

The sea boiled. Shapes swirled just beneath the surface, dark grey shapes swimming in patterns that moved ever closer to the beach. As the tide surged in, so did the shapes, until suddenly they catapulted out of the water and landed on the sand.

They were seals. An army of seals. All carrying cutlasses and wearing pirate hats. One had a wooden leg.

'Quack,' said the man. 'Duck,' said the duck.

The seals dragged themselves up the beach, frequently bumping into each other on account of their eyepatches, until they finally reached the harbour, which hadn't been there before but was now. Then they took their cutlasses and ceremoniously stuck them in their own bellies, cutting upwards until they had made slits right up to their heads. They pulled their skins off, revealing fish underneath.

'Fish,' said the fish.

The seals – which were somehow still there despite having discarded themselves – now raised their cutlasses and ran at the fish, shouting battle cries of 'Arf arf'. The fish stood their ground, which is difficult to do when you don't have legs, until the seals collided with them and then –

And then Ben woke up. There was an argument raging downstairs. A gruff man's voice was shouting, and a woman was trying to placate him. She sounded like she was holding her own, but there was fear in her voice. Ben ran downstairs to see what was going on. As he did, he heard a scream from the woman.

As he reached the lobby, a dark shape swept past him, pushing him to the floor. It was the stranger from the *Sapphire*. As he reached the door, it opened and Adam came in. The man roughly pushed Adam out of the way, causing him to collide painfully with the door frame, and strode off as if he had swatted a fly.

Ben and Adam picked themselves up and looked along the passage. Baabie was lying on the floor, blood streaming from her nose. Her cat lay in a bloody mess next to her. Ben reached her first, but Adam was soon after him, and between them they helped Baabie to sit up.

'Thank you, lads,' she said, her voice trembling. 'I'll be fine.' She looked sadly at the remains of her cat. 'The old devil!' she spat.

'What did he want?' asked Ben. 'Why did he hurt you?'

'Cos he never was any good at holdin' his temper.'

'You know him?' asked Adam in surprise.

'Aye, I know him,' she said darkly. 'I know him far too weel. He's ma husband.'

XXI. The Walking Stones

One stormy night, a ship was cast on the rocks and wrecked on the coast. The only survivor was a young man, and he barely survived at that. When they found him, at first they thought he was dead, but his head stirred and he moaned, and so they carried him to the nearest village, where an old couple took him in and looked after him, and slowly nursed him back to health. He was grateful to them, and stayed on and worked hard the whole year round for them, chopping wood, cutting peat, doing odd jobs and all the things they were getting too old to manage for themselves.

Nearby stood the Great Ring, and the old couple had often told him the stones walked at Yule. The young man longed to see such a sight, but they warned him not to try, for it would be far too dangerous, because the stones had once been giants, and surely they were again when they walked. But the young man said he wisna afraid o' a big stone, and on Yule night he would set out for the Ring to see for himself, and then come back and tell them if the legend was true.

No matter how hard they tried to reason with him, he would not be deterred, and so sure enough, when Yule came he left for the Ring, and everyone in the village locked their doors and barred their windows and trembled in fear for him.

No-one knows what happened that night, for there were no witnesses, and no sound was ever heard, but the sailor did not come back to the village. They went looking for him next morning, and the whole of the village trooped up to the Great Ring with fear in their hearts.

293

And sure enough they found him, and the old couple wished he'd heeded their warnings, because there was his broken and battered body, lying crushed at the foot o' the Odin Stane itself.

22

It was a fine, crisp morning for the wedding. The sky was cloudless, and there was a good chance it would warm up by the afternoon. Preparations were well underway in the Seatown, where it was pretty much the only thing on anyone's mind. Now that the shadow of mortasheen had been lifted, everyone was looking forward to a happier time. Involving lots of food and alcohol.

Adam had taken care of the remains of Baabie's cat, while Ben had helped her to clean herself up. Her nosebleed had turned out to be nothing more than that, but when they came down for breakfast there was a dark purple bruise around her eye. She had been reluctant to say any more about her husband last night, but when the Palatine heard what had happened, he had drawn her aside to have a word in private.

'I realise that your private life is none of my affair,' he said carefully, 'but I must ask if the man is a danger to the community.'

'I ken whit it is ye really want know, and I'll answer ye straight,' she replied. 'Yes. He is capable o' killin' a man, and he could be the one that killed poor Matheeus. But I've nae idea if he did it. And I'll no be the one that asks him. And if ye've any sense, neither will you.'

Before the Palatine could question her further, Mary and Murgen had bustled in, their faces masks of concern.

'Oh Baabie,' soothed Mary, 'we heard whit happened. Yer poor wee cat! Are you all richt?'

'I'll live,' said Baabie pragmatically.

'Ye've got a richt shiner, that's for sure,' observed Murgen. 'I hope ye gave him one back.'

Mary turned to the Palatine. 'Should something no be done aboot him? Folk canna go aroond given people hidins like yon.'

'He certainly needs to be kept an eye on,' agreed the Palatine, 'but I believe that legally this was a domestic matter, and it's entirely up to Baabie whether she wishes to take it further.'

'No,' said Baabie firmly. 'Best leave weel alone. I dinna want onybody else gettin' hurt.'

The Palatine bowed slightly. 'I'll ensure that he's discreetly watched, to make certain he causes no further trouble.'

By now Ben and Adam had wandered over.

'Will Jana still be coming to the wedding?' Mary asked Adam, a concerned look on her face.

'I think so,' smiled Adam. 'If she's finished nursing her injured bird.'

'Injured bird?'

'Yeah, it flew into the glass at the lighthouse.'

Mary's face fell. 'A bird flew into the window?'

'An' you saw that owl on the rooftop earlier,' said Murgen gravely.

'So?' asked Adam.

'They're both death omens,' explained Mary, a worried look on her face. 'It means someone's going to die.'

'Death omens?' began Adam incredulously, but Ben saw how the conversation would go and jumped in.

'How are you feeling, Baabie?'

'Dinna worry aboot me, young Ben. It taks mair than a black eye to finish me off.'

'It's weird,' said Ben, 'but just before it happened I was dreaming about people fighting.'

The three spae-wives all turned their heads towards him and gave him a curious look.

'What?' he asked.

'You dreamed it would happen?' asked Murgen.

'I didn't say that. I said I – '

'Dreamed aboot a ficht,' completed Murgen.

'Yes, but not between Baabie and that man. Not even people at all.'

'Tell us aboot it,' said Mary.

'It was just a silly dream. They never – '

'Tell us!'

Ben wilted under their three stern gazes, and told them about the army of pirate seals attacking the fish that had been inside their skins. 'The pirate stuff was because of another dream. About pirates,' he concluded lamely.

'Ye've been having other dreams?' pressed Murgen.

'Everyone dreams.'

'Tell us.'

He told them about the pirate ship and then, because he knew they would ask, he told them about the one-eyed lizard-horse-man creature as well. At this last, the spae-wives all looked at each other in astonishment, but before they could speak, Adam chimed in.

'One-eyed lizard? That's the Skentys.'

'I know – ' began Ben but Murgen interrupted.

'Not when it was growin' oot o' a horse. That was the Nuckleavee. And you dreamed o' it just before the mortasheen struck.'

'I believe Albert has established that your crop blight was not supernatural,' interjected the Palatine.

'That's as maybe,' said Mary, 'but it was still mortasheen, and young Ben's dream foresaw it.'

'Foresaw?' asked Adam.

'Aye. He's got the sicht.'

'The sicht?'

'The sicht.'

'I believe she's saying "the sight," ' said the Palatine.

'That's whit I said,' agreed Mary.

'Dreams can tell the future,' explained Murgen, 'and young Ben's got the power o' it. He saw the Nuckleavee, and the crops were struck as if it was mortasheen. He dreamed aboot the ship, and it's oot there noo.'

'Not fighting pirates, though,' reasoned the Palatine.

'Maybe no, but it's there. And he dreamed o' a ficht between seals who took their skins off, and fish people.'

'That'll be selkies and mermaids,' said Mary.

'Aye, Baabie may just be the start o' it.'

As they talked on, none of them saw Jana peer around the door. Satisfied no-one was looking, she darted past, quickly followed by

Merrow. They slipped quietly into the private rooms and knocked on Ceasg's door.

'Ceasg? It's Jana. Can I come in?'

'Come in, Jana,' came Ceasg's voice.

Jana stepped in, keeping Merrow concealed by the door for the moment. 'Ceasg, I've brought someone to see you. Is that alright?'

'Yes,' said Ceasg brightly. 'It's nice to have visitors. Who is it?'

Jana beckoned and Merrow came in, closing the door behind her,

'*Bures*, Ceasg,' said Merrow.

Ceasg looked at her curiously for a while and then smiled in dreamy recognition. 'Merrow! I haven't seen you in ages. It's nice of you to visit me. Sit down, won't you?'

Jana relaxed a little. Merrow really was Ceasg's sister.

'I have been looking for you, Ceasg. I came to take you home.'

'But I *am* home,' laughed Ceasg.

'I mean Væringjar.'

'Oh, that.' There was no indication of her feelings on the matter. She looked at Merrow's clothes. 'I see you still have your skin. Mine's in there.' She pointed at the locker behind the shelves. 'Matheeus keeps it locked in there. I mean kept. He's dead now. It's very sad.'

Jana stood up and walked to the locker. Ceasg had said she would return to the sea if she had her skin. 'Maybe it's time we got your skin out of there.' She grabbed the stack of shelves and started pulling on them. Taking the cue, Merrow joined her, and they pulled together. Slowly, the shelves inched forward until they had moved enough to let the locker open. The padlock was still securely fastened. Merrow began searching the room, but Jana stopped her.

'The key won't be here. It wouldn't be anywhere that Ceasg could find it. Matheeus would have kept it on him.'

Merrow looked at her nervously. 'Do you mean what I am thinking?'

Jana nodded grimly. 'It must be on the body.'

After Adam's head had been checked by Doctor Vleerman, the spaewives had herded their party down to the Seatown. They had tried to

encourage Ceasg to come, but she had mysteriously said she was waiting for news, and it was eventually agreed there would be no harm in leaving her. Ben had brought Serena, and after their help dealing with the mortasheen, Albert and the Palatine had been invited too. As they arrived, Liban ran over and hugged Albert's leg, before running back to Donny.

The entire population of the Seatown had congregated outside Maisie's family's house to embark on what they called the Wedding Walk, a sort of formal march to the Odin Stane. Adam looked around but saw no sign of Jana. Hopefully she would turn up later.

Pilot stood in what looked like pride of place, holding a fiddle. All eyes seemed to be on him as Mae emerged carrying a plate of some kind of meat. There were cheers as it was presented to Pilot and he began to eat.

Mary leaned over to Adam's party and explained quietly, 'That's the hot-tail pudding of a pig. He has to eat it all.'

'Er, why?' asked Albert.

'Tradition,' said Ben knowledgeably. Serena smiled and kissed him.

'Aye, ye could say that,' smirked Mary. 'It's traditional to line the fiddler's stomach so's he disnae get drunk too quick, and can play for longer.'

More cheers rose up as Pilot finished the meal, and then he took up his fiddle and began to play a jaunty tune, setting off on the march as he did so. Behind him came Abgal and Meg, who was the chief bridesmaid, followed by Maisie and Adaro, who was best man. Then came Mae and her husband, and then Abgal's parents. After them, everyone fell in line in whatever order they chose, and so began the march to the Odin Stane. Right at the back were Mairi and Shona, each dragging a broom made of twigs behind them.

'They're the tail sweepers,' explained Mary. 'They're sweepin' oor tracks so nae trows can follow us.'

Two of Abgal's friends stayed behind. 'They're watchin' the hoose.'

'In case of trows?' asked Adam.

'You catch on quick. Ye'll go far.'

The procession did not go straight to the stone, but instead detoured so it crossed a part of the river narrow enough for everyone to step or jump across. Several people carried pots and spoons, and banged them loudly as they walked.

Father Langstok was waiting for them at the Odin Stane. This was the first time Adam had seen it up close. It was large and irregularly shaped, wider at the bottom than the top, and with a cleft running all the way down its middle, so it looked almost like two stones joined together. Low down on one side was a large, round hole passing right through the stone.

Maisie and Abgal stood one either side of the stone, holding hands through the hole. The ceremony was simple and brief, with no singing or sermon. The happy couple recited their vows and Father Langstock pronounced them husband and wife. It took only a few minutes. On the way back, the bride and groom walked together, while the best man and bridesmaid now formed a couple. Once again, they detoured so they crossed the river, and people banged pots.

'Trows?' asked Adam.

'Trows,' confirmed Mary.

When they got back to the house, Willemena was sitting outside on a chair, with a plate of bread and cheese in one hand, which she offered to the bridal party. Her other arm cradled a baby. Adam looked questioningly at Mary, but she just held up a finger to indicate he'd have to wait.

While the bread and cheese were being eaten, Murgen had slipped into the house, and came back out carrying a large round cake. More tea brak, thought Adam but, to his surprise, she walked over to Maisie, held the cake above the bride's head and broke it into pieces, letting the whole thing tumble on to the grass. Everyone suddenly dived to try and grab a piece of the cake, while the bridal party laughed at the chaos around them. Some of the younger women seemed to be hunting for something, and finally Shona sprang up triumphantly to much applause, holding her arm up high. Held between her finger and thumb was a ring.

'That means she'll marry soon,' explained Mary, a little wistfully as she remembered Jana's experience the night before.

People were still scrambling for cake, and then Liban emerged from the throng clutching something small and shiny in her hand. This was greeted not so much with applause as awkward indifference. As Liban skipped past him, Adam saw her prize was not a ring but a thimble.

'What does the thimble mean?' asked the Palatine casually.

Mary didn't look him in the eye. 'Whoever finds the thimble ... isnae very likely to get married.'

'Ah,' said the Palatine lightly, and Adam got the feeling he'd already known the answer and had asked the question purely to make Mary say it out loud. Liban, however, seemed delighted with her find, and ran around happily showing it to whoever would pay her any attention.

Once the cake had all been snapped up, Maisie stepped back over to Willemena who, assisted in her frailty by one of the young men who had stayed to watch the house, handed the baby to her. The crowd fell silent as they all watched the baby carefully. At first nothing seemed to happen, and then, brought on by nothing that Adam had noticed, they all let out a sigh of satisfaction and Maisie returned the baby.

'What just happened?' Adam asked.

'That's the hansel-bairn' explained Mary. 'The youngest child in the Seatown. He lifted his left foot. That means Maisie's own bairns will be mostly boys.'

This appeared to mark the end of the rituals, and now Pilot struck up a new tune and the procession set off again, this time towards the barn. Inside, which was now devoid of horses, it had been decorated with garlands for the wedding. Makeshift tables had been set up by laying long planks on top of barrels. As everyone sat down, Adam looked around again for Jana, but still saw no sign of her. He wondered if she was still sitting brooding in the lighthouse. His thoughts were interrupted by Baabie placing a bowl of broth and a plate of oatcakes in front of him. The wedding feast was about to begin.

It was simple, rustic fare, but every bit as tasty as the expensive meal last night. The food was all washed down by a potent ale, but no-one had their own cup. Instead, each table had a number of large drinking vessels that were constantly passed around. These resembled miniature washtubs with two upright handles rising from their brims, and Mary explained that these were the wedding cogs.

As they ate, there was another cheer, and everyone turned to see that Maisie's father had stood up. He was holding another cog, which stood out from the others because it was made from alternate vertical strips of light and dark wood.

'That's the goodman's cog,' whispered Mary.

The cog was passed from right to left along the top table, each person taking a drink from it before handing it on. Once it got to the end, it was passed to the next table, and it soon became clear it was to be drunk from by every one of the guests. Adam watched to see what they would do when it was empty, and was soon rewarded by the sight of it being refilled from a tap in one of the barrels the tables rested on.

The broth was followed by a meat course, and Adam noted that while he and Albert had been served goose, the Palatine and Mary were eating rabbit, but Ben and Serena had what looked like mutton. Mary explained that no family in the Seatown could ever afford to feed all of their wedding guests themselves, so it was usual for the guests to contribute gifts of food themselves. Adam immediately felt guilty about not having brought anything, but Mary reassured him that, as they did not know, none of the six outsiders would have been expected to bring anything, and besides, as members of Albert's party, they were all guests of honour.

The meat course was followed by scones, pancakes and small cakes called bannocks. Once this last course was finished, it was Father Langstok's turn to stand up, and after making a short toast to the bride and groom, drink form a second of the more elaborate cogs. Once again, this was passed from right to left around the guests, and Adam now realised it was moving clockwise.

As the second cog made its journey, people began to call out, 'A song! Who's singin' the first song?' This seemed to be rhetorical, though, because it quickly became apparent this task was reserved once again for Pilot, who stood and walked to the end of the barn so everyone could see him. The noise quietened down, and everyone listened attentively as he began to sing.

'I heard a mother lull her bairn,
'Aye sleep well, my bairn within,
I ken not who thy father is,
nor yet the land that he dwells in."

It was a haunting tune, and Pilot had a fine, deep voice.

'An' then in cam a grey selchie
sayin' 'Oh how sound as thou dost sleep,
I'll tell where thy bairn's father is,
he's sittin' close at thy bed's feet,

I am a man upon the land,
I am a selchie on the sea,
an' when I'm far fae ev'ry strand
my dwelling is in Sule Skerry.

Thou wilt nurse my little wee son
for seven years upon thy knee
an' after seven years have passed
I'll come and pay the nursin' fee.'

An' at the end o' seven long years
he cam to pay the nursin' fee,
he had a coffer fu' o' gold
and anither fu' o' the white money.

'But how shall I my young son ken
When thou ha taen him far frae me?'
'I'll put a gold chain round his neck,
The wan wi' the chain shall he be.

An thou wilt wed a hunter good
an' a richt good gunner he wilt be
an' he'll go oot wan fine mornin'
an' shoot the son and the grey selchie.'

'Alas, alas, this woeful fate,
This fate that has been laid for me.'
An' wance or twice she sobbed an' sighed
an' her tender heart did brak in three.'

As Pilot finished his song to enthusiastic applause, Albert noticed the Palatine was watching spellbound. Albert sighed and braced himself for the inevitable singsong.

Unknown to Adam, Jana had confided in the Palatine before leaving the hotel. She had caught him as he came out of the dining room, taken him aside, and explained Matheeus had a key on him that Ceasg needed urgently. She hadn't mentioned the sealskin or Merrow. As the body was currently being held by the navy, and Jana was only known to two crewmembers of the *Invincible*, would Lord Reitherman write her a short letter of introduction? He had been only too happy to, and once he had gone upstairs, Jana and Merrow had slipped out of the hotel and gone to the naval base. The letter had got them a meeting with the ship's surgeon, who was still ashore. However, to their dismay, no key had been found on the body. This was a little surprising, as they would have expected him to at least have some hotel keys. They waited until they had left the base before voicing the obvious conclusion: Matheeus must have dropped his keys in the tunnel.

They returned to the cave, removed the seaweed and Merrow's boat, lit their lantern and descended the steps. They walked slowly, with the lantern held low so they could comb the rock floor for the missing keys. By the time they got to roughly the spot where Jana remembered finding Matheeus's body, there had still been no sign. Had he gone further down the tunnel and dropped the keys on the way back?

They kept going. The passage seemed fairly straight, so surely they must be well out under the sea. In fact, they were probably under the sea bed. Why was there a passage under the sea bed? Where did it go? Jana remembered what the Palatine had said about finding the covered walkway, but surely that was just an old story to explain the existence of the passage in the first place. On the other hand, the steps at least had been made by someone, so didn't that mean the passage wasn't natural?

These thoughts had distracted Jana enough that she had not really been paying attention to where they were going. Her eyes had still been on the floor, but her mind had been elsewhere, and she almost jumped when Merrow's voice came out of the darkness.

'Did you notice that the tunnel has been going up again?'

'Has it? No, I hadn't noticed.'

'It means we will be coming soon out of the sea bed.'

Jana peered at her through the gloom. 'Coming out into what?'

'We will see.'

Jana looked around, frowning. 'Is it just me, or is it getting lighter?'

'You saw that? It has been growing lighter for some time. It is not the rock that is glowing, it is something more down the tunnel.'

They carried on, but now it was hard to keep their eyes on the ground, because they wanted to see where the light was coming from. After a few more minutes Jana said, 'I've just had a worrying thought.'

'What is it?'

'If Matheeus had dropped his keys down here, he'd have heard it.'

'So you think we are wasting our time?'

'Either that or he had a reason for not stopping to pick them up.'

'What reason?'

'He was running from something.'

'I see why that worries you,' agreed Merrow. 'Now it worries me.'

They went on in silence for a while, before Merrow said, 'Do you think that what he ran from caught him and killed him?'

Jana avoided looking at her. 'I do now.'

Suddenly there was a jingling of metal. Jana's foot had kicked something. She bent down and picked it up. It was a bunch of keys.

'Good,' said Merrow evenly. ''Do we now go back with what we came here for?'

Jana gave her a shrewd look. 'Don't be silly.'

Merrow nodded once and they kept walking. Now they could keep their eyes ahead of them, they realised that they didn't need the lantern any more. Merrow extinguished it and they looked around them. The light was definitely up ahead, but it was strong enough to bathe the whole passage in a dim glow. They allowed their eyes to adjust and carried on.

It was fully fifteen minutes before they saw, literally, the light at the end of the tunnel. It had been growing gradually brighter with every step, and now it was almost like daylight. And it emanated from straight ahead. They couldn't see an object that might be the source. Instead, it seemed as if the end of the passage itself was alight. As they drew close, they both gasped. None of the things they had imagined it might be had prepared them for what they actually saw.

The passage ended not in rock but in water. The end was simply open to what they knew must be the sea because of the fish that kept swimming by.

'Why does not the water come in?' breathed Merrow.

Jana didn't answer. Tentatively, she reached out her hand until it touched the wall of water. It was cold and wet. She hesitated and then plunged her hand in.

Immediately she drew it back and tucked it painfully under her arm. 'It's freezing!'

'We are very far under the sea,' said Merrow reasonably. 'It is really water?'

'Yes.' Jana rubbed the life back into her hand as a squid propelled itself past.

'Why do not the fish swim through?'

Jana shook her head.

They still couldn't see the actual source of the light, but it was somewhere further out in the sea. Something was shining brightly enough to light up the passage from a distance. Through a wall of water.

They didn't know how long they stood and stared, but eventually they realised there was nothing else they could learn here, and so reluctantly, they turned and walked away. They hardly spoke the whole way back to the hotel. They had both seen the same thing and neither of them had any explanation for it. Magic perhaps – Jana certainly knew of no science that could accomplish it – but whose magic and why?

When they arrived back at Ceasg's room, Jana took the keys from her pocket. 'Do you know which one it is?'

'No,' said Ceasg dreamily. 'I never saw Matheeus lock or unlock it. But I suppose it must be one of them.'

There were around thirty keys on the ring. Presumably Matheeus had a spare one for each of the guest rooms, as well as the ones he would use every day. She tried each key in the padlock in turn. One by one they failed to open it. Finally there was only one left. She glanced at Merrow and Ceasg before taking a breath and inserting it in the padlock. There was the sound of metal scraping on metal and then she turned to meet their expectant gazes.

'None of them fits. The key isn't here.'

The entertainment had continued into the afternoon. Various people had taken turns at singing, and to Albert's mortification, the Palatine had enthusiastically introduced the Seatowners to the song about the man with the cream cheese hat. There had been dancing, Pilot had played his fiddle several times and Willemena had produced an accordion. Now they were duetting with a small crowd gathered around them.

Meanwhile, Murgen had gathered the children and some of the adults into another corner and began telling stories. Liban had jumped up onto Albert's knee, and she sat happily munching on an apple while Draatsie had curled herself around Adam's feet. The Palatine had also joined this group and was listening attentively.

There were tales of mermaids and trows, of witches and ghosts, and of seal people and the mysterious Finfolk. There were stories of how the Væringjar had come to Orknejar and then the Seatowners had come from Orknejar to Anterwendt.

As he listened, Adam felt he was beginning to understand a lot more about the Seatowners and their heritage. And then he began to think that he might be gaining an insight into more than just the Seatowners. As Draatsie shifted on his feet and Murgen began her next tale, he glanced at the Palatine, leaned forward and listened more carefully.

XXII. The Oath on the Odin Stane

*I*t wis a dark and stormy nicht. Black clouds gathered in the sky, thunder rumbled, and rain fell in big heavy spots. Mary Tait stood at her cottage door and shivered in the cold wind.

'Get yersel' inside,' said Walter Coulston as he turned from the door. 'Think weel on whit I've said. Think o' the bairns. No oath should be binding after death. I'll come back in the morning for your answer.'

'I will,' she promised. 'And thank you for your offer. It's very kind.'

She watched him walk away, and saw that he stopped for a moment as he reached the great standing stone with the hole through the middle. He shook his head at it and then vanished into the storm.

Mary closed the door and went into the parlour. The cold was shut outside, but it still chilled her heart to think about what breaking the oath meant. The fire was burning low, but she had used up all the peat and had no money for more. She sat and tried to knit, but she had to get up mair than once to comfort the youngest bairn and put a fresh cloth on his fevered brow.

Restless, she rose again, went to the shelf and took down a book, one of the only two in the hoose. She opened it up, and pressed between its pages, found the letter. She unfolded it, and in the dim licht of the candle that was near burned oot, read its yellowed page, even though she knew the words by heart.

'My beloved Mary, mind oor oath' that we made when we held hands through the hole in the Odin Stane, never to marry another. I would come back from death itself for my bairns if you should wed a man like my mither wed. I'll be going up north in the morning but when I come back … '

Except he never did come back. The icy waters of the river had taken him, and Mary had been left alone wi' the bairns. His pay had never been great, but withoot it Mary and the bairns had struggled each and every day for the last five years.

As the youngest coughed again, Mary whispered, 'Aye, I remember, Andrew. I've missed you every day o' these last five years, but that oath has cost us dear. And noo it stands between us and the food and warmth Walter Coulston offers us. Walter that was aye your friend. Would you deny us that, Andrew? Would you see us starve for an oath?'

After a few minutes, she wiped away her tears, folded up the letter and closed the pages over it. She placed the book back on the shelf and took up her knitting again, but soon her hands dropped and so did her head, and she fell into a fitful sleep.

When she woke, the candle and the fire had both burned oot. Something made her look at the door, but it was still closed and barred as she had left it. Not knowing why, she took the book down and opened its pages. She unfolded the letter and gasped at whit she saw. Save for Andrew's signature, the page was blank.

The knock at the door made her jump. Still shaking, she hurried over and opened it.

'Well, Mary, whit do ye say? My hoose is yours and your bairns if ye'll have me.'

Wordlessly, Mary held up the letter in her trembling hand. Walter looked at it and looked at Mary, a question in his eyes.

'He must have been here last nicht, Walter. The oath's gone!'

Walter looked at the page again and then nodded solemnly. 'I'll go and speak to the priest.'

23

As Murgen finished her latest story, Adam's mind was spinning. He wasn't sure why, but some of it sounded familiar. There was something he felt he should be seeing, some connection he should be making, but for now it eluded him. He looked again at the Palatine and saw that he too was deep in thought.

He felt a hand on his shoulder and turned his head to see Jana.

'I didn't think you were coming.'

'I'm sorry,' she said meekly. 'Something came up. How's your head?'

'Fine, thanks. Are you okay?'

'Yes, but there's something I need to show you. And someone you should meet.'

'What's been happening?'

'She's just outside. Come and – '

She broke off as a new sound filled the air and the whole barn fell silent. It was the most beautiful sound any of them had ever heard. All heads turned to see where it was coming from.

Serena stood in the centre of the barn singing. There were no words, but the sweet sound that came from her didn't need any. There wasn't exactly a melody either, but it was still utterly compelling. It snaked around the soul of every person who heard it. And Adam knew he had heard something like it before. Not on land but out at sea, on the *Renown*. It was similar to the sound he had heard just before the storm, when they had seen the illusion of the merman. Ben had called it whalesong.

Serena's was not exactly the same. For one thing, she didn't have size on her side to amplify the sound in the same way. But whatever she was doing, it didn't involve her voice. Her mouth wasn't even open. She just stood there with this indescribably beautiful sound emanating from her while the whole room listened enraptured.

Adam glanced sidelong at Jana. She was staring at Serena, but he couldn't read her expression.

After what seemed like both an eternity and not nearly long enough, Serena's song came to a close. The crowd sat in utter silence.

And then someone screamed.

Everyone looked around in confusion, until they saw a finger pointing up at the rafters. All eyes looked up and saw them. Two little figures sitting on one of the beams. They had round, yellow faces with large red eyes. Spindly arms poked out of their grey jackets and ended in hands clad in brown woolen mittens. Their legs were just as spindly, and their chests equally skinny, as if they had no muscles at all.

They had been as captivated by the singing as everyone else, but now they jerked up in fear and scrambled about looking for an escape. In the end they tripped over each other and plummeted to the ground. For a short while they lay there winded, but then they finally sat up and stared aroud them.

They were completely surrounded, but no-one made a move towards them. The Seatowners were clearly afraid of them, and the interlopers were no less scared of the Seatowners. They all stared at each other in terror.

And then someone made a move. It was Liban. She pushed through the crowd and walked fearlessly across the space to the two creatures, with her hand held out. In it was the doll that Jana had given her. She stood in front of the creatures, and when nothing happened, she shook the doll a little.

'Ta,' she said encouragingly.

The creatures looked at each other in amazement. Then, cautiously, one stretched out a hand towards the doll. It stopped just short of touching it, and hesitated uncertainly.

Liban smiled her best smile. The creature cocked its head and then its lips parted to bare green, spiky teeth. It took the doll and made a show of cuddling it. Then it handed the doll back to Liban. Pleased, she sat down cross-legged.

'What are they?' whispered Adam.

'They're trows,' breathed Murgen fearfully.

'I saw one at the circus,' whispered Jana. 'That's what the clowns caught.'

Adam thought about the stories he had just listened to Murgen telling. Many of them spoke of the trows as dangerous creatures who would steal children and cause trouble. But some told of friendly and even helpful trows, and come to think of it, even the troublemakers mostly just had parties that went on too long. The two sitting nervously in the centre of the barn while Liban tried to teach them how to play pat-a-cake, didn't seem particularly scary. If anything, they were just as scared as everyone else.

'Liban!'

The little girl sat bolt upright and the trows cowered a little more.

Ben Varrey stood on the edge of the crowd with a face like thunder. 'Get over here now!' He noticeably did not walk towards the trows, but just held out his hand.

Liban looked upset as she turned her head between her angry father and her new playmates. 'Playing,' she said in a small, quavering voice.

'We're going home, Liban. Don't make me ask again.'

She sprang up in terror and ran to her father, shouting, 'Sorry Daddy sorry Daddy sorry Daddy!'

He grabbed her by the wrist and swung her roughly in front of him. His other hand thrashed her across the backside, and she wailed. He walked three steps and found Jana in his way. She didn't move, and he gave her a black look before pushing past and leaving the barn, dragging the tearful Liban behind him. The trows watched them leave, shaking their heads sadly.

'Peedie ting's sabauy,' said one in a slow, reedy voice.

''Sa fjandin o a dedy.'

'Wull hannj klaksa er?'

'Avsetten! Maks min bleud bile!'

'They don't appear to be hostile,' ventured the Palatine calmly.

'They're trows,' said Pilot nervously. 'They're dangerous. They probably caused the mortasheen.'

'Mortasheen?' repeated one of the trows fearfully.

'Sna mortasheen,' said the other. 'Bugga fallsjon.'

'It wasn't mortasheen,' Albert reminded them. 'It was ergot.'

'Aye but you said someone did it deliberately. Well there's yer culprits rich there.'

A murmur of assent went up among the Seatowners, but it died to a hush when Jana took a step towards the trows. The two creatures huddled together nervously.

'It's alright,' said Jana reassuringly. 'I'm not going to hurt you.' She crouched down to their level and held out a hand. In it was a piece of tea brak. The trows looked at her suspiciously then sniffed the air. They looked at each other, and then one tentatively stretched a hand towards Jana. It snatched the cake and broke it in two, giving half to its companion. They nibbled at the cake and then smiled at each other.

'Tea brak!' they exclaimed in unison and happily devoured the rest.

'They don't appear to be harming her,' observed the Palatine wryly. 'And they seemed positively friendly towards young Liban.'

'Liban's a trowie bairn,' said Mae darkly. 'She's one o' theirs.'

Jana shot her a black look. Before she could say anything, the Palatine was at her shoulder.

'I think I understand about that,' he murmured. 'Let's talk about it later. For the moment, perhaps we should focus on avoiding any bloodshed here.'

'Alright,' said Jana with difficulty. 'How do you suggest we do that? These people seem to have made their minds up.'

'Then we have to change them.' He stood back up and addressed the tense ring of faces. 'It occurs to me that these may not be dangerous trows at all. They may, in fact, be hogboons.'

'Hog what?' muttered Jana.

'You should have been here for the storytelling. Most educational.'

'Hogboons?' repeated Pilot uncertainly.

The crowd began muttering, until Baabie walked into the circle and her voice cut through the noise.

'His Lordship's richt,' she said in a voice that brooked no contradiction. 'They've done us nae harm, and if we're good to them, they'll be good back tae us.'

Hearing this from a spae-wife seemed to settle the matter almost immediately. The mood of the Seatowners changed, and soon people were smiling and relaxing again. Even Mae came over with a plate of food and, contritely, said. 'I'm sorry I spoke ill of you.'

Then Maisie stood up with the third of the ornamental drinking vessels. 'The bride's cog,' she announced, and after drinking from it herself, made a point of passing it to the surprised trows first.

'Dakk,' said the first trow to her and took a swig.

'Fa mjer dikk,' its companion said to it, pulling the cog away. It took a draught and then, apparently familiar with the tradition, passed it to Jana.

'Far's dat spjelmann?' asked the first, looking around. Its eye fell on Pilot and it scampered over and thrust the fiddle into his hands with an encouraging smile. 'Gisa viseckky.' Pilot hesitated and then struck up a tune. Pleased, the trows began dancing, and soon the Seatowners were clapping them on as if the earlier tension had never happened.

Baabie nudged the Palatine. 'Ye're good, I'll say that for ye.'

'Thank you for being so open-minded,' he replied.

'Has anyone any idea what they're saying?' asked Jana.

'I'm no sure, but I think it might be Norn,' said Murgen.

'What's Norn?'

'When the settlers first came to Orknejar, they brought their own language wi' them. It changed a bit ower the years, an' the version that wis spoken in Orknejar was called Norn. Naebody speaks it any more, but I once heard my granny recite a poem in Norn, an' that sounded a wee bit like it. Hang on a minute.'

She walked over to Willemena and consulted with her, then came back. 'Aye, Willemena thinks the same. But naebody here can speak it.'

'We might know someone who can help,' said Adam.

Jana looked at him and then realised who he meant. 'Oh, yes!'

'We might be a while though.'

'Take my coach if it'll help,' offered the Palatine. 'Albert and I will stay here to make sure the trows are alright, although I think the worry's past now.'

As they ran out, Adam and Jana passed Merrow.

'Oh, Adam, this is who I wanted you to meet! This is Merrow.'

Jana grabbed Merrow's hand and dragged her aboard the coach with them. As the vehicle rattled on its way, Jana told Adam of their meeting and the wall of water. Ten minutes later, before Adam could give any real thought to what he had heard, they were at the circus. Adam ran to the freak show, but it had already closed. He soon found the tattooed man, however, who directed him to the caravan of Lionel the dog-faced boy.

'We need your linguistic skills,' Adam explained before telling Lionel about the trows. Intrigued, Lionel agreed to come at once, and was soon sitting with them in the coach. He was introduced to Merrow and immediately noticed something.

'That accent's not local. Is it Væringjari?'

'Yes, you are right,' said Merrow.

Adam stared at her and then at Jana. 'You didn't mention that bit before.'

'Didn't I?' said Jana. 'Sorry. Why? Does it matter?'

'The settlers who brought Norn to Orknejar were from Væringjar. You could have saved us a journey!'

'Oh. Sorry,' said Jana.

'I may not be as helpful as you think,' said Merrow. 'I am not of the Væringjari who went in ships to find the new lands. I am from the far north of Væringjar. My people are called Saami.'

'The languages are related,' said Lionel. 'I'm sure you'd still be useful to me.'

Merrow blushed. 'I will try.'

'I've heard of the Saami,' said Adam. 'It's said you're great sorcerers.'

'That is what the Væringjari say. But it is because they do not understand our ways. They fear what they do not understand.'

'Doesn't everyone?' said Lionel archly.

'But you're shamans, aren't you?' pressed Adam.

'What is shamans?'

'Well, you go into trances to contact the spirit world,' answered Adam, trying to give the best explanation he could remember from what Malchus had taught him.

'Our noaidi do. I think you would call them priests? It is a part of what we believe. They leave their bodies to talk to the gods, and to the nature spirits, and to the, er ...' She looked to Lionel for help. 'Máatar?'

'Ancestors,' suggested Lionel after a moment's thought.

'Yes. And the Væringjari think it is evil magic.'

Adam leaned forward. 'And they have a different name for you, don't they?'

'In their language we are called Finnar.'

Adam fell silent. He sat back, deep in thought, and didn't speak for the rest of the journey. Most of the conversation on the way back to the Seatown was between Merrow and Lionel who, Jana noticed, were getting on very well. Normally that would raise a mischievous smile, but now it just made her feel worse.

When they got back to the barn, the party was in full swing and it was as if the trows were old friends. Merrow stopped in her tracks when she saw them. Lionel was less suprised, and just looked at them curiously. The trows, on the other hand, stopped dancing and stared at him. Eventually one nudged the other and said, 'Ist a krupp ra hund?'

''Sa hjogfinni.'

Lionel turned to Merrow. 'They think I'm a dog.'

'You ken whit they're sayin'?' gasped Murgen. The Seatowners had stared at Lionel too, but had tried to be less obvious about it.

'Well, that one was fairly simple,' replied Lionel. 'We'll see how much more I manage.' He turned back to the trows. 'Haust,' he said.

The trows started and widened their eyes in surprise.

'Eg er Lionel. Issi Merrow. Du?'

The trows looked at each other in amazement. 'Hannj ikke braka!'

'They're impressed they can understand me.'

The two translators took the trows over to a quiet corner and set to work. Jana suddenly found herself alone. She looked around and saw that Adam was deep in conversation with the Palatine. She felt a little superfluous, and allowed her gaze to wander around the room. Until it fell on Ben and Serena. They were sitting on the floor, listening to Willemena play her accordion. Ben had an arm around Serena's waist, and she had her head on his shoulder. She kissed him and then settled her head again. In spite of herself, or possibly because of herself, Jana watched them for a few minutes until she sensed someone at her elbow.

'Ye should probably find something else to look at,' suggested Mary. 'Starin' at thon two'll just hurt yer eyes.'

'Our free circus tickets are for tonight,' said Jana, the thought coming out of nowhere.

'Mebbe ye should go then. Mae and Abgal'll no mind.'

'I might go later. I want to hear what the trows have to say first.' She suddenly realised she hadn't eaten all day. 'Is there any food left?'

Mary led her to a table and surrounded her with food, taking care to seat her so her back was to Ben and Serena. Jana ate ravenously, and only paused when Albert sidled over in his apologetic manner.

'Come and join me, Albert,' she said taking another swig of the potent brew in the cog. 'How drunk can you get?'

Albert sat down. 'Do you think the little girl will be alright?'

Jana put the cog down and met his eyes. 'You noticed too, eh? Everyone else just seems to turn a blind eye. Your lord and master said he had some clever opinion on that. I'd be fascinated to hear it.'

'I think I might know what he meant.'

'Then pray enlighten me,' said Jana, picking up the cog and not noticing how much she spilled.

'These are essentially poor people. Not starving, but they live from hand to mouth. They can't afford luxuries. They even have to bring their own food to a wedding.'

'So?'

'As soon as they're able, their children are set to work, because they need every pair of hands they can get just to survive. But a child like Liban who's, well, perhaps a little slow, or one who maybe has something wrong with their legs, for instance, and can't walk properly. Well they, dare I say it, can be something of a burden.' He saw Jana's mouth open to speak and hastily interrupted her. 'I don't mean I agree with that view. It's just, to these people, a child like that is an extra mouth to feed, an extra drain on what little they have, who can't contribute anything.'

'That's not her fault,' insisted Jana, but Albert held up his hands placatingly.

'I know, I know, but it's hard for people like these. And they're drenched in superstition. So they invent an explanation for it, one that makes them feel better.'

'That she's a trowie bairn.'

'A changeling,' said Albert. 'Left by the fairies, who have taken the real child away. That gives them something to blame for their misfortune.'

'But they're just blaming the child! That's not fair.'

'I agree. But it helps them to cope with it. And perhaps gives them licence … ' He tailed off.

'Licence to what?' she asked suspiciously.

'We heard Murgen telling some of their folk tales earlier. One was about a changeling and how it should be dealt with.'

'And how *was* it dealt with?'

'The child was beaten,' said Albert quietly, 'and left outside to die.'

'You're saying they use this changeling rubbish as an excuse to beat children?'

'I'm saying they use it as a way of coping with something they're not equipped to cope with. Oh, I don't think they'd really hurt a child – '

'I think her father would.'

'Perhaps, but I think the story is just a story. And perhaps a little wishful thinking. The solution their consciences won't allow them to try. But it means they can turn a blind eye and treat Liban differently, because she *is* different. And did you see how they all stared at the circus man when he arrived?'

'You mean Lionel?'

'Is that his name? I wasn't introduced. But it's just the same.'

'They'd all have heart attacks if they went to the freak show,' said Jana wryly. She suddenly lurched forward and grabbed Albert by the arm. 'You know, there's more to you than meets the, you know, the eye, Albert Munster. And you still aren't drunk enough. Drink up.'

'Er, I think something's happening,' said Albert. 'Look.'

Lionel had gone to speak to Adam, and now they and the Palatine walked over to the trows, where a crowd was starting to gather. Albert and Jana joined them, Jana taking a slightly circuitous route until Albert steered her in the right direction.

'We're managing to understand each other,' said Lionel. 'Mostly. There are some words we can't get.'

'But you have done well,' Merrow encouraged him.

'With your help.'

She blushed.

'That's all very lovely,' said Jana loudly, 'but what are they saying?'

'This is Truncherface,' said Lionel quickly.

'Haust,' waved one of the trows.

'And this is Bannafeet.'

'Haust.'

There were a few titters until Jana shouted, 'Don' laugh at people's names!'

'They've come from Orknejar,' continued Lionel.

'Orknejar!' said Bannafeet enthusiastically, looking around hopefully at the Seatowners. Truncherface nodded and smiled. They seemed to be trying to establish common ground.

'They're looking for their, er … ' Lionel looked at Merrow for help.

'Blodfrind,' she said. 'Kinsmen.'

'Whit kinsmen?' asked Pilot.

'Well, they are what you call trows,' said Lionel. 'Their word is "buman."'

'Buman, ja,' said Truncherface, pointing at his own chest.

'Then they're lookin' for ither trows,' said Pilot. 'Here?'

'There's a bit more to it than that. They're looking for "the trows that were taken". Or stolen.'

'Or changed,' added Merrow. 'It is not clear which word they mean.'

'It may be both. They say they were taken by the huldufolk.'

''Whit are the huldufolk?' asked Pilot.

'In Væringjar, they are what you would call fairies, I think,' said Merrow. 'The huldu men were ugly, but the women were beautiful and very good at singing. But the women had the tails of cows and had to marry a man – what do you say, a *mortal* man – and then their tail will fall off. They lived on farms on islands that can not be seen, and those come up out of the sea. If you could find one of these islands, it would become yours.'

'That sounds a wee bitty like the Finfolk,' said Murgen.

A murmur of assent went around the room.

'Finfolk?' asked Merrow. She looked at Adam, remembering what he had said on the coach.

'What was it you said the Væringjari call your people?' he asked her.

'Finnar.'

'And what's the name of the invisible island that the Finfolk live on, Murgen?'

'Hildaland.'

'Hildaland, Huldufolk. And the Finfolk are supposed to have magic boats they can row at incredible speeds, is that right?'

'Aye. They can cross the sea in seven strokes.'

'How fast would you say your boat is Merrow?'

'Oh, very fast. Because it is so light.'

'Very manoeuvrable too, I imagine.'

'Yes. I can turn it right around in a moment.'

'And tell them about the sealskin, Jana.'

'What? Oh, yeah. She wears clothes made of sealskin to keep the water out. When she takes them off it looks like a seal turning into a woman. *Adam saw her naked!*' She sniggered. 'Sorry, might be lil bit drunk.'

'Are you saying the Saami people are these Finfolk?' asked Merrow.

'Think about it,' said Adam. 'The Væringjari travel to Orknejar and take their legends of the huldufolk with them. And their belief that the Saami, or Finnar, are great sorcerers. It all gets mixed up with local Orknejar legends and comes out as the Finfolk. And the selkies.'

'Selchie!' said Bannafeet excitedly.

'Whisht!' Truncherface hit him.

''Salright, eryone already knows,' Jana reassured him. 'Ceasg things she's a selkie.'

'So,' began Pilot, trying to follow, 'this pair think the ither trows were taken by the Finfolk?'

'Taken – or changed – using "frolik", which we think means "old magic," ' said Lionel.

'Changed into what?'

'Sjupilti,' said Merrow. 'I think it means a water demon.'

'Sjupilti,' repeated Bannafeet.

'Njuggel,' said Truncherface.

'Whit did he say?' asked Pilot in a worried voice.

321

'Njuggel. It is another word for a water demon.'

'It soonds like nuckelavee.'

'What is nuckelavee?'

'That's one o' oor demons. The one that causes mortasheen.'

'Sna mortasheen,' said Truncherface firmly. 'Bugga fallsjon.'

'Whit did he say?'

'He said it's not mortasheen, whatever that is,' translated Lionel. 'It's a disease of the barley.'

'Ergot,' agreed Albert. 'We've already established that.'

'Aye,' agreed Pilot, 'but you said someone did it deliberate.' He looked hard at the trows.

Lionel and Merrow conferred with them for a moment.

'They say it was not them,' said Merrow. 'There is a huldu nearby. He made the disease.'

'Are you sayin' there's Finfolk here? In Anterwendt?'

'Where is she?'

Everyone turned to see the owner of the unexpected voice. Pieter Fredericks stood in the doorway. Rutger lurked at his shoulder. Donny Varrey strode over to them.

'Naebody here wants any trouble, Pieter.'

'Then give us the mermaid and there won't be any.'

'Ye're a bit outnumbered are ye not?'

'Your brother isn't here to fight your battles for you.'

Father Langstok rushed over. 'Pieter, please. This is Mae and Abgal's wedding.'

'Just give us the mermaid.' He looked around and saw Serena. 'There she is.' He took a step forward.

'Come an' gedder.' Jana was barring his way.

'Get out of the way, darling,' said Pieter.

'Don' darling me. I'm bad tempered at the besht of times, an' right now I'm off my face. So if you wanner, come an' gedder.'

Pieter laughed. 'Your brother's not here, so you've got your women fighting for you instead!'

Suddenly Jana was flanked by two diminutive figures. Truncherface and Bannafeet stood either side of her. Bannafeet growled.

'Bofi take dog!' spat Truncherface.

Pieter and Rutger both jumped back.

'What the hell are those?' yelped Pieter.

'Let's get out of here, Pieter,' Rutger implored him.

'It's bad enough they're harbouring mermaids, but they're in league with demons too! Come on, Rutger.'

They backed away until they reached the door, and then they turned and fled.

Jana nodded to the trows. 'You two are alright.' Then she threw up.

There was suddenly a lot of talking, as the tension was released and everyone's relief spilled out. When the commotion died down, Lionel spoke up.

'Um, we hadn't finished telling you what the trows told us.'

'What is it?' asked Adam.

'I said that were looking for their kinfolk. Well, they say they found some of them. Dead. They've taken the bodies to ... ' He tailed off.

'To where?'

'Wherever they've been living, I think. We couldn't translate the word properly.'

'Velsi,' said Merrow. 'The closest I can think is a tall, round thing.'

'Tall round thing?' repeated Adam.

'Like a cylinder?' asked Jana, wiping her mouth.

'Could be,' agreed Lionel. 'We're not sure.'

'Yeah we are,' she said. 'It's the lighthouse.'

XXIII. The Freeing of Eynhallow

When Teran made the storms rage and the seas boil, the Finfolk returned to the magical undersea kingdom of Finfolkaheem. Towers of white coral, encrusted with precious stones, spiralled upwards from gardens of seaweed of all colours, littered with giant pearls. Its great halls were made of crystal and coral, and were decorated with curtains that changed colours like the northern lights. It was never dark in the kingdom of Finfolkaheem, because it was lit by the phosphorescent glow of the ocean. In the surrounding waters, the Finfolk herded whales for their milk, and rode on them to hunt sea creatures.

But when the Sea Mither had won the Vore Tullye and bound Teran at the bottom of the sea, the Finfolk would leave their undersea kingdom to dwell on their summer home, the hidden island of Hildaland. Their magic made it invisible to mortal eyes, although occasionally someone caught a glimpse of it. Some said it was hidden by magical mists and fog banks. Others claimed that it rose up out of the sea. And still others said it was simply invisible and could not be perceived by mortals.

Hildaland was a beautiful paradise, with lush green meadows, glistening streams and fertile fields of corn and barley. The sun always shone, the breeze was always gentle and warm, and the cattle were always fat.

There was once a fisherman who had three sons. His wife died when the sons were grown, and their father married another wife. She was young and beautiful and he loved her dearly.

One day, the fisherman and his wife were down on the beach. She was closer to the water's edge than he was. His shoelace had come untied and he sat on a rock to tie it. He had his back to her when suddenly he heard her scream. Turning to see what was wrong, he was shocked to see a tall, dark man dragging her towards a boat. The fisherman ran to help his wife, but the stranger already had her aboard the boat. The fisherman waded out towards them, but the stranger picked up his oars, and with one stroke the boat had disappeared into the distance. The fisherman knew at once the stranger must be a Finman, and he swore vengeance on the accursed Finfolk.

He visited the spae-wife, who told him the greatest punishment he could inflict on the Finfolk would be to take Hildaland from them. She also told him how to get the power of seeing Hildaland with his mortal eyes, and what he should do once he found it.

For nine full moons at midnight, he went around the great Odin Stone on his bare knees. For nine full moons at midnight, he looked through the hole in the Great Odin Stane. And after nine full moons, he summoned his three sons and gave them each a straw basket. He himself took a metal chest, and off they rowed in search of Hildaland.

Eventually, the fisherman spied a beautiful green island where never had there been an island before. 'Fill the baskets,' he roared, and he pulled in the direction of the island. The sons filled their baskets with salt from the chest, but they were confused because they had not the power of seeing Hildaland, and they could see nothing but open water.

Suddenly the boat was surrounded by whales. The sons wanted to drive the whales away, but their father ordered them to row straight at the monsters. Then one rose up in front of them and opened a mouth big enough to swallow the boat whole. The fisherman stood up and threw a handful of salt into the whale's mouth, and the beast vanished, for the salt had been blessed by the priests. Encouraged by this, the sons threw salt at the other whales, and soon they were all gone, just phantoms conjured by Finfolk magic.

As they neared the island, two beautiful mermaids rose up out of the water. Their song enchanted the sons and they slowed their stroke, but their father gave them a sharp kick and they quickened the pace *again. Their father threw salt at the mermaids, who gave terrible shrieks and plunged back into the water.*

As the boat touched the shore, another monster stood in their path. It had great tusks as long as a man's arm, blazing eyes, and when it opened its mouth it breathed fire at them. The sons quailed in fear, but their father was undeterred. He threw a handful of salt between the creature's eyes and it vanished, but in its place stood a tall dark man with a sword in his hand. The fisherman knew him for the very man who had dragged his wife from the beach.

'Go back, thief,' he growled. 'You come to steal from the Finfolk, but go back or there'll be mortal blood spilled this day.'

The sons begged their father to come back to the boat, but he stood his ground and stared defiantly at the Finman. At that, the Finman struck at him with the sword, but the fisherman stepped to one side and threw the blessed salt in the Finman's face. The Finman roared out in pain, and fled.

The fisherman ordered his sons to bring the salt from the boat. They walked around the island, scattering the salt as they went. Nine times around the island they went, until nine rings of salt they had scattered, and as they did there was a terrible clamour from among the Finfolk and their livestock. They ran from the houses and the sheds, and sped down to the shore, howling and lowing. There they met the mermaids, who shrieked in response. Every last one of them headed out to sea and never again returned to the island. Their homes crumbled, and their crops withered and the enchantments fell, so the island was visible to all.

From that day, Hildaland no more belonged to the Finfolk. It was renamed Eynhallow, the holy island, and a church was built on it.

But mortals did not live there for long. The place remains haunted. If you cut grain there after sunset, it will bleed, and horses left tethered will always be found running loose after dark. Eynhallow is still an accursed, magical place and no-one lives there now.

24

Mr Coco and Mr Wobbly stood in the empty tent staring at the mirror. Mr Wobbly was playing with a yo-yo.

You still haven't brought me a mermaid.

'The local fixers turned out to be a bit unreliable,' explained Mr Coco. 'And the mermaid is being harboured by the people with the funny accents.'

Then we need more foot soldiers. See to it after the performance.

'If you say so. With or without pies?'

There was a sigh of despair.

Mr Coco, custard pies are no use as weapons in a real fight.

'Then what about – '

Neither are soda siphons.

'If you say so, but it won't be as much fun.'

The search of the boat was unsuccessful.

'They didn't find it. Either he's hidden it somewhere else, or he doesn't have it yet.'

He brought it with him. And the other is still beyond our reach. Although ...

'Although?'

There may be a way of obtaining it. As a last resort. But it would be easier to get the first one.

'Only if we knew where it was. If it's not on the – *Mr Wobbly,*' – toot toot – '*will you stop playing with that bloody yo-yo!*'

'Sorry Mr Coco. I was trying to master the Man on the Flying Trapeze.'

'What are you talking about?'

'The Man on the Flying Trapeze. It's a yo-yo trick. You start with a – '

'Shut up!'

'No need to be like that,' mumbled Mr Wobbly unhappily. 'I was just amusin' meself.'

'As I was saying,' continued Mr Coco with barely disguised exasperation.

'Sometimes I get bored.'

'If it's not on the boat,' continued Mr Coco loudly, 'where would he have hidden it?'

That's for you to discover. But first you have a performance to give. And then muster your troops.

'Why wait till after?' asked Mr Coco. 'We could kill two monkeys with one pie.'

There was a pause, as if the unseen speaker was considering.

Very well. Send in the clowns.

The coach was now heading to the lighthouse, as full as it had ever been. Adam and Jana were taking Bannafeet to show them whatever it was he wanted to show them, and Lionel and Merrow had been taken to translate. They sat next to each other, and chatted and laughed the whole time. Jana felt a pang of jealousy. The Palatine had chosen not to go because he wanted to press Murgen for more stories, and Albert had been told in no uncertain terms that, as a hero to the Seatowners for his efforts with the mortasheen, he would not be allowed to leave the festivities until he was good and drunk, and had danced something called the Bobadybouster.

The sixth seat had been intended for Truncherface, and he had left the barn with them, after insisting on hugging Maisie and Abgal and telling them, 'Gud wadirty. Eg bomfisin. Dakk,' which Lionel told them meant he was thanking them for having him at the wedding. He had then, very politely, implored them, 'Fa mjer vatnsdollja sob?' which meant he was asking for some milk to take away. Bemused, they had arranged for a small pail of milk, which Truncherface had handed over to Bannafeet. Both trows had bowed and made their exit, but then Truncherface had disappeared somewhere between the barn and the coach, and Bannafeet was evasive about his companion's whereabouts.

Bannafeet spent most of the coach journey marvelling at the plush velvet seats, and drinking the contents of the onboard bar. When they reached the lighthouse, he led them up to the middle door. Adam tried it but it was still locked. Bannafeet gave a sly smirk. Then he reached up and gave the handle a twist. They heard the lock sliding back, and the door fell open. As he pushed it in, there was a familiar shrieking from somewhere outside. Bannafeet looked upwards.

'Bofi whitemaa,' he muttered in annoyance. 'Aye skreckin'.'

'I think he's complaining about the noise the seagulls make,' Lionel translated.

The trow stepped into the room, and beckoned them to follow. 'Hannja.' Then he put a finger to his lips. 'Kyrr. Shh.'

Jana sniggered and put her own finger to her lips. 'Shhhh!'

Bannafeet turned and gave her a stern look. 'Kyrr!'

Jana held up her hand in apology. Satisfied, Bannafeet led them in.

The room was dimly lit by a small candle – too dimly to be obvious from outside, even at night, but just enough to provide light once your eyes adjusted, especially if you were already good at seeing in the dark, and also enough to give it a cosy atmosphere. For that reason, they heard before they saw. There was a sharp intake of breath from further into the room, followed by Bannafeet's reassuring voice.

'Ikke fashedy, Belia. Hann mog. Dir veru vinar.'

He was answered by another reedy voice, but higher pitched and timorous. 'Bannafeet! Eg var affrayit.'

Through the gloom, they could make out a small figure, and as their eyes grew accustomed, they saw that it was another trow. This one wore similar clothes to Bannafeet and Truncherface, but with the addition of a long skirt. She held a bundle of some sort in her arms.

'Hannja, hannja.' Bannafeet encouraged the group to come further into the room. He held his hand out to indicate the female trow. 'Hun heder Belia. Mjer heimelt,' he added proudly.

'This is Belia,' Lionel translated. 'Bannafeet's wife.'

Bannafeet introduced each of his guests by name, and Belia smiled shyly at them in turn. They could now see more of the room, and realised it was the lighthouse keeper's quarters. There was a bed on one side, and a small cupboard and a chair on the other. Lying on the chair were some torn strips of material. Two of the strips had cuffs, and another was a collar.

'Ishat ... Doc'r Vleerman's shirt?' asked Jana. 'You stole it?'

Adam looked at Belia's bundle. 'And I wouldn't be surprised if those are Father van Bleric's blankets.'

'What will they need them for?' wondered Merrow.

And then the bundle cried.

Jana gasped. 'Is that ... ?'

Belia took a protective step back, but Bannafeet reassured her again. 'Ikke fashedy, ikke fashedy.' He smiled at Jana, and beckoned her over. He pulled the blankets aside enough for her to see the baby. It was human, not trow. And was still crying.

Bannafeet dipped his finger in the pail of milk, and held it to the baby's mouth. The baby turned its head away and kept crying.

'That's not how you stop a baby crying,' said Jana. She reached out her arms. Belia gave her an anxious look, and then turned to Bannafeet for confirmation. He nodded encouragingly. Reluctantly, Belia handed the baby over to Jana.

'Husa,' she said.

Jana gently rocked the baby in her arms, making the sorts of noises people make to babies even when they're not drunk.

Lionel leaned across to Adam and whispered, 'Is she sober enough to be holding a baby?'

'You try taking it off her.'

Jana began singing softly, some song Adam had never heard involving babies falling out of trees. He wasn't at all sure that it would calm an already distressed infant. But somehow it did. Gradually, the crying subsided and the baby started making soft cooing noises that sounded only marginally less intelligent than the ones Jana had been making a minute ago.

'Ah, kirrabaw!' said Belia as if there had been some great revelation.

'She had not thought of a lullabye,' explained Merrow.

With the baby now quiet, Jana opened the blankets further, to reveal the infant's lower half. It was wrapped in a makeshift nappy made from a strip of shirt material held together with – 'Hey, that's my earring!' And it was a lower half that was completely unmistakable. 'It's Lorelei.'

'Bannj fra brennek,' said Bannafeet, looking at Lionel and Merrow expectantly.

'He says the baby is the child from the end of the rainbow,' said Lionel, bemused.

'Pilot said something about a rainbow predicting a birth,' Adam remembered, 'but he said it meant a boy.'

'Moder vara hintet,' added Bannafeet, tapping his temple.

'Er,' said Lionel embarrassed, 'he says the mother, um … ' He looked uncomfortably at Merrow. She clasped his hand and smiled.

'It is fine. I know what he said. The mother is not right in the head. Ceasg has always had difficulty.'

'Kallj tug bolk onjder gloamr,' Bannafeet continued, and Lionel and Merrow attempted to keep up with the tale he told them. A man had come with a bundle at night. He put it into the sea and went away. The trows had gone to see what it was, and found a baby floating in the water. If they hadn't been there, its blanket would have dragged it under.

'Illhaited, dubjasafit,' was how Belia described the child: deformed and sickly.

She and Bannafeet had taken the baby up to the lighthouse, while Truncherface had followed the man 'i gaba, onjda bor,' – into the cave and under the hole, which the humans took to mean down the underground passage. At the end was the 'granderi veda', the magic water, where the man had stood calling out. After a while, he grew worried, and then he turned and ran back up the passage. But when he saw Truncherface, he was surprised, and tripped and fell, 'blaget.' Dead.

'It sounds like Matheeus was expecting something to happen,' mused Adam, 'and when it didn't, he panicked for some reason.'

'I think he was expecting something to save Lorelei,' agreed Jana, 'but then he realised it wasn't going to happen.'

'Expecting what though?'

'The tunnel's supposed to be used by mermaids,' suggested Jana. 'And it ends with that weird wall of water. And Matheeus originally came from Haerlem, where Father Langstok's mermaid lived. Maybe he grew up believing in mermaids, and finding the tunnel would just have confirmed it to him.'

'You think he was expecting mermaids to save the baby?' asked Merrow.

'Maybe he thought she really was a mermaid, and would be better off with her own kind. Or,' she continued, remembering her conversation with Albert, 'maybe he convinced himself of that to avoid dealing with the truth.'

'And these took care of the baby this whole time?' asked Merrow, not sounding entirely convinced.

At this, Bannafeet launched into a string of what sounded like complaints. 'Gratska, dao virpa, dao dyba a! Onjgdi drit, onjgdi innrid! Eg aga jartfallj.'

'Bannafeet!' Belia scolded him.

'He, er,' began Lionel, 'he says the baby's a bit noisy and, er, smelly.'

Something in Merrow's expression told Jana that Lionel's translation had been somewhat toned down from the original.

His rant out of his system, Bannafeet appeared to remember something else. 'Hannja, hannja,' he beckoned, heading towards the door.

'You go,' said Merrow. 'I will stay here with the child of my sister.'

The others followed Bannafeet down the stairs and around the back of the lighthouse, to the mound Adam had seen from the gallery. Once again, he remembered Murgen's stories.

'It's a howe. Or a knowe. One of the two.'

'A what?' asked Jana.

'A trow mound. It's where they live.'

'They live in the lighthouse.'

'Yeah, strange that. Maybe they've got something else in there.'

'In it? It's a lump in the ground. All that's in it's more lump.'

'Then where's Bannafeet gone?'

They all looked. There was no sign of the trow, although he had been there only a moment before. Jana walked around the mound and back, but didn't find him. And then suddenly his head poked out of a hole they had barely noticed.

'Hannja. Dvarga!' He looked around at them and saw the problem.

'Fjagers!' he said irritably. He disappeared inside the mound again, and there was a faint scuffling sound. After a few minutes, the area around the hole caved in, creating a much bigger space. Bannafeet looked at his handiwork and shook his head with a sigh. 'Whitna steer.'

The space was just big enough for them to squeeze through, which was evidently what Bannafeet expected. They had to push through about three feet of earth before it opened into a small chamber. It had been roughly excavated, and was undecorated, unlike the howes in the stories Murgen had told. The light from the entrance was just enough for them to see that the chamber contained three objects, all very similar. The first, still in its case, was the Haerlem mermaid from Father Langstok's museum. The second was the Feejee mermaid from the circus. The third was unfamiliar to Adam, Jana and Lionel, but Albert and Lord Reitherman would have recognised it as the mermaid from Albertus Seba's collection.

'Blodfrind,' said Bannafeet sadly.

'These ... these are the dead kinsmen they found,' Lionel translated, his voice hollow.

The three humans stared in shock. They could see now that the top halves of the creatures were indeed trows, somehow joined to fishlike tails.

'Who did this to them?' asked Jana at last.

'And how?' added Lionel.

'Never mind how,' said Jana, the anger building in her voice. 'Why? Why would anyone do ... this?'

'The trows that were taken,' Adam quoted.

'Or changed,' Lionel added.

'Huldufolk,' said Bannafeet sadly. 'Frolik.'

'The Finfolk and their old magic,' said Adam.

'And they think there's one in Anterwendt?' Jana remembered.

Adam didn't reply, but he was thinking it wasn't too hard to guess who. He walked over to the three mermaids for a closer look. He had thought they were unconvincing when he saw them in their various exhibitions, but now he was forced to look again. You really couldn't see the joins. There were no signs of stitching or any other means of connecting the two halves. His original assessment that it must be a

335

fish and something else joined together still held, it was just a different something else. He had previously thought it grotesque, but now he upgraded that to monstrous. The sightless eyes and the drawn-back lips now looked frightened rather than frightening. Something terrible had happened to these trows, not just when they had been turned into mermaids, but also when they had died. And what creatures had been sacrificed to make their tails? He remembered Murgen's story of the mermaid who had her tail changed into legs by the Storm Witch, and then he thought of Serena's scarred legs, apparently made of porpoise blubber. Trows had been given fish tails, and a woman had once had a porpoise tail, which had been split and reformed into legs. They had to be related. Made by the same 'old magic'. Or perhaps the same old science. A nasty thought was growing in his mind.

He felt Jana at his shoulder. Or rather he realised that she had been at his shoulder and had now suddenly moved. He turned to see her squeezing frantically back through the entrance. Once she was outside, she ran to the edge of the cliff, threw herself on the ground and vomited over the side.

A very surprised seagull screeched loudly and flew to the sea to wash itself off.

She gulped air a few times and then sat up, her head a little clearer. Adam was standing next to her.

'I think we've seen all there is to see here. When you're ready you can show me that wall of water.'

Half an hour later they stood staring at the water at the end of the tunnel. Adam examined it carefully, running his fingers around the edge of the rock, peering into the distance and finally touching the water for just a second, having been warned by Jana about its cold-ness.

'So how's it done?' Jana asked him, after she felt he'd been silent for longer than was polite.

'Search me. I've never heard of any kind of magic that can do this.'

Bannafeet tugged urgently at Lionel's jacket, and pointed into the water. 'Mareld,' he said, a note of awe in his voice. 'Dekk.'

'What did he say?' asked Jana.

' "Dekk" is the bottom of the sea,' said Lionel, 'but "mareld" is more difficult. I'm not sure that there is an exact translation. The closest I can think of is "the light beneath the waves." '

'Does he know what it is?' asked Adam.

Lionel asked him, and the trow struggled to articulate whatever he wanted to say. Eventually he shrugged and simply said, 'Derg.'

'Something important or valuable, I think' said Lionel.

'We'd better get back to the lighthouse,' said Adam unexpectedly. He turned and headed back along the passage. The others exchanged surprised looks and followed him.

Back in the bedroom, Merrow and Belia were still cooing over the baby. When the others arrived, Merrow looked up and said to Jana, 'We have to tell Ceasg.'

Jana sat down on the bed next to her. 'Merrow, have you thought about what's going to happen to them both?'

'What do you mean?'

'Well, Ceasg can't look after Lorelei on her own. She can barely look after herself. And you came to take her home with you. But you can't take a baby in that boat, can you?'

Merrow looked at the floor and then at Lorelei. 'What do you think we must do?'

Jana thought about it. Her fingers brushed the tickets in her pocket.

'I think we should go to the circus.'

They never understood how Bannafeet opened the padlock. He simply gave it a pull and it opened. He grinned at their surprise, but he offered no explanation.

Adam had taken Lionel back to the circus, while Jana and Merrow had taken Lorelei back to her mother. Belia had been reluctant, but eventually gave in after Bannafeet had whispered something to her that none of the others had heard. She had then seemed happy to wait alone in the lighthouse, while her husband went to open the locker.

Bannafeet swung the door open and climbed up into the locker. A few seconds later, he emerged dragging the sealskin behind him. He let it fall to the ground, and then he scrambled down the shelves. Ceasg handed Lorelei to Merrow, leaped up and swept the skin from the floor, hugging it to her chest. Then she held it up, allowing it to hang down so they could see all of it.

'It's an actual sealskin,' said Jana in surprise.

'This was not what I was expecting,' said Merrow. 'Those are not her clothes for paddling a kayak.'

'Maybe that's not the point,' said Jana thoughtfully.

'What do you mean?'

'Maybe Matheeus never had her clothes. Her boat's gone. He found her living in the cave. Maybe she spoke about her skin and he didn't know what she meant. But he knew she was, well, a bit confused, and vulnerable too. And he'd heard about selkies from the Seatowners. So he got a sealskin and locked it in the cupboard to keep Ceasg from going back to the sea. Maybe he thought he was protecting her. From herself as much as anything else.'

'Matheeus always protects me,' agreed Ceasg.

Jana looked at her sadly. 'Ceasg, you do remember that Matheeus died, don't you?'

'Oh yes, so he did. It was very sad. But I have my skin now. And my baby. I can go back to the sea.'

Jana sat Ceasg down on the bed, and then sat next to her. 'Ceasg, you can't take a baby into the sea. Or on a long journey back to your home-land.'

'But she's a mermaid, Jana. She belongs in the sea.'

'No, Ceasg. She's not a mermaid. She's just very, very sick. Which reminds me: we should get Doctor Vleerman to check her out and make sure she's okay.'

'But I have to go back to the sea, Jana. It's been too long.' There was a note of agitation in Ceasg's voice, and she looked anxiously at Lorelei.

'Then you must decide,' said Merrow. 'Which is more important? Staying here with Lorelei, or coming home with me. Sadly, you can not do both.'

Ceasg thought. 'It's been so long since I was home, and I've missed everyone very much. And I long to go back to the sea. And when you think about it really, I haven't known Lorelei for very long, and I don't really know how to look after her properly, so I should probably leave her with Bannafeet and his wife. Mrs Bannafeet.' She said all of this in her dreamy, matter-of-fact way, as if it was the most normal thing in the world.

'I don't think we can leave her with the trows,' said Jana, 'but I do have another idea.'

As she explained it, Bannafeet was looking curiously at the locker. He shinned back up the shelves and disappeared inside.

'It's a good plan,' said Ceasg with no hint of sadness. 'And it sounds like fun. Let's do that.'

'But there is still only one kayak,' Marrow reminded them.

'I think I know how to deal with that too,' said Jana. 'We might need Bannafeet's help. Where is he?'

Bannafeet poked his head out form the locker and grinned. 'Hannja,' he beckoned. 'Bjarga derg.'

'He said there is, I think, a hidden, um, a treasure that is hidden,' Merrow faltered. 'Lionel is better at this than I am. I wish he was here.'

I bet you do, thought Jana, and then felt bad about it. They all stood and walked to the locker, Merrow still holding the baby.

'Ljus,' demanded Bannafeet, pointing at the lamp beside the bed.

Jana lit it and brought it over, so it illuminated the inside of the locker. Bannafeet scuttled to the back, and then turned and held up a finger, as if telling them to wait. Then he indicated the back of the locker, like a conjurer pointing out the perfectly ordinary trick box. He rapped twice sharply on the wood, looked back at them, and winked. He cracked his knuckles, and finally pressed a spot on the wood. A section of it slid open to reveal a secret compartment.

'Ei!' he exclaimed triumphantly. He reached into the space and pulled out a small book, which he handed to Jana. She flicked through it, and then stared into space, amazed at what she had read.

'What is it, Jana?' asked Ceasg.

'It's Matheeus's journal. He really did believe you were a mermaid.'

'I'm a selkie, not a mermaid.'

'He thought you came through the wall of water. From – ' She looked at Bannafeet. 'From what he called "the light beneath the waves." '

'That sounds pretty.'

'He says that mermaids came and went through the wall of water all

339

the time. And when he went to the wall himself ... ' She looked at Merrow in disbelief. 'They'd come and talk to him.'

'That is why he thought they would come that night,' breathed Merrow. 'Do you think it was real, or was he mad in the head?'

'I don't know. But the wall of water's real enough. And so were those bodies in the mound.' She closed the book and put it down on the bed. 'I'll go and fetch the doctor. Then I'll ask one of the spae-wives to look after Lorelei while we go to the show.'

The *Sapphire* stood silent in the harbour, the water lapping at its barnacle-encrusted hull. All the other boats sat side-on to the wall for easy access, but the *Sapphire* had its pointy end – Adam didn't know the correct terminology – facing inland, making it harder to get on or off. Presumably the belligerent man who had salvaged it either used the rope ladder, or had to jump the distance from the boat to the wall. Adam was sure he was capable of it. His voluminous layers of clothes would probably catch the wind and let him glide gently to the ground.

Getting up was much harder though. It wasn't actually that high – in fact the harbour was designed so the side of a boat, the point where you would normally get on, was more or less level with the wall, but the *Sapphire* sloped up at the front, so Adam had to jump up and catch hold of the edge, and then try to haul himself upwards.

At least until a hand clamped around his wrist and dragged him up on to the deck. As Adam was dropped in a heap, he noted the man had done it *with just one hand*. He looked up into the foreboding face of the mystery man who, to Adam at least, was no longer a mystery.

'What're ye doin' on my boat?' the man snarled.

Adam warily got to his feet, never taking an eye off the man. 'I know who you are.'

'Do ye now?' The man gave no indication that this might bother him.

'The flowing clothes, the bad temper, the impossible manoeuvres with the boat. You're a Finman.'

'I already know who I am. What of it?'

'In the stories, you're supposed to be able to cause storms. You wrecked the *Intrepid*, didn't you? And only you would know enough about mortasheen to poison the Seatowners' barley.'

'The boat was too close. And the villagers needed to be broken. They have something that I want.'

'I think they have more than one thing that you want, don't they?'

'Why are you here, boy?'

'Because you know how mermaids are made, don't you? And where.'

'You're not the one I'm supposed to give it to.'

'So that *is* why you're here.'

For the first time the Finman's face registered surprise. 'You think you can play me, boy?'

Adam didn't see the huge fist coming at him, but he felt it strike his temple. And then he felt himself hit the water, just before everything went black.

XXIV. The Mermaid's Tears

*T*here was once a mermaid, who saw a young monk walking on the beach. She thought him very handsome, and used to come and watch him every day from behind a rock as he walked. But one day he spied her and smiled at her. By now, she had fallen in love with her young monk, and so she needed no further encouragement to come out from hiding and swim up to the beach to talk to him. At first he was surprised when he saw her tail, but he soon got over it, and they sat and talked until he had to go and take care of his duties in the monastery.

Every day for a week they met and talked, and at last the mermaid could hold back no more, and confessed her love to the monk. But mermaids have no souls, and the monk told her that she must gain one. She thought gaining a soul would enable him to love her, but alas, she did not realise that he only wished for her to go to heaven, for he was a monk and could never marry.

She asked him how she could gain a soul, and he told her she must forsake the sea and come to live on land. This saddened her greatly, for she knew that she could never leave the sea.

But she loved the monk dearly, so every night she came ashore and went right up to his window. There he would pray that she might gain an immortal soul and go to heaven; and she would pray for a soul so the monk would marry her. And every night, she realised her prayers had still not been answered, and she would run back to the sea crying.

When her tears touched the ground, they formed green pebbles that still litter the beach, and are to this day known as mermaid's tears. It's said that if you carry one with you, you'll never drown.

One day the mermaid stopped coming, and the monk felt sad. Perhaps it was because he knew she had chosen the sea over an immortal soul. Or maybe he'd finally realised, too late, that he loved her after all.

25

Ben Varrey put down the bottle with a thump. He'd come home in a bad mood, and had now drunk himself into a rage. He could no longer remember what it was he was angry about, but that wasn't the point. He was good and angry, and that was all that mattered. And now he had to do something about it.

He did what he always did. He got up – which took two or three attempts – and staggered through the door to the bedroom. Liban's cot sat next to Ben's own bed. She was too old for it now, but Ben had never replaced it because it would cost money, and he still saw her as a baby. The blanket was pulled over her huddled form.

'Liban!'

She didn't stir.

'Liban! Wake up till I gie ye a thrashin'.'

There was still no response. His rage mounting, Ben clenched his fist into a tight ball and hauled back the blanket with his other hand.

The thing that sat up and grinned at him definitely wasn't Liban.

'Haust,' said Truncherface, and punched him between the eyes.

'My name is Coco the clown – but you can call me *Mister* Coco. And this is my associate Mr Wobbly.' *Toot toot.*

The big top was full, and the crowd was chattering excitedly. The smells of hot food wafted throughout the tent from the stalls outside, and the various examples being eaten by the audience. Occasionally, more sellers walked among them trying to tempt them further with bags of roast chestnuts, honeyed apples or their latest delicacy, trifle doughnuts. The clowns stood in the ring doing their routine, and introducing the other acts.

Jana looked around the crowd and saw a number of familiar faces. Father Langstok had evidently slipped away from the wedding festivities, and sat munching a trifle doughnut, and occasionally sucking drops of jam or custard off hs sleeve. He saw her, and waved happily. She waved back.

The two fishermen who had thrown stones at the mission and then disrupted the wedding were also there, looking somewhat uncomfortable in the back row. Vleerman had turned up too, and he nodded to her, unsmiling. Right at the front, exactly where Jana would have expected him, sat the Palatine, who seemed to have bought some-thing from every food stall. She noticed Albert wasn't with him, but then she didn't think this would be Albert's sort of thing. Perhaps he was still at the wedding, feeling overwhelmed by his guest of honour status.

Merrow looked a little bemused by the whole place, but Ceasg sat smiling and clapping her hands in her childlike way.

'Oh Jana, this is so exciting! Thank you for bringing me here. And I think it's a wonderful idea.'

Before entering the big top, they had taken time to wander around the sideshows and visited the freak show, allowing the sisters to soak up the entire atmosphere of the circus. And allowing Merrow to steal a few minutes with Lionel, which turned into a surprisingly intense whispered conversation.

Murgen had agreed to leave the wedding to look after Lorelei, and had taken no persuasion whatsoever. The news that the baby had been found had caused a sensation among the wedding guests, and many had wanted to go and see her immediately, or asked that she be brought to the barn for everyone to dote on. But it was agreed that the noise and crowds were the last thing little Lorelei needed, and they could all could visit her later, in dribs and drabs. Before that, Doctor Vleerman had been called to examine the baby, and had been amazed at how good her condition seemed to be. The trows had taken surprisingly good care of her, and she was evidently stronger than he would have imagined possible.

The first act was an acrobatic troupe, and everyone oohed and aahed at their daring, and presumably very uncomfortable exploits. Merrow seemed particularly impressed by the bulging muscles of the men, and applauded enthusiastically throughout. Jana enjoyed them too, but found her attention unaccountably slipping. Her head felt a little fuzzy for a moment, and then suddenly cleared, leaving her with a slight headache. It was as if a fly had been buzzing around inside her mind and then flown out again. She shook her head to clear it. She noticed that Merrow looked slightly confused, although Ceasg was just as happy as she had been all evening. By now the acrobats were finishing, and the clowns returned.

'And now for something *different*,' announced Mr Coco. 'If you don't like things that are *different,* then you know what you can do.'

Jana felt that this joke fell a bit flat, but most of the audience seemed to love it and cheered. The next act featured horses doing things like walking on their hind legs, and moving in time to music. Jana thought they were very clever, but knew Adam would disapprove.

When the clowns reappeared, their patter continued to take a bizarre turn. 'Well, people of Anterwendt, we've had a look round your town, and noticed you've got a harbour where you land your fish, people of Anterwendt.'

'Where's that, Mr Coco?'

'Out there, Mr Wobbly.' *Toot toot.* Laughter. 'See? Town, harbour, fish, people.'

For some strange reason, most of the audience loved this, but Jana found it baffling. Was she missing something? She looked at Merrow, who was equally bemused. Ceasg was still smiling, but there was a suggestion that she was no longer sure what she was smiling at. Jana looked across at Father Langstok, and he too bore a quizzical expression. Doctor Vleerman looked stern, and she couldn't see the Palatine's face.

And so it went on. Human cannonballs, and fire eaters and trapeze artists came and went, animals did things that were very impressive because they were so contrary to nature, and in between, the clowns came on and made laboured remarks that pleased the crowd but left

Jana wondering if they were speaking in some code she couldn't discern. At one point, they performed a card trick and dragged the extremely willing Palatine up on stage to help them. Of course, it went spectacularly wrong, to much hilarity, but by now Jana felt the clowns' appeal was waning. At the end of the trick, instead of returning to his seat, the Palatine left, which Jana found just as odd as everything else. Still, Ceasg looked happy, which was the main thing, and Merrow still seemed to be enjoying herself, despite the clowns, which was just as important.

Jana decided to distract herself from the weird clowns by sampling a trifle doughnut. It tasted good, but she'd probably have to throw this shirt out.

It was the rhythmic pressure on his stomach that shocked Adam into consciousness. That and the fact he was vomiting water, which was difficult to ignore. As he groggily took in his surroundings, it occurred to him that being rendered unconscious was becoming something of a habit lately, and perhaps he should consider giving it up.

He was lying on the wooden floor of what he soon realised was a boat. Not the *Sapphire* though. A much bigger boat. Did that make it a ship? Was there a difference? It definitely wasn't a fishing boat, and he quickly realised that there were only two vessels in the vicinity this large. As the deck wasn't crawling with Imperial navymen demanding an explanation for his presence here, it had to be the *Venture*, which would be much easier to get aboard, considering its crew was stood down awaiting the captain's return from his family illness.

The person pumping Adam's stomach turned out to be Baabie. She was as wet through as he was.

'Ye're aye alive then,' she remarked, sitting back with a sigh. 'I'm affy glad, cos I couldna hae done that much longer.'

Adam sat up and looked at her wet clothes in disbelief. 'Did you pull me out of the water?'

She laughed. 'And why not? Because I'm old and fat, is that it?'

'I didn't say that.'

'Just as well. But ye thocht it a' the same. Well it shouldna be such a surprise to ye. Ye ken who he is – I heard ye talkin' tae him – and I told you he wis ma husband. So what does that mak me?'

Adam hung his head in annoyance at missing that link. 'You're a Finwife.'

'And one thing the Finfolk can do is swim.'

Adam suddenly looked up. 'But that means you used to be a mermaid, doesn't it?.'

She laughed again. 'The stories are a bit ravelled. Mixed up. Ah'm no mermaid and never was. But I was sent here tae spy on the Seatowners, and earn white metal to send back to him. I just saw it as a chance tae escape, and I became one o' them.'

'But he came and found you. And gave you a black eye for your troubles.'

'It's no the first,' she said tersely. 'You shouldna hae tried to tak him on by yersel. Ye're lucky I wis keepin' an eye on him, or ye'd be at the bottom o' the harbour by noo.'

'Thank you.'

'An' noo that ye're here, ye can stay and aye keep watch wi' me. There's dark deeds afoot the nicht.'

'What sort of dark deeds?'

'We'll hae to wait an' see. But I think this is the nicht he's going to do what he came here for.'

Adam pulled himself up to his knees and crawled to the side of the ship to get a view of the *Sapphire*. 'Then he'll have a meeting arranged. Maybe two.'

'You ken more aboot this than ye've been letin' on, young Adam.'

'Yes. Jana hates that about me.'

'Aye, she told me.'

Adam decided to let this pass, and settled down to wait for the night's drama to play out.

The audience spilled out of the big top, all heading back to wherever they were heading. Except rather a lot of them were all heading in the same direction. Crowds didn't normally do that. They usually all headed off in lots of different directions. But the greater proportion of this crowd was, there was no other word for it, flocking. They were walking purposefully away from the playing fields in the direction of the sea front. At their head were the two fishermen who'd gatecrashed the wedding, and a man in priest's robes.

Jana looked around for Father Langstok and Doctor Vleerman, and steered Merrow and Ceasg towards them.

'It *is* odd, isn't it?' agreed Father Langstok. 'Very odd. Where do you think they're going?'

'With those two fisherman leading them, I'd guess they're going to the Seatown for Serena,' said Jana.

'We should follow them,' said Vleerman. 'Not that we can do much against so many, but we can't just ignore them.'

As they walked away after the crowd, Mr Coco and Mr Wobbly stood watching from the entrance to the big top.

'D'you wanna go and watch, Mr Coco?' asked Mr Wobbly, casually taking a bite out of a trifle doughnut.

'Why not?'

'Well, I can't think of a reason why not,' replied Mr Wobbly in confusion. 'I was the one suggested we should do it in the first place, so really I was thinkin' of reasons why, not reasons why not.'

'It was rhetorical, you doughnut,' said Mr Coco irritably.

'Rhetorical. That means a question that doesn't need an answer, doesn't it? What I can't understand is, why bother asking it at all if it doesn't need an answer? Just a waste of time if you ask me.'

'Shut up and eat your doughnut, you doughnut.'

They took a couple of steps towards the crowd, but suddenly found their way blocked by an imposing yet decorative figure.

'Can we have a word?' asked the tattooed man.

It still wasn't real, it was still a dream. Fish and other marine creatures were dancing and singing. Not the haunting whalesong, but real, melodic music. Several of them were playing musical instruments, some of which he didn't recognise. An octopus played lots of different drums, a stick in each tentacle. A seal performed an erotic dance, stripping off its skin to reveal a woman underneath, and then stripping off that skin to reveal another seal. The whole ensemble was conducted by an excitable lobster, and watched by a mermaid who danced in time to the music. The lyrics seemed to be mainly about how much better life was on the sea bed because fish all love music, or something, and included couplets such as, 'We're all in luck down here in the muck, "Quack" said the man, "Duck" said the duck.'

Lights danced around them, illuminating the scene and changing colour in a way that somehow added to the spectacle. And yet he felt someone was missing, although he couldn't think who.

As the song reached its climax, the performers all swirled around in a frenzy, kicking up clouds of sand, which suddenly dispersed in exactly the way they never would in real life, at the precise moment the music stopped.

The mermaid was gone.

Ben sat bolt upright where he had fallen asleep on the makeshift wedding table, and suddenly remembered who was missing.

'Jana!'

He looked around the barn at the revellers. There was no sign of Jana. And there was no sign of Serena either. Jana could be anywhere, but Serena wouldn't have gone far from Ben. Something was wrong. But at the same time, something was right. His head felt clear for the first time in days. And now that it did, he didn't know what to do.

'We're a bit busy, really,' protested Mr Coco, as the tattooed man steered him into the freak show tent.

'Things to do, people to humiliate,' added Mr Wobbly.

'This won't take long,' said the tattooed man, indicating the entrance to Prince Randian's tent.

Inside were all of the freak show performers, as well as several of the big top acts. They all wore unhappy expressions.

'You all look thoroughly miserable,' said Mr Wobbly gravely. 'I think our work here is done.'

'You could be right,' said the tattooed man.

'What does that mean?' asked Mr Coco.

'Something weird happened in the big top tonight,' said the tattooed man. 'In fact, we think something weird's been happening here for a while.'

'We're all weird,' replied Mr Coco. 'It's a circus.'

'When did you pair actually join?' asked Randian. 'None of us can remember. It's like you were just here and no-one noticed.'

'That's hardly our fault,' said Mr Coco.

'Isn't it?' asked Lionel. 'That mermaid you caught when you went fishing. It wasn't a mermaid at all. It was a trow.'

'Anyone can make a mistake,' said Mr Wobbly reasonably.

'Except,' pressed Lionel, 'it turns out the trows *are* related to the mermaids after all.'

'Then we got it right. You can't have it both ways.'

'How did you know?'

'Well, it's just basic common sense - '

'How did you know about the trows?'

'Why were you mermaid hunting in the first place?' asked Randian, before they could answer.

'Who really runs the circus?' asked the tattooed man. 'Who runs *you?*'

'Look,' said Mr Coco, 'this is all very entertaining – '

'Not really,' interrupted Mr Wobbly.

'No, not really,' agreed Mr Coco, 'but we've got a rather pressing engagement.

As the clowns turned towards the entrance, the tattooed man stepped in their way.

'I think we'd rather have this out first.'

Mr Coco only raised his hand slightly.

Mr Wobbly grabbed the tattooed man by the throat, and simultaneously kneed him in the groin. As the tattooed man sagged, Mr Wobbly took him by the shoulders, whirled around and sent him flying into the group, knocking several of them over.

The clowns didn't even bother to look back as they left.

No-one followed them.

As Adam and Baabie watched the harbour, their attention was distracted by lights. In the far distance, there were several lights moving down the street from the direction of the playing fields. A crowd was heading in the direction of the sea front. Crowds moving purposefully were never good.

'Maybe we should go and see what's happening,' said Adam, starting to get up.

Baabie pulled him down again. 'Look.'

Coming down a different street was the unmistakable figure of the Palatine, and he was heading straight for the *Sapphire*.

'Is that who you were expecting?' whispered Baabie in surprise.

'Yes. I'm not entirely sure what he's up to, but I thought he'd come.'

As the Palatine reached the harbour, he saw the crowd in the distance and stopped to watch. Instead of continuing along the promenade, they turned towards the Seatown.

'Whit's that a' aboot?' asked Baabie anxiously.

'I'd say those two fishermen who came for Serena earlier on have come back with reinforcements.'

'Whit do we do?'

'We can't do anything now. If we move from here, we'll disturb Lord Reitherman's meeting.'

They stayed where they were and continued to watch, but now they were breathing more heavily, as their anxiety mounted.

The crowd made its way through the Seatown to the barn. There were no flaming torches, but many carried lanterns. One actually had a pitchfork. They stopped outside, and Pieter hammered on the door.

'Come out and face us.' There was no answer, and there was still the noise of merrymaking from inside. He hammered again. 'Come out!'

'Pieter, what are you doing?' Father Langstok came around the side of the crowd with Jana, Merrow and Doctor Vleerman.

'Get out of the way, Father, our quarrel's not with you.'

'Why is there any quarrel at all?'

'You know why.'

'Oh, not this mermaid business again. You're causing arguments over fairy stories.'

'You know that's not true. I've seen your museum.'

'That's just a bit of fun, Pieter! But this is getting out of hand.'

Pieter spoke over his shoulder. 'Tell him, Father.'

Father van Bleric stepped forward. 'Mermaids are fallen angels who have no souls.' A murmur of agreement rippled through the crowd. 'And they'll stop at nothing to gain one. Nothing!' The murmur grew louder. 'They live in their undersea kingdom, and create storms to cause shipwrecks, so they can drag sailors down to eat their flesh.'

'Like the crew of the *Intrepid*,' shouted Pieter, and the crowd roared its approval.

'They tear them to pieces with their green spiky teeth.' The crowd cheered. 'Their lustful natures endanger our immortal souls.' Another cheer. 'They are a threat to our very way of life.'

It was virtually the same speech he had given to Adam in the church, but now it was spoken with a great deal more conviction, and it was working the crowd up. Jana noticed the Scary Clowns lurking in the background, casually watching the proceedings.

'Listen to yourself,' Father Langstok implored him. 'This is madness.'

'Don't get in our way, Father,' Pieter warned him.

'And what is it that you're going to do, Pieter?'

'Just give us the mermaid.'

'So you can do what with her?'

By now the noise of the crowd had penetrated the music inside the barn, and the door opened. Mary Player and Donny Varrey stood there.

'Whit's goin' on oot here?' demanded Mary.

'We've come for the mermaid,' Pieter said again.

'Can't any of you see some reason?' implored Father Langstok. 'You, Rutger. You're a reasonable man. I know you are. Can't you talk some sense into Pieter?'

Rutger looked confused. 'I ... ' There was a pleading in his eyes, but then he looked at Pieter, and the expression turned to fear. He bowed his head, avoiding eye contact with anyone.

'Give us the mermaid,' repeated Father van Bleric. 'Then the cancer at the heart of the Seatown will be torn out, and the rest of you can live in peace.'

'Is that supposed to be a threat?' asked Mary. 'It sounds awfy like one. Will ye no' let us live in peace if we don't do whit ye ask?'

'Don't stand in our way, Mary.'

'So ye do know who I am, Pieter Fredericks. I helped deliver you when the doctor couldn't come. Don't think ye're too big to go over my knee now.'

There were a few sniggers from the crowd. The clowns looked on with interest, but did nothing.

'I don't think you want to put that to the test,' said Pieter darkly. The sniggering stopped. There was a pause before Mary replied, and when she did, her voice sounded just a fraction less certain.

'Then it's a good job we'll no have to. Serena's no here.'

'I saw her before.'

'Aye but she's gone now. Disappeared.'

At this, Jana's ears pricked up. She squeezed past Mary into the barn. Merrow followed her. Father Langstok and Doctor Vleerman remained outside, facing the crowd. Pieter took a step forward, as if to follow Jana, but a commotion at the back made him stop. Members of the crowd were being pushed aside as someone forced their way through. No-one was standing up to whoever it was, and it soon became clear why when Ben Varrey barged his way to the front. On seeing his brother, he walked straight to him.

'Where's Liban?'

'What do ye mean? She wis with you.'

'An' noo she's gone. One o' those trows wis in her bed. If she's come back here – '

'She's no. Hiv you lost her?' There was a darker shade than usual in Donny's voice.

'She's been taen by her ain kind. An' they'll hae taen her back here so a' you trowie lovers can dance wi them.'

'She's no here, Ben. If anything's happened to her – '

'You'll what?' Donny fell silent. 'Ye havena the guts. Oot o' my road.' He pushed roughly past Donny and into the barn. The crowd was reluctant to follow.

Inside, Jana had quickly established that Serena was nowhere to be seen. She also spotted Bannafeet and Truncherface sitting on the beam, swinging their legs and eating what looked suspiciously like trifle doughnuts. Before she could do anything, Ben had come running over to her. She gritted her teeth and said, 'I know, I heard: Serena's missing. And I suppose you'll want me to help you look for her. Alright. Who saw her last?'

To her surprise, Ben clasped her hand. 'Jana, I'm sorry.'

'What?'

'I've treated you so badly. I don't know what came over me, but it's like I've suddenly woken up and remembered you. Can you forgive me?'

Jana stared at him, speechless. She remembered what Adam had said about Ben being under a spell, and their guesses about the so-called special scent. And then she remembered all the times she had seen Serena kissing Ben. She'd probably breathed air in to his mouth when she rescued him. Was that the chemical exchange? Was each kiss a way of reinforcing it? And now that she had been gone for too long it had worn off.

She smiled at him, just slightly. 'You were under her spell.'

'And now I'm free.' He smiled back.

Up in the beams, Bannafeet nudged Truncherface. 'Aww, de drenga.'

Truncherface leaned forward eagerly. 'Kuss! Kuss, kuss, kuss, kuss!'

Ben leaned forward and kissed Jana. To his immense relief – and the trows' delight – she kissed him back. A long, passionate kiss with lips and hands and everything, that made him tingle and her melt.

Truncherface punched the air. 'Kuss!'

The moment was interrupted by Ben Varrey bursting in.

'Liban!' he shouted. 'Come here now, or I'll gie ye a hot backside.'

'Fjagers!' snarled Truncherface.

'Bofi bruit!

They both jumped down, to land in front of Ben Varrey. At the same time, Donny strode up behind him, and Jana and young Ben turned to face him. Ben Varrey glared at them all.

'Get oota ma way, the lot o' ye. An' bring me ma daughter. Now!'

Seeing the confused looks, Donny explained, 'Liban's missing.'

'Liban *and* Serena?' Jana looked at Merrow, but said nothing more.

By now, all sounds of merriment had stopped, and everyone was watching the confrontation.

Ben Varrey focused his attention on the trows. 'Look at ye all. Dancin' wi devils an' evil spirits. The whole lot o' you should be given to the witch-finders.'

'Eviltu,' growled Truncherface in a warning tone.

Ben Varrey stared at the trows, but his expression showed he was still afraid of them. Instead, he swung around and spoke to Donny. 'Where is she? If ye don't bring her here now, I swear I'll brak ye into wee pieces.'

Donny was breathing heavily, obviously scared of his brother. 'Let's go and look for her together. Let's – '

Ben Varrey raised a fist. There was a gasp from the Seatowners. Then there was a *thunk,* and Ben Varrey dropped to the ground. He clutched the gash on his head, and stared up in confusion at Albert Munster, who stood holding a bloodstained cog in his hand.

'If you ever touch that little girl again,' he said, his voice quavering, 'I'll find something much bigger to hit you with.'

Ben Varrey tried to sit up, but the trows suddenly leaped on top of him and pinned him to the ground.

'Haust,' grinned Truncherface, and punched him between the eyes.

'You should leave,' said Donny, 'while they'll still let ye. An' maybe tomorrow we'll decide if ye get to stay in the Seatoon or no.'

The trows slid down off Ben Varrey's chest, and Truncherface kicked him for good measure. Somewhere that meant leaving would be a bit more difficult for him. Ben Varrey looked around at the sea of angry faces, and fled from the barn.

There was a cheer, and suddenly Albert was surrounded by people slapping him on the bag and plying him with alcohol. Some were shaking Donny's hand, and most gave the trows an appreciative smile.

'Someone shoulda had the courage to stand up to him years ago,' said Pilot.

Jana knelt down to speak to the trows.

'You know where she is, don't you?'

Truncherface grinned. 'De havda duster. Dolk bost dokka. Mog byrsten. Eg gera um. Min benidju brari. Bensdotter i velsi.'

'Um, he says he was angry with the big ugly man for shouting at the little girl. So he changed places with her and hit him. The girl is in the lighthouse.'

'I thought so,' said Jana. 'The trows don't steal children. They save them. And I wouldn't be surprised if Serena's there too.'

As she spoke, the door burst open again and Mary, Father Langstok and Doctor Vleerman were forced inside as the leaders of the mob pushed their way in. Jana noticed the clowns were just behind them, but they immediately turned and walked away with a purposeful gait.

'Majuggelti blannablura,' said Bannafeet worriedly.

'Magic? Juggling tricks?' guessed Merrow.

'The clowns?' suggested Jana.

'Ah, yes, the clowns. He says they are mixed in a conspiracy, or a bad deed.'

'They must have heard me saying where Serena is! Come on!'

She stood up, but saw that the door was completely blocked by Pieter and his followers.

'There! You heard it from one of their own,' intoned Father van Bleric. ' "Dancing with devils and evil spirits." And there they are right before our eyes.' He pointed at the trows.

Jana bent down again, and whispered to Truncherface. 'Quick, go. We can't get out but you can. Protect Serena.'

The trow didn't seem to need a translation. He grabbed Bannafeet, and they scrambled up the wall to the roof. They ran lightly along the beams, and squeezed out through a tiny hole.

'See how your demon friends desert you?' Father van Bleric waved his hands expansively. 'They will not save you now. Give us the other demon, and you will be spared.'

'Spared?' repeated Father Langstok in disbelief. 'What's wrong with you, Nicolas?'

'It's you who are in the wrong, Francis. Give us the mermaid so your immortal soul might be saved.'

'I already told ye, she's no here,' said Mary firmly.

'And I suppose those other demons weren't here either?'

358

'They're no demons, they're trows.'

'It doesn't matter what you call them.'

'That's enough talking,' snarled Pieter. 'If they won't hand her over, we'll have to tear the place apart and find her ourselves.'

He strode further into the barn, and the crowd started pouring in behind him.

After pausing to watch the crowd for a short time, the Palatine had continued on his way to the *Sapphire*. When he reached its prow, he simply stood there, waiting. It was several minutes before the Finman emerged from the hatch and strode across the deck. Without breaking stride, he jumped down on to the harbour wall, and stood before the Palatine.

'Ye're on time,' he grunted. 'Never trust a punctual man.'

'I apologise. Next time we cross paths I shall endeavour to be late. Or early. Do you have a preference?'

'Ye're full o' clever words an' smug humour. My only preference is that ye shut yer mooth and make good yer master's promises.'

'Very well. Straight to business then. You have the artefact?'

The Finman reached into his voluminous clothes, and drew out a large object that was essentially a drum shape with a thick handle. It appeared to be made of coral.

'Never leaves ma side.'

'Nowhere safer,' agreed the Palatine. 'And easily concealed in those bulky clothes. May I examine it?'

'Just don't try anything.' The Finman handed the object over.

'I wouldn't dream of it.' The Palatine pulled the Emperor's envelope from his pocket, and compared the object to the carving.

'Satisfied?' asked the Finman impatiently.

'Certainly. I think we're ready to proceed.'

'Then you'll purge the vermin?'

The Palatine nodded out to sea. 'Our ship is in place. I only need to give the signal.'

'Aye, well you do that. Until you do I'll take back – '

He was interrupted by a loud bang. He whirled around to see the sea erupting skywards, not far from the *Invincible*. There had been a massive explosion underwater. He turned back to the Palatine, his face livid. The Palatine looked shocked, but the Finman didn't even register this.

'Ye traitor! You and yer Emperor. Double-cross me, wid ye?'

'No! I don't know what's happened, but it wasn't our doing.'

'Ye're a liar! And ye'll get nothin' fae me.' He snatched back the coral object, and swung it at the Palatine's head. Lord Reitherman dropped to the ground, blood oozing from a gash on his temple.

The Finman reached up and grabbed the prow of the boat, hauling himself up with ease. He went straight to the wheelhouse, and within seconds, the *Sapphire* was moving, despite the lack of wind. It swung around in an impossibly tight circle, scraping against the boats on either side of it, and smashing a hole in one. Once it had come around a hundred and eighty degrees, it surged forwards and out of the harbour.

By this time, Adam and Baabie had come running from the *Intrepid*, and now knelt by the Palatine. Baabie examined him carefully.

'He's alive. But he needs the doctor.'

'It'll be quicker if we use his coach. We can get him back to the hotel and fetch Doctor Vleerman. I think it's still down at the Seatown. You stay with him while I run and get it.'

As Adam got up, he glanced at the *Sapphire* speeding away. 'What about your husband?'

'Oh, dinna worry aboot him,' said Baabie. 'If ye paid attention to the stories ye'll mind somethin' else we Finfolk are good at. Putting holes in boats.'

Adam stared at her. 'You didn't.'

'Whit de ye think I was doin' in the water?'

'But he can swim.'

'It's a long way home withoot a boat. Now go.'

A lot had happened in a very short space of time. The mob had surged into the barn, and most of the wedding guests had backed away until they were corralled against the far wall. Those who had stood their ground had been grabbed and roughly held with their arms pinioned, while the barn was searched, tables were overturned, and children and adults burst into tears. Violence hadn't quite erupted yet, but the air was thick with it, and it was only a matter of time.

And then they had all heard the explosion. There were shouts from those who were still outside, while those inside were thrown into disarray. It was almost as if the noise had shaken them out of their immediate state of mind, and it took them a few moments to recover. Then they released their prisoners and rushed outside to see what was going on. Only Pieter seemed unaffected, and shouted after them to come back, but they ignored him and left. Jana, Ben, Merrow, Albert, Father Langstok, Doctor Vleerman, Pilot, and Donny followed them, while Mary rushed to attend to the rest of the Seatowners.

Outside, they all watched the plume of water in astonishment. As it died down, the crowd all looked at each other in confusion. It was as if they didn't know what they were doing here, and for a while they just milled around, until gradually they started to disperse.

Pieter now stood alone, glaring wildly at the wedding guests. But Jana ran straight past him.

'Come on,' she urged. 'We've got to get to the lighthouse. Quick! The clowns'll be halfway there by now.'

Ben and Merrow followed her. The others remained, not taking their eyes off of Pieter. His mouth tightened and his breathing increased as he considered his options. Then he turned and ran.

The first thing they noticed was that the light was on. The weather wasn't bad, so it must be for another reason. A signal. And it must have been Belia who had lit it. So she must be signalling that something was wrong. Signalling for help.

Bannafeet and Truncherface quickened their pace. They didn't need to go the long way around by the road. They just scrambled up the low cliff, and then bounded up the stairs to the middle room. The door lay open, and there was no-one inside. Bannafeet scampered up to the lamp room, while Truncherface checked the other two rooms. When they met a few minutes later, their expressions told each other they had found no-one.

'Fjagers!' cursed Bannafeet, a note of panic creeping into his voice.

An idea struck Truncherface. 'Hannja!' he called, and ran back outside. Bannafeet followed, and soon they were at the entrance to the knowe. 'Bjarga i knowe,' suggested Truncherface.

But there was no-one there either. There was a rattling noise outside, and they ran to see what it was. The Palatine's coach drew up, and Jana, Ben and Merrow leaped out. They had passed Adam on the road, but had not stopped to see why he was waving his arms at them.

Before the humans could even ask, the trows shrugged and shook their heads. They all stood at a loss for a few minutes, until Jana suddenly said, 'The tunnel! Serena would go to the wall of water.'

The trows scrambled back down the rocks, while the others had to take the longer route via the dunes. They ran into the cave and down the rough steps to the passage. It was only then that they realised they had no lanterns. They could hear the trows' running footsteps somewhere up ahead of them, but the humans had to go slowly in the dark. Presumably the trows had better night vision. However, after a while, the mysterious glow from up ahead illuminated the passage, and they were able to go more quickly. Now there were shouts from ahead, and they realised one of the voices was a man. There was also another sound in the distance, but it was difficult to make out.

A short time later, they came across a scene that explained everything. Truncherface and Bannafeet were poised in a sort of stand-off with their quarry. Pieter, who knew all the streets and short cuts of Anterwendt much better than any of them, had managed to get to the lighthouse ahead of them all. He now stood with a terrified Liban gripped tightly in his arms, a knife at her throat. A tearful Belia had been forced to lead Pieter here. As the others caught up, he raised the knife just slightly, to make sure they had all seen it.

'Stay right there.'

'Sorry, Daddy,' wailed Liban.

'Shut up!' Pieter held the knife closer to her throat and she fell silent, but tears streamed down her cheeks. She desperately clutched the rag doll to her chest for what little comfort it could give her.

'Let her go, Pieter,' said Jana in as level a voice as she could manage.

'Shut up, all of you! I say what happens here.'

'Alright. Just tell us what you want us to do.'

Pieter hesitated. He hadn't planned for this. He hadn't really planned any of it, but he'd more or less known what he was doing until they had all found him. He flattened himself against the wall.

'You all go in front, where I can see you. One at a time! No-one tries anything, or I swear I'll cut her throat.'

The trows went first, and Belia was allowed to join them. She embraced Bannafeet, who kept a protective arm around her. Merrow went next, then Ben and finally Jana. Once they had all passed, Pieter followed, still keeping a tight grip on poor Liban. As they walked and the light grew stronger, the strange sound became clearer too, and they all knew what it was before they reached it.

Soon they were at the wall of water, and found Serena standing in front of it, singing. She broke off and turned around as she heard them arrive. Seeing Ben, she rushed over and threw her arms around him. Too late, Jana realised what was about to happen.

Serena kissed him.

It had happened before Ben realised.

'No!' shouted Jana, but it was already done. Almost immediately, his eyes took on that glazed expression he had worn for the last few days. Jana stared at him in hurt disbelief.

'You!' ordered Pieter, looking at Ben. 'Bring the mermaid over here.'

Ben pulled Serena close to him. 'I don't think so.'

'Bring her now, or the girl dies!' Pieter's voice was desperate.

'I said no.'

Pieter opened his mouth, but another voice cut him off.

'I've never seen one of them before, Mr Coco.'

Pieter whirled around. The Scary clowns were standing just a few feet behind him, looking curiously at the wall of water.

'Me neither, Mr Wobbly.' *Toot toot.* The horn echoed eerily in the rock passage. 'And oh look. There's our mermaid.'

'She's mine,' said Pieter warningly.

'I think you'll find we had a deal,' Mr Coco reminded him. 'One that worked to everyone's advantage, but especially ours.'

'The deal's off,' said Pieter, not entirely sure what he was going to do now. He just knew that he no longer had any intention of handing the mermaid over to someone else. He would deal with her himself.

'I wouldn't advise you to cross us,' warned Mr Coco.

'In fact,' added Mr Wobbly, '*I'd* advise you *not* to.'

'That's what I just said,' muttered Mr Coco irritably.

'No, what *you* just said was – '

'Why do you always have to do this in front of people? Just shut up and let me do the talking.'

'You two are mad,' said Pieter.

'Then that probably makes us more dangerous,' reasoned Mr Coco.

'But *you* haven't got a knife.'

'No, but we *have* got pies. And some of the custard's pretty thick.'

'You're the ones that are thick.'

'I think he's insulting us, Mr Wobbly.' He paused, waiting for the toots, but they didn't come. 'I *said* – '

'I'm sulking.'

'Oh, for crying out loud.'

'Shut up, the pair of you!' Pieter was visibly shaking now, completely out of his depth, and thoroughly confused by the clowns' behaviour.

At that moment, all three trows suddenly sprang at Pieter. Belia leaped on to his shoulders and started pounding at his head with her little fists. Truncherface and Bannafeet attached themselves to an arm each, and bit as hard as they could. Pieter cried out in pain and released both Liban and the knife. Liban fell, but Truncherface was quicker. He somersaulted to the ground, and caught Liban before she landed. She was actually bigger than him, but he braced himself so she landed reasonably softly, and he himself stayed upright.

Pieter swung his other arm, and Bannafeet was flung off, crashing into the wall. Belia bit into Pieter's neck, and Truncherface launched himself head first into the man's groin. As Pieter doubled up in pain, Truncherface pulled him to the ground, grabbed the fallen knife and stood over him. The trow didn't notice the read smear on the blade. Pieter writhed in pain, and made no attempt to get up.

Mr Coco clapped, and after a few seconds, Mr Wobbly joined in.

'Very good,' said Mr Coco. 'Very impressive.'

'Yeah,' agreed Mr Wobbly. 'Impressive.'

'And now,' continued Mr Coco, 'our mermaid please.'

Serena looked at him, and then turned to face the wall of water. Ben turned with her.

Jana's face filled with panic. 'Ben, no!' Her voice was shaking. Her eyes glistened. 'Please, Ben ... '

He turned his head and smiled at her, then turned back and took Serena's hand. Serena kissed him, a long, lingering kiss on the lips. Then she stepped forward and into the water. Ben followed. Serena kicked her legs expertly, and swam upwards, pulling Ben behind her. Within seconds, they were out of sight.

Jana sank to her knees sobbing. Merrow knelt down and put a comforting arm around her shoulder.

'No!' Pieter sprang to his feet, sending Truncherface reeling to the ground, and ran forward to the wall of water. Without stopping, he ran straight through.

Immediately, the freezing cold coursed through his body, and he fought to breathe. In a very few seconds, he too disappeared upwards, but he was floating, not swimming, and completely lifeless.

There was a long, silent pause.

'Well, that was unexpected,' said Mr Coco.

'A bit disappointing really,' added Mr Wobbly.

And they simply turned and walked away.

Belia helped Truncherface to his feet, and they rushed over to the still form of Bannafeet, who hadn't moved since being flung against the wall. They now saw why. The back of his head had cracked completely open, and there was also a gash on his chest where the stray knife had caught him.

Belia sat down heavily, and held Bannafeet's head to her chest, in tears. Truncherface collapsed beside her, holding his head in his hands and shaking it dazedly.

Liban picked herself up off the ground, and wiped her nose on her sleeve. She looked around at them all, as if trying to decide who to go to. Then she walked hesitantly to Jana, and put a hand gently under her chin. Jana looked up at her. Liban held out the rag doll.

'Ta,' she said quietly.

Jana pulled Liban close and hugged her for dear life.

XXV. The Drowned Land

*T*he River Anter had many fertile lands along its banks, and many prosperous towns grew up on these lands, but the most prosperous of all was Saeftinghe.

Long before Anterwendt was built, the land extended further into the sea, and there at the estuary stood Saeftinghe. It was surrounded by green fields filled with rich crops, good grazing and lush meadows. The cattle were strong and gave good milk, and the fishing was plentiful.

But the town's prosperity made its people proud and vain. The farmers dressed in silk, the horses had silver on their saddles and reins, and the doors of the houses had gold frames and thresholds.

The wealth brought poor people, looking for work or charity, but the people of Saeftinghe had grown greedy and had no compassion. They chased the poor away with sticks, set dogs on them and refused to part with their wealth.

One foggy morning, a fisherman felt something heavy tugging at his net. Thinking that he must have secured an unusually large catch, he drew the net in, and was surprised when he saw a woman caught in it. But as he drew the net closer, he saw it was not a human woman at all, but a mermaid with a glistening tail. She begged him to free her, but he refused, hoping there might be money to be made from such a prize.

At this, she began to sing, and soon her song called another of her kind – her husband, a merman. He too demanded that the fisherman free his wife, but the fisherman shouted and threw stones at him. The merman cursed the fisherman and the whole town, snarling, 'The lands of Saeftinghe will fall, and only its towers will stand tall.'

The people of Saeftinghe continued in their greed, but they forgot to look after their dikes, and that was their downfall. One day, a maid went to the well for water, and was surprised to see cod swimming in the bottom. When it was drawn, the water from the well tasted of salt. The sea was seeping into the town.

Then, one winter's day, there was a great storm, with waves higher than anyone had ever seen. The dikes broke, and the sea flooded the town in a huge tidal wave. The people were drowned in their finery, and not one soul survived. The fields and meadows turned to swamp, and the town sank down into it, until only the tops of its highest towers showed that there had ever been a town at all. Finally, even they sank, and there was nothing left of proud Saeftinghe.

But on foggy days, the tower bells ring out to remind anyone who hears them of the Drowned Lands of Saeftinghe.

Bannafeet's little body lay on a bed of straw in the barn, his feet pointing towards the door, and a plate of salt perched on his chest. The Seatowners declined to explain the purpose of the salt, saying only that it was important. However, they had made clear no-one was to use his name, in case it summoned his spirit back. Instead, he was to be referred to only as 'him that was taen.'

The sounds of sawing and hammering outside indicated Pilot and Donny were making a coffin. Donny had been to his brother's house earlier but had not found him, and no-one had seen him since he fled the barn last night.

Belia sat on a stool next to her husband's body. Food and drink were brought to her regularly, but she hadn't touched any of it. Truncherface had gone off on an errand for Jana, promising to be back later.

'How's Lord Reitherman?' Jana asked Albert quietly, standing a respectful distance away from Bannafeet and Belia.

'He hasn't woken up yet. Doctor Vleerman says he's lucky to be alive. If Adam and Baabie hadn't been watching, we might not have reached him in time. They're with him now. I'll go back with Murgen a little later, to relieve them.'

The door opened and Merrow slipped in. She looked across at Belia, sitting silently next to the body. 'How is she?'

'She hasn't spoken all morning,' said Jana. 'Or eaten or drunk anything. She just sits there. It's so sad. How did you get on?'

'The clowns have not been back to the circus. No-one knows where they are. When I told Lionel what happened, he made a meeting for everyone to talk about it. They will not let the clowns back. They will send them away if they do. The circus will leave without them.'

'Then the plan's still on?'

'Yes. It will be alright.'

'What plan?' asked Albert.

'Nothing for you to worry about,' said Jana. 'We'll tell you after.'

The door opened again and Mary came in, leading a wide-eyed Liban by the hand. Draatsie was sniffing around outside, but wasn't allowed in. Mary smiled at them as she passed, and led Liban over to the body. Jana, Merrow and Albert all gave each other concerned looks, and followed them. Mary knelt down and moved Liban's hand towards Bannafeet's corpse.

Realising what was about to happen, Albert snatched the girl up into his arms. 'What are you doing?'

'It's one o' the rites,' Mary explained patiently. 'A child has to touch him that was taen, to stop his spirit comin' back. He needs to be reassured his bloodline'll go on, so he has to be touched by the youngest o' his family, the latest o' that bloodline.'

'She's not a trow!' said Jana hotly. Belia glanced up at them and Jana lowered her voice. 'She's not a trow,' she said quietly.

Liban tapped her on the arm, and when Jana looked at her, the girl held out the rag doll. Unsure what it meant, Jana took the doll. Liban then put a finger to her lips. 'Sh. All better.'

Jana realised she had been given the doll to comfort her and to keep her quiet!

Liban turned to give Albert a solemn look. Then she turned to look at the body, and stretched her hand towards it. She turned her head back to Albert and gave him that smile. Albert nodded, and reluctantly put her down next to Bannafeet. She reached out and stroked Bannafeet's face. Then she clasped his hand, and kissed him on the forehead. She turned to Jana and held out her own hand. 'Ta.' Jana handed back the doll, and Liban gently tucked it underneath Bannafeet's folded hands. Finally, she walked over to Belia and gave her a hug. Then she smiled at them all, and skipped off to find Draatsie.

As she left, Jana noticed Truncherface scuttling along the beams. When he reached the ground and sat down next to Belia, he gave Jana a nod of confirmation. She nodded back, and then nudged Merrow.

'Let's go and get Ceasg.'

An hour later, they stood on the beach with Ceasg and Lionel, who was cradling Lorelei in his arms. Merrow's kayak sat on the sand next to the one Truncherface had liberated from Albertus Seba's collection. He had also found Ceasg's waterproof clothes amongst the exhibits, and Donny had taken time out from coffin-making to carve a second paddle to Merrow's specifications.

'You're sure about this?' Jana asked again.

'Of course I am,' said Ceasg happily. 'I told you, it's a good plan. And Lorelei will be much better off than she would with me. I'm hopeless.'

'We'll take good care of her,' said Lionel. And she'll have a life with us that makes her legs an advantage. We'll make her a star.'

'They really will take care of her,' Jana reassured the sisters. 'They've got lots of experience.'

'I know,' said Ceasg. 'Stop fussing.'

Merrow put her hand on Lionel's arm. 'You will come to our village?'

'Randian's already planning the itinerary.'

They kissed briefly. Jana turned away, and Merrow looked at her guiltily.

'Come, Ceasg. Time for us to go home.' She smiled at Lionel, 'I will miss you.'

'I'll see you soon,' he said.

Merrow and Ceasg climbed into their kayaks, and Jana pushed them into the water.

''Bye,' said Ceasg with a smile. 'It's been really nice meeting you both. Look after Lorelei for me.'

'Goodbye, Jana,' said Merrow. 'Thank you for everything.'

The kayaks paddled off into the distance. Jana and Lionel stood and watched until they were just specks, and then they walked back along the beach.

The Palatine's nose twitched. 'Bacon?' he murmured. His eyes flickered open and he moaned in pain. 'How much of my head is missing?'

'It's all still there,' smiled Adam. 'A bit bashed up, but the doctor says it'll heal, and you'll soon be beautiful again.'

'Ha!' He winced again. 'How long have I been unconscious? What have I missed?'

'It's just the next morning. A mob turned up at the wedding, looking for Serena.'

'Is she alright?'

'She and Ben went through the wall of water.'

'Ah. You ignored my instruction not to go back into the tunnel then. I rather thought you might.'

'You didn't actually tell us not to go. You just said you didn't want the public going in.

'Yes, very good.'

'Will Ben be alright? The guy that followed them wasn't.'

'I imagine Serena would have ensured Ben's survival, just as she did when she rescued him.'

'The clowns turned out to be behind it all.'

'Clowns? Oh, the circus. We must go there later today.'

'Must we? Why.'

'We'll go into that later. What else?'

'Well your friend's boat sunk.' Adam waited to see the Palatine's reaction. There was a wry smile but nothing else. 'Is it even worth asking what that was all that about?'

The Palatine gave a resigned sigh. 'As you already know, he was a Finman, a sorcerer from Orknejar folklore. You'll recall from Murgen's stories, they live on a hidden island that rises out of the sea. And there are various stories of how mermaids were created.'

'Some of the stories said they were the daughters of Finfolk.'

'Indeed. I believe that island to be real, and I believe it was once occupied by the Skentys.' Adam gasped. 'And I think the Skentys created the mermaids.'

'The legends say they created all magical creatures,' Adam reminded him.

'True. But I think they specifically created them on this island. And it took them a few attempts to get it right. They started by splicing together trows with fish.'

372

'The Feejee mermaids,' said Adam, remembering the mound behind the lighthouse.

'Quite. But those weren't entirely successful.'

'Fish and mammals don't go.'

'I'm sorry?'

'A conversation we had with Doctor Vleerman. He said Serena's legs were made of something like whale blubber, and they'd originally been joined together like a tail. They'd been surgically separated.'

'Oh yes. Humans and dolphins were a far better match.'

'Porpoises actually. So Ben said'

'Really? Well the Finfolk island still has the Skentys artefacts that make mermaids. The tools to join the different parts together, and another one that enables them to breathe underwater. Although it reconstructs the breathing apparatus so the mermaids are no longer able to speak.'

'The Finman told you all of this?'

'Some of it. Some I learned from a very erudite local man, some Albert and I worked out for ourselves, and some was told to us by the Emperor.'

'The Emperor? Oh yes, your secret mission. I suppose you're still not going to tell me that part.'

'On the contrary,' said the Palatine to Adam's surprise. 'The situation has changed dramatically. You see, there's another Skentys island right here, off the coast of Anterwendt.'

'The light beneath the waves!' exclaimed Adam, remembering the mysterious light beyond the wall of water, and the phrase used by the trows.

'Very apt. It has the same tools for creating mermaids. And the Emperor would very much like access to them. Particularly the artefact that enables one to breathe underwater.'

'Why?'

'Well, he has developed a certain interest in what could loosely be termed occult artefacts. But more than that, think of the military applications. Soldiers who can breathe underwater.'

'So that's why the *Intrepid's* here? And why it cordoned off the area.'

'Precisely. The island lies directly below.'

'How can you be sure?'

'Oh, it's there. I've seen it.'

'So did you need the Finman to show you how the artefact works?'

'No, Lazlo Winter, the court wizard, will study it. The Finman was here to strike a bargain. As you know, the Finfolk are cruel.'

'Yes, I experienced that first hand.'

'Really? Well, the mermaids left the Finfolk long ago, and many of them settled in the undersea island here. But now the Finfolk want to expand their territory. They want that island. And they want it purged of mermaids.'

'In return for the artefact.'

'Exactly. The Finfolk have no use for it. The Finman brought the one from his own island, and was to hand it over once the *Intrepid* had removed the mermaids. But the Emperor betrayed us both.'

'The explosion. He blew up the island?'

'So it would seem. Captain Hofstadt must have had orders I wasn't privy to.'

'But why? Now you haven't got the artefact. And why wouldn't he tell you?'

'I think the Emperor was putting me in my place. I was very much just a lackey. But I'm still not sure why he jeapordised gaining possession of the artefact. Unless ... '

'What?'

'I need to get back out to the *Intrepid*.' He struggled to sit up.

'You're in no condition to go anywhere. You need rest.'

'Later. There's too much to do. And we have to go to the circus. If you're up to it.'

'Up to it? What do you mean?'

'Why do you think the clowns want a mermaid? They're after the artefact too.'

'What would they want it for?'

'Not what. Who. Who do we know that's interested in experimenting with human development?'

Adam thought. 'Baphomet!'

'Baphomet must be somewhere in the circus.'

Adam had a vague memory of something. Was there a floating head?

'Yes! I'd already worked that out. I went to confront him ... it. And then I ... I forgot.'

'Baphomet must have affected your memory somehow,' guessed the Palatine, pulling on his shirt.

' "Run away and join the circus," ' murmured Adam.

'What? Would you mind facing the other way for a moment?'

'Baphomet kept saying that to me.'

'Perhaps he's trying to recruit you. Could you pass me my boots?'

'Recruit me for what?'

'Let's go and ask him.'

They took the coach, and were at the playing fields less than ten minutes later. There was no sign of the circus. Adam looked around the empty field in amazement.

'How could they have packed up so quickly?'

'Interesting, isn't it?'

'Surely we'd be able to catch them.' Adam was already climbing back on board the coach, but the Palatine put a hand on his shoulder.

'Somehow I doubt it. They're gone.'

'But they didn't get what they were after.'

'No. They didn't.' The Palatine frowned in thought.

'What?'

Suddenly the Palatine leaped on to the coach. 'There's no time to waste. Come on!'

It was a clear, calm day. Seagulls glided and screeched, occasionally diving for fish, or for people's unguarded lunches. The sun glittered off the water as it always did, and the *Intrepid* sat as a floating sentinel nearby.

Jana gazed out at nothing in particular, contemplating the events of the last few days. Mostly contemplating Ben and Serena. And trying not to cry. Well, not obviously, anyway.

Then she noticed something so obvious that it hadn't occurred to her before. She rubbed her eyes to clear them and looked again. Was it just today or had it always been like that? Surely it didn't mean anything.

Did it?

What had caught her eye was the light playing on the water. More specifically, it was which part of the water. It was very much inside the area cordoned off by the marker buoys. She remembered the First Mate of the *Venture* guessing the *Intrepid* was cordoning itself off, and she had more or less forgotten about it with everything else that had been going on, but now that she looked, she realised the cordon was actually some distance from the ship. And it surrounded a pool of light. There were other places where the sun sparkled on the water, but they were small and moving. In fact, now she thought about it, the light inside the cordon wasn't really sparkling at all. It was more like a glow. Then she thought about the light beyond the wall of water. The light beneath the waves.

She looked again. It was spreading. The light was getting bigger, covering a wider area. And the sea was starting to churn. Oh hell. It wasn't getting bigger. It was rising. Whatever it was, it was rising from the depths of the water. And it was big enough to make the *Intrepid* sway. In fact, she could see sailors running about on deck, letting out sails and raising anchor. They were moving the ship out of the way!

The churning of the water was now creating its own waves, enough that the sailors didn't need to bother about moving the ship them-selves, and could concentrate on the more important business of not capsizing.

By now, crowds were gathering all along the seafront to watch the spectacle. Something emerged from the boiling froth. It was white and pointed up at the sky, and as it continued to rise, it became clear it was a tower of some sort. It had windows, and reflected the sun with an unearthly glare. It appeared to be made of coral.

Gradually, more structures surfaced. A second tower, this one an artistic spiral, and studded with coloured gemstones. An archway decorated with intricately carved reliefs of sea creatures. Houses and cathedrals, spires and domes, some made of coral of all different co-lours, and others fashioned from crystal, so they shone in the sunlight. But that wasn't the reason for the underwater glow. There was some sort of phosphorescent light pervading the whole island. And it *was* an island, perhaps a quarter mile in area. The buildings were hemmed with gardens of seaweed and anemones, and ringed with a reef of multi-coloured coral. It was one of the most awe-inspiring sights Jana had ever set eyes on. It was breathtaking in its beauty. Anyone who saw it would say that they had lived. Anyone who heard about it later could never imagine it fully, and no description could ever do it justice. It was magnificent.

There was no sign of life. No mermaids, or seals or anything else. If anyone occupied it, they weren't showing themselves. But nor was there any sign of disrepair. If it was abandoned, it had worn very well. It just sat there, sparkling and silent.

And then Jana saw the speck. A small boat was rowing towards it. The boat was on the shore side, so the island was between it and the *Intrepid*, which had survived the island's appearance, but was now still bobbing precariously while the sea settled. She peered, but couldn't make out who was in the rowing boat. And then she heard a sound that told her all she needed to know.

Toot toot.

'Big, isn't it, Mr Coco?'

'I suppose it is.'

The rowing boat had almost reached the island, and was starting to sway precariously, as the water this close was still rough.

'Handy it comin' up outa the water like that, eh?' said Mr Wobbly. 'I dunno how we'd have got the thingy otherwise.'

'Thingy?' repeated Mr Coco in a long-suffering tone.

'Yeah, you know. The thingy. Can't remember the word. The thingy we're supposed to get.'

'The word you're failing to remember is "artefact". We're trying to find an ancient artefact.'

'Yeah, artefact. Where is it then?'

'What do you mean, where is it? It's on the island, you doughnut.'

'Yeah, I know that. I mean where exactly on the island?'

'How should I know?'

'How are we supposed to find it then?'

'Well we'll have to look, won't we?'

'Oh.' Mr Wobbly sounded disappointed.

'Will that be a problem, Mr Wobbly?'

Toot toot.

'Well, it's just that I 'aven't had any breakfast, and I'm gettin' hungry.'

Mr Coco sighed and reached into his pocket. He withdrew his hand, and passed Mr Wobbly a small paper bag.

'Trifle doughnuts!' said Mr Wobbly, almost happily. 'You're good to me, Mr Coco.'

'Stuff one of those in your gob. It'll stop you from talking.'

'Er, Mr Coco?'

Mr Coco sighed heavily. 'Yes?'

'Is it just me, or is the sea getting rougher all of a sudden.'

Mr Coco looked around at the water. 'I think you may be right. I think there may be something else coming out of the water.'

The sea in between the boat and the island bubbled, and from it rose a large wooden egg. It was the *Turtle*. The hatch opened and the Palatine waved out at the clowns.

'Good morning, gentlemen. I don't think we've met.'

'Oh dear,' said Mr Coco.

'Oh dear,' continued Mr Wobbly.

'Oh dear,' concluded Mr Coco.

Mr Wobbly whipped off his top hat – revealing a smaller top hat underneath – and threw it deftly at the Palatine. It stayed upright, spinning on its own axis. It hit him square in the chest.

And dropped harmlessly into the sea.

'Oh,' said Mr Wobbly lamely. 'That's disappointing.'

'Isn't it?' agreed Mr Coco.

'What are we going to do now?'

'Have you got any of those trifle doughnuts left?'

'Yeah, why?'

'Try throwing them. Maybe some seagulls'll attack him.'

Mr Wobbly reached into the bag, but the boat suddenly lurched, and the bag went flying into the water. The clowns looked around in alarm. A pair of arms had come out of the water and grabbed the side of the boat, and were now rocking it.

'What's going on?' shouted Mr Coco. 'Stop rocking the boat.'

More arms appeared and joined in. The clowns started hammering on the fingers, and trying to prize them off, but finally the duo fell head-long into the water, and the boat capsized. The clowns disappeared under the water, and all that was left were two hats and a green wig. The arms disappeared, and there was a flash of what looked like a dolphin tail. Then the sea became calm.

The Palatine stared into the water, but there was no sign of anyone. He shook his head and manoeuvred the *Turtle* to the the edge of the island. He stepped ashore and walked towards the buildings.

For a few minutes there was silence, and then the hats floating on the water rose up to reveal two heads underneath. The clowns doggy paddled towards the *Turtle*, Mr Coco collecting his wig on the way.

'There's only enough room for one, Mr Coco.'

'Not a problem. We're clowns.'

'Oh yeah.'

Mr Coco pulled himself out of the water and into the submersible. Mr Wobbly followed him, even though there shouldn't have been space for him. As the hatch closed and the *Turtle* began to submerge, their voices could still be heard.

'This gives me an idea for a new act, Mr Coco.'

'Oh yes?'

'We could have an endless stream of clowns coming out of one of these. And then a monkey.'

'That isn't even slightly funny. I like it. How do you steer this thing?'

After leaving the Palatine at the Naval base, Adam had taken the coach to look for Jana. He found her staring at the island.

'Do you think Ben and Serena are on that somewhere?' she asked without looking at him.

'I don't know. Lord Reitherman knew it was there. I think he's gone out to investigate it.'

'And left us here. Imperial business, I suppose. The clowns are out there too.'

'Are they? But the circus has left.'

She looked at him for the first time. 'Has it? That's strange. I hope Lorelei'll be safe.'

'What do you mean?'

'I haven't had time to tell you. Ceasg left with Merrow, but they couldn't take Lorelei with them, so we gave her to Lionel to look after.'

Adam stared at her. 'You did *what?*'

'She'll be much better off with the freak show. They'll be more understanding, and they'll know how to take care of her. She'll have a chance with them.'

'But Baphomet runs the circus!'

'What? Why didn't you tell me? You never tell me!'

'I didn't know! Well, I did but I forgot. Look, it's complicated. We've got to catch up with them.'

'How? We don't know where they are.'

Adam thought about it. Then he remembered something. 'Yes we do! There are posters all over town saying where they're going next.'

'But they've got a head start on us.'

'They've got caravans to pull. If we uncouple the horses from the coach, we'll be faster and we can overtake them. Come on!'

The Palatine wasn't sure what he was looking for, so he walked in and out of the buildings, hoping something would give him a clue.

The island was just as Murgen had described in her story of the Finfolk's ancestral home, Finfolkaheem. The structures did indeed seem to be made from coral, not just white, but all sorts of colours. Some were encrusted with polished gemstones, which caught the light and sparkled majestically. Every one of the buildings was set in its own garden of seaweed, but not the drab green stuff that adorned the beach. There were all different shapes and colours, and scattered among them were anemones and myriad other undersea plants the Palatine didn't know the names of. These were all arranged on more corals, which resembled something between a reef and a rock garden. And, most astonishing of all, many of the gardens really were littered with giant pearls, the size of boulders.

Inside, many of the buildings had walls fashioned from crystal. They weren't the straight, square walls of human dwellings, but rather followed the natural facets of the minerals, just as the outsides took the existing shapes of the coral. Chairs and beds were made of sumptuous sponges, and most of the rooms were decorated with frescos made of shells, depicting scenes of people riding whales, or mermaids frolicking in the sea. For all the sour disposition of the Finfolk in the legends, thought the Palatine, their dwellings were in complete contrast. But then he remembered that this one wasn't yet occupied by Finfolk, and he wondered if it was an insight to the Skentys instead.

Every now and again, he fancied he saw something moving out of the corner of his eye, but when he looked there was nothing, and he returned his attention to the buildings. The smaller ones on the outskirts seemed to be simple dwellings, but as he moved closer to the centre, the structures became bigger and more functional. One seemed to be a meeting hall, and another might have been an administrative building. But it was the large central one full of beds that looked most promising. This seemed almost like a hospital, and was the most likely place for the surgery that turned people into mermaids. Somewhere in here would probably be another artefact like the one the Finman had shown him.

The real clincher, though, was the Finman himself, standing over a rather complicated-looking piece of machinery, from which he was extracting an exact duplicate of the artefact. He looked up angrily.

'Thocht ye could double cross me, did ye?'

'I assure you I knew nothing about it. I was as shocked as you were.'

'Ye pretended to destroy the island so I'd leave and yer Emperor could have it for himself. And it micht ha worked if that wife o' mine hadna holed ma boat.'

'What are you planning to do now? You can't stay here as an enemy of the Empire.'

The Finman grunted, and put the artefact in his pocket. He walked out of the building, and the Palatine ran after him.

'We could still come to an arrangement.'

The Finman ignored him, and walked towards what the Palatine had assumed was the administrative building. The Palatine caught up and grabbed him by the sleeve, but the Finman shook him off violently and sent him reeling. As he picked himself up, the Palatine thought he saw movement up above. He looked and saw a seagull perched on one of the towers, which was topped with a thin crystal spire. He got to his feet, and ran after the Finman, who had already entered the building.

Inside, he found him bent over another piece of machinery, pulling levers and turning valves. The Finman glanced up, and then returned to his task.

'What are you doing?' asked the Palatine.

'Revenge.'

He turned another dial, and there was a sound like a thunderclap, and at the same time, a blinding light followed by a distant explosion.

'What was that?' asked the Palatine, worried.

'That wis yer ship,' replied the Finman with a grim smile.

The Palatine rushed outside and around the building to get a view of the *Intrepid*. It was on fire, with thick black smoke rising from the wreckage.

The ground lurched, and the Palatine almost fell over. He saw the Finman come out of the building.

'Hope ye've got a boat,' he laughed.

The ground continued to shake, and the Palatine realised with horror that the island must be sinking back into the sea. He had to get back to the *Turtle*. But as he turned to run, he felt the Finman's powerful hand grab him and throw him to the ground. A giant fresco of an octopus loomed towards him as his face hit it. He tried to get up, but the Finman kicked him and he fell again.

'I don't need a boat,' said the Finman. 'Get up.'

The Palatine sat on the ground trying to catch his breath, but the Finman hauled him to his feet.

'I said get up.'

The Palatine looked at him, only to see the Finman's fist coming towards his face. He went down again. Water was starting to lap around him. He felt the huge hand grab his collar, and prepared for the worst. Then he heard a crack from somewhere above, followed by a sickening thud and a gurgling scream. The Finman's grip slackened. Lord

Reitherman looked up, and saw the Finman was still standing there, pinned to the ground by the crystal spire that had impaled him. The Palatine looked to the top of the tower, and saw Truncherface sitting there. Then he lost consciousness.

Neither Adam nor Jana rode horses often, but they both knew how. It made galloping a bit hairy, and they clung on for dear life as the black stallions made the most of a freedom they rarely got to enjoy.

The poster had said the circus was visiting Haerlem next, meaning it would take the main road south past the playing fields. Of course, there was no way of knowing how long ago it had left, particularly considering how remarkably quickly it had been packed up, so it was impossible to be sure they would catch it up at all, but they reasoned the circus would have to travel by main roads, would have to stop sometime, and the Palatine's horses would still be faster, so surely they'd catch it eventually. Adam knew by that time he'd probably be unable to walk again.

As it turned out, they didn't have to go too far. They had only been riding about a quarter of an hour (although it felt much longer) when they saw the familiar sight of garish caravans on the road ahead. Jana spurred her horse on, and Adam groaned as his matched the pace and gave his gentleman's vegetables another battering.

After another few minutes, they were almost level with the hindmost caravan, and Jana started shouting for them to stop. As they began to pass the caravans, a buzz began to go around, as the circus folk wondered what was going on. Finally, the riders reached the front of the convoy, where they found Lionel and the tattooed man. Confused, the tattooed man signalled for everyone else to stop, and gradually the procession ground to a halt.

'What's going on?'

'Lionel,' Jana said breathlessly, 'where's Lorelei?'

'She's with the twins, why?'

'Can we see her?'

'Of course. But she's fine. They're really good with kids, and everyone wants a turn with her.'

He led them to the caravan occupied by the joined twins, which to no-one's surprise any more, was being driven by Randian, by means of a complicated system of pulleys attached to the reins, so he could control them without losing his teeth. Inside, the twins were cooing over the baby, who was smiling and gurgling happily.

'You don't want her back?' asked Lionel anxiously.

'No,' said Jana. 'We just needed to check.'

'Where are the freak show tents?' asked Adam.

'Packed away. All the tents are.'

'Then where does it live when the tents aren't up?' Adam said, more to himself than anyone else.

'Where does what live?'

Adam looked along the line of caravans until his eye fell on one in particular. He ran towards it and stopped outside. 'In here.'

Painted on the side of the caravan were the disembodied heads of the Scary Clowns.

'They're not there,' said Lionel as the others caught up. 'They weren't around when we packed up, so we just left without them.'

Adam ignored him and pulled the hinged steps down, flung the door open and stepped inside. He wasn't sure whether he'd expected it to be dark and foreboding or brightly coloured, but it turned out to be neither. Instead, it was rather tastefully decorated with pastel shades, a few small paintings and a floral tea set. On a shelf sat two eggs with the faces of Mr Coco and Mr Wobbly painted on them, along with miniature replicas of their hats and one of Mr Coco's wigs.

'I told you, they're not here,' said Lionel as he, Jana and the tattooed man all crowded in behind Adam.

'It's not the clowns I'm looking for.'

'Then what?'

I think he might be looking for me.

The voice came from nowhere. Everyone looked wildly around for a source, but there was nothing.

Oh, you don't like what you can't see, do you? Does this help?

A bearded head appeared, hanging in mid-air. It had a vacant stare, and its lips didn't move when the voice spoke.

Better?

'Is that what you really look like?' asked Adam.

It's just something to make you all feel more comfortable.

'What the hell is it?' asked the tattooed man.

'This,' said Adam, 'is Baphomet.' There was a chuckle.

I haven't heard that name for a while. But alright, if you like. I'm so glad you came. Are you joining the circus?

'You keep saying that. What do you want from me?'

We could do so much together. The magician who thinks like a scientist. You could play such a part in the new world order.

'New world order? Is that the one where you tamper with evolution and sacrifice innocent people for your own curiosity?'

Oh, that's just a part of it. There's far more to it than that. We could change the world, you and I.

'What the hell *is* this?' There was anger in the tattooed man's voice, and probably fear too. 'Why have the clowns got a weird floating head in their caravan? Is it a trick they've been working on?'

'It's not a trick,' said Jana, 'it's evil.'

Oh, such an emotional word. Typical of you, of course. That's why Adam is so much more suitable. He doesn't let his emotions rule him. He's a far better scientist than you could ever hope to be.

'Is this who the clowns have been working for?' asked Lionel, as Jana's hackles rose.

'Yes,' she said darkly. 'This is who's been manipulating you all.'

'Get out,' said Lionel. 'We don't want you here. You're not welcome.'

How inhospitable of you. But not to worry. I had no further use for you anyway. You've been a bit of a disappointment really.

'Good.'

Oh dear. I know when I'm not wanted. But I'm sure some of us will meet again. Until then.

The head faded out of existence. Lionel turned and walked out of the caravan. 'Burn it.'

The others rushed to catch up with him. 'I don't think that'll help' cautioned Adam. 'It's escaped a fire before.'

'It'll make us feel better,' said Lionel. 'Burn it.'

Ten minutes later, the circus was on its way, leaving a lone burning caravan behind it. Adam and Jana watched them disappear into the distance.

'Do you think Baphomet's really left them?' asked Jana.

'I hope so. But it'll turn up again, somewhere.'

'Looking for you?'

Adam didn't reply. They watched the fire for a few minutes, before turning their horses around and heading back to Anterwendt.

They were never sure how the Palatine had ended up on the beach. He remembered nothing, and Truncherface had refused to say. The island had disappeared back into the water, taking the wreck of the *Intrepid* in its wake, and the sea no longer glowed.

The next morning, a procession of Seatowners walked solemnly to the Anterwendt cemetery, Father Langstok at their head, ringing a bell. Behind him came Pilot, the oldest man in the community, and then the tiny coffin, carried by Adam, Donny, Albert and Truncherface, who had to hold his arms up high to keep his corner at the same height as the other three. After the funeral, there was a wake in the barn. Unsurprisingly, cogs of home brew featured heavily.

No-one saw the trows again after that. They simply disappeared, and the knowe was empty. Ben Varrey was never seen again either. Nothing had been taken from his house, but he never came back, and Liban went to live with Donny.

The Palatine was still bruised when he and Albert got into the coach to leave.

'Good luck in Nazca,' he said to Adam and Jana. 'Let me know when you get back. I'm sure you'll have lots of stories to tell.'

'What'll happen to the island?' asked Adam.

'I imagine the Emperor will send a team to investigate it. There's obviously a very powerful weapon down there. Of course, the loss of the *Turtle* will make that expedition somewhat more difficult, but I'm sure they'll manage something.'

'And the wall of water?' asked Jana. 'Anyone could still find it.'

'Oh, I had that bricked up. And the passage caved in for good measure. Too dangerous to leave that open to the public.'

'Did you get the artefact?' asked Adam.

'Unfortunately not. The Emperor will not be pleased. But presumably it's still down there somewhere. Perhaps both of them. They may still be recovered.'

As the coach rolled away, Albert said, 'It really is a shame that you didn't manage to save at least one of the artefacts, sir. It could have been valuable to us in working out what the Emperor's up to.'

'Indeed, Albert. And even better if I had recovered both, and had one to give to the Emperor, and could therefore keep the other without arousing suspicion.' He patted the small chest on the seat beside him. 'A great shame.'

The room was large and wood-panelled, with high vaulted windows. The curtains were drawn, and the long oak table was dimly lit with a single candle, and surrounded by high-backed leather chairs. Lazlo Winter stood at the end of the table, facing the seated figures.

'Does the Emperor have his artefact, Winter?'

'He does. It's being examined as we speak.'

'And the other?'

'We believe Lord Reitherman has it.'

'Not quite as planned, but acceptable. It may even benefit us. Presumably the Emperor knows nothing of this.'

'Of course not. He has accepted Lord Reitherman's story that the second artefact was lost.'

'Good. Overall a successful endeavour, in spite of the unexpected developments. I'm glad Lord Reitherman survived. He could prove useful.'

'He could also prove dangerous.'

'This whole business is dangerous. We look forward to hearing about your findings from the examination of the artefact. Keep an eye on the Emperor. We will arrange for an eye to be kept on Lord Reitherman.'

As the *Venture* cast off, Adam joined Jana on the deck. They had put their luggage into their rooms – berths the sailors called them – and now had to settle themselves down for the long voyage. They watched Anterwendt getting further away, and they waved to the group of Seatowners who had come to the harbour to see them off.

'Do you think the Empire will still be there when we get back?' Jana asked.

'You think the Emperor's preparing for war?'

'I think he's preparing for something, and whatever it is, it's not good.'

'Right now I'm wondering if we'll get back at all. Nazca's bound to be much more dangerous than here.'

'Oh. Good. That's … comforting. Very comforting.'

She hadn't looked at him the whole time.

'Are you going to be okay?' he asked her.

'No. But let's pretend I am.'

They stood in silence as the ship headed out to open sea, and they felt the wind in their hair, listened to the screeching of the seagulls, and watched the sun sparkling off the water.

Printed in Great Britain
by Amazon.co.uk, Ltd.,
Marston Gate.